Beguiled by a Baron

Heart of a Duke Series

For more information about the author:
www.christicaldwell.com
christicaldwellauthor@gmail.com
Twitter: @ChristiCaldwell
Or on Facebook at: Christi Caldwell Author

For first glimpse at covers, excerpts, and free bonus material, be sure to sign up for my monthly newsletter!
Printed in the USA.

Cover Design and Interior Format

Beguiled by a Baron

Heart
of a
Duke

THE
SERIES

USA TODAY BESTSELLER
CHRISTI
CALDWELL

Other Titles by
Christi Caldwell

THE HEART OF A SCANDAL

In Need of a Duke—Prequel Novella

For Love of the Duke

More than a Duke

The Love of a Rogue

Loved by a Duke

To Love a Lord

The Heart of a Scoundrel

To Wed His Christmas Lady

To Trust a Rogue

The Lure of a Rake

To Woo a Widow

To Redeem a Rake

One Winter with a Baron

To Enchant a Wicked Duke

Beguiled by a Baron

THE HEART OF A SCANDAL

In Need of a Knight—Prequel Novella

Schooling the Duke

LORDS OF HONOR

Seduced by a Lady's Heart

Captivated by a Lady's Charm

Rescued by a Lady's Love

Tempted by a Lady's Smile

DEDICATION

To Reagan and Riley: my strong, smart, loving,
and kindhearted daughters.

Vail and Bridget's story is for you.

CHAPTER

1

Leeds, England
Spring 1820

LADY BRIDGET HAMILTON HAD BELIEVED she'd made her last great sacrifice where her brother, the ruthless, soulless Marquess of Atbrooke, was concerned. She should have learned better—long ago.

Bridget gave thanks for having the foresight to leave her ten-year-old son, Virgil, in the care of their maid-of-all-purposes, Miss Nettie, who'd been with them since Bridget herself was a babe in the cradle. Keeping her son away from Archibald ensured he'd never grow up like the ruthless bastard.

"I beg your pardon?" Bridget said in frosty tones.

Born partially deaf in her left ear, it was possible she'd misheard Archibald. She had certainly failed to detect lesser words and tones than the ones he'd uttered. Yet, by the mercenary glitter in his ruthless eyes, she'd all the confirmation she needed.

He reclined in his seat; an upholstered chair with faded fabric and tears showing its age. "Oh, come, you make more of it than it is," he drawled. His words forced her back to a different time. To the first and only time she'd left that remote, crumbling estate her family kept, with Archibald's child in tow. In the end, Bridget had left with unexpected work from an old book collector…and also her nephew, rejected by his father. That same miserable bastard who now kicked his feet up. He dropped his gleaming black boots upon the French refectory table. "You've certainly undertaken far more than this small favor."

Bridget lingered her gaze on his immaculate, and what was more, expensive footwear. Fine boots when he was in dun territory chasing a fortune and being hunted for the money he owed others. Costly articles when she and her son should live in the squalor that they did, in this ramshackle cottage. "Yes," she said quietly. But those decisions had been ones she'd made…not to help her derelict, reprobate brother but rather to right the wrongs he'd inflicted upon others. "I have. As such, you should be ashamed to come here and put any requests to me." As soon as the words left her mouth, she flattened her lips. Archibald was incapable of shame or regret. He'd been born with a black soul that not even the Devil would have a use for.

A flash of fury sparked in his eyes and he surged forward. "But there is where you are wrong, Bridget. I asked you for nothing. I demanded it of you." It was not, however, the palpable outrage in his words that gave her pause, but rather the location of his feet. His dirt-stained heels kissed the edge of a document she'd been studying, prior to his arrival. That venerated script that she'd been asked to evaluate and study by a London scholar who'd no qualms in dealing with a young lady adept in antiquities. Those revered pages would provide much-needed coin and were also to be respected for the history contained within them. "Goddamn it, Bridget," he shouted, cupping his hands around his mouth. "It is a chore to pay you any damned visit, even when you serve a purpose."

So, he'd mistaken her silence for an inability to hear him. That had been a cherished tool she'd used over the years to gather the thoughts, words, plans, and opinions of the soulless siblings she'd been saddled with.

With her white-gloved fingers, she rescued the book and tucked it under the table—out of his reach, vision, and feet. She'd learned long ago that her brother's attention was sparse at best. He could be distracted the same way a dog might when thrown a bone.

"You don't have a use for antiquities," she finally said.

Archibald smirked. "I've developed a newfound appreciation for them."

"Oh," she bit out. "Since when did you care about anything?" Anything that was not a coin or a bottle of spirits.

"Since I learned the cost of this particular artifact," he supplied, looking altogether smug. "Lord Chilton has it." A crazed glitter lit his eyes. "And I want it. Need it," he whispered.

So, he'd learned the value of those books. She curled her hands into balls. He'd never been the bookish sort. He'd mocked her and jeered her love of literature and ancient texts and documents. Only to now, all these years later, find the value of them. Of course, it should come to be because of his own financial failings. He'd been living in hiding these past two years, which was no doubt because of the creditors after him. And yet, he always crawled out to the Kent countryside like a determined rodent that Cook would never succeed in ridding from the kitchens. "You want me to enter a nobleman's household, masquerade as a servant in his employ, and rob him while he sleeps?" Mad. Her brother was as mad as their sister, who'd just been committed for the attempted murder of the young Duchess of Huntly.

Archibald scoffed. "You're rot at subterfuge, Bridget. You don't need to wait until the dead of night. The gentleman is off seeing to business most days and nights. The time will really be yours to choose."

"Which particular book?" she asked with an inquiry that came forth more of her passion for those records and less to aid him in his plans of theft. She'd sacrificed enough in her life: her respectable name, her ability to move freely in the world. She'd not also now sacrifice her honor. Not for a material scrap or coin. Not even a small fortune.

"It is the first edition of Chaucer's *Canterbury Tales.*"

Her breath caught and she froze, unmoving. "Chaucer," she breathed. Impossible. Predating the fifteenth century, that great work was a rarity that every last bibliophile would be champing at the bit for.

And my brother wants me to steal it.

Bitterness and hatred turned her blood hot. Bridget shoved to her feet. "I cannot help you in this." *Not even if I wanted to*, which she most decidedly did not. "One cannot simply steal a first edition of Chaucer's work and then sell it without the whole of the world knowing one was complicit in that crime."

Archibald wagged a finger. "Ah, yes. But, you see, I've already found a buyer." Of course he had. The rotted bastard. The men and women he kept company with were people whose souls would one day make up Satan's army. "We've made arrangements. I acquire the copy and he'll turn over twenty-five thousand pounds."

She choked on her swallow. Her brother named a vast sum that could ensure the livelihood and security of an entire family for two generations to come. "You'll simply squander those monies on whores and your clubs and wicked parties, Archibald." Bridget gave her head a disgusted shake. "I'll not steal for you. You'll do your own theft," she said, infusing an air of finality to that vow. "I've done much for you." Certainly more than he'd ever done for her. No, Archibald had only ever brought shame, pain, and turmoil. "But I'll not do this." She took a step toward the door. "We're done—"

He jumped up. "What you've done for me? The only reason you've found work with Lowery—"

"Lowell," she forced out past her fear. The funds she received from the ancient bookkeeper were what afforded her the money to feed her son and see him cared for. If Archibald yanked that away, with it would go the fragile security Bridget had established for her boy. "His name is Mr. Lowell."

"Regardless. You have your employment because *I* secured work for you with those bloody books of his."

Indignation driving back fury, she went toe-to-toe with him. "Do not pretend you've done any of this for me, or…Virgil," she seethed. "You were always self-serving." The funds she earned were split half with her wastrel brother, all because he'd found her the post. "You simply used my skills to pay for your gaming and whoring."

The air slid from her lips on a painful hiss as he shot a hand about her wrist. He crushed the delicate bones in a punishing grip. Tears dotted her vision. "You do not end discussions, Bridget," he whispered against her right ear. "The only reason you exist in any way is because I allow it," he threatened, tightening his hold.

She bit the inside of her cheek to keep from crying out, refusing to let him see he hurt her. Not allowing him to know he terrified her still. She knew the evil he was capable of and didn't doubt he'd choke the life from her without compunction if the mood struck him. But she also knew that to answer him now and cede this point would only empower him.

With a growl, he flung her arm. She resisted the urge to rub the tender flesh and, instead, planted her feet. "Damn it, I need that book, Bridget."

He asked her to steal and risk her name, reputation, and very life. And then, where would Virgil be? Unbidden, her gaze went to the closed doorway and, for the first time since Archibald had put to her his scheme, dread iced her spine. For this plan moved beyond her and the greedy monster before her. It involved her ten-year-old son, Virgil, who'd find himself motherless if she were caught in a criminal act…against a nobleman. "I have responsibilities here in Kent. I earn coin that you benefit from, I'd remind you."

"Pfft." He scoffed. "A damned pittance that won't solve—"

"—the mess you've made of the Hamilton fortunes," she cut in. And he'd demanded her hard-earned coin countless times or he'd threatened to reveal her identity to the community as no widow, but an unwed whore of seven and twenty as he'd too often called her.

"This will solve all my problems, though," he said with a pleased smile.

His problems. In short, she'd benefit not at all from the book he expected her to steal. Not that she'd seek or take a pence of stolen coin but, nonetheless, it still spoke to her brother's self-centeredness. He proceeded to enumerate a tidy list. "I'll not need to live in hiding anymore,"—she far preferred him slinking in shadows—"I'll pay off the damned bastards holding my debt. I'll wed a fat-in-the-pockets heiress who'll deepen my wealth. It's really quite brilliant."

Yes, as far as villainous plans, it rather was. "I won't," she said with an air of finality.

He let out a beleaguered sigh. "You've always been an obstinate one. Always trying to be proper and well-behaved. As though that would have earned you anyone's regard or note." She curled her fingers reflexively into tight balls. "No one will ever notice you. They never did," he said without inflection.

Bridget brought her shoulders back. "I'd rather be invisible than seen for a blackness in my soul, as you are."

Archibald lifted one shoulder in a casual shrug. "If I cared about another's opinion, I'd have been destroyed long ago. You, however, are the one hiding in the countryside, living a pretend life and poring over your," he nudged his chin at the books scattered upon the table. "Dull books." He caught his chin between his thumb and forefinger and proceeded to walk about her very much a predator sizing up its prey. "I wonder… hmm."

Bridget forced herself to remain still through his deliberate show. Questions screamed around her mind and she quelled them. A woman of seven and twenty, she'd been the brutalized sibling of two monsters and then eventually cast out. Neither of them knew anything about her. She'd far more calm and control than Archibald or Marianne had ever credited.

Her brother stopped before her. Nearly four inches taller than her own five-feet seven-inches, he still towered over her enough to command a space. He stuck his face close to hers. "You know you want to ask me what I'm thinking. You want to know what is going on inside my head."

"I know it can be nothing good," she rejoined.

"And that is enough," he continued as though she'd not spoken. "It is enough knowing that you care. Just as you care about the boy."

Despite her bid for control, her entire body recoiled. *Virgil.* The one person who truly mattered. A person she loved so wholly and who she'd sacrificed her own life to protect. Heart hammering, she swung her gaze to the doorway, grateful her son was away from this monster.

"You and I both know the truth about him." She'd wager every coin she'd earned evaluating antiquities that Archibald didn't even know the child's name.

"Don't," she whispered. Where did she find the steely strength to form that response? Where, when inside every nerve was stretched tight and she was poised for battle?

Archibald grinned a cold, unfeeling grin. He gripped her head tight in his hands and dragged her close. "He's not your boy," he taunted. "He's all mine. His mother was a whore who's dead at her own hand."

On a hiss, Bridget wrenched away from him, drew her arm back, and slapped his cheek. The crack of flesh hitting flesh echoed around the room, as the force of her blow jerked his head back.

She braced for the roar of outrage. Instead, her brother ran a distracted palm over the imprint left by her palm. "I see you understand, then."

Terror gripped her. Those dangerous words he'd uttered could shatter her and Virgil's very existence and happiness. It would see Virgil stripped from her care and turned over to this monster, for no one would dare believe the word of a scarred spinster, deaf in one ear and without a husband or gainful employment. "You'd risk your...my son's life." She may have not given birth to Virgil, but he was hers in every way. She'd loved him, cared for him when he was ill, held him when he'd fallen.

Archibald plucked a speck of dust from his sleeve and flicked it to the floor. "Without hesitation...and yours? I'll tell the world, a lonely, miserable, deaf spinster, you stole my child and passed it off as your own and invented a world for yourself. Why, I expect Society would even applaud me when I committed such a woman to Bedlam." He laughed uproariously.

"What do you want?" she entreated, hating the desperate plea there. She'd given up everything for Virgil. The threat her brother made now against her only brought a fear for what that would mean for her son.

"You know," he said coolly.

Bridget ran her hands over her face. When Virgil's mother had arrived at one of her family's country estates and abandoned her newborn babe in Bridget's arms—only after she'd revealed the depth of Archibald's treachery—Bridget had taken the babe to London. She'd demanded her brother do right by him. Doing right had involved him promising to turn the boy over to a foundling hospital.

And so, Bridget had taken on the babe as her own and disappeared into one of their family's small, run-down properties where she'd been ever since. She knew what kind of ugliness Archibald was capable of. She had borne the sting of his hateful words and his ruthless blows. He would do this. Virgil meant nothing to him. He never had nor would he ever. "Please, do not ask me to do this," she begged, hating that he'd reduced her to this. But she'd have laid herself down prone at his feet and offered her own life to protect Virgil.

"His name is Chilton," her brother said, ignoring her entreaty. "Lord Chilton."

Lord Chilton. Lord Chilton. She searched her mind. How did she recognize that—

"He has one of the vastest antiquities collections. Brings his items to auction and makes an obscene fortune."

Of course. That was how she knew of him. Referred to as the Bastard Baron in the papers that found their way to the country, she'd cared less about those personal details and more focused on whichever collection he was purported to have acquired or sold. If life had turned out differently for her, and followed an altered path, she would have paid a visit to the halls where he kept those cherished treasures. Mayhap, she would have plied him with questions and begged for a look, even as she could never have afforded even a scrap of parchment in his establishment.

"He's out a housekeeper. I've coordinated with the hiring agency responsible for staffing his London townhouse for you to fill the respective post."

"A servant," she repeated back.

He nodded.

Restless, Bridget wandered over to the small window that overlooked the overgrown front gardens. She stared blankly out, contemplating what her brother put to her. He'd have her serve on Lord Chilton's staff. Granted, a housekeeper, alongside the butler, was the most respected of the household positions. Nor had she truly been born for more than that. Having been shunned by her family for the birthmark that covered her left cheek, and being deaf in one ear, she'd been an outcast among their kin. It had never even been expected that she'd have a Season or marry. As she'd once read her parents' lips and heard them talking of the empty future awaiting her, she'd found her value deemed of little worth even by the people who'd sired her. She'd finally found a family, in Virgil and Miss Nettie…the one person who'd ever offered her kindness. And she'd do anything to protect them.

In the lead windowpane, she spied the guilt ravaging her features. "Just this once," her voice was a barely-there whisper. "I'll never steal for you again."

At his silence, she spun back. "I want a promise." *Do you truly believe your brother's word means anything?* She held a hand up when he opened his mouth and opted for a language he understood. "I want ten thousand pounds," she said bluntly, her skin crawling at the stolen monies she'd accept. "I'll not turn over that book until you give me those funds."

He eyed her with an appreciation that turned her stomach. "I never thought I'd see the day I was proud of you, Bridget. Until now."

I'm going to be ill.

"Five thousand," he said flatly.

"Eight."

"Seven and not a pence more," he said with a finality that marked the end of his bargaining.

She gave a tight nod.

"You begin in a week's time."

As he rambled through the perfunctory details of her assignment, a loud humming filled her ears. *I am complicit in this crime. I am sacrificing my honor… for my son's life.* That reminder brought her back from the precipice of despair.

"While you're gone, I'll remain here with the boy."

A denial burst from her lips and she sprang forward on the balls of her feet. "You'll not." She'd rather dance with the Devil on Sunday than leave Virgil alone in her brother's company.

He frowned. "Come, you hurt my feelings, Bridget." Archibald made a tsking sound. "Surely you don't think I'd hurt my own—" Her breath caught. "—nephew."

She'd conceded enough this day. She'd not allow him this. "No. I've agreed to help you and you have my word I'll do so. But I'll not have you staying with my son."

He pursed his lips and glanced around the room. He sighed. "Very well. It would be rather hideous living here." He eyed the paintings pinned to the wall; those precious gifts made by Virgil three years earlier. Her brother sneered.

"We are done here, Archibald," she said tightly and marched to the door.

Her brother lifted his head. "I say, you've hurt my feelings again, Bridget."

"You don't have any feelings to be hurt," she shot back.

"No." He grinned. "You are correct there. But you share my blood. And for all your failings and flaws, you have parts of the Hamilton determination inside you."

"Evil." Archibald cocked his head. "The Hamilton evil." Her parents had been a coldhearted pair who'd spawned even colder children. Was it a wonder she could so easily agree to help Archibald in this?

"Call it what you wish, but it will see me—and now you—survive."

Seething, Bridget yanked open the door. Her heart dropped to her stomach as Virgil stumbled into the room. Cheeks flushed and eyes downcast, he demonstrated the same lack of skill with subterfuge as she herself.

With the same crescent-shaped birthmark on his wrist and the same shade of brown hair as Bridget and her brother, he was very much a Hamilton—in appearance. Not in any other way, however. "Mum," he mumbled, scuffing the tip of his shoe along the floor.

"Virgil." She damned her reduced hearing that allowed him to sneak up on her. And then her stomach lurched. How much had he heard? She searched him for any indications. "His Lordship was just leaving," she said tightly.

"U-uncle Archibald," her son greeted.

With barely a glance for this boy he'd sired, Archibald stalked out of the room.

She instantly closed the door behind him. "I told you not to lurk at doorways, ever," she said sharply.

Virgil wrinkled his nose. "Why is he always so miserable?"

"Because he was born miserable," she said without thinking. And merciless and cutting. She winced. Regardless of the truths about that vile reprobate that was her brother, she'd no place interjecting her feelings about Archibald or anything. She gathered Virgil close, needing the soft, reassuring weight of his small frame. "Some people are just happy and some are—"

"Miserable," he finished and struggled away.

Her heart pulled. How often he drew back from those expressions of warmth. As a babe, he'd always been ready with a hug. As a young boy, he desperately craved and required a gentleman's influence. She steeled her jaw. Never one like Archibald. Which brought her back to Virgil's presence here before her now. "What were you doing listening at the door?" she asked in even tones. *What did you hear? How long were you there?*

"I went out to feed the sheep and saw his carriage."

So, he'd sneaked free of Miss Nettie. Nearing fifty, the older woman was growing more lax. And she'd be all Virgil had when Bridget went off to London. Suddenly, the wisdom in that course gave her pause.

"What did he want?" Virgil asked, with a surprising amount of world wariness in his eyes.

To destroy our future: yours and mine.

Opting to give him as much truth as she was able, she explained: "There are books in London. I've been asked to evaluate them."

Her son's eyes lit. For his earlier standoffishness, he threw himself at her, tugging at her sleeve the way he had as a young babe. "We're going to London? When do we leave?"

"We're not…" As soon as those two words left her lips, she froze. Her gaze locked on Virgil's dipping smile. *He can't remain here. I need him close.* Archibald would expect Bridget to comply and he'd know precisely where Virgil was at all times. "We're not set to leave for another week," she adjusted and, just like that, her son brightened. "However, I'll be required to live in the center where I'll be working."

Mayhap in a handful of more years, Virgil would possess the maturity to question that peculiarity. As it was, he peppered her with questions about where he'd be residing and what he'd be doing while he was there.

The sight of his enthusiasm: his wide, even-toothed smile, his dancing eyes briefly lessened her fear. And for a sliver of an instant, she could almost believe they were any other mother and son bound for an exciting journey to that great metropolis for Virgil's first trip. She gathered him into her arms again and squeezed hard. He grunted but, this time, folded his arms around her, returning that embrace. "What's that for?" he asked the usual question.

"Just because I love you." Her throat worked painfully as she gave him that familiar reply. *I'm going to crumple before him.* She fought desperately for a rapidly slipping control. "Run along," she urged, setting him aside. "I've to return to my work. Miss Nettie will be looking for you."

He nodded. "I love you," he said so easily. Growing up, there

had been a dearth of those words shared in the Hamilton household. When she'd first held Virgil, that babe without a name, she'd
vowed he'd know everything she'd been without.

"I love you, too," she said softly, staring after him as he darted
from the room.

She loved him. It was why she'd barter her honor and sell her
soul to deceive Lord Chilton and steal that coveted tome.

CHAPTER
2

Vail Basingstoke, Baron Chilton, had learned early on that passions and vices came in all forms.

Some gentlemen had scandalous bedroom proclivities that could only be carried out in the darkest streets of London. Others craved fine spirits that ultimately drowned them in their own weakness.

Everyone was generally of the opinion that a learned man was a respectable one; a man who favored literature and books embodied self-restraint, logic, and reason. Vail, however, a bastard-born son of a whore only titled through battlefield actions at Waterloo, had seen the darkest, depraved actions of men of all stations. From his late mother's keepers to the soldiers who'd cut down men in war to London's most learned scholars—all were rotted to the core.

It was that understanding that had allowed him to build himself a fortune and rule the world of his making. It was also what saw him riding down the dangerous cobblestones of King Street with night falling.

He guided his mount, Atlas, down the noisy, overflowing streets. Whores lingered on corners and dandies seeking a thrill on the wild side stumbled drunkenly along. Vail narrowed his eyes on the establishment at the end of King Street. It was not, however, whores, drink, or wagering that brought him here.

He brought Atlas to a stop outside Jack Spiggot's. Dismounting, he did a quick sweep, searching, and then finding. A small boy came bounding over. "Sorry, guv'nor," Jeremy Jon said in his coarse Cockney accent. "Oi was tied up." He collected the reins from Vail.

Having first met the lad one year earlier when Jeremy had attempted—unsuccessfully—to pick his pocket, Vail could wager his entire fortune, and win, just what had occupied him. "I just paid you," Vail said without recrimination. "Has it been lifted?"

Any of the drunken lords, sailors, and merchants stumbling about would assume they haggled over the fare…or something far more nefarious. That is if they weren't too deep in their cups to notice something outside their own lust for drink.

A ruddy flush stained the boy's cheeks. "No one lifts anything from me, guv'nor."

No, with the child's fleet feet and ability to wind his way like a specter through the streets of St. Giles, no constable could even come close to nabbing him. And yet, Vail had put Jeremy in his employ. "I don't want you picking pockets," he said in a hushed tone. He'd too much need for him and the truth was he'd come to care for the child.

Jeremy nudged his chin up at a belligerent angle. "Sister's having a baby, guv'nor."

Another one. The boy had revealed offhandedly some months ago that his sister was married to a cruel bruiser who kept her pregnant and beat her in equal measure. His own mother had been a well-cared for whore, but she'd still been knocked around enough times that Vail had developed a burning loathing for men who'd brutalize a woman. "Here." Reaching inside his jacket front, he withdrew a small purse and slipped it to the boy. "For watching my mount," he said from the corner of his mouth when the lad made to reject it. Jeremy Jon had more pride than most grown men combined.

The boy hesitated another moment and then pocketed the purse. Too many lords thinking to help a street urchin tossed those bags over without proper consideration that doing so in a public manner marked them instead…and invariably those coins would prove stolen by the leaders of London's underbelly. "I don't want you picking pockets," he said for the boy's ears alone. "You're too valuable." Those matter-of-fact words weren't ones he used to inflate the boy's self-confidence or sense of self-worth. Jeremy proved to be one set of eyes and ears Vail relied on in the Dials who found out the information Vail sought as a book buyer and seller. "If you need more, you tell me."

Stubborn as the day was long, Jeremy tightened his mouth and met that order with silence.

Vail lowered his head. "Are we clear?"

"Aye, guv'nor." Jeremy touched the brim of his cap in a smart salute. Vail, however, had told enough lies in his life to recognize them even now in this boy. Jeremy Jon was too proud to ask him for a pence more than he was paid. He'd rather rob and steal than humble himself.

"What have you heard?" he asked from the side of his mouth, as he tugged free his gloves and stuffed them in his jacket.

"Stanwicke was meetin' wit someone about that book." Whatever given assignment he doled out for the child, no titles, authors, or specifics were mentioned beyond the first time.

"And?"

"He was asking if he'd the funds to beat yar offer."

Beat his offer. Vail smiled coolly. The Earl of Stanwicke, notorious collector who'd beggared his family and estates to grow his obsession. Crazed as too many lords often were and all the while Vail profited. "Who was the gentleman?"

"A Lord Derby, sir." Jeremy adjusted the brim of his cap. "Tall. Bald. But he was dressed loike 'e wasn't a lord."

Vail glanced to the doorway of the Coaxing Tom. Like every other Black Legs, the door hung agape as it did morn through night, inviting the weakest of passersby to come sit at the tables and toss down their fortunes. "When did they meet?"

"Two in St. James' Street, guv'nor."

Of course. Two lords choosing to meet in the respectable ends of the Dials, they'd not think Vail, ruthless in his business pursuits, would deal on the proper side of London. What they'd miscalculated were the people he had all over London who brought him information just like that shared by Jeremy. "You've done well," he murmured. For the valuably obtained information, he slipped Jeremy another purse.

His informant hesitated, but then shot greedy fingers out and gathered the velvet sack. "Do yar need anything else, guv'nor?"

"Watch Atlas for now." He glanced about. "I'll also need you to monitor Derby when he comes 'round. See who he talks to." The Earl of Derby didn't deal directly or indirectly with Vail for his purchases and sales. As such, he wanted to know precisely who that nobleman's connections were.

"Aye, sir."

Angling his head slightly in that unspoken command he'd given Jeremy at the onset of their partnership, the boy bustled off with Atlas. A carriage rumbled by and Vail waited for it to pass. Then he made his way through the crowded streets. Where the fashionable end of London would be quiet in preparation for the upcoming balls and soirees, this hour was when the seediest hells and streets came to life. Senses alert for the hint of threat, he skimmed his gaze over his surroundings.

Where most every other titled gentleman saw in this area a place for inanity and wicked pursuits, Vail recognized the danger here. And he thrilled in it. His stare alighted on Mr. Andrew Barrett. Brother-in-law to his best friend, Nick Tallings, the Duke of Huntly, the young man had acquired a reputation for being a reprobate like his nearly impoverished father. The younger man wound his way through the streets and then entered through the open doors of The Pill Gilder. Vail gave his head a disgusted shake at the gentleman's lack of awareness of his surroundings. These areas would see a man, regardless of station, with a blade in his belly.

Vail climbed the steps of the Coaxing Tom. The loud din of raucous laughter attacked his ears. The pungent floral fragrances worn by the whores and gentlemen alike flooded his nose. Long ago, he'd become immune to those cloying scents. With a narrow-eyed gaze, he surveyed the crowded rooms.

The guards stationed at the front door gave him a quick once-over, and then nodded in recognition. "Yar Lordship."

Silent, Vail lifted his head in greeting. Business drove his purpose this evening. He spied Lord Derby seated at a back table. Portly, with bewhiskered cheeks, the man stole nervous glances about.

Yes, the bookish scholars Vail dealt with were men out of their element in these wicked hells. It was why he'd made a point early in his career to conduct all appointments inside one hell or another. Brooke's or White's put a gentleman at ease. Places such as the Coaxing Tom stripped a man of his usual control. Black cloak swirling about his ankles, Vail stalked through the club.

A voluptuous blonde-haired beauty stepped into his path. "Your Lordship," she purred, pressing herself against his chest. "How lovely it is to see you." Nearly eight inches shorter than his own six-feet four-inches, she had to go up on tiptoe to reach his mouth. She placed a kiss at the corner of his lips.

Vail lazily wrapped a hand about her waist and pulled her closer. "How long?"

"Been here for nearly an hour," she whispered close to his ear.

Maintaining the façade, he angled her head and pressed his lips to her throat. "Any company?"

She arched her head back and emitted an exaggerated moan. "None. Has a bag under his table. A pistol in his breeches that he keeps flashing when he checks his timepiece," the whore, Tabitha, said, barely parting her lips as she spoke.

To anyone observing them, they were no different than every other lord with wandering hands and an eager whore. Since the first time he'd taken Tabitha to the rooms abovestairs nearly four years earlier, however, they'd struck an unexpected-to-Society relationship. One devoid of any carnality, despite Tabitha's occasional offer to bed him. Theirs was strictly a business arrangement. She was his eyes and ears inside this club and when word needed to reach him, she found a way.

Feeling Lord Derby's stare on them, Vail cupped Tabitha about the nape of her neck. He dragged her mouth close and kissed her for the other man's benefit.

Tabitha instantly melted against him. This time, there was nothing false in her breathy moan.

Vail broke the kiss. "Mayhap later," he said loud enough for the gentlemen passing by them. He swatted her once on the buttocks and turned to go.

"Vail?" she called out, staying him.

Pausing, he looked back.

She drifted closer. "There can be a later," she murmured, fiddling with the lapels of his cloak. "I can…"

He pressed his fingertips to her lips, staying those words. She'd grown too close. Wanted more. Hoped for something he could not give her. Something he could not give any woman. He'd loved once and lost hard…a young woman who'd rejected him because he hadn't a coin to his name. From that betrayal, he'd learned to keep his guard up and let no one in.

Tabitha sighed. "You're the only bloody nob who's uninterested in a place in my bed, Vail Basingstoke," she muttered, though he detected the flash of regret in her eyes.

"I don't bed the women in my employ," he said to soften the blow of his rejection. Resuming his march to Derby's table, Vail didn't wait for an invitation and simply tugged out a chair.

The bald nobleman swallowed; that audible evidence of his nervousness stretched across the din of the room. "Ch-Chilton," he greeted, pushing an empty glass and bottle of brandy across the table. "A brandy."

Vail reclined in his seat and then steepled his fingertips together. He proceeded to tap them in a deliberate, silent staccato. "I'm displeased with you, Derby," he said in a frosty tone.

All the color leeched from the earl's cheeks. "W-with me?" he yanked frantically at his cravat, rumpling the perfectly tied gastronome knot. "C-Can't imagine why. I've done nothing."

Abandoning his casual pose, Vail leaned forward and placed his elbows on the surface of the table. "Haven't you?" he asked in a menacing whisper. "I don't take well to liars,"—the earl trembled, his legs shaking so hard, he knocked the table and his glass splattered droplets upon the scarred surface—"nor do I deal with men who break their word once an agreement has been reached. Why, those men, I won't even sell to." It was the ultimate trump for these men obsessed with their books and manuscripts. Some of the leading peers of Society would cull and hunt down first edition works and rare copies at the cost of their own names and reputations.

Derby lifted his palms in supplication. "Haven't broken anything. I wouldn't—"

Vail narrowed his eyes. "Think carefully before you finish that sentence," he warned.

The earl's shoulders sank. The book in question was Sir William Dugdale's first edition work of *The Baronage of England*. Having discovered it was in Derby's possession, Vail had taken advantage of the other man's desperate need for finances to win the script at a favorable price.

The pale nobleman matched Vail's pose and leaned across the table. "I've an explanation. One you can appreciate."

"Do not tell me what I can, will, or will never appreciate," he said, coating that warning in ice.

"Of course, of course. Forgive me." Derby spoke so quickly his words rolled together.

Vail would lay down his life for his siblings and the one person he called friend. But where members of the peerage were concerned, He'd fleece them of their fortunes with a smile and sleep at night all the better for it.

"I was trying to fetch more for it. Surely you can app…?" At Vail's pointed look, the man's throat muscles moved. "I want that Chaucer," he said, giving Vail the first honest truth since he'd joined him. "If I can fetch more, I can pay you more."

"And if you'd deny my payment for a spoken contract, then you'll never even set foot inside the auction house when bidding commences," Vail said flatly. "Are we clear?"

The other man had the look of one who'd imbibed too much and was about to toss the contents of his stomach up for it. "W-we are."

Vail motioned for Tabitha. The young woman instantly rushed over. "Can oi be of service," she purred, playing her part to such perfection a Drury Lane actress couldn't manage.

"If you'll clear the table?"

Pouting, she made quick work of putting the barely touched bottle of brandy and two glasses onto her tray. Expertly balancing that burden, she withdrew a clean rag from her bodice. Had Derby been cleverer—at all clever—he'd have noted the fabric was of a quality and cleanliness at odds with the establishment they now frequented. After Tabitha dusted the surface and sauntered off, Vail reached inside his jacket and fished out a specific pair of gloves. Carefully pulling on the white cotton articles, he peered down his nose at the earl. "The book."

"Yes. Yes. Here. I have it." The older nobleman leaned under the table and fiddled with his valise. He straightened and handed it over.

Collecting it, Vail proceeded to the front page. With the same expert eye that had shaped him into one of the most successful and most ruthless booksellers in England, he took in every detail of the volume in his possession. He noted the coloring and quality of the page and the vibrancy of the ink. Vail paused, lingering his perusal on the author's name marked on those pages. With his gaze, he traced the specific loops and turns of Dugdale's flourishing signature. With careful movements, he closed the book.

Wordlessly, he pulled out two items. First, he slid a one hundred pound note across the table. Then he fingered a special cloth sack he'd had made to shield and protect items he acquired. Vail stood. "Do not ever attempt to renege on a deal with me." He spoke those words as a lethal threat. "I do not take to being made a fool."

"My apologies, Chilton," Derby stammered, scrambling to his feet. "I–I'm still able to come bid, then? I've more items to sell you in the meantime. If you'd care to—"

"This is all I've a need for now." Never let a person know one's interest or eagerness. Let a person present the item for bid, then feign disinterest, and walk away…and then later strike the terms of an agreement that fit one's own desiring. Not bothering with another glance for the man, Vail marched the same path he'd traveled a short while ago and took his leave.

Once outside, he searched the streets, looking not for his mount, but—

His gaze landed on his black lacquer carriage emblazoned with the gold Chilton falcon. With its wings spread and talons curled, he was a predator about to pounce. It was an ideal symbol he'd inherited that perfectly matched the role of hunter he'd adopted. Vail stalked over to that conveyance. Everything about his meetings in King Street was perfectly orchestrated: from Jeremy who collected his reins, to the guards, attired as a driver and footman who returned and traded out Vail's mount for the carriage to escort him home.

"My lord," Ernest greeted, a question in his eyes.

Vail inclined his head in the silent, universal statement they'd adopted which confirmed everything had been met without conflict. Book in one arm, Vail climbed inside the carriage and, as the conveyance rolled away from the Coaxing Tom, he leaned back and relished his thrilling triumph over the nobility.

CHAPTER
3

"OH, LADY BRIDGET, I DO not like this. I still don't like it at all," Nettie repeated, wringing her hands.

There was something frustrating in going through life banished by one's parents, spurned by one's siblings, and not known by anyone in Society. Yet, to have the one woman who'd cared for you since your birth unable to, all these years later, refer to you with only your name went beyond that frustration.

Lady Bridget.

"I know that, Nettie," she said softly, surveying the rooms she'd rented in London. Bridget didn't like any of it. From the scheme her brother demanded she play part in, to the accommodations they'd call home for the next…however long it took her to obtain that book.

She studied the dirt-stained lead windows, the water stains upon the ceiling, and the discolored furnishings, and sighed. In all the times she'd dreamed of leaving the countryside and exploring the city of London, she'd never expected *this* would be where she and Virgil would reside. Only it wasn't her. It would just be her son and Nettie. Her heart constricted at the thought of being parted from him.

Tucked away on the outskirts of Piccadilly, in a townhouse that was dark, dank, and damp, there was no other place she wished to be but back in their small, familiar cottage.

"A waste of resources this one is," the graying, lifelong nurse-maid muttered.

"Yes." But at the end of this deception, there would be coin enough to free her of the manipulation at Archibald's hands. And there'd be enough money to last her, Virgil, and Nettie well into the future. "It is just for a short while."

Nettie tightened her mouth. "I don't understand what manner of man would expect you to take up residence in his household, all to evaluate books."

A dull blade of guilt twisted inside. For that was the lie she'd given this woman who'd made her entire life—hers and then Virgil's.

"It's not natural, I say," the woman said in hushed tones. "I don't care if he's one of those bookish scholars you deal with. They're wicked ones, too."

Warmth suffused her breast. The older woman might only ever refer to her as Lady Bridget, but Bridget had been invisible to her parents. Nettie had been far more a mother than had she given Bridget life. It was a bond she appreciated even more since she'd become a parent to Virgil. She wrapped her arms about the other woman's shoulders and squeezed. "I daresay there's no scholarly scoundrel with wicked intentions for a partially deaf, scarred widow," she said pragmatically. She was a woman of logic and reason. As such, she'd never given much worrying or regret to her appearance. It was a thing that could not be changed and certainly not a reason she'd ever want one to notice her.

Nettie swatted at her hand. "Don't speak ill of yourself."

Bridget bussed her nursemaid on a wrinkled cheek. "You know I only ever speak the truth. I hardly have any vanity where things such as my looks should ever matter."

"Humph, the only reason some gent hasn't absconded with you is because you've been hidden away for your whole life."

Repressing a smile, Bridget gave Nettie's shoulders another light squeeze. The nursemaid may as well be a proud mama for how she'd always spoken of her. "Well, I promise, I shan't run off anywhere unless I have you and Virgil with me."

"Where are we going?"

They both looked up as Virgil skidded into the room.

Both women spoke in unison. "Slow."

Cheeks flushed red with excitement and his eyes glowing, Virgil wore his joy tangibly like a mark upon his face.

"We are not going anywhere," Bridget said, walking over. She ruffled the top of his chocolate brown tresses. When his face fell, she added, "You and Nettie, however, will be exploring London." As much as they could afford. All their resources had gone to rent these rooms for the next two months. She'd not proffered coin for any additional ones. That was the time she'd set for herself to see this through.

"Why can't you stay?" And with the faint pleading there, Virgil was very much the tiny babe she'd cradled in her arms, and not this little person who wavered between babe and boy.

"I will be busy shut away evaluating old books."

"And you'll love it all the while," he groused, though his lips pulled slightly at the corners. For all his protestations to the contrary, Virgil had an equal love and skill with antiquated texts.

But how well he knew her. And yes, normally she would have traded the slim material possessions to their name to examine some of the most prized first edition books and tomes of Lord Chilton's collection. From this point forward, she'd never look upon another without seeing Archibald's evil and her own complicity. Ravaged with guilt at taking part in this scheme and leaving her son behind, she dropped to a knee so she could look him squarely in the eyes. "I'll return every Sunday," she vowed. As housekeeper there were many benefits that came with the post. Not only would she acquire thirty pounds each month she served in the baron's household but she also had the freedom of movement one day each week.

"And we'll do something wonderful on those days?" he pressed.

Bridget caught him to her, knocking him off-kilter. "Are you daring to suggest it's not just wonderful being with me?" She tickled him in his sides until peals of laughter rang from his lips.

"S-stop. S-stop," he pleaded, fighting against her hold.

Tickling him once more for good measure, she leaned up and kissed his cheek. "Something wonderful," she hedged. For the truth remained, she could not be caught out in the fashionable ends of London and risk being spied by her employer in Virgil's company.

At her back, Nettie cleared her throat and pain lanced through her. "'Tis time, Lady Bridget."

It had been inevitable, that pronouncement. And yet, hearing it somehow cemented the finality of her decision and her departure. Biting the inside of her cheek, she forced herself to stand slowly. She'd not have Virgil see her pain and trepidation in leaving. Her son's lower lip quivered and the sight of his quiet suffering ravaged her. From behind her, Nettie's crying filled the small parlor. *I'm going to splinter apart right in front of them.* "Until Sunday," she said hoarsely. And before she dissolved into a puddle of tears at his feet, Bridget grabbed her valise and rushed from the room.

Virgil's soft weeping followed behind her and she quickened her footsteps, fighting the urge to return. If she did so, she'd be useless to him. He'd see her break down and would only find greater misery. With every step, Nettie's hushed reassurances grew fainter and fainter until they dissolved altogether. Her muslin cloak whipped noisily about her ankles and, shifting her cumbersome valise to her other hand, she rushed down the hall to the foyer.

Lords and ladies had housekeepers and butlers. But even as Bridget's own family had been in possession of a once plentiful staff, she herself had forever been without that luxury. In time, after she'd been scuttled off to the country with Archibald's son, she'd opened her own doors and brewed her own teas. She let herself out the front door.

An overcast London morn greeted her; the dreary day a perfect match to her mood. Shoving aside such maudlin sentiments, she scanned the streets of Piccadilly. No good had ever come in wallowing in regrets. She located a hack. Shifting the burden of her valise to her other hand, she started over. "To Lord Chilton's Mayfair residence. Number Fifteen."

The young man eyed her a moment and then, jumping down, he drew the door open. He collected her bag. First, he helped Bridget up and then tossed her valise inside after her. It landed with an unceremonious thump at her feet. "Thank—" The silent driver slammed the door shut. "—you," she muttered under her breath. The carriage lurched forward and she gasped. Grabbing the edge of the seat to keep from flying forward, she held tight.

The torn, faded, velvet curtains whipped wildly. The passing streets of London danced in and out of focus like the kaleido-scope she'd gifted Virgil years earlier. Bridget stared absently out at the foreign streets and used the remaining time to prepare for her introduction to the baron's household. As the senior member of Lord Chilton's staff, she'd be permitted freedom of movement within the household which should make her task of finding the Chaucer and—

She pressed her eyes closed. "I've become a common thief," she whispered into the carriage. For the first time, Bridget forced herself to utter those words aloud and own them. She was sacrificing her honor to save Virgil. If she were being truthful with herself at last in this instant, she was saving herself, too. Because she'd witnessed over the years the evil Archibald was capable of. She knew what he did to those who'd thwarted him. And she did not doubt he'd have her committed as he'd vowed if she didn't do this.

Fueled by that, she set her shoulders and shifted her thoughts to something safer—her upcoming meeting.

My name is Bridget Hamlet.

Given that she'd spent her childhood days in one of her family's far-flung country estates and then chose self-exile so she might raise Virgil, none either knew or remembered a third Hamilton child.

Bridget silently mouthed all the details she'd worked out for her fictional existence. ...*I'm a widow. My late husband was a bookseller. My family landed gentry...*

Having read every book inside her family's once well-stocked Yorkshire estate, she'd read enough gothic tales of ladies sneaking inside a powerful nobleman's household. Every last one included surprise that the employer should ask probing questions and so commenced the stammering. Bridget, however, was too logical to make that mistake.

The carriage rolled to a stop and a peculiar still gripped her. Where were the lurching stomach and the panicky thoughts? But then, mayhap this calm was just further testament that her blood was as evil as that of Archibald and Marianne.

"Here we are, miss," the driver called, yanking the door open.

Gathering her valise by the worn leather handle, she held on to it with one hand. With the other, she accepted the hackney driver's offer of help. Bridget reached inside her cloak and withdrew coin for the fare, and the young man grabbed it with quick fingers. He tucked the coin inside his jacket, scrambled back atop his box, and drove off.

Alone, she remained planted on the pavement and directed her attention up the brick finish of the townhouse. The structure and windows facing the streets and lanes marked it one of the first-rate houses, and stood as a sign of Lord Chilton's wealth. But then, a man in possession of one of the most coveted tomes, no doubt, had fortunes to rival the king's.

He'll not miss that one book, then. He'll survive and thrive even with it gone, whereas I have no hope of existence without it.

That reminder ricocheted around her mind. Even as it propelled her forward and up the steps of Lord Chilton's residence, guilt stung her throat like vinegar and made it hard to swallow. Bridget set her valise at her feet and knocked once.

When no one rushed to open the door, she shifted back and forth on her feet. Her skin pricked with the feel of stares trained on her. Unbidden, she looked out. Several ladies strolling arm in arm gawked. The same hideous fascination that accompanied any other stranger upon first spying the crescent-shaped mark upon her cheek. Their lips rapidly moved but Bridget had always been rot at gathering a jot of what another person said after they'd moved their lips away from her line of focus.

Drawing her bonnet up higher, she faced the arched entranceway, and frowned. Where in blazes was the butler? Or any household servant, for that matter?

As a girl, her earliest remembrances of her dictatorial father had been a man who'd railed at servants and sacked them if they failed to answer a door in a single rap. What manner of man was the baron who'd serve as her employer? Was he an absentee noble-man, whose servants carried on as they wished because of it? She knocked again.

The panel was drawn open with such alacrity, she gasped. A young servant in dark garments and an easy grin on his lips stared back. He passed his gaze over her, lingering on her valise. "Mrs. Hamlet," he greeted with the warmth of a lifelong friend who'd been reunited as he motioned her forward. "You've arrived. Early. I am Mr. Lodge—" She opened her mouth to return the salu-tation—but he spoke hurriedly. "That is, I take it you are Mrs.

Hamlet?"

Grateful to have that wood panel as a barrier between the gaping passersby and herself, she rushed inside. "I am."

A dark-clad footman came forward to collect her valise and she turned it over to his hands.

"Mr. Winterly will meet with you and go through your responsibilities. When His Lordship returns, it is Winterly who'll perform the necessary introductions," the butler prattled.

Bridget furrowed her brow. *Who?*

"Forgive me. Mr. Winterly is Lord Chilton's man-of-affairs. A business partner and," the servant dropped his voice to a low whisper, and she carefully watched his mouth, "brother." He stole a secretive glance about. "Given you'll be responsible for the female staff, I daresay it isn't gossip, mentioning Mr. Winterly is also a bastard child of the Duke of Ravenscourt like Lord Chilton."

Her mind spun under the flurry of gossip flying from this man's lips.

"Shall we?" Not waiting to see if she followed, Mr. Lodge started forward.

Fiddling with her clasp, Bridget hurriedly shed her cloak and dropped it into the hands of the patiently waiting footman, and rushed after the head servant.

"You'll find His Lordship exceedingly…" His words pulling in and out of focus, she cursed her partial deafness and quickened her steps until she walked alongside the loquacious servant. "…fair, generous, and kind to his staff," the butler directed that assurance forward.

Fair, generous, and kind. In short, all things her father, brother, mother, and sister hadn't ever been. She bit the inside of her cheek. Why couldn't Lord Chilton be spoken of with loathing and disdain by his staff? It wouldn't erase the wrongs of her actions here, but it would ease some of the guilt.

"…extremely successful and… Ah, here we are," Mr. Lodge stopped abruptly at the end of the corridor. He pushed the door open and motioned her forward.

She hesitated, as an irrational fear needled around her insides that this was all some kind of grand trap and, at any moment, someone would jump forward, finger pointed, and calls for the constable flying from his lips.

"Hmm," Mr. Lodge said with a frown, as he perused the room. He brightened. "Mr. Winterly should arrive shortly. If you'll but wait until he returns?"

Bridget turned to offer her thanks but the words died on her lips, finding him already halfway down the hall. She stared bemusedly after him. What a…peculiar man. But then, she had spent so many years with only Nettie and Virgil for company that she'd settled into a largely quiet existence.

Taking a step inside the room, she assessed the office. The gleaming surface of the mahogany furniture and the leather button sofas and winged chairs all bespoke wealth and masculine elegance. It was not, however, the Chippendale furniture that commanded her notice. Motionless, she stood frozen, her gaze trained on the floor-length shelving that wrapped around the sprawling room. For all intents and purposes, it was a library. Yet, the pedestal desk on plinth bases with its leather top, and folios and ledgers gathered there marked it an office.

It was a perfect room for a man who dealt in first editions and had made a fortune on ancient tomes. Her fingers twitched. The need to pull each edition from the shelf and assess its age and history gripped her with a potent force. Surely there would be no harm in examining them? Except, given her intentions for Lord Chilton's household, it would be an inauspicious beginning to be found poring over any of those tomes. As an inner battle waged between restraint and her own hungering, she cast a look over her shoulder. The hum of silence lingered in her one good ear. In the end, the pull of those books, however, proved too much.

Bridget drifted over to the front of the room, close to Lord Chilton's desk and stopped. A foot away from the bookcases, she skimmed her gaze over the volumes.

Richard Verstegen: *A Restitution of Decayed Intelligence: In Antiquities.*

Edward Coke, Sir John Swinton, George Baker Quinta pars relationum Edwardi Coke Equitis aurati, Regij Attornati Generalis / The fifth part of the reports of Sr. Edward Coke Knight, the Kings Attorney Generall.

She mouthed the titles of book after book. Seventeenth century works, they'd each been reprinted numerous times in that century alone. Closing her eyes, Bridget breathed deep the scent of the old works. That scent, beautiful and rich, filled her nose, calming her.

And for the first time since she'd agreed to help Archibald, there was something more than fear and regret—there was excitement at working beside books she'd never touch in the whole of her existence.

Magnifying glass in hand, Vail examined Johann Coler's astrological works he'd acquired from auction.

"Torn pages," Edward Winterly, Vail's brother, business partner, and man-of-affairs, stood at his shoulder as he viewed Vail's morning acquisitions.

"Several of the books," he conceded, setting aside the glass and book. "But the set can be broken up and will earn considerable coin for the copies that are intact."

Edward snorted. "I hope yesterday's purchase from Derby fares in better shape."

By way of answer, Vail swiped the drawstring velvet bag from the edge and held it over. "Near flawless." He rolled his shoulders to ease some of the tension he'd amassed from being bent over his work.

His brother grinned. Not unlike Vail himself, Edward revealed a tangible excitement in triumphing over members of the peerage. "So the transaction was a success, then." White gloves already donned, his brother carefully loosened the drawstrings and withdrew the volume in question. He laid it on the satin fabric draped over the table.

"Yes," he agreed as Edward examined the recent addition to his collection. Vail tightened his mouth as annoyance with Derby's actions stirred back to life. "But not before Derby tried to maneuver another purchaser." His brother briefly lifted his attention from that coveted tome. "Wanted to secure funds to compete for the Chaucer." That first edition work men would fight, kill, or steal for, and for that reason it had been carefully hidden away until it went to auction.

"Ahh," Edward said understandingly. "No one ever claimed Derby had a brain in his head."

"A love of books and literature hardly determines how grounded or logical a person is," Vail agreed.

Edward, engrossed in that copy, devoted all his attentions to Vail's most recent acquisition. "It lacks the tract *De iure Regis ecclesiastico*, as found in most copies," Edward correctly observed.

"Yes." It was a testament to its rarity. A wave of pride filled him. Born to different mothers but also both bastards of the Duke of Ravenscourt, Vail had discovered Edward four years earlier, mucking out the stables of a pompous lord. It was the last horse shite any one of his kin would shovel. From then on, Vail had resolved to find his siblings where he could and help them all make better lives for themselves. Since he'd joined Vail's employ, his brother had proven adept at assessing the value, worth, and integrity of coveted books and documents. Whereas Vail didn't care about the words on those pages past the fortunes they earned him, Edward had an abiding appreciation for the profits and the content in those books.

"Are you ready for me to locate a buyer for it?" He directed that question towards the book. Vail set prices and drove meetings and decisions but, as his man-of-affairs, Edward oversaw the acquisition of purchasers.

Vail shook his head. "I would still have the pages and cover cloth dusted first and—"

A knock sounded at the door. His butler and brother, Gavin Lodge, entered, and looked between Vail and Edward. He cleared his throat. "My lord," he greeted.

"I've already told you, you needn't call me 'my lord'," Vail said gently.

"I can't call you by your Christian name. You're my employer," Gavin groused. "I hardly need the staff believing the only reason I head your staff is because I'm your brother and—"

"I expect a debate on what you might call Vail is hardly the reason you've come 'round," Edward drawled, turning the page of his book.

Their younger sibling cleared his throat. "You're correct. A Mrs. Hamlet arrived a short while ago. I took the liberty of escorting her to your office."

Mrs. Hamlet? Vail stared back with befuddlement. "Who is—?"

Edward snapped his head up and cursed. "Your housekeeper."

What in blazes had happened to Mrs. Kelly? "I *have* a housekeeper."

Man-of-affairs and butler exchanged a look. "*Had* a housekeeper, my lord. *Had* a housekeeper," Lodge explained.

"She instructed your maids to set fires in every room." Edward's face turned red.

Vail narrowed his eyes. "In every room?"

"She insisted it was unnatural to not have lit hearths, even after I'd explained the reason for it, she did so anyway." As a rule, regardless of whether it was a freezing winter's day in London or a hot, humid summer one, no fires were lit, no windows opened in any place where his books were kept.

"I've found you a new housekeeper. Mrs.—"

"Hamlet," Gavin cut in, always eager to be involved in a discussion or exchange, regardless of whether or not it affected him.

"She's the widow of a late bookshop owner and, given that, I felt her experience marked her ideal for your household." Edward returned his focus to the book. He proceeded to pass the magnifying glass over the pages of that text, lost as he invariably became in those antique editions.

Gavin made a clearing sound with his throat. "I might point out that the young woman is waiting," he whispered.

Lingering beside the leather tome, Edward gave Vail a pleading look.

Oh, blast. "I'll do it," he muttered, grabbing his jacket from a nearby cranberry upholstered armchair. He started for the front of the room.

"Thank you," Edward called after him.

"This is the extent of my dealings with the staff," he warned, not deigning to look back. It wasn't that he believed household duties beneath him. Minted a baron after Waterloo, he still didn't put much value behind a title. He'd been a whore's son who'd varied between having a full belly and fine shelter or having an empty belly and tattered garments. Ultimately, it had always come down to whether his mother had a protector at any given moment. Furthermore, seeing as the last woman had compromised a fortune's worth of his collections, he'd be wise to at least oversee this particular task.

"Vail!"

He stopped and glanced back.

Gavin came sprinting down the hall. "I forgot," he said faintly, breathless. He handed over a note. "This arrived earlier."

The fragrant hint of jasmine flowers that clung to the scrap was familiar and once beloved. Now, it was nothing more than a reminder of his own foolishness. Accepting the missive, he needlessly scanned the flourishing scrawl. "Thank you," he said, dismissing his brother. "That will be all."

With a jaunty wave, Gavin skipped off.

His youngest sibling gone, he unfolded the page and hurriedly read yet another note from Lady Adrina Mast, the Countess of Buchanan, and recent widow. There had been a time when any word she'd written would have had him at her side. He'd been a boy when he gave his heart to her. Now, he felt nothing but a detached indifference to her desperate notes. Stuffing it inside his jacket he resumed the walk to his office.

He entered the room and stopped. The woman who'd been hired for the role of housekeeper was positioned behind his desk and remained wholly engrossed in the titles before her. She stood on tiptoes, surveying the shelves that contained the most recent additions to his collection.

Having dealt with thieves, scoundrels, and thugs who'd fight for and steal prized collections, he'd learned a proper wariness of anyone who came too close to his books. Particularly a servant new to his employ, who'd commandeered a place behind his desk. He entered the room but, engrossed as she was, Mrs. Hamlet continued to work her gaze frantically over the titles. Vail folded his arms at his chest. "Mrs. Hamlet," he said in hushed, icy tones. No one would ever accuse him of being unfair or cruel to his staff, but neither was he a man who'd tolerate a person entering his household and infringing upon his space.

The auburn-haired woman muttered something to herself and then bent down. At her blatant ignoring of him, he cocked his head. What in blazes?

Mrs. Hamlet froze and reached long, gloved fingers for a volume—

"Mrs. Hamlet," he barked.

The woman cried out and, knocked off-kilter, she tumbled against the shelving unit.

"Have a care with my—" That frosty warning died on Vail's lips as she faced him. In possession of auburn curls that shimmered hues of red, Mrs. Hamlet had a delicate, heart-shaped face and impossibly wide, almond-shaped, blue eyes that would have marked her a great beauty in any court—except for the large crescent-shaped birthmark upon her left cheek. The unusual crimson mark spanned half her face, transforming someone who Society would have considered a flawless beauty into someone wholly unique.

At his scrutiny, she brought her shoulders back and glared. "Forgive me, Mr. Winterly," she said with a surprising strength, wholly devoid of an apology from this woman who'd been caught sneaking about his offices. There was fiery glitter in her pretty, cornflower blue eyes; eyes that mocked him for his scrutiny. Yet, having battled Society's condemnation for the whole of his life, Vail saw something more behind that brave showing—insecurity.

Then her address registered. Ah, she'd mistaken him for his brother, then. "Lord Chilton," he offered, correcting her error. He'd neither the time, nor inclination for cases of mistaken identity.

Mrs. Hamlet wheeled her gaze to the doorway and then searched the room.

Vail shot a hand up and waved his fingers. "Me, Mrs. Hamlet. I'm your—"

"Oh, bloody hell," she whispered.

He started.

The young woman gasped and slapped a palm over her mouth. "Oh, dear."

A laugh escaped him and he quickly tamped it down. Why, she was refreshing. Wordlessly, he motioned to the pair of seats. She instantly scrambled to claim the nearest Louis XV carved walnut fauteuil à la Reine.

With slow, measured steps he stalked over and took up the leather chair behind his desk. Leaning back in his seat, he clasped his hands over his flat belly. "Tell me, were you interested in what you saw?"

"I hardly had time to assess enough to determine the overall value of your collection," she said with a perfunctory businesslike manner better suited a potential buyer or seller than a just-hired housekeeper. "However, I did identify one—"

"I was being sarcastic, Mrs. Hamlet," he said dryly.

The lady studied his mouth as he spoke. A pretty blush stained the lady's cheeks and turned that stark white crescent red. "Oh." The young woman briefly dipped her gaze to her lap and he used her distraction as a moment to study her. Slender, with an ample décolletage and generously curved hips now concealed by her repose, she couldn't be more different than the white-haired matron who'd held the post prior.

"Most employers would turn you out for snooping about a desk."

Mrs. Hamlet smoothed her palms over the front of her dark blue skirts. An outdated garment that bespoke the status of her wealth and finances. "Given I've been hired to oversee your female staff and have a right to the silver, I daresay examining your shelving would hardly merit a call to the constable," she said with such drollness his lips twitched.

Apparently, he'd been of an erroneous opinion earlier that her bluntness at his entrance had been a product of mistaken identity.

"Fair enough, Mrs. Hamlet," he said. He'd not point out that those books she'd been studying could fetch more than a small fortune. As the Bastard Baron, wanton women and widows vied for a place in his bed. But beyond that, respectable ladies averted their eyes whenever he, the Bastard Baron, was near. There was something refreshing in Mrs. Hamlet's frank reply. "Well, which was it then?"

Confusion glimmered in her eyes.

"The single copy among all these volumes." He gestured about the room. "That called you from your seat and around my desk."

The lady shook her head. "You are mistaken." His new house-keeper's chignon looked one more quick movement away from tumbling free of its pins. "I was never seated."

"Ah." He arched an eyebrow. "One of the obedient servants standing until the employer entered?"

"An appreciator of books who made the most of your absence," she demurred. The unexpectedness of that pulled another laugh from him. Since he'd returned from Waterloo, hailed a war hero, he'd become accustomed to women practiced in their words and praise. His servants averted their gazes and weighed their responses. How much more he preferred this directness.

A little frown marred Mrs. Hamlet's lips. "I wasn't jesting."

"Your honesty is appreciated." He lifted his head. "I apologize to have kept you waiting."

"Apologize," she repeated back slowly.

Mayhap, she was one of the few in London who did not know of his history. She couldn't know that he wasn't, nor would ever be one of those snobbish nobles who gave a jot for his rank. "Are you surprised?"

"That you should make apologies for your tardiness?" She nodded. "The nobility as a rule…" Mrs. Hamlet promptly closed her mouth and he had to resist the urge to press for her to complete her thought. "Forgive me," she said instead. "I expect you'd rather discuss my responsibilities and then return to your business matters."

Her cultured tones and grasp of the peerage indicated she was, mayhap, from one of those noble families, down on her fortune. "Which was the title?" he asked quietly, bringing them back to his earlier query.

Mrs. Hamlet's gaze wandered beyond his shoulder. For a long moment, she said nothing. He thought she'd ignore his question. Nor, as she'd accurately pointed out, should it altogether matter. He'd a meeting in a short while with his friend, Huntly, at Brooke's, and one immediately after with a deep in debt Lord Darbyshire for the first right to assess his collection. So why did he linger with a lively housekeeper? Mayhap, it was the honesty of her.

"Basile's *Petrosinella*," she murmured.

"Ah." Absently, he opened his middle desk drawer and withdrew one of six immaculate, white, cloth gloves. Standing, he drew them on slowly and wandered over to the shelf. "A classic damsel in distress archetype." He immediately found that copy and carefully tugged it free, all the while aware of Mrs. Hamlet's eyes on his every movement. He flipped the brown leather cover open.

"You've not read it, then," she ventured, her words more a statement than anything. Mrs. Hamlet eyed the book in his hands the way a lady might a lover. He snapped it shut.

"On what did you base that opinion, Mrs. Hamlet?"

She lifted her shoulders in a little shrug. "Because if you had, you'd have noted Basile's telling included a heroine who battled the ogress with her own magic tools. She was a woman who partnered with the prince and fought for her freedom." His housekeeper lifted an index finger. "It was only in later versions, Schulz's *Rapunzel* and de Caumont de La Force's *Persinette*, where Petrosinella's role shifted."

Vail's mouth fell open and he stared over the book, bemused at the clever woman opposite him. From but a handful of moments of meeting her and that quite impressive set-down on his incorrect opinion of that work in question, she'd the qualities of one he'd hire for his business and not the running of his household.

"Are you certain you're here as my housekeeper?"

"I am, my lord." There was something so very endearing in her literal take on every rhetorical or teasing question he put to her. "It is my understanding I was hired because of my experience in the handling, treatment, and care of books and manuscripts." As she spoke, Mrs. Hamlet alternated her focus between his face and the copy of *Petrosinella*.

In a silent test, he held out the book.

His housekeeper hesitated. She darted the tip of her tongue out and trailed it along the seam of her bow-shaped lips. Test forgotten, his mind stalled as he lingered on that slight movement. *I am lusting after a servant in my employ. I'm going to hell. There was nothing else for it.* Shame sank like a stone in his belly.

"I cannot," she said, in regret-laden tones that pulled his attention away from her mouth. "Unless you have gloves?" she ventured, hope lighting her eyes.

And for his hungering of moments ago, a different appreciation filled him.

Collecting a pair from within his center drawer, with his spare hand he tossed them over. Mrs. Hamlet quickly shot her hands out and caught them to her chest. She hurriedly pulled them on, the way one who feared a gift would be yanked away at any moment. Then with a reverence to her graceful movements, she accepted the copy and set it down on the surface of his desk.

Joining her, he specifically studied her handling of that first edition text: the delicate turn of the cover and first page. The last housekeeper his brother had hired may have nearly destroyed those precious copies stored inside this household. However, in finding and employing Mrs. Hamlet, he'd quite atoned for that mistake. This woman handled *Petrosinella* with the skill of a master seller.

She ran her gaze frantically over the vibrantly sketched images contained within the pages. "Quite impressive, are they not?" Himself not anything more than a seller of most ancient texts, he still had an appreciation for the artwork and words expertly joined in the volume. "It's a recent acquisition." One that would fetch a hefty sum.

Mrs. Hamlet gave no indication she'd either heard or agreed with his observation.

At last, she straightened and faced him.

"I understand you've experience with collecting." He propped his hip on the edge of the broad, mahogany piece.

The lady stiffened. "My husband," she said softly. "My late husband," she amended. "Served as an evaluator of fine texts and volumes." The long, graceful column of her throat moved. So theirs had been a love match. Only, where Vail had built a fortune, Mr. Hamlet had left his wife without security or safety.

Eager to replace that melancholy in her expressive blue eyes, he spoke. "My collections are vast. They largely exist for re-sale purposes." Nearly all of them, really. Nothing was too important that couldn't be sold to deepen his wealth. It was far easier not becoming attached to anyone or anything that could be taken away.

His young housekeeper stared at him with stricken eyes. "How very sad." She looked back at Basile's work.

"And yet they bring fortunes that allow for security and stability." For all his siblings. As such, he expected she'd appreciate the value in that.

"But to sell them all?" Mrs. Hamlet gave her head a pitying shake.

At her overt disapproval, he fought back a frown. The money he acquired allowed him to keep his siblings close and cared for. It was a detail he'd not share with anyone, particularly not a stranger. "With regards to your assignment…" He removed his gloves and tossed them aside. "…you'll of course be responsible for the female servants. I'll have you inventory the cellar stores and ascertain which shipments are needed and when. I'll also have you personally see to the care of my collection rooms." Surprise lit her eyes. "Matters of bookkeeping will be overseen by my man-of-affairs, Mr. Winterly." Mrs. Hamlet's skills were best served elsewhere. He'd speak to Edward about best utilizing her talents. "I would have you speak with the staff about proper treatment of the texts inside this household."

Removing her own gloves, she placed them down on his desk. "Yes, my lord."

And just like that, his perfunctory list restored the station divide between them. He frowned, far preferring the camaraderie they'd briefly enjoyed. Nonetheless, he stood and the lady stared expectantly back.

"Given your care of my Collection Rooms is the most important aspect of your assignment, I'd provide you a brief tour." He motioned Mrs. Hamlet ahead of him.

She eyed him with a hesitancy in her expressive eyes, and then they fell into a like step, with a companionable silence between them. Most women would have scrambled to fill the void, however, there was a confident assurance to his new housekeeper.

They reached the end of the hall and he brought them to a stop. Opening the doorway, he gestured for her to enter. "This room contains solely text predating the fifteenth century." From the corner of his eye, he detected the lady's awe-filled appreciation as she devoured the floor-length shelving lining the room. "Given that all the works here predate the printing press they are—"

"In folio form," she breathed.

He cast a surprised glance in her direction. So she knew they'd be in loose pages, then. "My previous housekeeper thought the room was too drafty and instructed the maids to set a raging fire in the hearth."

Mrs. Hamlet winced. "Surely not."

"Surely," he drawled. His brother may have failed to find an appropriate housekeeper in the last woman to hold the post, but there could be no doubting this one's skill and knowledge. "Shall we?" Not waiting to see if she followed, he guided her from his most rare Collection Room to the one in the next hall. "In here, you'll find all works of Western artists. From Shakespeare to his friends Herminge and Condell, you'll find all the greatest here."

He stole another peek at his housekeeper in time to detect the disapproving way in which she wrinkled her nose. "Only Western artists?"

Tamping down a grin, he guided her across the hallway to the adjacent room. "The finest of the Oriental literary masters is shelved in here." Letting them inside, Vail displayed some of his finest books. "*The Tale of Genji*—"

"Genji Monogatari," she whispered, touching a hand to her mouth.

"As well as *Makura no Soshi*," he finished, supplying that Japanese title. He tamped down his tangible surprise at the depth of her proficiency in text. He wasn't so snobbish that he'd be startled by a young woman's mastery of Oriental literature, but neither was he so connected to women who had a grasp of even Western texts. His appreciation grew for the composed Mrs. Hamlet. "Shall we?"

The lady nodded eagerly. "Have you read all these titles?" she asked, as they resumed their tour.

"Many. Not most. My collections are too vast," he said without inflection. It was a matter of fact, more than anything. "Not as impressive as Lord Dandridge's, whose floors caved in from all the books he kept."

A startled laugh spilled from the lady's lips. Enchanted by the husky beauty of it, he looked over.

"You joke," she charged, a sparkle in her eyes.

He swallowed hard. Blast if he wasn't captivated by her wit and her bloody smile. "Indeed, not," he forced himself to answer. Affixing a grin to his face, he leaned close to her ear. "Hardly as shocking as Lord Templeton who has a problem with rats and shoots them at all hours of the night to keep them from his texts."

The lady widened her eyes. "Surely you jest *now*?"

Actually he'd didn't. Mrs. Hamlet revealed her naiveté where his world was concerned and he far preferred her as just a woman with a deep appreciation for literature. Not wanting to disillusion her with the ugliness he'd witnessed, Vail winked, earning another laugh. The sound of it did funny things to his heart's rhythm. Unnerved, he hurried through the remainder of the tour, showing his housekeeper the seven rooms where his titles were kept. After they'd finished, the lady fell silent.

"Well?" he urged as they arrived at his office.

She gave her head a wistful shake. "It is a shame someone else will have possession of all these great works."

And just like that, she'd brought them 'round back to her earlier disapproval. Not knowing why that should matter, just that it did, Vail rang the bell, needing a restoration of his own logic where Mrs. Hamlet was concerned. "Mr. Lodge will show you to your

rooms. You may have the day to familiarize yourself with the residence and have Mr. Lodge perform your introductions to the
staff."

Footsteps sounded in the hall. Vail opened the door before his
brother, Gavin, could let himself in. "Vail…" The younger man
grumbled. "I…" He swiftly remembered himself and his cheeks
colored. "Forgive me, Your Lordship."

Mrs. Hamlet's clever gaze took in every aspect of their exchange.

"If you'll escort Mrs. Hamlet to her rooms?"

"Of course. Of course." Gavin dashed from the room.

Vail searched for evidence of the same disapproval so many had
shown his youngest sibling—or the youngest of the ones he'd
located of Ravenscourt. Gavin had once been a legendary street
fighter. When he'd located the young man and questioned those
in the streets who'd known him, they'd all spoken of a man who,
after his fighting days, had never been completely right in the
head. Vail's housekeeper, however, demonstrated none of the scorn
so many others had shown the young man.

Gavin scurried back in. "I forgot Mrs. Hamlet," he said mournfully.

"Quite fine," Vail assured him, motioning for the newest addition to his household to join the young man.

The young lady smiled. "I would be most appreciative for the
escort," she said with more kindness than most showed Gavin. "I'll
certainly require your skill and understanding of Lord Chilton's
household in order to properly oversee my responsibilities."

Gavin puffed his chest out like a country rooster. "It would be
my honor," he said offering a sweeping bow.

Mrs. Hamlet glanced back to Vail and sank into a flawless curtsy.
"My lord."

A moment later, Gavin's prattling as he chatted the housekeeper's ears off faded.

After she'd left, Mrs. Hamlet's earlier censure whispered forward.
Gathering the one book she'd examined, with a frown he restored
it to its proper place on the shelf. His new housekeeper had passed
judgment on his business drive. However, Vail had lived the first
thirteen years of his existence, devoid of stability. From year to
year, as his mother moved among protectors and searched out her
next, there had been fleeting moments of comfort. That comfort

had been yanked away so many times he'd been marked by it and for it, he'd been indelibly changed. Instilled in him an appreciation to rely on no one, help those he called friend and family, and amass a fortune. It was why his investments stretched from the ruthless men obsessed with books, to steam, millinery, and factory investments.

And anyone who mistook his kindness for weakness was destined to find themselves destroyed.

CHAPTER 4

BRIDGET HAD BEEN BUT FIVE the first time she'd seen her father strike a servant. A maid had sloshed tea over the cup as she'd set it down before him and she'd been rewarded with a sharp slap for her misstep.

From that point on, she'd noticed details she'd been previously too small to note: the fearful glances servants cast whenever her parents and siblings were about, the occasional bruise or awkward gait as young maids went about their work. And she had realized from that moment the abuse her family's staff suffered inside the Hamilton household.

Having herself been spurned by her own family and witness to their cruelty, she'd taken the whole of the peerage guilty of those same affronts.

Until she'd met Lord Chilton.

Dinner now served in Lord Chilton's household, Bridget, as housekeeper, found herself at the leisure only afforded to the senior members of a household staff, until her meeting with Mr. Lodge. Tonight, he'd show her about the stores and discuss the ordering of necessary household items. Until then, with a large round key ring containing keys for every door, she continued familiarizing herself with the baron's household.

It was a privilege afforded only the most elevated servants and would invariably aid in her search for the first edition Chaucer, and both those truths made her hate herself all the more.

Bridget paused beside a doorway and admitted herself to another room—a portrait room. She made to exit the darkened space, lined with heavy gold frames, and yet froze. Beckoned forward, she hesitantly entered and drifted over to the nearest portrait.

She cocked her head, easily recognizing the smiling butler, Mr. Lodge. With a boyish glimmer in his eyes and a loose black curl tumbled over his brow, there was an air of innocence to him. Perplexed, she moved on to the next. A young woman, no more than fifteen or sixteen years with golden blonde curls and a dimpled cheek stared back. By the fine robin's egg blue of her gown and the diamond, heart-shaped combs tucked artfully in her hair, she was a lady of noble origins. Earlier reservations forgotten, intrigue pulled Bridget from portrait to portrait. Some figures forever memorialized within those frames were children, many years away from adulthood. All finely dressed. She lingered before the portrait of Mr. Winterly.

"The man-of-affairs, too," she mouthed.

The garments and hairstyles of every last person captured there all spoke to recent portraits done. And yet…only a nobleman's family was memorialized within those frames. Or that had been the way, as she herself had known it, in the Hamilton household.

A gold frame from the corner of her eye snagged her notice. Drawn to the child there, Bridget stopped before it. Craning her head back, she examined the small boy. He could not be more than nine or ten years of age and he was not unlike so many of the other figures whose likenesses had been preserved within this room. And yet—she angled her head left and right, squinting in the dark to better study him—there was something different about him…this wisp of a child. Tiny of frame, and with high-set ears and slightly slanted eyes, he was set visually apart from the other subjects whose paintings hung about the room. His smile, even with his significantly crooked teeth, however, bespoke of a similar kindness and warmth to the other strangers she had previously examined.

A vise squeezed at her heart as she thought of a different child she'd been forced to leave in coming here. It was just a day she'd been a way from Virgil, but since he'd been abandoned to her care, there'd not been a single day they'd spent apart. Was he sad? Was he happy? She preferred to think of him grinning like the nameless boy in the portrait, filled with excitement for the adventure he'd embarked on.

She forced her gaze away from the joyous child and her eyes slammed into the adjacent portrait. Her breath caught.

Lord Chilton.

Never breaking contact with the powerful man frozen on that frame, she wandered several steps closer until she stood directly beneath his likeness. A few inches past six feet, the dark-haired gentleman with his aquiline nose and high brow had the air of greatness. With Society's standard views of perfection, his chiseled cheeks and rugged jaw were too sharp to ever be considered classically beautiful as those sculptures done by Donatello but it lent him an air of realness. One that was matched by the glitter in his eyes. Going up on tiptoe, she closely scrutinized their emerald depths. For there were warring sentiments in his eyes: a warmth that had the power to reach all the way through the canvas to a viewer and a fierce glint, so very contradictory to the ghost of a smile on his lips.

Who was this man? Ruthless business owner, as her brother had purported him to be? One who'd cut down the man or woman who entered his home to deceive him? Or kind-eyed gentleman who kept an eclectic mix of images inside his portrait room?

Hands on hips, Bridget did a slow sweep of the room, trying to make sense of it all—and she gasped. Her gaze collided with the dark-clad figure lounging against the doorjamb. His lips were moving and even as his words pulled in and out of focus, she struggled through her shock at finding him here, to make sense of his body language. "…wondering about…"

She shook her head frantically and took several lurching steps closer to Lord Chilton and then stopped. Smoothing her palms over her skirts, she waited as he approached.

He stopped before her and, folding his arms at his broad chest, stared expectantly back.

Over the years, she'd come to accept that some women were born beautiful like her sister, Marianne. Some men were born athletic, as Archibald. And then others, such as her, were born wholly imperfect with scarred visages and flawed hearing. Never more had she regretted the loss of that sound than she did in this instant.

"Or mayhap I was wrong, then?" he drawled. His lips turned up in a lazy grin; it dimpled his right cheek and did funny things to her senses. "It would not be the first time since we've met."

Bridget waged a silent debate with herself. She could brave her way through his questioning or she could offer the truth. "Forgive me, I did not hear your earlier query," she admitted quietly. Her stomach muscles clenched. "I'm partially deaf." As soon as that admission slipped out, she curled her toes into the soles of her serviceable black boots.

Surprise lit the baron's jade-green eyes.

"My left ear," she said weakly, uselessly motioning to the respective one in question. *As though there could be another, you stupid chit.* She braced for his inevitable pity or scorn. After all, how many times had her own siblings played cruel games at her expense or had she been railed at by her parents for being the shame of the Hamilton family?

The baron worked his gaze over her face. "That is why you did not hear my approach yesterday morn," he observed in somber tones.

Bridget nodded, the movement stiff and jerky. Where was his icy derision? "My right ear is perfectly fine," she spoke on a rush, to assure him of her worth. The disabled had little place in Society. Her own family hadn't even wanted her underfoot. "I simply have to…compensate in other ways," she finished lamely.

Lord Chilton let his arms drop to his sides and nudged his chin at the closest painting: the golden-haired, flawlessly perfect English beauty whose painting she'd studied earlier. "I suspected you were wondering about the paintings."

That was it. A statement to her purpose and thoughts in being here. Not any questions or pitying statements about her partial deafness. Warmth unfurled inside her breast and fanned out, spreading to every corner of her being. How very beautiful it was simply being…any other young lady. "I was," she confessed.

"They are my siblings."

She blinked slowly and then whipped her gaze about the room, silently counting: one, two, three, four, five—

"Twelve," he supplied for her. "My siblings. I'm one of the Duke of Ravenscourt's many bastard children." So that was the reason behind that mocking address of Bastard Baron, as Archibald had shared. The baron's lips peeled up in an ugly remnant of an empty smile devoid of all warmth and a chill scraped along her spine. How easily this hardened man before her had replaced the gently smiling one of moments ago. It proved the artist who'd painted Lord Chilton's likeness, a master at his craft. "Thus far, I've found ten brothers and one unwed sister." He paused. "Two were already married before I'd identified them as kin."

With more and more evidence of his kindness, she strolled back to Mr. Lodge's painting near the front of the room, unnerved. "Mr. Lodge?" she asked, shooting a glance over her shoulder.

"My brother."

And Mr. Winterly, too, then.

"Winterly, my man-of-affairs and business partner, as well," he said as though he'd heard hear unspoken question. "All of them," he confirmed once more, with a negligent wave about the portrait room. He pulled out a pair of elegant leather gloves and drew them on. Those articles served as another statement of his wealth. They stood a marked juxtaposition, however, to his long, tanned, callused fingers. "I've made it my business finding all the men and women my bastard of a father sired, and setting up futures for them."

"Where are they all?" she asked, unable to quell the bold wondering. He was her employer and a peer of the realm, she'd no place putting intimate queries to him, and, yet, a need to know outweighed propriety.

Lord Chilton motioned her forward and proceeded to escort her about the white, Italian marble floor. It did not escape her notice that he'd deliberately positioned himself away from the painting of the small boy. "Theodore and Leonard have established their own businesses," he indicated two blond gentlemen, elegantly attired, somewhere in their twentieth years. "Several work on my various properties as stewards. One is a Bow Street Runner. My sister is at finishing school. Others are just boys at Eton or Cambridge." They reached the painting of the tiny child with his crooked, joy-filled smile.

"And what of him?" she asked softly, not knowing what it was in that small boy's visage that called to her. Bridget registered the absolute silence and, believing her hearing had failed her once more, she faced the baron.

The ruggedly beautiful planes of his face were contorted in an anguished mask. He gave his head a shake. She stood an interloper in his private grief. His slight negation indicated he neither wanted, nor expected any questions about the boy…of like age to her Virgil, but the evidence of his quiet suffering ravaged her until she ached to wrap her arms about this man—a mere stranger. *It's not my place to know…a thief in his household who means even less than nothing to him.*

Wanting to rid him of the sorrow there, she cleared her throat. "They are so fortunate to have you as their brother," she said softly, speaking to herself more than anything. Hardly believing such a truth was possible. The only thing her own kin had ever wanted for her was to forget her existence and be free of her completely.

If it was possible to love a man one had known for just a day's time, Bridget was certain she lost every piece of her heart to the one before her.

"They control their own future," he said with a modesty most nobles would never be able to manage in the whole of their existence. "I merely provide the posts or opportunities and they fulfill their responsibilities admirably." Lord Chilton spoke with such casualness she may as well have imagined his earlier grief. But it had been there. As one who'd known pain, she recognized it in another.

Or did he truly not know the impact he had on those siblings fortunate enough to call him kin? She moved closer until only a foot of space separated them. "Do not diminish what you do for your family," she spoke with a firm resolve that demanded he see that truth. "Whether they are servants in your employ or young girls and boys receiving an education, you have provided them a future, my lord."

His midnight lashes swept low; those thick, long lashes that most would have traded their smallest little fingers for. Lord Chilton's gaze remained fixed on her mouth and, for one heart-stopping, endless moment, she believed he'd kiss her. Which was utter foolery. None would ever dare a hint of an impropriety with the scarred Hamilton. But in this instance, she could almost believe that this man not only could…but wanted to. Her pulse hammered loudly in her head.

"Vail."

She wetted her lips. "M–My lord?" her breath emerged breathless to her own ear.

"Given your role in my staff, I'd ask you to call me by my given name."

Vail. She tested it silently in her mind. Even as he spoke the truth to her elevated position in the household and the close dealings she'd have with him because of her status, propriety still didn't give her leave to use it. And what was more, with every day spent here betraying him, she'd even less right to his name. "I can't," she said, dropping her eyes to his immaculately folded white satin cravat.

He brushed his knuckles along her jaw, bringing her gaze back to his. "A woman who challenged me upon our first meeting, I certainly expect can take to calling me by my Christian name, at least in private." A tempting smile, a dangerous one, tilted his lips at a roguish angle. No woman, herself included, would be wont to deny this man anything in this given instance.

"Bridget," she said reluctantly.

"Bridget," he repeated, wrapping those two syllables in a husky baritone. A name her parents hadn't even bothered to give her but who'd instead ceded the chore to her nursemaid. "It suits you," he murmured and their gazes locked.

Her heart raced with a thousand and one questions for those three words he'd so casually stated. But every nerve thrummed to life at his nearness as he dipped his head lower. Bridget's breath hitched and she fluttered her lashes. *He is going to k—*

"There you are, Mrs. Hamlet." That loud booming voice had the same effect as jumping naked into the lake outside her family's Yorkshire estate. She and Vail backed quickly away from one another.

His brother, Mr. Lodge, a perpetual smile fixed on his face, sprinted over. "I thought we might begin our inspection of the stores," he said with such innocence he revealed no indication that he'd stumbled upon Vail and his housekeeper moments away from...from what? To conceal her trembling fingers, Bridget clasped them at her back.

Then the kindly butler glanced to his brother. "Vail," he blurted. Color suffused his cheeks. "My lord," he swiftly corrected and dropped a formal bow.

"Gavin," he said quietly. "I assured you it's entirely fine to—"

The younger man glowered at him.

Bridget watched their exchange with fascination; that a powerful nobleman could and would willingly cede an argument to preserve his sibling's pride was a kindness she'd believed a member of the peerage incapable of.

Mr. Lodge pulled his shoulders back. "I've seen your horse readied, my lord."

"Thank you, Lodge," he said, deferring to the formality his brother displayed. "Mrs. Hamlet."

Bridget sank into a deep curtsy. "My lord." And yet, as she stared after him, an unexpected wave of disappointment that their exchange had come to an end gripped her.

CHAPTER 5

VAIL HAD LONG-PRIDED HIMSELF ON his rigid self-control, restraint, and practicality. Those strengths were what had allowed him to rise up, the bastard son of a whore, to make a way for himself, and then enabled him to survive and thrive on the battlefields of Waterloo. After he'd returned, fighting different demons, he'd managed mastery of his demons and converted earnings given him for battlefield heroics into a vast fortune.

Two nights earlier, with Bridget Hamlet, nearly every attribute that had gone into making him the success he was, he'd been close to tossing out the proverbial window.

That wicked hungering for the lady had kept him far away from his household and the young woman.

Seated at his back table at Brooke's, Vail downed the remaining contents of his brandy in one long, smooth swallow. It stung his throat and, grimacing, he welcomed the fiery burn. It did little to ease his restlessness.

Setting the glass down with a *thunk* on the round mahogany tabletop, he swiftly grabbed the barely touched bottle and poured himself another. Thought better of it, and added several fingerfuls.

It was madness enough that he'd relieved his damned house-keeper of her housekeeperly duties but, bloody hell, he'd almost kissed her. And would have done so if his brother hadn't the poor timing to interrupt.

Poor timing?

Vail had gone mad, indeed. He chased the staggering truth with another long swallow.

"Bad night." The tall, familiar figure of his friend, Nick Tallings, the Duke of Huntly, hovered at the foot of his table.

A bad *two* nights. Vail spared him a brief glance. "You're late," he snapped as the other man slid into the empty chair across from him.

"Never tell me that is what has you wallowing in your spirits."

"I'm not wallowing in my—" Vail caught his friend's far-too-amused expression. "Oh, go to hell," he muttered, eliciting a deep laugh from Huntly.

Best friends in the village Vail's mother had finally retired in, they'd each come from difficult origins and risen to greatness for it. The bonds they shared went deep, but there were certain things a man never shared with another—lusting after a servant in one's employ was decidedly one of those things.

Huntly reached for the empty, untouched glass Vail had ordered upon his arrival. "Problems with business?"

Quite the opposite. A rather enjoyable one, with the unconventional Bridget Hamlet. "My upcoming auction has led to a bloodlust among the *ton's* leading book collectors," he settled for. "Marlborough's still determined to keep me from purchasing his damned collection and I'm to host another damned ball." He despised those infernal affairs. Yet, they were all periodically planned and held to host the buyers and sellers amongst the peerage.

"Ah," Huntly directed that at his snifter as he filled the glass. "A bloodlust for books," he said with disgust in his voice. His friend had always been a lover of poetry and had once dreamed of a life as a writer, but he'd not the blackness in his soul like the men Vail dealt with daily. Even if the other man had once set out to destroy a young lady in a game of revenge, in the end, Huntly had proven himself different than those ruthless others.

"And how is Her Grace, Lady Huntly?" he asked, settling for a less contentious discussion.

A besotted glimmer sparked in his friend's eyes. "Splendid," he said with a crooked grin. "Very well." Since he'd married, happiness had erased the other man's once cynical edge.

Discomfited with that show of emotion, Vail briefly looked at his drink. Once, long ago, he'd also found love…except, where Huntly knew happiness with his new duchess, the young woman he'd given his heart to had chosen a titled lord. The irony of his changed circumstances that had come *after* her rejection remained with him still. At the very least he'd been spared an entire lifetime with a schemer. "What calls you away from Lady Justina?"

"That actually is why I requested a meeting." Huntly set his glass down and leaned forward. "I'd enlist your help with a gift."

The duke had been compelled, by his young duchess' shared love of literature, to create a salon for her. Periodically, the lady held lectures and discussions where other enlightened individuals came to discuss a given topic or works. "What do you require?" Vail asked without hesitation. Given the length and depth of their friendship there wasn't any favor he'd deny the man.

"I understand you have the original text for Basile's *Petrosinella*," Huntly explained.

Mrs. Hamlet's animated visage as she'd been regaling him with the relevance of that very work, flashed to his mind. "It would be that one," he muttered. What in blazes was it with women and that particular title, one already promised to Lord Cartwright for an outrageous sum?

A frown turned Huntly's lips at the corner. "I beg your pardon?"

"Nothing. Nothing," Vail said with a wave.

"Would you be willing to loan Justina that copy for her upcoming salon?" His friend cleared his throat. "I understand it is a tremendous favor and, had I learned of her interest in that title, I'd have purchased it before it was promised to Cartwright."

Had anyone else put such a request to him, he'd have called them mad and pointed them in the direction of Bedlam. That particular volume would earn him more than ten thousand pounds. To renege on the agreement Vail had reached with the marquess would ruin his name in the book-purchasing community. He finished his drink. "The transaction is to be finalized in a fortnight. I can't loan it beyond that date."

"A week from Friday, then."

Vail set his glass down. "I'll bring the copy for you to present her." He'd trust Huntly with his life. As such, he'd no hesitation turning the coveted volume over to the other man's care. A bachelor who invariably spent his nights at his clubs conducting business tonight, however, there was a peculiar restlessness since Bridget Hamlet had entered his household. "If you'll excuse me?"

Huntly looked up and then shot his eyebrows to his hairline. "You're leaving, now?"

"I've business to attend," he offered evasively, hoping that this was one of the nights Huntly didn't probe.

The other man jumped to his feet. "I'll accompany you out." Of course, it would only have been a secret gift for Huntly's wife that called him away. Since their recent marriage, the young duke was scarcely away from his wife, except for the once weekly rides in Hyde Park he still took with Vail.

They fell into step, walking at a brisk clip through Brooke's. Gentlemen seated at their reserved tables and games of whist and faro called out jovial hellos. Smoothing his features to conceal his antipathy, Vail returned those useless greetings.

"Rotters, the lot of them," Huntly muttered from the side of his mouth.

"A title and a fortune will tend to see doors opened, though, won't it?" he rejoined, as they exited the distinguished establishment. They could all go hang, those self-centered lords who littered London with their bastards and carried on their respectable days and nights with people of their own station. "Send my best to Justina," he said, as he collected the reins for his mount.

"What affairs call you at this hour?"

At Huntly's question, teeming with curiosity, Vail froze, his leg suspended. He forced himself to complete the motion until he was seated astride the magnificent creature. "Beg pardon?"

Huntly stared up at him curiously. "You'd indicated you were off to a meeting."

Bloody hell. Vail's mind raced. In his damned eagerness to return home, he'd not given thought to a proper explanation or lie. A lie is what it was. "I've a new member of my staff overseeing my collection," he managed belatedly, coming as close to the truth as he was comfortable.

"And you're forcing the poor bastard to work at this late hour?" Huntly called up as he swung himself atop his own mount. A carriage rumbled too close and the tall stallion danced around skittishly. "You are as ruthless in business matters, then, as Society purports you to be, if that is the case." With a chuckle, Huntly expertly handled the reins, righting his horse.

Vail stiffened, braced for further blasted probing.

Instead, his friend touched his fingers to the brim of his black Oxonian hat and rode on toward his Grosvenor Square residence. Continuing on at a slower pace, Vail guided Atlas through the fashionable and busy streets of London, toward his townhouse…and Mrs. Bridget Hamlet.

Again, the crimson hue of her full-lips surged forward in his memory and, with it, that same hungering to know the taste of them. No, the lady, with her crescent-shaped mark upon her cheek and auburn tresses didn't fit with any woman he'd taken to his bed before, but he'd been enthralled with her for that very reason. That was not, however, the only reason. The lady hadn't shown so much as a hint of fear, reverence, or regard for his title. She'd not expressed any of the same horror displayed by lords and ladies about the Bastard Baron's vast number of siblings. Instead, she'd looked up at him with a doe-eyed innocence and wonder that he'd not even witnessed in Adrina, the one woman he'd thought faithful to him. His housekeeper of one damned day had asked more questions than anyone, including Huntly, had ever put to him and the raw honesty of her response had fueled this dangerous hunger. "There is nothing for it, you are a reprobate bastard," he mumbled, directing Atlas down the end of St. James Street.

His horse whinnied his equine agreement.

Adjusting the reins, Vail leaned forward. "So much for loyalty." He followed that teasing jibe for the horse with a pat on his neck. A short while later, he dismounted and handed his mount over to the waiting servant who rushed to claim the reins. With a word of thanks, he bounded up the steps and skidded to a stop.

Drumming his gloved fingertips together, he proceeded to wait. The same way Gavin took pride in his position and form of address, so, too, did he value being the one to oversee that front doorway.

Erasmus' small face flashed behind his mind's eye and a wave of sorrow struck as fresh as the day his brother had drawn his last breath in Vail's arms. Simple, but in possession of only goodness,

Erasmus had been turned out and sent to die in a hospital. And with his passing, Vail had resolved to find every last kin Ravenscourt had failed and spare them from the cruelty that was life. Gavin Lodge, slightly touched in the head after too many punches, had been the first he'd managed to locate.

The door opened. "Vail." His brother beamed. "My lord, that is." Gavin helped him from his cloak.

He glanced about. "How does Mrs. Hamlet fare in her new post?" It was a casual query. One any gentleman had a right to ask of the woman responsible for one's female staff.

"I quite like her," Gavin said excitedly.

"Do you?" The household maids, though not outright unkind, were unsure of Gavin. Vail still had overheard the whispers as he'd passed servants at work in rooms throughout his household. Questions about Gavin's mental faculties.

"Oh, yes. We spent the evening talking about coffee. Then Mrs. Hamlet insisted she make a cup for me to try and we talked about preserves. Her favorite is strawberry but she makes an exceptionally wonderfully raspberry one, and—" They reached Vail's offices. "It really is such a shame that you've removed her from preserve making. For now, we'll never know." Gavin's eyes lit. "I don't suppose you might reconsider?"

Repressing a smile, he patted Gavin on the shoulder. "Perhaps after the next auction, I might see about reallocating some of Mrs. Hamlet's time."

With a widening grin, Gavin nodded excitedly. "Splendid." Then, whipping about on his heel, his brother rushed off.

Letting himself inside his office, Vail closed the door behind him. Gavin's high praise for Bridget and his ramblings about her ability stirred further curiosity. Who was this woman with the cultured tones of a peer who was familiar with valuable texts and also made her own preserves and coffee?

And more, why did he have a need to know more about her?

"Enough," he gritted out. He stalked across the room to the well-stocked sideboard and grabbed the nearest glass and bottle. The clink of crystal striking crystal filled the midnight quiet. Carrying his drink and glass over to a leather-button sofa beside the hearth, he claimed a spot there and poured himself his third drink of the night. With the works he collected and sold, and his desk being a cornerstone of where many of those titles were assessed and a place where transactions occurred, by a rule, Vail didn't consume brandy or any spirits there.

He stared over the rim of his snifter into the cold grate. As a child, he'd borne witness to the heartache and uncertainty that was his mother's life. A pretty maid in the Duke of Ravenscourt's employ, she'd caught her master's eye, and fallen helplessly and hopelessly in love.

Vail grimaced.

Or that was how she'd romanticized it in her telling over the years. The part she'd omitted about that pathetic tale was how the powerful duke had ultimately tired of her—only after she'd given him a son. How had that rich and powerful lord cared for his illegitimate child and the lover who bore him? By passing her on to her next partner, another peer. And so, her existence continued from one protectorship to the next…until she'd the funds to retire in the countryside.

Through it, Vail had been forever marked by his mother's fall. When he'd returned from Waterloo and been titled for his actions, he'd vowed to never become his father. He would treat all his staff—men, women, and children—with deserved respect. And he'd certainly never lust after a woman in his employ.

That first evening, a breath away from kissing the unconventional Bridget Hamlet, and he'd proven that his father's rotted blood coursed in his veins.

Vail took a sip of his brandy.

I'm making more of it than it is.

Just because he'd asked after her and thought of her, and wanted to explore the contours of her crimson, bow-shaped lips, didn't make him evil. It made him human.

But humans were flawed. The ruthlessness he'd witnessed from the men he did business with was proof of that.

And this unwitting fascination with his young housekeeper was proof that Vail himself was as weak and flawed as the Devil who'd sired him.

CHAPTER 6

AFTER JUST A SHORT TIME working in Lord Chilton's employ, Bridget discovered something about herself: she had been born a Hamilton, but she was rot at treachery.

During the days, as she inventoried Vail's latest purchases, it had been too easy to pretend that she was, in fact, a record keeper for a powerful bookseller. All the while, she'd searched—to no avail—for that coveted Chaucer tome. Under the guise of familiarizing herself with Vail's prized collection, she'd systematically gone through room after room in search of that blasted title. There, however, remained two rooms she'd yet to search—another library…and Vail's office.

Her stomach twisted in vicious knots. A tray of coffee and pastries in her hands, Bridget made her way from the kitchens. The servants had sought out their beds for the evening and Vail was otherwise at his clubs. She took advantage of his absence and the quiet to search for that bloody copy.

As she wound her way abovestairs to Vail's office, she contemplated their last meeting—in the portrait room—and everything he'd revealed about himself…and the people whose portraits hung inside his household.

Her brother had painted Vail Basingstoke, Lord Chilton, as a ruthless businessman who cared about nothing and no one, except his own material gains. As unpalatable as it had been to stomach the idea of committing theft from *anyone*, it had been, if not easy, somewhat palatable, to imagine she was sharing a roof with a man who was just like her brother and father.

Only to find in a handful of brief meetings, that the man, Vail, who thought nothing of conversing with a servant and who cared for his brothers and sisters, couldn't be more different from Archibald than the Lord himself was from Lucifer. *What he is or who he is cannot matter.* No one mattered more than Virgil.

Her resolve strengthened, Bridget stopped outside Vail's office. Shifting the burden of her tray, she rapped once and waited. She strained her ear to make out a call or hint of sound within that room. When only the sharp hum of silence rang in the corridors, she knocked again. *No one is here. Get inside and conduct your search now.* The sooner she found that book, the sooner she could be free of this household and Vail would become nothing more than a memory.

Adjusting her grip on the burden she carried, she let herself inside his office. The tray clattered in her hand as she immediately caught her gaze on a lone occupant in the room—Vail. Her heart climbed to her throat and she braced for him to jump up with shouts for a constable.

A bleating snore filtered from where he rested. Her heart warmed at the sight of him, seated at his desk littered with books. The baron's head was down on his right arm, which occupied the only available space on that surface. He'd the look of a student asleep at his studies. Carefully, she set the tray down on a nearby table.

I should go. She could hardly conduct a search with him slumbering a handful of feet away and there was otherwise no reason for her to stay.

Bridget wet her lips. She briefly contemplated the hallway, but then made the mistake of looking at him, once more…more specifically, his left arm. That long limb hung down before him. Having fallen asleep too many times while tending the accounting, she knew what it was to eventually awake from that stiff, uncomfortable slumber. "Do not," she silently mouthed. He was not her affair. The only reasons she'd come were to serve as his housekeeper and steal, and how he slept or didn't sleep or whether he enjoyed the raspberry puff pastries or the chocolate tarts were all irrelevant in the scheme of what Archibald had concocted.

She briefly closed her eyes. Her sister, Marianne, had always called her the ugliest and the weakest of the Hamilton siblings.

And though she'd never doubted the former argument, she'd strenuously protested—at least to herself—the latter. Until now.

Her true purpose in being here briefly set aside, Bridget moved quietly forward and stopped beside the baron. The great space of the cavernous office now erased, her ear picked up the bleating snores that filtered past his lips. Another dratted sliver of warmth snaked through her. With him sleeping on, she used the moment to study him…

Her breath caught.

Nay, appreciate him. Half his face was concealed by his arm and the other half was partially concealed by a curtain of black hair, given to a slight curl, that fanned his face. A thick, dark growth marred his chiseled cheeks, giving him the look of a medieval warrior. The sight of him was one of a male beauty of which she'd never before seen, even in the books she'd studied and examined. As she carefully cleared a spot, she continued to steal furtive looks, ascertaining that he still slept on. Her lips twisted wryly as she reached for the baron's limp arm. Not that she'd had an opportunity to appreciate the male form outside of those art books she'd once read and researched for Mr. Lowell. Bridget froze.

…*What good does she do me? No man will ever want her. And, why should he? She is hideous and now deaf, to go with her ugliness…?*

Her father's thunderous voice echoed in her mind all these years later; his venomous recrimination bellowed at the doctor who'd tended a then four-year-old girl. And with it, her own flaws stood out a stark contrast to the baron's perfection. Flaws she'd believed herself long at peace over.

She firmed her mouth. *Enough.* She *had* shed her last tear and applied her last hopeful concoction to her marked cheek long, long ago. She'd not let those memories force their way back into her life now. Disgusted with herself for that fleeting moment of caring still, she lifted Vail's heavy forearm. The heat of his skin penetrated through the dupioni silk shirt he wore, burning her fingers. She laid that muscled limb upon the place she'd cleared on his desk.

He emitted a broken snore and she froze.

But then his breathing settled into a smooth, even cadence.

Bridget hovered at his desk, taking note of the details that had previously escaped her until this moment. For the earlier clutter she'd taken his work space for, there—upon closer inspection—appeared an order to Lord Chilton's work. Leather folios occupied one parcel of space, matching leather ledgers another, and every other left unoccupied sliver had been claimed by aged texts and manuscripts.

Her gaze went to the book and magnifying glass that rested near the baron's fingertips.

What manner of gentleman was Lord Chilton? Weren't noblemen supposed to spend their evenings at balls and soirees and then travel off to their wicked clubs? Or mayhap only their wicked clubs? Instead, this man spent his days and nights dealing in antiquated texts.

She spared a brief glance at the snoring baron, and then leaned over him to examine the open book before him, when her gaze snagged upon a folded note there. The pungent scent of jasmine slapped at her nostrils. Jasmine. A floral, feminine scent. Was it a letter from a lover? The ugly tendrils of jealousy wrapped her in its hold and, unbidden, she read the first two lines.

Vail…

Mistakes were made. Please, I miss you…

Heart racing, she quickly yanked her attention away from that private note. In the scheme of her many crimes, reading his letters would certainly fall as the lesser of the evils. And yet, she'd not intrude on those delicate missives.

Unbidden, she stole another sideways peek.

Enough…

Returning her attention to the original object to secure her notice, she sank to her knees and craned her head around to look at the gold leather cover, etched in dark green lettering. The crimson and green mark in the middle marked it as that great seventeenth century work. Squinting—Bridget cursed the dim lighting—and yet, something of that page gave her pause. She shifted her gaze to her still slumbering employer and, holding her breath, she reached past him. She closed her fingers around the gold handle of the magnifying glass and brought it to her eye so she might examine the page.

Bridget quickly worked her gaze over it. "No shadows," she whispered.

"That is, if one doesn't count one's hovering housekeeper," Lord

Chilton said in sleep-laden tones.

She gasped and swiveled sideways. Seated upright, his hair hanging about his shoulders, Lord Chilton's thick lashes obscured all hint of emotion in his eyes. The magnifying glass slid from her fingers and clattered noisily in the quiet of the room. Silently cursing her blasted fascination with any and every antiquated book, she jumped up. "You're awake," she blurted.

He arched a midnight eyebrow.

And for the first time since she entered his office, she gave thanks for the dim lighting that hid her burning cheeks. "That is, my lord," she said weakly, dipping a belated curtsy. "I brought you coffee and pastries." She pointed over at the silver tray, giving thanks for the hindsight she'd had to bring along that offering. He followed her stare and, then again, met her gaze.

Bridget braced for the deserved fury from him. She'd no place touching, snooping, or interfering in his business. *Mayhap, he'll sack me.* And for a sliver of a moment, instead of the terror that prospect should raise, there was a fledgling hope. For then, Archibald would have no use for her and she might not have the fortune from the Chaucer tome but she'd have freedom with Virgil and Nettie in their small corner of Leeds. *Archibald will never let me be free.* The truth of that stung like vinegar in her throat.

Lord Chilton rolled his shoulders. "Well?"

Oh, God. Memories of her father's harsh, cruel dressing-downs ran through her mind. The vicious cries of one maid as Archibald had struck her across the cheek. "It will not happen again," she said on a threadbare whisper. "I'd no right approaching you while you slept. I..." She swallowed hard. "It won't happen a–again."

The baron folded his arms at his broad chest. *Sans* jacket and attired in nothing more than his stark white shirtsleeves, it revealed the broadness of his chest and the faint wisp of midnight curls exposed there. Her mouth went dry. *Look away. It is shameful and wanton staring as I am.* But then, mayhap she was just like her younger sister who'd often cavorted with stable boys and footmen, for she could no sooner tear her gaze away from Lord Chilton than she could pluck out her eyelashes.

Then, slowly, he unfurled to his whole six-foot, four-inches, towering over her. The momentary pull of madness was shattered.

She took a hasty step back, but he merely turned on his heel and continued around the other side of the desk. Bridget watched in abject confusion as he crossed to the front of the room and picked up that small pot she'd brewed a short while ago.

The tinkling clink of porcelain touching porcelain, followed by the steady stream of liquid as he poured himself a cup, filled the room. That porcelain cup looked dainty in his large grip. He took a small, experimental sip, revealing nothing. Then, freeing one of his hands, he passed his fingers over the tray.

Which would he select? One could always tell much about a person by the sincerity of their smile…their eyes…and the dessert one selected.

Lord Chilton settled on a Banbury cake, the simplest of all those elaborate treats. Then, cup and dessert in hand, he moved to the center of the room and stopped so they were directly across from one another. Quickly dusting off that small cake, he downed his coffee and set his cup down on a side table. "I referred to the book," he finally said.

Bridget shook her head. "I don't understand."

He nudged his chin at the Shakespearean tome. "You've again demonstrated an inordinate interest in my collection and I wondered what you thought of that piece."

She eyed him suspiciously. Invariably, in the rare times Archibald came 'round, whenever he presented questions to her, there was a trick contained within them.

The baron chuckled, that deep rumble easy. "I assure you, this is no test. Sometimes, a question is simply a question."

"Yes. But sometimes, it is more, too," she pointed out.

His lips tipped up in the right corner into a heart-stopping half-grin. "This is not one of those times."

"It's a beautiful book," she gave him the words he, as a bookseller, hoped for. But she could not offer half-truths in this. "Although… not an original." She winced, waiting for an explosion of fury and thunderous questions.

The smile melted from his lips. "Beg pardon?"

What does it matter whether he believes he's in possession of an original text? And yet, no self-serving aficionado on books could dare let such a truth slide. "Here." Not bothering with permission, she collected his gold-handled magnifying glass and held it out.

Lord Chilton joined her at the desk and collected that fine piece in his hands.

"As you know, until the eighteenth century all molds had the same design." She drew the proverbial rectangle with her fingers. "And there was the widely-spaced, vertical, wooden ribs with a chain wire lace to the top of each and…"

Pausing in his examination, he looked at her through baffled eyes.

Bridget coughed into her hand. "Ah, yes, laid paper. You know it was all laid paper with a latticework pattern that—"

"Revealed a watermark," he finished, turning his glass back upon that page.

"Exactly. A watermark."

Lord Chilton shifted the lens back and forth. "This has the requisite one."

"But not *the* one," she pointed out. "The vertical stripes have a graduated shadow." Bridget held her palm out. "May I?"

The baron eyed her palm a moment and then turned it over… when surely any other nobleman would have turned her out for her insolence. Nay, when any other gentleman wouldn't have even asked for her opinion in the first place. Encouraged by his silence, she placed the magnifying glass at the center of the page and leaned close. "Do you see how it's lighter down the middle but darker at the edges?"

He dropped his head beside hers and eyed the watermark in silent contemplation. "This is antique laid paper that came along when mold designs improved," she explained. Unnerved by his silence, she folded her hands before her.

What was he thinking?

GIVEN HIS BODY'S RESPONSE TO his housekeeper, Vail had intended to keep his distance from the enthralling young woman.

He'd gone through the week seeing to his business, doing an admirable job of carrying on as he always had with his affairs, confident that he was not at all like the father who'd sired him.

Then he'd caught the lady hovering over him as he slept. Or rather, as he'd feigned sleep. After she'd come around his desk, he'd awakened, but he'd been too damned intrigued by her boldness to question just what she was up to.

And then she'd moved his arm in an attempt to make him comfortable as he'd slept; in a gesture that was so tender, it went against the very life he lived and the business he conducted. He'd been so frozen by that tenderness that he'd almost forgotten his pretend bid at sleep.

Now, for his earlier resolve, he could not put distance between them for altogether different reasons.

Vail whistled through clenched lips. "By God, I've been swindled."

His skin pricked with Mrs. Hamlet's eyes on him. He looked away from the book and met her gaze. She eyed him with a world's worth of wariness. He frowned. What had put that look in her eyes? "I'm sorry," she said softly. She did not, however, attempt to assuage his ego or doubt her own opinion. She rose in his opinion for that honesty and self-confidence.

Setting down the glass, he crossed his arms before him. "I'd believed the extent of your knowledge was of the care and keep of antiquated books."

A droll grin curled those bow-shaped lips, revealing a flash of even, pearl-white teeth. Desire ran through him, as all manner of wicked thoughts whispered forward. "Because I'm a woman?"

His neck went hot and he ripped his focus away from her mouth. *I'm a depraved letch.* "Because I, apparently, was given to two miscalculations this evening." He waved a hand lazily between the book and her. He inclined his head. "I apologize for both."

The lady stared at him as if he'd sprang a second head. "Apologize?"

"Are you unaccustomed to a gentleman apologizing?" he asked, curious about her life before she'd entered his household.

"Actually, I am. I—" She abruptly cut her words off and he cursed that small glimpse she'd been about to provide.

Eyes weary from a night of poring over that damned volume, Vail scrubbed a palm over his face. He dropped his arm to his side. "So now that I've discovered you in my office, again examining my works, what are we to do with you, Mrs. Hamlet?" he asked, pushing away from the desk. He took a step toward her.

Mrs. Hamlet backed up. "D-Do?"

Vail continued his approach. "I hired you as a housekeeper. Are you not content in that role?"

"Yes. No. Yes." The young lady's eyes formed round saucers in her face.

His lips twitched. "Which is it, Mrs. Hamlet?" he murmured. Detecting her quick retreat, he stopped.

"I'm content," she said quickly, continuing to back away from him, anyway.

"I'm afraid, though you do brew a tremendous cup of coffee, the role of housekeeper is not one you're entirely suited for." Vail folded his hands at his back. "I'd have you take on some of the responsibilities overseeing my inventorying."

Her breath exploded from her on a noisy gasp. "What?" She backed into the wall. That abrupt movement knocked her chignon loose and several crimson-kissed strands tumbled over her shoulder. The whispery hint of a country garden clung to her skin and that delicate scent wafted about his senses, intoxicating in its innocence, and so wholly different from the sharp, cloying fragrances used by the women he'd taken to his bed. Shock brought her mouth open. "You would turn such important tasks over to a housekeeper?"

"If she was as capable as you are, then yes."

"But…" She again shook her head.

"Your services would be entirely wasted dealing with mutton and perfumery." He paused. "Unless, you otherwise wish to deal with them."

"No." She shook her head frantically. "The altered assignment would be…is perfect," she whispered. He may as well have gifted her the task of caring for the Queen's crown for the reverent awe there.

He opened his mouth to offer some glib reply, but she touched a hand to her heart, bringing his gaze back to those loose strands. Vail clenched and unclenched his hands several times, at war with himself.

In the end, the temptation proved too great. He caught one of those curls in his fingers, and rubbed the satiny soft tress between his thumb and forefinger. "I've never met a woman who was so adept at antiquated books," he said softly, puzzling through the mystery that was his new housekeeper.

Her lips parted and a soft whispery exhalation slipped forward.

She fluttered her lashes.

The muscles of his stomach clenched as a wave of hunger took root and held him frozen. "If you do not leave now, Bridget, I am going to kiss you," his voice emerged hoarse to his own ears.

His shameful admission should have sent her fleeing. Instead, she wetted her lips. "Wh-what if I wanted you t—?"

Vail swallowed the remainder of that question, taking her mouth under his as he'd ached to since she'd first entered his household. She hesitated, and then lifted her palms between them. For an agonizing moment, he believed she'd push him away. Instead, she gingerly twined her fingers about his neck and melted into him.

With a groan, he took her lips under his again and again, exploring the plump contours of that generous flesh. She boldly met his strokes and a little moan filtered from her. He slid his tongue inside and laid claim to that moist cavern. She tasted of chocolate and mint, and he was enthralled by the innocence of her.

Bridget collapsed against the wall and he went with her, anchoring her between his arms. He broke contact with her lips and her little protesting cry filled the room; it echoed off the soaring ceiling in an erotic melody.

He kissed the corner of her mouth and moved lower, exploring all of her, until he reached that graceful column of her neck. Vail found the place where her pulse beat hard.

Footsteps sounded in the hallway, cutting across the thick haze of desire that had dulled all logic and reason. He wrenched away from Bridget and she slumped against the wall. Their chests rose and fell in a like, desperate rhythm.

He backed away, as a slow, dawning shame replaced his hungering for this woman.

I am my father.

Riddled with the horror of that truth, he spun away from her, putting space between them—

Just as Gavin entered, his lips wreathed in a perpetual smile. "Vail," he greeted, "I'd forgotten to bring you coffee and—oh." He stopped abruptly as his gaze landed on Bridget. "Mrs. Hamlet," he said cheerfully. "Whatever are you doing here this late?"

An awkward pall descended on the room. Vail, who'd dallied with any number of wicked widows and unhappily married wives and ballet dancers, found himself unable to utter a smooth, deflective reply.

The high color on the lady's cheeks deepened and she looked helplessly to Vail.

Gavin's smile dipped and he glanced about. His stare landed on the empty coffee cup. "Oh, how good of you to remember." He glanced to Vail. "She makes far better brew than I do," he said on a loud whisper, as though it was a secret he intended to take to his grave.

Avoiding Vail's eyes, Bridget dropped a swift curtsy. "If there is nothing else you require, my lord, I will leave you to your business." Without seeking or awaiting permission, the lady darted around his shoulder and bolted past Gavin.

"And she's quick," Gavin said with rounded eyes. "I suspect she was quite good at blind man's bluff."

Vail's shame deepened. As innocent as his brother was, he could not see the truth of the depravity that had gripped him moments ago. "I suspect you're right. Gavin, going forward, given Mrs. Hamlet's skillful knowledge of books, her responsibilities of the stores and perfumery are to fall to another."

Four lines creased the younger man's brow. "But…but…you've just hired her." Whenever Gavin's usual household routines were altered, he demonstrated confusion and worry.

"I'll have Edward find someone to take on the tasks," he said in calming tones, when inside he was still in tumult.

Some of the tension left Gavin's wiry frame and he again smiled. Without so much as a parting word, he spun on his heel and left.

As soon as he'd gone, Vail unleashed a streak of black curses. By God in heaven, he'd kissed her. Nay, he'd backed her against a wall and passed his mouth over her skin, exploring her…and he would have continued had Gavin not interrupted.

Filled with a restiveness, he claimed a seat beside the fraudulent Shakespearean book…the one Bridget had brought to his unknowing eyes and attention. Given that, he should be focused on his fury with Lord Aberdeen and frustration with his own mistake.

Instead, desire gripped him still and a hungering to know more of the clever young woman who could identify a fake from a real antiquated book, and who smelled of a countryside meadow.

This inexplicable pull she had went against every moral standard

he held himself to. Vail gave his head a hard, clearing shake, determined to dispel her from his thoughts.

He returned to his work. All the while, shame ate away at him
and left a hollow, empty void inside.

CHAPTER
7

THE NEXT DAY, SEATED IN one of Lord Chilton's Collection Rooms, Bridget hummed a discordant tune as she oversaw her new responsibilities. Charged by Vail's man-of-affairs and brother with inventorying a complete set of Dante's *Inferno*, *Purgatorio*, and *Paradiso*, she recorded the dates and cover condition of each volume.

Over the years, she'd found occasional work evaluating the authenticity and worth of certain documents for a book buyer in London. In a world where women were remarkably without options, she'd appreciated that small gift. Tucked away in the country, with Virgil and Nettie, that existence had been the best she could hope for—for all of them.

As a young woman, she'd never dared allow herself the dream of a husband or children. One of the only talks she recalled ever having with her mother had been a bored, quick explanation about the fate that awaited deaf women: husband-less, child-less, and purpose-less. That future, the late marchioness had insisted, was even more bleak for one with a crescent-sized, crimson birthmark marring one's face. She'd been told so many times by her kin that no man would ever want her, that she'd simply believed it as fact.

Until Vail.

Bridget paused in her writings. Her lips burned still with the memory of his kiss. Dropping her pen, she raised trembling fingertips to her mouth. He'd kissed her. It had been the most erotic moment of her entire seven and twenty years. One she'd thought to never know. And as he'd kissed her, exploring the curve of her neck and the sensitive flesh of her earlobe, she'd understood, at last, why women tossed away their reputations and virtues. Vail's embrace had been a potent spell that she'd gladly have traded a sliver of her soul to know more of. She briefly closed her eyes. Only, it hadn't been solely his kiss that had this eddying effect on her senses. He'd implicitly trusted her judgment over his own. Why, even Mr. Lowell, whom she'd sought out all those years ago on the one trip she'd taken to London, had resisted hiring her for several days. She, with her brother's strong-arming as a marquess, had ultimately earned the position, but she'd had to continually prove herself. How very different Vail was even of all others she'd ever known. He was the manner of man Virgil had deserved as a father…

Giving her head a little shake, she returned to the task at hand. A wistful smile played about her lips as she set aside one canto and, with her gloves donned, she reached for the next. She picked up the heavy leather copy of *Inferno*. With slow, meticulous movements, she laid the book on the velvet cloth before her and opened it, turning to the year of publication.

Comento di Christophoro Landino fiorentino sopra la Comedia di Dante Alighieri Venice Pietro di Piasi

Her fingers trembled at the significance of the date. It was the first fully illustrated print edition. A book older and more valuable than anything she had personally owned, and in Vail's possession. It was just another mark of his wealth and influence…only—distractedly she turned another page—he was not one of the powerful lords who collected these treasured works.

"Impressive, is it not?" the loud question sounded from the doorway.

She turned to greet Mr. Winterly. He came forward, a smile on his face. However, she did not miss the intent way in which he studied her handling of Dante's work. His jade-green eyes had the ability to pierce a person's thoughts and rattle one's nerves. "Forgive me," she said quickly. "I did not believe we were scheduled to meet—"

He waved off her apology. "I was here for an appointment with

His Lordship." *Vail.* "I merely thought I'd pay a visit to see how you fare with your new responsibilities." He worked his astute gaze over the columns she'd completed that morning.

In short—he was checking on her.

She could hardly fault him for the diligence with which he oversaw his brother's collections. He and Vail were wary enough to not blindly trust a person who'd only just entered the baron's household. It made her task in locating the Chaucer all the more difficult and lengthened the amount of time she'd be forced to remain.

"What do you think?"

She followed his nod to the heavy leather tomes. "The set is magnificent," she said softly.

"It will fetch a heavy sum."

Despite it being best that Vail remain a stranger to her, a need to know more about him won out. "His business is very important to him," she observed.

"It is." But for his height and jade-green eyes, the gentleman, with his wiry frame and halo of blond curls could not be more different than Vail. And yet, he lounged his hip against the table with the same casual elegance. "Far more important than the title he received."

Their world driven by birthright and rank existed to keep out all those not born to that cold, cruel world…and yet he'd found himself titled. "How did he become a baron?" she asked, unable to keep the question back.

"His Lordship received the honor in recognition for his services at Waterloo. A score of French soldiers were riding at Wellington and Vail…His Lordship prevented that attack."

Her fingers curled reflexively. "He is a war hero," she said blankly.

"Yes." Mr. Winterly grinned and dropped his voice to a whisper. "But never allow him to hear you say as much. Quite despises all the fanfare."

She briefly closed her eyes. She'd been set to steal from a man who'd saved Wellington's life, returned from war to establish his own business so he might care for twelve siblings, *and* he didn't care to speak of his accomplishments? Her heart pounded hard. Vail was a bloody paragon; a man larger than proverbial life. His greatness when presented with her total inability to look after the two people in her care, only highlighted the weakness and ugliness of her own character.

Edward pulled out his timepiece. "If you'll excuse me. I have a meeting with His Lordship."

"Of course."

As he tucked that gold chain back inside his jacket, something he'd said earlier registered. "You said *would*," she blurted.

Having taken several steps, Vail's brother again faced her, his brow creased.

She hurried to clarify. "It is just you'd said the collection would fetch a heavy sum: not, will. He does not intend to sell this one, then."

Mr. Winterly offered a half-grin that was also very much Vail's lazy smile. "My brother is known as a ruthless businessman who believes every book can be bought and sold."

She worried the inside of her cheek with her teeth. What did it say that Edward would describe Vail as ruthless? After all, she'd observed her own brother and read Society's writings of him in the gossip columns to know he was referred to in the same light. Aware of Mr. Winterly's gaze on her, she met his stare. "How very unfortunate to go through life where everything only ever exists for a profit." She'd but a ramshackle cottage and meager posses-sions to her name and, yet, she still appreciated the gifts in those books she was fortunate enough to touch.

Edward frowned. "Being a ruthless businessman does not mean my brother is without a heart. Most nobles would use their for-tunes on frivolous pursuits and scandalous activities." And yet that was not his brother. His statement hung there at the end of the sentence as clear as if he'd spoken it. "His Lordship cares for men, women, and children, who, until recently, were nothing more than mere strangers. Some who are still nearly complete strangers. So occasionally, from ruthlessness comes good. Vail is one of those circumstances."

That impassioned defense spoke to the depths of Mr. Winterly's regard for his brother…and his respect. If a pistol had been placed to Bridget's temple with an order to name a single redeeming aspect of her own brother's character, she'd have said a prayer and prepared to meet her maker.

With Mr. Winterly's words ringing in the room still, she looked to Dante's collection. "He's kept this one, though," she ventured, more than half-wanting Vail's brother to explain the baron's connection to this set.

Mr. Winterly nodded. "He indicated this was special and it was to remain out of the auction."

Bridget curled her fingers into reflexive balls. It was as though the Devil himself took vicious glee in taunting her. Of course, of all the works Vail might keep, he should hold on to this allegory of human life that had long served as a warning for individuals to stay on a path of righteousness. She should let him go. Let this topic die. In the end, her need to know proved too great. "Do you know what made him keep this one?"

Mr. Winterly shrugged. "Who can ever say what he is thinking? That is a question best reserved for His Lordship. I'd come by to determine whether or not you require anything, Mrs. Hamlet?" he asked, his meaning clear: he'd not share any further details about Vail with her.

She shook her head. "No, thank you."

He nodded and, with a short bow, left.

Bridget stared after him long after he'd gone, considering the significant pieces he'd revealed about Vail Basingstoke, Lord Chilton.

How different he was from every other peer.

Vail was a nobleman who'd established a lucrative and prosperous business. His very life was anathema to everything she'd believed about how gentlemen lived their lives. Her brother and late father had lived extravagantly, wagering away fortunes and frivolously spending coin where there was none. Even when their wastrel ways had strained the Hamilton's coffers, placing them nearly in dun territory, they still had never *sullied* their hands with trade.

Vail, however, revealed no shame in the work he did. That depth of character set him apart from the reprobates she'd been—and still was—unfortunate enough to call family.

And he did it for his family. Absently, she flipped through Dante's *Inferno*. That blasted, dangerous heat inside her heart flickered to life. Despite her greatest efforts for it to cease, it continued to expand and grow, leaving her warm from the inside out. For Vail was not solely a man driven by material gains. He was a man who'd, according to his brother, grown his fortunes so he might help his kin find stability in an uncertain world.

And I will betray him. She paused, mid-turn of a page.

Lucifer's woodcut image stared mockingly back; that bearded, horned demon with all the sinners about him.

Working with treasured tomes and manuscripts had been all too easy to make believe that this was, in fact, real…that she was here to assist a bookseller with his collections. And after that night-time exchange with Vail where, for one breathless moment, she'd known his kiss, she'd seen neither hint nor hair of him.

She'd simply slipped into the role of a worker in his employ, living in this fictional state. It was far safer that way. For the man he'd been in her short time here—the man who'd taken her in his arms, and shared parts and pieces of his family, who'd spoken of the brothers and a sister he cared for—made him dangerous. Just as Edward's words from moments ago made it even more so.

It made Vail *real* and someone she respected and admired. Some-one who deserved far more than a faithless housekeeper who'd come to betray him with an act of theft.

With wooden fingers, she collected the *Inferno* and turned page after page, and then stopped: on Canto XXIV.

Bolgia 7-Thieves

Remorse churning in her belly, she frantically scraped her gaze over the words written there of Dante and Virgil as they left the Bolgia of the Hypocrites.

Oh, God. Seeing her son's name there, an ironic reminder no doubt from God Himself of her complicity in evil, intensified the shame and guilt cleaving at her. A chill iced the room, and she shivered, forcing herself to continue reading of those thieves being chased by monstrous serpents.

She froze on the story of the sinner, Vanni Fucci, bitten by a ser-pent at the jugular vein, to then burst into flames, and be re-formed in the ashes, only to face the same fate at the Devil's hands.

Bridget pressed her eyes closed. Surely the ends justified the proverbial means? In committing this act of thievery, Archibald had demanded she sacrifice her honor, and she'd agreed. Yet, how great a crime was it truly to steal from a man richer than Croesus to save Virgil?

"I'm only attempting to make myself feel better," she whispered, forcing her eyes open.

And failing miserably.

CHAPTER

8

SINCE HE'D TAKEN BRIDGET IN his arms, Vail had done an impressive job of avoiding his bibliophile housekeeper. He'd kept a wide berth; conducting his business the same way he had before she'd arrived, away from his residence, at meetings. And when he wasn't overseeing upcoming transactions and finalizing sales, he was attending the business of his siblings.

Given that, it would be his damned vexing brother, Edward, who forced her back into his thoughts.

"I came to visit Mrs. Hamlet."

Disgruntled, Vail continued reviewing his upcoming meetings with clients and potential clients, "Did you?" So that is why he'd come then when there'd been no planned meeting. Feigning nonchalance, he continued skimming the page. "And how does Br—Mrs. Hamlet fare in her new post?" Mrs. Hamlet whom he'd taken pains to avoid.

At Edward's answering silence, he looked up. Standing between the wingback leather chairs, there was a besotted glitter in Edward's eyes. Vail thinned his own. Why…why…his book-loving brother was fascinated by the lady. It shouldn't matter. It didn't matter. And yet…he growled.

Edward spoke, slashing across that damning sound of his fury. "I must confess, when I'd initially received her credentials from Lord Stanwicke, I was, at best, skeptical."

Good. Talk of Stanwicke and the lady's references was far safer than an irrational annoyance with Edward's fascination of Vail's new housekeeper. "Anything coming from Stanwicke should be received in such a way," he agreed.

Now that he had secured Vail's attention, Edward claimed one of the chairs. "In my requests with the employment agency, they provided me Stanwicke's references of the young woman. He'd spoken with such high praise for her handling of his texts and her keen understanding of their content that I'd doubted that such a woman existed." Edward gave his head a bemused shake.

It was not uncommon for London's leading book collectors to staff households with men and women who knew how to care for those valuable tomes. And yet, even with Bridget's skill and competence, that man had released her from his employ? Vail frowned as, for the first time, doubts were born. "If Stanwicke was so pleased, how did the lady come to be looking for work?"

"A disagreement with the Lady Stanwicke," Edward explained, looping his ankle over his opposite knee. "The marchioness took umbrage with the inordinate amount of time Mrs. Hamlet spent within the marquess' office."

The sliver of doubt about the lady's presence here gave way, replaced, instead, with a dark, simmering fury…and different questions flitted forward. Ones about the lady's previous employer. Nor could there be any doubt with Bridget's proficiency in literature and her cultured tones, she was anything but a lady. "Did the gentleman…?" He left that question vague, even as a red, hot fury burned under the surface and threatened to spill over.

"Stanwicke?" Edward scoffed. "With his obsessive fascination with his books, I'm stunned the man's gotten an heir and a spare on his wife."

Yes, but the man's wife was not in possession of Bridget's talents…those skills would earn any bibliophile's attentions. That dark, unwanted possibility that the lady had fled after a handsy employer forced his attentions on her.

Edward grinned, that affable expression at odds with Vail's dark thoughts. "You know I don't conduct my work seeking praise…"

At the unfinished thought, Vail tossed his pen down. "Good. Then do not begin now." He blighted that teasing set-down with a grin.

Edward's smug smile deepened. "However—"

"You intend to begin now, then?"

"—given my rather poor showing in hiring Mrs. Peach, Mrs. Batch, and, most recently, Mrs. Kelly, I've quite outdone myself with your new housekeeper."

Who could have imagined that finding a reliable, effective housekeeper who knew her way around his books would have been such a bloody chore? "She's been here but five days," he said, far more grudging in the appreciation he favored a new person on his staff. "I believe applauding yourself and extoling the lady is premature at this time."

"Ah, yes," his brother dropped his other foot to the floor and, leaning forward, wagged a finger. "But I'm the one who has spent the better part of the week with her."

Edward's words conjured images of the pair, tucked away in Vail's library—alone. And this time, it was not Vail who had her in his arms, but his brother. Something insidious slithered around inside. Something that felt remarkably like…jealousy. He scoffed. Jealousy? The lady had lived in his household for *less* than a week. In that time, he'd had three meetings and a handful of other polite, perfunctory exchanges when she brought coffee—which Gavin had, in fact, been correct on. The woman brewed a masterful cup. What in blazes…?

"Are you listening to me?" Edward asked impatiently, snapping Vail back to the moment.

"Yes." *No.*

His entirely too-besotted brother proceeded to tick off on his fingers. "The woman knows how to properly handle antique books. She not only knows how to care for them, but also has an appreciation for the contents within. *And* she fluently reads and speaks Latin, French, Italian, German, *and* Spanish." And with Edward's regard for literature, his awestruck visage told the tale of a man more than half in love with Mrs. Bridget Hamlet.

Having already gathered her skill with antiquated texts, only one revelation about his new housekeeper commanded Vail's attention. "Latin, French, Italian, German, and Spanish?" Surely, he'd misheard the other man.

Edward nodded.

Vail opened and closed his mouth several times. Only wealthy, highborn ladies were generally in possession of those skills. And even then, how many were fluent in Spanish, as well? Further questions about his peculiar housekeeper whispered forward, deepening his suspicions.

"Mm, mm," Edward protested, already shaking his head. "Don't you do that."

"Do what?" Vail sat back in the comfortable folds of his chair.

"You've got the same cynical stare you don when dealing with purchasers and sellers."

At that accurate charge, Vail remained silent.

"You don't deny it?" Edward asked, relentless.

"I don't think there is reason to." He'd not make apologies for being skeptical…of anyone. He'd witnessed firsthand, as a boy, then as a soldier, and then as a baron doing business with the *ton's* leading nobles, the evil a person was capable of.

"I've already found you the ideal housekeeper. If she could brew a perfect cup of coffee, then I'm fairly certain she'd be the perfect woman."

"She does brew—" Vail closed his mouth. Alas the damage was already done.

His brother rounded his eyes.

"It is among her responsibilities," he grumbled, resisting the urge to squirm. When she set one of those cups down at the front table in his offices each night and inquired about the books he studied, it had become one of the unexpected pleasures of his day.

"Humph." Edward hopped up. "Then, it is official: accomplished in foreign tongues, capable with antique books, keen of mind, and skilled at making coffee? I've found you the perfect woman. No thank you is necessary," he said, starting for the door.

"Where are you off to?"

Edward paused at the doorway. He glanced back. "I've a meeting with Lord Tennyson." In deep from too many years of whoring, wagering, and drinking, the man had a recent reversal of fortune at the tables—which he'd promptly lost. And each time he did, he sold off another parcel of his collection. Edward, with his knowledge of books, was always the first to make contact and inventory the titles. "I just came to see how Mrs. Hamlet fared her first day without supervision."

"How very devoted you are to Mrs. Hamlet," he said in even

tones, eliciting a blush from his brother.

"Yes, well, then." Color on his cheeks deepening, Edward touched his brim and made to go…but then stopped. "I understand why you're wary of people." Having found Edward in one of those seedy clubs in the Dials, his younger brother's life was largely a mystery that he didn't speak on, and one that Vail didn't force him with questions over. "But sometimes," Edward said, the same way a tutor might dole out instruction to his student. "A person is exactly as they seem."

And sometimes they weren't. "I didn't say she wasn't." He'd merely identified peculiarities about the lady.

Edward snorted. "I may only know you these five years now, but I know you well enough to gather precisely what you're thinking about the young woman."

The fortunes Vail earned in the course of his sales were what allowed him to care for the children Ravenscourt had littered about England, and see they no longer struggled or suffered. Erasmus' face trickled forward, once more… "You'd ask me to trust a fortune over to a stranger's care?" A ball of regret and sorrow lodged in his throat.

"Hardly," Edward shot back. "You can spend time with her yourself and ascertain whether or not your cryptic worrying is, in fact, merited. Or have Colin investigate her as he does those dregs of London Society," he drawled.

"I'm not employing Colin to investigate her." Not because he was at all opposed to using Colin's services. His brother, Colin Lockhart, was one of the best Runners in London. He'd taken on plenty of work about clients and members of Vail's staff over the years.

With a doubtful snort, Edward lifted his hand in parting and left.

"Cryptic worrying," he muttered. Vail would hardly characterize cautiousness as a flaw on his part. As Edward had accurately pointed out, life had given each of them proper reason to be wary of all. He drummed his fingertips together and stared contemplatively over them at the doorway. After kissing his housekeeper, he'd resolved to keep his distance from Bridget. Mayhap, his brother was correct in this regard. After all, it would be unwise business to not monitor her work…at least periodically.

Shoving to his feet, Vail quit his rooms. A short while later, he found himself at the entrance to one of his seven Collection Rooms. He stood a long moment in the open doorway.

I should enter. I should, at the very least, announce myself loudly, so she might hear my approach.

Instead, he lingered, proving himself a literal and figurative bastard, and observed her at work. Her back presented to him, she'd the regal bearing most queens couldn't master, a noble carriage that only further cemented this woman's connection to the peerage. And yet…it was not questions of her origins, background, or history that compelled him in this given instance—he swallowed hard—but rather the pull of the sapphire muslin fabric as it stretched at her trim waist and generously flared hips. Fighting an inner battle—and losing—Vail dipped his gaze downward, to her rounded buttocks. Even in her modest muslin gown, Bridget Hamlet was a study of lush carnality. Lust bolted through him.

You depraved bastard. You are your father's son. Get a damned grip on yourself, you lecher.

Mindful of what she'd revealed earlier that week in regards to her left ear, he called out loudly, belatedly alerting her to his presence. "Never tell me you're cataloguing out of order?"

Bridget cried out and spun around. A book slipped from her fingers and she made a desperate grab for it. It landed with a dull, unsatisfying thump on the hardwood floor.

Silence hung in the cavernous room.

Horror and fear wreathed the lady's delicate features. "Oh, God," she whispered, the words coming out as a prayer. She hurriedly sank to the floor.

Vail rushed over and dropped to a knee. *Pietro di Piasi.* One of the titles he'd intended to keep for his own collection.

"I'm so sorry," she whispered, reaching for the copy now lying indignantly on its spine. "Oh, God," she repeated, as she rescued the book.

"It is fine," he said in the tones he'd used with Atlas when he'd gone fractious just before battle. "It's not even intended for auction," he said as a way of reassurance. Even if it hadn't been, he still wasn't one of those ruthless employers who beat his servants or sacked them for errors.

"But it matters to you," she protested. "You've indicated everything," she motioned about the room. "Can be purchased or sold and, yet, not these copies. So, they matter to you and therefore are more important than the ones you'd sell."

Vail paused. His whole life he'd taken a person's appreciation for material items as a vile attribute of the nobility. Whereas he? He'd operated for so long as profit-driven, and a need to amass an even greater fortune so he could know security for himself and his family. What this woman before him spoke of ran anathema to everything he'd based his existence on. "I'd not thought of it that way before," he said, clearing his throat.

"Well, you should," she said softly. "It is all right to prize things for what they mean to you and not what they show off to others."

How did she see so much about him…things he'd not even known about himself? That is precisely how he'd come to view all material possessions. They were just another sign of the peerage's misplaced priorities. With a gentle smile, Bridget returned her attention to her organization of those books, even as her words ran through him.

The lady spoke her mind and stated her beliefs with such ease. Existing amongst Polite Society, more an outsider than anything, he'd found the *ton's* ability to prevaricate, exasperating. Not a single person—lord, lady, or servant—had demonstrated an ability to freely speak their mind. How very…refreshing it was.

I should go. Even as his brain urged his legs to move, he remained rooted. "Have you read those titles?"

She briefly glanced up, with some surprise. Was it the fact that he remained here, putting personal questions to her, still? Or had she dismissed his presence? That thought oddly grated. No man cared to be forgotten. Particularly not by a woman who'd some inexplicable hold on him. "I have," she said guardedly, studying him as he started back over. "They're dark. Bleak. And there's enough misery that I never really cared to read them again."

Of course, having been a bookseller's wife, she'd no doubt been exposed to many volumes and collections. Did the lady realize she also painted an image of the life she herself had known? "On the contrary," he said, picking up the previously dropped book.

She paused and studied his handling of it, lingering her gaze on his hands.

"As a child, I witnessed the vices that men and women of any station were capable of. Greed. Gluttony. Lust. Envy. Dante presented the world in such a way where we have control over all of it. That we determine our path." He set his jaw. "We set our fate."

Bridget met his stare. "One might say that is naïve of you, my lord."

His annoyance stirred at both the station barrier she'd resurrected between them and also her ill opinion. He'd countless other matters that commanded his attention at any given day and time. This one was no exception, and yet he could not bring himself to abandon a debate with the direct woman before him. "You disagree, then? You'd make excuses for Dante's sinners?"

"Not excuses," she protested, shaking her head. "I, however, would not find all sinners the same."

"Neither did Dante," he pointed out, collecting *Purgatoria*. He flipped to one of the wood-carved plates of a winged serpent guarding the entrance surrounded by mournful souls. "There are different degrees of sinners and, inevitably, they all end up in hell, just varying places within it, for their crimes."

A small, sad smile played at Bridget's lips. "Do you know, my lord," she began, moving around the table so she stood directly opposite him. "When I was just five, I had a governess who insisted I paint." She waved a hand about. "She claimed all ladies needed to be proficient painters and insisted I memorize the twelve colors upon the color diagram."

At the unexpected turn of the discourse, he cocked his head. "And, did you enjoy it?" he asked, attempting to follow that abrupt shift.

"Painting?" An inelegant snort escaped her. "I hated it. I was rot at it. My sister was quite skilled, but drawing images I'd created with my own hand never spoke to me the way the written word did."

Her gaze grew distant and she went silent for a long moment. He used her distraction to study her. The lady had a sister. Not for the first time, he wondered about the circumstances that had found her in her current station. Had she abandoned all for the love of a bookish man?

Bridget chuckled. "One day, my governess fell asleep in the middle of my lesson." A mischievous smile on her lips, she lowered her voice to a conspiratorial whisper. "I despised her as much as I did painting. So, I was quite content to let her slumber away."

A smile pulled at his lips as he imagined her, as she would have been, a girl too clever for even her own governesses. "While she dozed, I experimented with those twelve colors. I mixed every color together. Ones that she said should never be paired," she spoke with an animated glimmer in her eyes, gesticulating wildly as she spoke. "Green and red, purple and blue, orange and blue. With those colors, I made black and white, and from that, gray. Do you know how many shades there are of that dreary color?"

He shook his head. "How many?"

"Thirty," she said, widening her eyes. "Thirty variations of it. Can you imagine?"

"No," he said quietly, mesmerized by her telling and enthusiasm.

Her smile dipped; a somberness erased that earlier glimmer and he mourned the loss of it. "One might see red and green and yellow and purple, but sometimes buried within are other shades…" She paused. "Like gray." Bridget held his eyes and the significance of her words settled in. "Life, much like color, doesn't exist in a neat, orderly way, no matter how much easier it might be to categorize it." She turned her palms up, as if in supplication. "People are no different. You cannot neatly file them as sinners or saints. We are all simply people, flawed by our own rights…surviving in an uncertain world."

The solemnity of her words ushered in a heavy silence. He curled his fingers around the antique text in his hands. She'd ask him to challenge every basis with which he'd made sense of his existence and that of everyone around him. She might accuse him of naiveté, however, he'd witnessed the scores of lovers his mother had taken, he'd given his heart to a woman whose avarice had triumphed over love, and, now, a man grown, met daily with men whose souls were just as black. And then there had been Erasmus, put into a place not even fit for a rabid beast. His throat worked as the same piercing agony of finding his brother that day slammed into him as fresh as when he'd stepped inside that rancid hospital. "Your words are poetic," he said at last, filling the void. "But ultimately, the decisions we make define who we are."

Something flashed in her eyes and he tried to make sense of the silver flecks dancing in those cerulean depths. Was it pity? Sadness? Regret?

"Yes, mayhap you're right." And he knew the moment she'd

marked their discussion at an end and had restored him to the role of employer. *Which is what I am.*

Swiftly setting down the book, he bowed his head. "Is there anything you require?"

She shook her head. "No, thank you."

He hesitated and turned to go. But stopped. Puzzling his brow, he faced her once more. "How did you know those titles mattered to me?"

A pretty blush stained her cheeks. "Mr. Winterly mentioned…" So Edward had been chatting about him with Bridget.

"And what did he mention exactly?" he encouraged. Had the lady asked questions about him? Or had Edward freely volunteered it? And Vail wasn't certain why that should matter…and yet, it did.

She gave her head a shake as he came closer. He walked a path around her. The scent of her, a blend of hyacinth, lilac, and fresh rosewater, wafted about his senses, intoxicating him. "Do you think I'd sack my brother?" he asked, infusing a droll edge to that query. He stopped before her, so she might see his lips.

Bridget chewed at her lower lip. "I don't know?"

"There is a question there," he pointed out. He didn't have a right to be offended by her truthfulness, especially given his own earlier reservations and Edward's charges.

"No question," she said quietly.

He'd taken many lovers to his bed. Inventive women, obvious in their ploys, who'd emphasized their physical attributes. How much more appealing and enticing Bridget's husky contralto, in fact, was.

She must have mistaken his silence for displeasure for she spoke on a rush. "I don't know you, beyond a handful of conversations and our brief exchanges when I bring you coffee and pastries in the evening. I can't truly know what kind of man you are in the short time I've been here: whether you're kind to servants. Or whether you'd berate a clumsy maid who dropped a book," Bridget looked to the forgotten leather tome. "Particularly one worth more than most country cottages and some estates."

Her words hit him. "Do you think I'd do that?" The question exploded from his lungs, harsh and shocked.

Bridget shook her head. "I don't. But I don't truly know you."

The meaning of what she spoke pierced his hurt indignation.

His brother's earlier revelations about her previous employment slipped forward. She didn't speak of him. She spoke of…another. "Do you know something of that, Bridget?" he asked quietly.

"No," she said quickly, twining her hands before her.

Having attended every last detail of a person's movements and actions had saved him more times than he'd deserved on the battlefields of Europe. As such, the telltale twisting of her fingers, those long digits clenched so tight she'd drained them of blood, spoke more truth than her words did. The sight of it roused a primitive fury inside. He managed two words: a name. "Lord Stanwicke?"

Surprise alighted in the lady's eyes and she swiftly swept her thick, long auburn lashes down, concealing all emotion there. "I don't—"

"Did he put his hands on you?" Because if he did, Vail would take him apart with *his* bare hands and do it quite gladly. His mother had one protector who'd left marks upon her neck and arms. As a boy, Vail had vowed to never be one of those reprobates and, more, he'd promised himself he'd knock a bastard out who did so.

"He never put his hands on me," she spoke so softly he strained to hear, but he did.

"And yet you witnessed such treatment?" Had it been a husband?

She skimmed her fingertips along the edge of the table, and he followed that back and forth distracted movement. "I did."

That was it: two words that confirmed that which he'd already suspected since Edward had broached the topic of Stanwicke.

Who? The urge to ask that of her hit him like a physical force.

Bridget trained her gaze on the gilded lettering of Dante's *Inferno*. "I'd simply come to expect that intemperate lords quick to anger, and even quicker to exercise their fury, was just the way all noblemen were."

It wasn't. Not the way all noblemen were. His friend, Huntly, was proof that there were some powerful peers who treated others, regardless of station, with decency. And yet…Vail moved closer, placing himself close to her right ear. "Many of them are careless in their restraint," he agreed. "I witnessed that as a child."

She lifted her gaze.

"I'm the Bastard Baron, son of a courtesan." He paused, letting the enormity of that settle between them.

Bridget stared up at him for a long moment. "And do you expect that should matter to me?" she asked, her question rich with disappointment. Not for the first time, he questioned the life she'd known before this. Her cultured tones and grasp of classic texts marked her highborn.

Only the most ardent bibliophiles and desperate lords in need of a fortune pushed their unwed daughters into his path. "It matters to everyone," he said, veiling his eyes. It had mattered to Adrina, who'd married an old, doddering earl, and only came to Vail years later when he'd been titled and rich by his own work. It mattered to everyone, it would seem, except *this* woman.

Bridget claimed his hand in hers, twining their digits. His heart pounded. Odd, in all the carnal acts he'd known with clever lovers and wanton widows, never had he properly appreciated how the simplicity of joined palms could elicit such a potent eroticism. "Society has its views of what perfection is and who belongs amidst their noble ranks." Her husky contralto washed over him. "If one is a bastard or not of noble birth, or…" She laid his hand upon that large crescent mark upon her cheek. "Otherwise, imperfect, one is treated the same." She held his gaze. "I would never be a person to treat anyone differently."

How could she not see her beauty? "Imperfect?" he murmured. "The *ton* is full of fools." She fluttered her lashes and leaned into his touch. Soft as satin and despite the words she'd uttered to the contrary, ones that rang with conviction—she was beautiful.

It was Bridget who broke the quixotic spell between them and he mourned the shattered connection. She disentangled their hands. That movement forced his hand back to his side.

Recalled to the moment, he looked at a point over the top of her head. "Your opinion is far more forgiving than members of Society. Through my mother, however, and what she did to survive, I encountered all different levels of humanity. Some of her protectors were kind." Men who'd voluntarily offered funds to pay for a tutor as long as Vail's mother had been their mistress. His jaw tightened as a memory slid forward. His mother, with a cold cloth pressed against a swollen cheek.

Bridget caught his hand again. "And the others?" she gently urged.

"Most were self-serving. And then others were ruthlessly violent."

Her gaze softened. "That is the reason for your opinion on the vices of men."

"Not just men. Men and women alike are capable of the same degrees of treachery, deception, and evil."

She gave his fingers a slight squeeze. "I'm so sorry," she said gently.

All the muscles in his body jerked to tautness under the staggering realization—she sought to comfort him. What had begun as a discussion to learn more about the woman he'd trusted his collection to, had dissolved into something intimate, details of himself he'd shared with no other soul—not Huntly, or Huntly's sister, Cecily, whom he'd called friend since he was a child. Not the brothers or sisters he'd tracked down through the years.

Feeling exposed, Vail drew back. "I should leave you to your task." And he who'd faced soldiers with blades, guns, and bayonets drawn on him on the battlefield, for the first time in the whole of his existence did something he'd never done before—he retreated.

CHAPTER
9

THERE ARE DIFFERENT DEGREES OF *sinners and, inevitably, they all end up in hell, just varying places within it, for their crimes.*

Later that night, her responsibilities as housekeeper completed for the day, Bridget made her way through the darkened halls. Vail's accurate pronouncement echoed around her mind; a mocking reminder of the truth of them.

He'd divided the world into sinners and saints, and she would always fall in the former category. As they'd spoken, and he'd presented his concrete view of people and goodness, she'd accepted the reality—Vail would never understand, nor forgive her betrayal. A crime was a crime, and when he discovered what had brought her here, it wouldn't matter that everything had been for Virgil. Bridget would forever be just a thief in his eyes.

And that is what I am.

Creeping around, in the dead of night while the household slept on, was just further proof. Bridget tiptoed down the hall; the chill of the hardwood floor penetrated her bare feet. She folded her arms and rubbed in a bid to bring warmth back into her limbs. This cold, however, was more than just the night air. This was also the shame of her actions. She stepped on a loose floorboard and the wood groaned loudly in protest. She stopped, her heart racing, and she held her breath in dreaded anticipation of someone rushing forward with fingers pointed and charges raised against her.

"Don't be silly," she muttered to herself and resumed her path to one of Vail's Collection Rooms. What reason had she given him or his family to be suspicious? Her stomach muscles tightened, for that made it all the worse. He and his entire household had welcomed her within their fold. During the day, the female staff looked to her for guidance and that was when she was not fielding visits from Vail's kindly brothers.

The faint glow of a candle at the end of the hall brought her up short. The Portrait Room. Given the manner of work Vail dealt in, she'd carefully explained to the servants as to which rooms were to have fires lit and which should be doused in darkness at the end of a day. With the canvases covering those walls, the maids had been instructed to never leave the sconces lit.

Casting a restless glance over her shoulder to the library she'd come down to search, she briefly closed her eyes. Forgotten candles could wait long enough until she'd conducted a once over of that enormous library. The longer she lingered in these rooms and halls, the closer she came to other members of the household waking to see to the start of their daily assignment. She scrubbed her hands over her face. "Bloody hell," she muttered and shifted course, making for that Portrait Room. Shadows danced off the walls, those irregular shapes melded with the paintings of Vail's family. An eerie chill scraped along her spine as the stares of his kin bore into her. Swallowing nervously, she forced her legs to move until she stopped beside one lit sconce.

Bridget leaned up on tiptoe when, from the corner of her eye, the ominous shape of a large shadow slipped into focus. She gasped and spun about. Heart thundering against her ribcage, she slapped a hand to her heart. Vail sat on the French Rococo Louis XV sofa with a bottle of brandy at his feet and a glass in hand. "My lord," she winced as her voice echoed loudly in the quiet. "Forgive me. I believed the room was empty."

"Only the ghosts of Falcots lost." Vail followed that peculiar statement with a small laugh. He lifted his glass in salute and then dismissively redirected his focus to the painting directly before him.

Worrying at her lower lip, she warred with herself. *I should go.* Unbidden, her eyes went to that snifter. Her own brother had, as long as she'd had the misfortune of residing with him, never been without a drink. Experience had taught her those dangerous spirits turned ordinary men into inordinately cruel ones. This was the first time, however, she'd witnessed Vail with a drink in his hand. She followed his stare to the portrait commanding all his notice and then, against all her better judgment, she drifted over to where he sat. She hovered a moment, before joining him on the sofa.

Wordlessly, he held out his glass in silent offering. "It is all your fault, you kknoww." There was the faintest slur to that last word, hinting at a man who'd consumed too much. Yet, where Archibald was raucously loud in his laughter and speech, Vail was as contemplative as he was in the light of a sober day.

"Of which crime have you found me guilty?" Or the ones he knew of, anyway?

"You have me speak of matters that are better off never discussed." He chuckled again and took a long swallow from his nearly full glass. "And then you make me question what I already know to be true. I resent you for that, Bridget Hamlettt."

She puzzled her brow.

"Your lesson on the color grayyy," he explained, stretching his long legs out before him.

Bridget cleared her throat. "It was a lesson on all colors," she felt inclined to point out. Her gaze, of its own volition, went to the thick-corded muscles of his thighs that strained the black fabric. Oh, God. No man had a right to such perfection. Giving thanks for the dark cover of the room that concealed the blush burning up her cheeks, she spoke gently. "I feel I should also make mention that it wasn't a lesson on colors per se, but rather—"

"Hell."

Gooseflesh dotted her skin. How bleak and desolate that quietly spoken word was from his mouth. He spoke as one who'd personally visited that dark place and returned to battle the demons that haunted him still.

He tossed back the remainder of his drink and then reached for his bottle.

Bridget shot a hand out, intercepting his efforts. She firmly wrested the glass from his fingers and set it on the floor. She'd witnessed what spirits did to a man. She'd not see Vail make himself weak for that dangerous drink. She prepared for his snarling protests; the same ones she'd had her ears blistered when Archibald came to the country and forced his presence upon her and her family. Vail, once again, proved how very different he was from her ruthless brother.

Falling into the scalloped back of the sofa, he dusted a hand over the day's growth on his cheeks.

They all battled demons—some were living, as was in her case, and others fought ones that now dwelled only in one's mind. Her gaze drifted up to the cheerful boy on that canvas, instinctually knowing from Vail's evasiveness days earlier that this small child was the reason for his melancholy. Heart softening, she rested her fingers on the clenched fist resting on his leg. Through the terror that came in being forever manipulated by her ruthless brother, she'd sought to shield her fears, to protect her son and Nettie. She knew what it was to struggle in silence and how that weighted a person. She had secretly yearned for someone to simply be there beside her in facing Archibald's evil. As such, all a person some-times required was knowing one wasn't alone.

Feeling Vail's stare on her, she looked up.

"No questions?" he asked.

"They aren't my place to ask," she confessed. His expression grew instantly shuttered. "But sometimes there can come good in talking about what that hell is. It strips away the darkness and makes it real and real is something one can confront and face."

He lifted his stare back to that painting and his face crumpled. "His name was Erasmus."

His name was Erasmus.

Those handful of words given to Bridget when he'd not let him-self talk about or even make mention of that name.

Mayhap, it was too much drink that had pulled it forth. Or may-hap, it was that Bridget Hamlet was, in fact, a siren who could lure a man into giving up his secrets and very life if she wished it. But in uttering Erasmus' name, and giving him life once more, Bridget, his housekeeper skilled in books, proved herself correct in this, as well—there was an easing in his chest.

Had she pressed him for details and peppered him with questions, he'd have retreated. Instead, she sat in a patient silence—waiting;

her meaning clear: she'd not force him to share more than he wished.

"Back in one of your first days here, you asked who he was." His heart spasmed. "He was my brother," he said hoarsely, those words emerging through a thickened throat.

Bridget stared up wistfully at the portrait. Even in the dark of the room, the sheen of tears glowed bright in her eyes. "I know that l-look." Her voice broke. "A little boy whom one cannot keep up with, who'd chase the rising sun all the way to its setting to experience all that a day brings."

She spoke as one who knew and, mayhap, that unconfirmed supposition made it easier to lower the walls he'd erected.

"Erasmus is…was one of the duke's children." That bastard who'd given Vail and so many others life, and had never properly cared for them. "He was simple and, for it, after his mother's passing, he was sent to a *hospital*."

Bridget gasped, and her fingers reflexively clenched and unclenched about his hand. Yes, for even as people like his brother, deemed imperfect by Society were sent away to be forgotten… the world still knew what those institutions, in fact, were. She did not, however, offer false platitudes and for that he was grateful. "I should have known about his existence long before. But I did not," he said, his voice gravelly from regret and shame. "Because I was self-absorbed."

She made a sound of protest.

"I was," he said, matter-of-factly. "For the earliest years of my life we moved from place to place. All I wanted was a home and a family and when my mother retired in a small Suffolk village, I was determined to have that. I found friendship, and then I found a young lady, and she ensnared me from the instant I spied her in Sunday services." His gaze grew distant, as he recalled that first meeting. "She was a squire's daughter. Beautiful. Respectable. And I was determined that she'd be mine."

"What happened to her?" There was a hesitancy to Bridget's query.

"What happened to her?" He made a sound of disgust and shoved angrily to his feet. Wanting to escape the memories of his greatest follies and, yet, at the same time, wanting to torturously walk that same path, again. "Rather, what happened to me? She couldn't marry a man with no prospects. She couldn't marry a gentleman not linked to the peerage," he amended. Restless, he wandered over to the floor-length window alongside Erasmus' portrait. Peeling back the gold brocade, he stared out into the streets.

…You are a duke's son, Vail… that means something…you mean something because of it…

The floorboards groaned, indicating Bridget had moved. She settled a hand on his shoulder, encouraging him to finish. "Then I revealed I was a duke's son." It had been the last time he'd ever touted his connection to Ravenscourt. "She urged me to go to him and seek a commission in the King's Army." So, he'd choked down his pride and gone to that man who'd so callously cast his mother out. "I would have done anything for her." Even fight a war. He sucked in a shuddery breath. *When the only people I should have done anything for were my siblings.*

"Oh, Vail," she said achingly.

He gave a dismissive wave of his hand. The sting of Adrina's betrayal had faded long ago. All that remained now was the shame of his own selfishness. "I returned and found she'd married an earl. I was so mired in my own grief I drank and whored and lived a decadent lifestyle, ignoring all correspondences I'd received. They grew and grew. Until one day, I sobered, opened one, and learned of Erasmus. His mother had discovered who I was and, while she was sick and dying, wrote to me." He squeezed his eyes shut. "And I never even read those notes until after she'd gone. She didn't know her son would be cared for." His voice broke. "She knew nothing but fear in death."

Bridget moved into his arms and he stiffened as she folded him in her embrace. He fluttered his hands about her; this woman who'd been a mere stranger days ago, who'd somehow slipped inside and managed to pull the darkest secrets from him. Vail settled his arms about her, taking that undeserved comfort she offered. He inhaled deep of her floral fragrance.

"You having shut the world out because of your heartbreak did not make you selfish. It made you human." She rested her cheek upon his chest. "You have this unrealistic sense of what human beings are. You allow no missteps or mistakes but, yet, that is what we all inevitably do—falter."

Her words ran through his mind and he sighed. "Some are

greater than others."

Bridget drifted from his arms, and he ached to call her back and take the solace she offered. Except, she continued on to Erasmus' portrait. "He looks happy here," she observed.

Clasping his hands behind him, he rocked on his heels. "What he suffered through would have broken most grown men." He'd witnessed soldiers before battle crumple from far less. He glanced up at the first sibling he'd managed to locate. "He was tiny. So small. And yet emerged from that experience smiling, still." Though the child he'd managed to track down to a hospital had been limited in the words he had and the ease with which one understood him, there had been a depth to Erasmus' spirit, unrivaled by any man, woman, or child he'd known before. "Where many boys his age would speak of ponies and revel in making mischief, Erasmus was content to sit in the walled in gardens outside, with a cloth doll his mother had made." A painful laugh escaped him, as remembrances of his brother lost in the wonderful world he'd created in his own mind slid forward. "He was also weak. His heart..." His own clenched at the memory of the doctors he'd brought out to care for his brother. "If one placed an ear against his chest, there was the faintest murmur. And then he was no more," he whispered, achingly into the quiet.

"That would not have changed had you found him earlier," she said gently.

"But it might have," he pointed out. "I, however, was seeking Society's approval. A woman's love and, in the end, left to battle Boney's forces, not even thinking of the others I knew existed." He'd simply read of those Ravenscourt bastards with a detached indifference. Until he'd read that letter from Erasmus' mother and found that those men, women, and children were, in fact—siblings.

Bridget wandered away from him and he followed the gentle, graceful sway of her hips like a moth drawn to a flame. She stroked her fingers over the sapphire blue satin wallpaper and raised her touch higher, caressing the gold frame that contained his brother Colin's portrait. "Who is he?" she asked curiously.

"Colin. He's a Bow Street Runner. One of the best in London," he said with a pride he expected a father should feel.

"Was he one when you found him?"

He shook his head tightly. Another sibling he'd failed. "He'd been living in the streets of St. Giles. Picking pockets to survive and care for our sister," he said, tossing out that reminder of the man he was, for a woman who'd make foolish pardons.

Bridget eyed Colin's portrait for a long moment, head cocked at a little angle. "Yet, he's a Bow Street Runner. One of the finest, you said?" she asked, tossing a glance over her shoulder.

He nodded.

Sighing, Bridget drifted over. "You don't see. You would lash out at yourself for the remainder of your life for giving your heart to a woman undeserving of that gift. For going off to fight. You focus on that and you fail to see what happened because you did. None of these people," she gestured to the framed portraits about the room. "Would have the stability and security they do if you hadn't been titled and had the monies to begin your business. So sometimes, from great darkness, comes good. And it would be wrong to miss all that good because you're mired in what brought you there."

Her words cascaded over him, filling him inside and out with an odd lightness.

Their gazes locked and a charged moment passed between them.

Bridget cleared her throat "I should return to my rooms." Without awaiting a reply, she started for the door.

"Bridget," he called out.

She paused, glancing back.

"Thank you." Vail held her eyes. Wanting her to stay. Wanting this stolen moment with her to go on.

Lifting her head in a slight acknowledgement, she left.

CHAPTER 10

THERE WERE MANY BENEFITS TO being a housekeeper. For a servant, it was a coveted post for the elevated station one enjoyed in one's employer's household.

With her Sunday her own, and now spent alone in Hyde Park with Virgil and Nettie, seated on the grounds watching them, Bridget appreciated her role—albeit her temporary role—all the more.

In fact, with the morning cry of the kestrel and the dew on the emerald green grass, she could almost believe they were back in Leeds. She could imagine them rising before the sun fully crested the dawn sky and breaking from the responsibilities that came with each day.

Except, she was not in Leeds. She was in London to steal from Vail. A nobleman who genuinely loved his siblings and looked after them, and erroneously blamed himself for the suffering they'd known.

Her purpose here in London had been loathsome when she'd been first presented with it by Archibald. What she'd underestimated was just how agonizing the task would be to carry out... particularly when her employer had moved from nameless stranger to honorable, admirable gentleman.

A memory slid forward of Vail as he'd spoken of his departed brother; a small child whom Society cast out because he'd been born different, but whom he had loved and cared for anyway.

A cinch squeezed about her heart, wrenching the organ. For last evening, Vail had let her inside to who he'd been as a boy and then as a young man who'd dedicated his life to helping his siblings… and who blamed himself for the one he'd been unable to aid.

Not unlike her, he'd lived firsthand the violence of the world around him. She'd witnessed the horror and disquiet in his eyes, at the path their discourse had traveled. Who was the fool woman who'd thrown away the gift of his love? Was it the same woman from the note she'd spied upon his desk when he'd been sleeping?

Fighting back the pit of jealousy low in her belly, Bridget sighed. Where she had only reasons to be ashamed, Vail had proven himself a man of honor. For just as he'd pointed out in their debate on Dante, he had taken control of his future and blazed a path for himself.

And what have I done with my honor? I've followed blindly where my evil brother would lead me.

It spoke depths of the difference between her and Vail. And telling herself in the light of a new day that a woman was with fewer options didn't do anything to dull the sharp blade of guilt twisting inside.

"You aren't paying attention," Virgil complained. Dropping his battledoor to his side, her son planted his hands on his hips and glared at her.

Shifting back and forth on her feet, Bridget shoved aside thoughts of Vail and was filled with a new wave of guilt. *I'm failing everyone in this.* "I am paying attention." *Liar.* She'd not seen him for six days now…the longest they'd ever been apart and she couldn't give him all her focus? What did that say about her as a person?

"The boy is right," Nettie called from her spot upon a blanket at the lakeside. The old nursemaid didn't even deign to lift her head from her embroidering. "You aren't paying attention."

Exasperated—even if they were both in the right—Bridget tossed her arms up. "There is no way you could have noted that. You aren't even looking."

"I cradled you when you were a babe. I don't have to." At last, Nettie picked her head up and favored Bridget with a wink.

Dropping her battledoor, she strode over to Virgil and gripped him by the shoulders. "Forgive me," she said softly. "I was distracted."

"Those books," he groused, kicking the grass with the tip of his shoe.

"I'm paying attention now. I promise." She gave him a slight squeeze and, reluctantly, he lifted his gaze. "Another match, please."

He set his mouth and then sighed. "Another, match."

Bussing him on the cheek, she rushed back and reclaimed her battledoor. Virgil was correct. Their time in London, until she had her hands on that Chaucer, was limited. As such, he deserved her entire focus. "I'm ready," she called out and he hit that ball and feathers at her.

Devoting all her attention to the back and forth movement of the ball that they, together, kept in the air, she called out, "Left. Left. Left."

Her son darted sideways and, with a backhand stroke, kept the shuttlecock aloft in the air. Breathless, Bridget sprinted over to the ball and smacked it just before it hit the ground. Virgil let out a jubilant cry, cheering her on.

What if I don't commit the theft? What if I tell Archibald to go hang and see to his damned thievery himself?

Frustration slammed into her. She'd risk Virgil's very life and happiness because of a man she'd known just a short while.

"Right, right," Virgil cried.

Startled back to the moment, Bridget, reached, lunged, and missed. Quickly bending, she slipped the netting under the shuttlecock and propelled it back into place. An early morn breeze caught it and whipped it about the air.

"That is cheating," Virgil charged, even as he hit it back. Only, instead of his earlier annoyance, his innocent laughter pealed around the empty grounds of Hyde Park, the sound of his childlike mirth, infectious, and caused a dull ache inside. For there could be no doubt that if her brother followed through with his plans to destroy her and take possession of his son, that all Virgil's mirth and innocence would, in fact, die. The shuttlecock landed with a noiseless thump in the grass at her feet and she stared blankly down at it.

"Mama?" Virgil called loudly, bringing her head up.

Bridget swiftly rescued the ball and feathers, and caught Nettie's eyes. Worry in their depths, the older woman dropped her knitting and scrambled to her feet. "Why don't you allow your mother a break for a bit and play with your bilbocatch." The woman grabbed the wooden cup and handle.

"Bilbocatches are for babies," he protested. The reminder that the babe who'd first come to her was now a boy and, would one day soon be a young man, sent terror unfurling in her breast. As he rushed over and launched into an argument with Nettie, Bridget stood frozen.

Until she'd come to London, she'd existed in this almost make believe world, where Virgil remained an unaging little boy, and she and Nettie carried on with the daily chores about their Leeds cottage. Leaving that life for the first time in ten years, the reality that was life hit her with all the force of a fast-moving carriage.

Virgil belonged at Eton and then Oxford. He couldn't stay with her forever. What became of a boy who dwelled on the fringe of the world, a marquess' unacknowledged bastard, raised by his spinster aunt? For he eventually deserved the truth…and then what? The enormity of the questions continued coming, rolling unto one another, and her breath came in frantic little spurts. The racket slipped forgotten from her fingers as she pressed her palms against her temples.

From over the top of the back of Virgil's head, Nettie caught her gaze. She said something to the boy. He glanced briefly back, with his usual boyish grin. Giving her a wave, he grabbed the bilbocatch, and proceeded to heft the tethered ball to the cup, counting as he went, the sound growing muffled as he walked further and further around the lake.

Virgil's attention was devoted to that wooden cup. Nettie came bounding over, with a speed better suited for a woman twenty years her junior. She took up position at Bridget's side and they stared after the little boy whom they'd both cared for in equal measure over the years.

"I haven't seen you troubled like this since the day she showed up with a child at your doorway, my girl." Virgil's true mother; a young woman from a neighboring village who'd been cruelly taken advantage of by Archibald. She'd shown up sobbing, in tears, and Archibald had been at sea.

"It's because I haven't been," she said hoarsely, watching Virgil all the while. A girl of seventeen, she'd been panicked as the woman from a nearby village placed her screaming, crying baby in Bridget's arms. For all her pleading and protestations, that woman had vanished…and she'd later learned had been found hanging in the parish village.

"You weren't made for theft," the older woman said suddenly, unexpectedly. Somehow, in hearing those five words spoken aloud, it made Bridget's intended crime all the more real.

"I was though," she said bitterly. "You always see undeserved good in me." And because of it, she'd tricked herself into believing she was different from all the other Hamiltons. "I'm a Hamilton." That vile surname forever attached to her stung like rancid vinegar on her tongue.

Nettie swatted her arm. "You aren't one of them. You never were and never could be. The fact that you're as bothered as you are, is proof of that."

"Feeling guilty and still making a choice to commit a crime, are entirely different things," she spat. Restless, Bridget wandered to the edge of the lake and sat at the edge where she could best watch Virgil on the opposite side. She registered Nettie's presence as she claimed a spot next to her. Bridget dragged her knees up and dropped her chin atop them.

"Sometimes not," the old nursemaid said with the same naiveté Bridget had shown…before her discussion on Dante's levels of sin and hell with Vail. "Sometimes we've no other choice and we make the best ones we can…even when they are the wrong ones by Society's standards."

"We only say those things to make ourselves feel better," she said softly. Only, this crime was not one Nettie would carry out…it was one that Bridget would be in complete and rightful ownership of. "At the end of the day, when I do this," which there could be no denying she would and must. "I'm a thief and history knows the fate of those people." That woodcarving held in Vail's fingers with the winged serpent slid forward and she shivered within the folds of her cloak. "And he'll know as well," she whispered, squeezing her eyes shut. Vail would know he'd entrusted his collection to a woman whose soul was as black as Archibald's and Marianne's. Would such a man rest after she'd made off with that prized tome? Or would he find her and…? Her breath came hard and fast as she forced herself to consider all the horrifying possibilities she'd not thought of before this moment. Aside from Nettie, he'd been the only one to show her warmth and kindness. He'd not treated her as though she were somehow less because she'd only partial use of her hearing and ugly because of an unfortunate mark that marred her skin.

Nettie placed a hand on her trembling fingers. "This is about more than the theft," she stated more as a matter-of-fact.

Bridget swiveled her head to face the old nursemaid who'd always seen too much.

With a tender smile, Nettie patted her briefly on the cheek. "You forget that I cared for you the same way you care for that boy over there." They both looked over to Virgil, engrossed in his game of bilbocatch. "You didn't birth him, but do you think you could have loved him anymore had you given him life?"

Bridget's throat thickened and she tried to swallow. She gave her head a shake. She loved Virgil as her own. She'd nursed him through illness and cheered him along as he'd taken his first steps, and cradled him close when he'd stumbled and fallen.

"Tell me about Lord Chilton."

She stiffened. "What is there to say?" Other than he had a heart bigger than she'd ever believed a nobleman capable. That he'd kissed her and she had hungered to know his embrace again, ever since. "He's a book collector who sells those antiquated texts for a small fortune." Bridget curled her toes into the soles of her boots. How very wrong it felt speaking of him in those cool, perfunctory words, when he was a man who cared for his siblings the way her own brother and sister never had or would. And whose embrace had set her afire.

"Humph."

Don't ask what that little grunt means. Do not ask. She wants you to… "What?" she asked, the question pulled from her.

Nettie moved her gaze over to Bridget. A glimmer lit the old woman's eyes. "If that was all the gentleman was, you'd not be blushing to meet the morning sun."

Bridget bit the inside of her cheek, hating her cream white cheeks that allowed her not a single secret. "What would you have me say? I've been there but a week?"

"Do you think you'd need more than that to tell what manner

of man your brother is?"

She wrinkled her nose. Point taken. "He takes care of his siblings," she finally brought herself to say. Bridget looked away from where Virgil played. "He has more than twelve brothers and sisters and he's resolved to help them all find a stable future." She implored Nettie with her eyes. "What manner of man does that?

"A good one," her nursemaid murmured.

"Precisely. And I have to steal from him," she spat, hating Archibald all over again for putting this demand to her and hating herself just as much for being so weak to go along with it. The thundering beat of horses' hooves sounded in the distance, signifying the end to this stolen moment. She sighed. "We cannot stay here." Even as she was unknown in London Society, being out with Virgil was far too dangerous. "I have to return," she said, hating this life of subterfuge, but knowing with the logic she'd always been in possession of that the more time she spent with her family, the greater the risk she put them all in.

"I'll go gather the boy," Nettie murmured.

Returning to the blanket, Bridget popped open Nettie's old wood basket carried from the countryside, all the way to London. She placed the battledoor game inside, and, grabbing the grass-stained blanket, stood. She snapped the fabric once and a slight gust caught the lace edges. It fluttered and danced, and then settled back to the ground.

Bridget made quick work of folding it. Nettie's words ringing in her mind blending with Virgil's laughter in the distance, she stared absently out over the grounds of Hyde Park. For a brief time with Vail, she'd allowed herself a week's time of living a pretend existence. She'd carried on as though she were, in fact, a member of his staff, and had thrilled at every meeting with her employer.

Today, with Virgil and Nettie, reality had reared its head. The fact that Vail was a devoted brother, a kind employer, and a man of honor and decency didn't matter. It couldn't matter. Ultimately, in the end, the only thing that could save her son was betraying Vail. And not one week, nor one year, nor a lifetime in his household could change her course.

She briefly glanced over to where Nettie and Virgil made their way, toward her. Her son lifted his hand in greeting, waving excitedly. Forcing a smile for his benefit, she returned that exuberant gesture.

There'd been no greater gift in her life than Virgil. And yet for the first time in ten years, she wished her life could have also included a gentleman like Vail Basingstoke, Lord Chilton, in it.

CHAPTER 11

SUNDAY MORN WAS A DAY when most members of the *ton* adhered to at least a pretend civility and decorum. Having been born a bastard, Vail had never been saddled with lessons on the reasons or need for pretend—anything. Nor had he ever cared about how the world viewed him and he certainly hadn't coveted one of those titles he'd eventually be saddled with anyway. To Adrina Mast, his lack of power, wealth, and title had been all that mattered. And when she'd shattered his heart, his work had given him strength and purpose.

As such, Sunday was any other day when business transactions were handled and ruthless meetings held. By a rule, the men he dealt with were ones who respected nothing and no one outside of their collections and coin in hand.

Standing at his sideboard, sipping his brandy, Vail stole another glance at the long-case clock. Forty minutes past six o'clock in the morning. Also, forty minutes later than the agreed upon time for his appointment. Generally, the thrill of an upcoming meeting, and the battle that would ensue over price and then the eventual trading of notes filled him with exhilaration. Particularly a discussion he'd been struggling to make a reality for more than three years now.

Lord Marlborough, an aging earl who had the largest, most

revered collections in the whole of England was selling off the contents of his libraries. And he'd decided Vail, regardless of the coin he'd pay, was undeserving of his collection.

And yet, today, he remained oddly…detached from his appointment with Lord Marlborough. Where he should have his mind cleared, and be running through a script of that exchange justifying why he should receive first look at and right to purchase, instead he remained wholly distracted by thoughts of the young woman he'd fled from yesterday morning.

Bridget had challenged everything he'd believed to be fact where human nature was concerned. She'd insisted that there were shades that explained away a person's avarice, greed, and any other vice they were guilty of. It spoke to her innocence. It spoke of a woman who didn't deal with ugliness and evil and greed. A woman who, instead, on her day off slipped out the front door with a picnic basket and used a hired hack.

Frowning, he took a long swallow of his drink. Where in blazes had the lady been off to? Or rather…with whom? Those outings, though, usually took place later in the day, invariably occurring between gentlemen and young ladies. Vail clenched and unclenched his gloved hands in a reflexive gesture around his glass.

His office door opened and he looked up. "He's livid," Edward informed him, shutting the door.

He? He puzzled his brow.

His brother gave him a droll smile. "Marlborough. The Earl of Marlborough whom you've been angling for a meeting with for the better part of three years? I trust you remember the gentleman?"

What in blazes am I doing? Pondering a maid instead of his meeting. If ever there had been a doubt whom his sire, in fact, was, this was the proof. "Oh, I remember." The first meeting between Vail and that miserable old bastard had come five years ago when he had set himself apart as one of the most ruthless, knowledgeable collectors. Marlborough had kept him waiting nearly an hour and, all the while, he'd no intention of selling to the Bastard Baron, as he'd spat on Vail's way out. "He'll wait another ten minutes," he said quietly to himself. He was a master of restraint and control in all aspects of his life: from his business dealings to the lovers he took and he'd prided himself on that clear-headedness since

Adrina's betrayal all those years ago. He'd not compromise that for a quick-witted maid who was a master with his collections and proficient in more languages than Vail himself. Just as he'd not compromise his pride for a pompous lord like Marlborough. Ever since Vail had rejected a possible arrangement with the gentleman's eldest daughter, the earl had ended all business transactions between him and Vail.

"The gentleman insists he'll wait no more than another five," Edward warned.

"Gentleman," he muttered. There was nothing gentle, refined, or polite about the slender earl who hungered for old texts the way a glutton did prime steak. "He'll wait," he said, swirling his drink. Because his pride would not let him leave without ever receiving a proper greeting.

"I'm not in possession of your usual confidence this time," Edward countered, shaking his head.

"He'll wait," Vail repeated. They always did. Some of them threatened to walk off, but the madness that gripped them always proved far greater. Vail had discovered that long ago, and had grown his power and his wealth as one of the most renowned booksellers because of it.

"Your efforts to rile a client are better reserved for when you're selling. Need I remind you, today you're seeking privileged rights from the earl?" Edward cast a nervous glance over at the clock.

If Edward believed Marlborough had any intention of giving Vail the first rights to his collections, then he wasn't cut of the same ruthless cloth as men like him and the earl. Finishing his drink, Vail chuckled. "I'm always the seller." He set his glass down on the mahogany sideboard. "That is the difference between me and them. I don't give a jot for those books—"

"And Marlborough knows it."

"—outside the coin they'll fetch me," he spoke over him. Nor was he so much a fool that he didn't know precisely the reason the old earl had swallowed his pride and waited now for a meeting. For Marlborough, just like Stanwicke, Dunwithy, and every other rabid, antiquated text collector in London, was in want of a book—the same book. The Chaucer up for auction in three weeks' time had created a frenzy among those gentlemen, eager for that coveted tome…even ancient collectors like Marlborough who was selling off his own works.

At the end of the proverbial day, those books were merely a means to a greater fortune…*this one matters to you…and it is the most important because of it…*

A little niggling started low in his belly and he scowled. What sorcery was Bridget Hamlet capable of that she'd have him standing here questioning his views on those works and, more, the way he'd lived his life all these years?

"Perhaps I'll speak to him, once more."

"Do not," Vail called, staying him in his tracks. "I don't want him appeased." He'd sat through the earl's insults and taunting years ago. He'd not deny himself a long overdue exchange, where he was in control.

"Bloody hell, Vail," Edward muttered, checking the time once again.

As an appreciator of those fine texts, his younger brother, for all his business acumen, was more alike many of those collectors than Vail. Taken under the wing of one of his mother's late protectors, he'd benefited from a fine education at Eton and Oxford and, in turn, used those skills to shape his way in the world. Vail, however, had been schooled by tutors in rooms of the townhouses rented by whatever lover was keeping his mother. He'd not seen education as anything more than a way out of the uncertain life his mother had known.

Silence, punctuated by the ticking of the clock, stretched on. At last, the clock struck forty minutes past the hour. "I'm going," he said brusquely, pushing away from the sideboard.

"About bloody time," Edward grumbled. "There are other ways to woo a buyer, you know," he called after him.

"I'm not trying to woo him."

"You should."

Vail found his way through the townhouse and onward to the largest of his Collection Rooms. The place where, just yesterday, he'd shared parts of himself with Bridget that he'd never shared with another. Her veiled, but subtle, challenge to how he'd run his business and how he'd lived his life rang in his mind, again. Rearing itself when it had no place in his head before a meeting with a man willing to toss down a fortune for his obsession.

Setting aside thoughts of Bridget Hamlet, Vail stepped inside the

Collection Room.

"Forty minutes," the earl thundered from his seat on the leather button sofa in the front of the room. The man jumped up quickly, for one his age. "You'd arrange a meeting at six o'clock in the goddamned morning and keep me waiting here?"

At first glance, one would only ever take the bespectacled, old earl as a bookish lord, without a spine in his back. Vail had learned early on that appearances were as deceiving as people themselves. "Marlborough," he greeted with a veneer of false civility as he entered the room. "A pleasure as—"

"Don't you give me a bloody word of civilities or pleasantries," the man boomed, jabbing a finger at him. "After that insulting offer you made when we last met, I should have never bothered contacting you again."

"And yet, you did." He found wicked delight in pointing that out as he approached. The moment he'd learned of the Chaucer.

A ruddy flush stained the earl's pale cheeks. And there is where he revealed the depth of his weakness. Vail took up a place behind his desk and reclined in a deliberately negligent pose, daring the other man to leave.

His cheeks ruddy, Lord Marlborough puffed out his narrow chest and, with stiff movements, claimed the spot opposite Vail. "You insulted me, Chilton." He'd have to be deaf to miss the true source of his contention there—Marlborough's spinster daughter, an avid book lover, whom the earl had hoped to coordinate a match with.

"I offered you a fair price," he said, neatly focusing on the safer feud they'd fought: over DeFoe's *Robinson Crusoe*. Just over a century old, the book had hardly merited those accolades—at this time, and he'd been abundantly honest in that.

The earl sputtered. "A f-fair price? That work," he jabbed a furious finger at the velvet sack upon the viewing table. "Is a literary masterpiece. Ran through four editions within its first year of print. Four." He held up four ink-stained digits. "And fortunate for you, I've come with the purpose of allowing you to try and redeem yourself. You've the opportunity to add a first edition signed copy and the follow-up title, and you offered me two thousand pounds?"

This is what it was to be, then. A test. The bloody man hadn't forgiven the slight of Vail declining a courtship of his daughter and, by this, he wagered he never would.

He flattened his mouth. "I've not invited you to speak on past grievances or your DeFoe."

Some of the tension eased from the earl's frame and he preened. "Ah, yes. You'd make your appeal for right of first refusal on my collection."

The bastard was relishing this. Marlborough's library would fetch upward of two hundred thousand pounds, and Vail's driven desire to be the best at what he did. It had been dangled as a dowry for the man's eldest daughter. Vail, however, had little interest in whoring himself for a fortune.

"First, we'll talk about the copy of *Crusoe* you disrespected last time we met."

Vail studied the earl's set mouth, the triumphant glitter in his eyes. Vail's own want of that collection…the need to be the greatest of the sellers, had driven him to dance the same proverbial dance. Staring at Marlborough, he at last faced the truth—the inevitable result would be a denial. Lord Marlborough had no more intention of granting him access and control of his cherished volumes than he did setting them all afire and burning his own townhouse down.

"Very well," he drawled. "You wish to have me look again at DeFoe's works?" He nodded for the earl to remove the articles he'd brought.

The earl eyed him with a deserved wariness and then, drawing on his gloves, set to taking out each of the four copies. He set them up on four wooden display stands, and turned to Vail. "Have a look?" Three syllables and yet they contained a world of jeering mockery.

Vail shoved lazily to his feet and, as he joined Marlborough at the tableside, he made a show of studying the works. All the while, he repressed the same fury that had driven him to pummel those boys who'd mocked him as a child. Whatever street he and his mother had called their temporary home had inevitably found him fending off attacks and taunting jibes over the origins of his birth. Until he'd met Huntly, he'd thought the world, as a whole, incapable of seeing him as anything but an extension of his mother's occupation. After he'd gone to war, he'd vowed never again be an object of ridicule and shaped himself into a master of his own fate. He'd not ceded that for this priggish lord before him.

"Well?" the earl demanded.

"*The Farther Adventures of Robinson Crusoe?*" he drawled. "With the dearth of praise it receives even now, I expected you were merely including it as free per an agreement."

Lord Marlborough froze, and then shot his eyebrows up. A moment later, the earl unleashed a stinging diatribe on Vail's ancestry.

CHAPTER
12

℟ETURNED FROM HER TOO-SHORT VISIT with Virgil, Bridget moved through the halls of Vail's townhouse. Basket in hand, she turned at the end of the corridor and came to an abrupt stop.

His brother, Mr. Winterly, stood with his ears all but pressed to Vail's office door. Perplexed, she opened her mouth to greet him. "Good—"

"Shh." He whipped his head toward her and raised a finger in warning.

Well, then. Whatever held Vail's brother outside that paneled door like a naughty child didn't pertain to her, at all. The baron's business was his own. Oh, blast, her curiosity had always been her Achilles heel. Setting her basket down against the wall, she joined him at the doorway.

Mr. Winterly cast her a quick glance.

"What is it?" she mouthed.

Another bellow split the doorway. Even with only partial hearing, she'd have to be deaf as a post to fail and detect that.

"A business meeting," Edward muttered.

She stared perplexedly at the door. What manner of meeting was this?

The young man-of-affairs leaned closer. "The Earl of Marlborough is inside. He's—"

Bridget stifled a gasp behind her fingers.

"You've heard of him, then." There was a glimmer of approval there.

"I have," she whispered in return. Even tucked away in her corner of Leeds, she knew of the Earl of Marlborough. Mr. Lowell had brought her a handful of volumes to assess which had come from the earl's collection.

The same frustrated worry she'd spied earlier returned to Edward's gaze. He placed his mouth close to her ear and she angled her head giving him access to her right one. "Vail's vying for the rights to Marlborough's collection." All of it? "He's selling his works," he confirmed.

Noted among scholars everywhere for its greatness, it hardly made sense.

"Why?" she blurted and then promptly closed her lips.

The muffled shouts swallowed her quiet interruption. What were they arguing over in there? She damned her reduced hearing.

"According to the gossip, he's ill. The line will pass to a hated nephew, and he'd see his daughters cared for."

Envy—a wicked, dark emotion pulled at her heart for those nameless, unknown women whose father would part with his beloved tomes so he might protect his kin. On the heel of that was shame for her own self-absorption in light of the earl's sickness.

"…Bastard Baron is the perfect title for you," the earl bellowed those words distinctly reaching Bridget's ear. "I'd, however, argue you're a son of…" The remainder of that inventive insult singed her cheeks.

Well. This was the revered collector, regarded for his literary knowledge of all texts—ancient and new ones, alike. Through their heated argument, Bridget strained to detect a hint of Vail's replies or retorts…and yet, he remained stoically silent, allowing the outraged earl to fill his office with insults. "He's never going to grant him ownership of his collections," she murmured.

"No." She started, having failed to realize she'd spoken aloud. "Though…" Mr. Winterly looked to the door, and spoke in hushed tones, that even with her good ear, she strained to detect. "I suspect he never did. Vail knew that, and he's too much pride to let a person enter his household and make a fool of him."

Tendrils of dread snaked through her. Vail was a kind man, generous to those who were fortunate enough to call him family. Yet, by the fortunes he'd made and the people he dealt with, he was ruthless. She searched Edward for evidence that he knew of or hinted at her own duplicity but he had his effortful attention trained on the doorway. Lord Marlborough's thunderous bellowing reached a crescendo.

"…And I will be goddamned if I ever let you, of all sellers, near a damned book. Not even a child's primer…"

Reaching past Edward, she knocked once. Mr. Winterly hissed. "What are you…"

Without bothering for permission, she entered. The gaunt, bespectacled gentleman pacing before Vail's rectangular table didn't even break stride. For a moment, she stared in reverent awe at the famed owner of some of the greatest works. It was rumored that one of his country estates had been converted solely into a place where he stored his first edition, signed books.

If looks could kill, Vail would have smote her where she stood.

"My lord," she greeted. Mayhap, the sound of her voice snapped the earl from his tirade.

"Wh-who is this?" the other man demanded, indignantly. Despite his concave frame and frail appearance, he moved with a surprising alacrity placing himself between Bridget and his prized volumes resting on that table.

Vail stood quickly and came around his desk. He glowered at Bridget. "My housekeeper was just leaving." Logic said leave and let Vail to his failed transaction. The need to intervene—even when he neither wanted, nor realized he needed assistance—stayed her.

"Your housekeeper interrupting a business meeting? I've my doubts about the manner of seller you, in fact, are," the earl shot back.

Both men took a step toward one another and Bridget swiftly moved between them. With the air of civility stripped away and tensions high, how vastly different these meetings between the sellers were than the kindly visits paid her by Mr. Lowell "I came to inquire as to whether you required refreshments," she said hurriedly, glancing frantically about.

Vail stared pointedly at her empty hands.

"Refreshments with Chilton?" his guest spat, planting his hands on his hips. "I'd sooner take tea or coffee with—"

"*Robinson Crusoe*," she murmured, drifting over to the earl.

The gentleman stopped mid-sentence. "I was going to say the Devil…" The heated fury receded from the earl's tones.

"It is a magnificent work. Is it not?" she asked, raising her gaze briefly to his.

Through his round, wire-rimmed spectacles, he met her stare with wide-eyed shock. "You're familiar with it?" he asked, the question emerged grudgingly.

"Indeed," she replied, moving closer to the table. She leaned down to assess the watermarks upon those pages. Once, she'd been tasked with evaluating the authenticity of a second-generation copy. "Some dismiss DeFoe's *Crusoe* as a work of literary fiction and undeserving of the same respect shown more antiquated texts."

The earl folded his arms at his narrow chest. "And what is your opinion, Miss…?"

"Mrs. Hamlet," she supplied. Her skin pricked with the intensity of Vail's eyes, following her every movement. Since she'd entered his household, he had been far more generous than any other nobleman would have with how she'd inserted herself inside the collections. By the palpable fury emanating from his frame, there were certain boundaries he was unwilling to cede. Her commandeering a meeting with a powerful peer and business associate appeared to be the line against which he drew liberties permitted. She warred with herself. Inevitably, the lure to discuss those texts proved greater. "The narrative is simple," she finally said. The gentleman stitched his white eyebrows together in a single, disapproving line. "But that narrative does not preclude it from greatness. Even at the time," she gesticulated wildly to the books as she spoke. "DeFoe's style was unfamiliar but people recognized the significance of his voice and that work." She laughed. "After all, there is a reason that it went through four editions when it was not even a year old in print."

The gentleman eyed her suspiciously for a long moment and then he smiled. That upturn of his lips erased his earlier outrage, transforming him into an affable fellow. "Precisely." He jerked his head at Vail. "Tried to tell this one, to no avail." He drifted closer. "This is a first edition, you know." He spoke with the same pride Bridget had in talking of Virgil's first steps and words to the villagers in their parish.

"Is it?" Bridget arched her neck in a bid to see the front cover.

"Mrs. Hamlet," Vail said, a warning in those four syllables.

"Do you have experience with antiquated texts?" The earl countered, ignoring Vail's menacing form, hovering beyond their shoulders.

"I evaluated books and manuscripts for…" In her ease in speaking about the familiar and safe topic of her experience, she'd nearly forgotten the lies she'd given Vail about her background. "For my late husband," she finished somberly.

The earl withdrew a pair of white gloves and extended them toward her. She stole a sideways peek at Vail. Only where earlier there'd been a barely concealed outrage for her interference, now his face was a carefully set mask, carved of stone. Accepting the articles from his visitor, Bridget drew them on. With meticulous care, she lifted up the first copy and searched the front of the book as she'd been longing to since Lord Marlborough had shifted, revealing DeFoe's work laid out behind him. She scraped her gaze over that title page, noting the word mark, the age of the parchment. "It is a—"

"First edition," the earl supplied for her. "Yes." A muscle leapt at the corner of his eye. "And Chilton tried to rob—"

"Some believe DeFoe was inspired by Ibn Tufail's *Hayy ibn Yaqdhan*," she neatly interjected, in a bid to diffuse that resurgence of Lord Marlborough's indignation.

The earl caught his chin between his thumb and forefinger. "I'd read he was influenced by Robert—"

"Knox's abduction by the King of Ceylon." This time she finished for him. Bridget carefully tugged the too large gloves off and returned them. "I daresay it would be interesting to have the texts side by side to study."

"I've all of them," he whispered sounding years younger for his enthusiasm. "First editions."

She gasped and looked up. "Truly?"

For all the gentleman's earlier rancor, a silly, affable grin teased the corners of his mouth. "You're certain this one's a housekeeper, Chilton?" he called over jovially to the still silent baron.

Bridget faced Vail and braced for the evidence of his fury. The ghost of a smile hovered on his lips and a proud glimmer lit his eyes. Her heart did a funny flip.

"I noted her skill from the onset and relieved her of most of those responsibilities."

The earl snorted and stuffed his gloves back inside his jacket. "Then you're as much a damned fool as I took you for at the start of this meeting, for having her cut your mutton and cook your pastries is a waste of her real talents."

"Oh, I removed those tasks within her third day here."

Lord Marlborough chuckled. "Then, mayhap you're not as stupid as I'd taken you for, Chilton." Turning back to Bridget, the earl dismissed Vail once more. "And what do you think of *The Farther Adventures of Robinson Crusoe?*"

His was a test. She heard it in the challenge underscoring that question, as much as she picked it up in the glimmer in his rheumy eyes. Bridget carefully weighed her words. "DeFoe's work…there was nothing like it prior," she finally said. "It set the literary world upon its ear and earned places on everyone's shelves for not only its uniqueness but because the brilliance of that simple prose." Bridget gestured to the follow-up edition that had been met with nowhere near the accolades as the first. "Inevitably, all readers cannot help but compare a title to its predecessor, and it's hardly fair to the book or the author. So, if you look at it against DeFoe's first masterpiece, it cannot ever help but fall short." She dropped her voice to a conspiratorial whisper. "I, however, was always one who appreciated each title for its own worth and greatness." Bridget winked.

"Clever girl." The earl's eyes twinkled. "Nor did it escape my notice that you didn't put a price upon the volume." He laughed and she joined in until he dissolved into a paroxysm of coughing.

White lines strained the corners of his eyes, and he quickly yanked out a kerchief, covering his mouth. As he drew it back, she caught the bright flash of crimson and a wave of pity filled her. He stuffed the stained article back inside his jacket. When he looked to Vail, his earlier apathy was firmly back in place. "It is unfortunate your employer doesn't have the same appreciation for literature."

Vail rolled his shoulders. Except where earlier he'd baited his guest, now he remained somberly silent.

Bridget cleared her throat. "May I be so bold?"

"Bolder than bursting into a formal meeting?" Vail asked from the corner of his mouth.

Did she imagine the shared smile between the two combative gentlemen? "You're not wrong. His Lordship does not appreciate DeFoe's work." At her side, Vail stiffened. He gave her a quelling look. She ignored it and continued, directing her words at his guest. "But I've found in the short time I've been in his employ that though he might not appreciate that work, it doesn't mean he does not respect, admire, and even love other literary pieces."

"Humph," the earl said under his breath, however, without his earlier rancor.

"It's true. He might not like DeFoe but he's an ardent admirer of—"

"Mrs. Hamlet," Vail said tightly.

She continued. "Dante Alighieri's *Divine Comedy*."

"*Chilton?*" the earl asked, eying the other nobleman opposite him.

Bridget nodded. "Oh, yes and—"

"That will be all, Mrs. Hamlet," Vail said tersely and she fell silent. She clasped her hands before her. She'd overstepped.

"If you'll excuse me?" she said quietly, dropping a curtsy. She had the door's handle in her grip when Lord Marlborough stayed her.

"Mrs. Hamlet?" he boomed.

She slowly wheeled back.

"A pleasure. It was an absolute pleasure." He favored her with a wink.

Avoiding Vail's piercing gaze, she returned the earl's smile…and left.

Following his meeting with Lord Marlborough, Vail couldn't determine whether he should sack Bridget Hamlet for bursting in and commandeering the appointment, kiss her…or thank her. He was dangerously close to two of the possibilities, ones that had nothing to do with packing the lady up and sending her on her way.

Striding through the halls, he called for his brother, Gavin.

The younger man came skidding around the corner so quickly, he crashed into the wall. He caught himself against the plaster.

"Your L-Lordship," he called out, panting as he sprinted over. His trembling lower lip hinted at a man on the verge of tears. "I forgot to see him out," he blurted, and then covered his face with his hands.

Vail slapped him on the back. "It's quite fine. No harm has ever come to a gentleman who saw himself out." Whether people talked about the unconventional way Vail ran his household mattered as much as their opinion of him as a Ravenscourt bastard.

"B-but I knew he was leaving and then, after the yelling started, I ran for Edward." Gavin wrung his hands together. "And then it was just so much fighting, I didn't remain."

Through those worried ramblings, Vail gave his shoulder a slight squeeze. "The fighting ended." A credit to an impertinent house-keeper who'd interrupted his official meeting with Marlborough. "I'm looking for Bridge…Mrs. Hamlet," he amended.

"She was with Edward in the Inventory Room."

With Edward. His literature-loving, affable brother who also happened to be smitten with the young woman? "Sh-should he not be?" Gavin whispered.

No, he should not be. Given that Edward was to be meeting shortly with one of Vail's contacts at King Street, it certainly didn't merit that he was now closeted away with the same woman who'd charmed the un-charmable Lord Marlborough. Smoothing the involuntary frown, he shook his head. "No, that is fine. I—" As was his custom, Gavin spun on his heel and himself marked the end of the discussion. Wheeling back, he readjusted his path.

It hardly mattered whether Bridget was with his brother. Why… aside from Huntly, there was no one he trusted more than Edward. He'd proven himself skilled with keeping Vail's vast collections cat-alogued. In addition to his bookkeeping, the younger man had an urbane charm that had served Vail's business well. Why did those skills suddenly grate? As he came upon the Inventory Room, the sounds of their voices drifted to the hallway. Lively words flew back and forth.

"The volumes in one of Lord Chilton's Collection Rooms are rare not because of their value but because of who owned the titles," Edward was explaining.

"I always found that aspect of book collecting peculiar." Vail stood outside the room, transfixed by the quiet insistence of the young woman's voice. How many ladies whom he'd known before had any opinion on the art of collecting, either way? "It matters far more what's contained on those pages than whose hands they've been in."

Edward snorted. "You find it peculiar? Or obnoxious? Because I…"

At the intimate path their discourse followed, Vail entered.

The couple seated at the mahogany table, heads bent close, remained absorbed in their discussion. Edward said something that earned a husky laugh, and the sound of that wrapped around him. A bolt of lust went through him. So, this was the siren's song written of in those sailor's tales. Tempting. Enthralling. It had the power to keep a man frozen and batter him against the jagged rocks. It—

Edward's answering chuckle effectively doused his ardor. And then, even with the distance between them, he detected the subtle dip of his brother's gaze to Bridget's generous bodice. For all his earlier silent thoughts of the contrary, Vail cared…he cared very much. An answering growl rumbled in his chest.

From over Bridget's shoulder, Edward shifted his gaze. He scrambled to his feet and retreated several steps. "Vail."

Bridget instantly hopped up and faced him squarely. All laughter died from her lips and eyes. A charged intensity passed between them. He damned the lady's earlier ease with his damned brother, when she'd greet him with a stoic silence.

Edward cleared his throat. "I was just—"

"Meeting on King Street?" For all his attempts at dry humor, the completed question emerged clipped and impatient. Edward blushed. Not allowing him a reply, Vail looked again to Bridget. "I would speak to Mrs. Hamlet alone."

"Vail," Edward began, casting a concerned glance between them. "It is my understanding…" Leveling him with a glare, Vail managed to kill that defense. Edward's mouth tensed and, for a moment, he believed his younger brother intended to battle him right there. But then, with a curt bow, he stalked past Vail and took his leave.

The rapid rise and fall of Edward's footsteps faded, so that the only lingering sound was that of the inordinately loud long-case clock.

Never taking his gaze from Bridget, he reached behind him and drew the door closed. She followed his every movement with a proper wariness radiating from her eyes as he wandered over to where she stood.

His spirited housekeeper folded her hands primly before her. "W-Was your meeting successful, my lord?" That faint tremble was the only outward sign of the lady's unease.

"Oh, it would depend on which person you're inquiring after: me or Marlborough?"

Bridget wrinkled her pert nose. "Well, *you*, of course." A slight admonishment underscored her retort. She spoke so simply, so matter-of-factly as though there could be no doubt where her loyalties lay, that a peculiar, but not unwelcome warmth filled his chest. The spirited young lady sighed. "Very well. I should not have interfered."

"No," he murmured, continuing his advance. Only where she'd once retreated, now she remained proudly rooted to the floor; shoulders and head tilted back in a beautifully bold defiance.

"It was certainly not my place and I understand why you *might*," she stuck a finger up. "Be angry."

He stopped before her. The enticing floral scent that clung to her skin wafted about them. "And is that what you think?" he asked in hushed tones. Vail placed his mouth close to her temple. "That I am angry?"

Positioned as they were, his ears missed nothing: Bridget's audible swallow, the faint sound of her top teeth striking her bottom ones. "I-I suspect that is a l-logical reaction."

The evidence of her tangible nervousness grated on his nerves. Did she believe he'd harm her or turn her out for her earlier boldness? But then, how many lords would have done that very thing? He caught an errant curl that had, somewhere between Vail's meeting with Marlborough and his trek through the household, managed to escape its constraints. Gathering that silken lock, he tucked it back behind her ear. "And you are nothing if not logical, are you?"

His tempting housekeeper darted the tip of her tongue out. That pink flesh trailed a path over the seam of her lips. "I've been known to be referred to as such, Vail." Vail. For her reservations and unease, she still took ownership of his name and he reveled in that connection.

"And how else have others come to view you, Mrs. Hamlet?" he murmured, walking a small circle about her, studying her contemplatively. Wanting to know about the people who'd been in her life. Who was her family? Did she have any? Or was she now a widow with only herself in the world? The idea stuck painfully in his chest.

Bridget captured her chin in her right hand and tapped her index finger in a distracted beat against her cheek. She'd the look of a student considering the correct answer to a tutor's exam. "Practical," she said with a nod. "I've also been referred to as bookish." She opened her mouth to again speak, and then brightened. "Am I to take it to mean you've forgotten my whole interruption with Lord Marlborough?"

His lips twitched and he fought back that grin. "You should not take it to mean that."

Her expression fell. With her slumped shoulders and slight pout, she was so damned endearing. Had she been any other woman, he'd have accused her of artifice. Where Bridget Hamlet was concerned, there could never be anything but raw honesty. The lady wasn't capable of anything but. Then nodding, she flared her nostrils. "Very well, my lord. Let us cease dancing around the true matter between us. Yes, I did interrupt your meeting, however…" She raised that same finger. "…I should point out that you were handling it rather atrociously before my arrival."

Yes, he had been. And where he was not too proud to admit so, it was wholly more enjoyable taking in the lady's passion as she spoke. "Is that what you believe?" he asked, instead. Had anyone else challenged the way he conducted himself in his business dealings, he'd have sent them to the Devil.

She snorted. "It is what I know."

Goodness she was magnificent in her directness. Even Adrina, whom he'd considered himself in love with, had flirted with her eyes and left him guessing what she truly wanted, felt, or thought at a given moment in any day. "Very well." He lifted his chin. "Let us hear your opinion on my meeting with the earl."

"Taking a strong-arm approach with Lord Marlborough would never see you with the first right to view or purchase a single volume in his collection."

"And *you* presume to know the best way simply by listening at a keyhole?" His question was intended without recrimination. The men Vail dealt with were ones who fought boldly for supremacy and control.

"I've been told you are ruthless," she said, ignoring his question. Was that a deliberate evasion? An insult?

Except, he *was* ruthless. Where matters of his business and caring after his siblings were concerned, he didn't make apologies and certainty didn't make himself beholden to Societal rules of propriety. "Is that what you think?" Feigning nonchalance, he dropped his right hip onto the edge of the table, even as her answer mattered more than it should.

"I believe you care for your siblings," she put forth, unerringly accurate in that. "I trust that a man who hangs portraits of men, women, and children he's known but a few years speaks to someone who loves deeply." He shifted, disquieted by the ease with which she spoke of his emotions. "And do you know what else?"

Vail fought to draw forth a glib reply; one that would undercut the somberness of her pronouncements—but came up…empty. "What is that, Bridget?" he asked, strangely wanting her to complete that statement, to know precisely what she thought. When to Polite Society he was nothing more than the Bastard Baron; with his vast wealth and peculiar penchant for his business, she saw beyond it.

"You are not unlike Lord Marlborough."

That startled a laugh from him and his shoulders shook under the force of his hilarity. Nearly thirty years or so separated them and the other man lived, breathed, and slept his literary love.

Bridget pursed her mouth.

He instantly masked his features. "You were serious."

"Deadly." As she spoke, her gaze took on a distant quality and, though she was looking at him, her gaze penetrated through him. "He's not someone who wants wealth just to assuage his own greed. He's not been driven to collect over the years so he might have the largest and greatest library in England." Which the gentleman did and the fact that this woman knew as much spoke to an even greater skill in Vail's world. "He is merely a man who loves two things: literature and family. You and Marlborough both care for your kin." Bridget shook her head. "He's not selling his books so he might grow his fortune for greed but to see his daughters are cared for when he's gone."

A sad glimmer reflected in her eyes. And he wanted to know the reason for it. He wanted to ask question he had no right to. In her short time here, she'd gleaned much about his relationship with his brothers and sisters…and yet this woman before him still remained a mystery.

Bridget collected his hand in hers and gave a light squeeze. "You needn't treat all your clients the same. What strategies might work in acquiring the works from one man might be wholly unsuitable with another."

He started. The advice she gave flew in the face of every strategy he'd undertaken. He'd gone from a modest business to one of the most powerful fortunes in the kingdom.

She drew in a slow, shuddery breath. "I understand you might be angry at me for—"

Vail cupped his hand around her neck and gently brought his mouth down to hers. She instantly melted against him; her yielding lips pliant and eager as she returned his kiss. The last woman he'd shared any parts of himself with had ultimately betrayed him. Adrina had been so single-minded in her lust for Societal rank that she'd erroneously believed he, as a duke's bastard, could afford her that power. When he'd gone to war, she'd wed a titled gentleman. As such, he'd simply accepted as fact that all women were of similar grasping natures. Until Bridget Hamlet.

She parted her lips, and he slipped his tongue inside the moist cavern to duel with hers. A fire burned in his blood for this woman and he'd already accepted that in hungering for her as he did, it marked him very much Ravenscourt's son. But in this, Vail could not rouse sufficient—any—regret.

Reluctantly, he drew back and a little groan spilled past her full lips. He laid his cheek along the top of her head. "Marlborough has agreed to let me evaluate his collection and present him with first offer on his tomes."

Bridget looked at him through dazed eyes. And then she widened them. "Oh, Vail. That is wonderful."

"Under one condition," he murmured, brushing a loose strand behind her ear. "I'm not allowed anywhere near his titles unless I bring along the delightful Mrs. Hamlet." Given her open love and regard for antiquated texts, he expected that familiar eager glimmer whenever she came upon a book.

She opened and closed her mouth several times like a trout tossed ashore. "What?"

He grinned. "You'll accompany me." In part because the earl had ordered him to not bother darkening his door unless she was there. In larger part, because she belonged there. In the short time she'd been in his employ, she'd demonstrated not only a remarkable skill with precious books but also an appreciation. As such, no one deserved to be there more than she did. She met that news with an intractable silence. "You'll join me for my meeting at the Earl of Marlborough's townhouse," he finally said, clarifying when she still said nothing. He braced for the familiar glimmer of excitement always revealed in her expressive eyes.

Bridget gave her head a negating shake. "No."

He frowned. That was it? No? And yet, though he'd believe he proffered a gift in the opportunity for her to see Marlborough's collection, neither had it been a request, either. "No," he repeated, slowly, cautiously. This woman who loved literature and lost herself in evaluating valuable texts would decline?

Then in a wholly dismissive move, she returned to the table and devoted her attentions to gathering her leather journals and pens. "I cannot go there," she said tightly. Bridget filled her arms with those books and tools. "If you'll excuse me, my lord." She dipped a curtsy and made to step around him.

Vail instantly slid into her path. "I've known you a short while," he began.

"A week," she needlessly supplied.

He started. That was all the time that had passed? Yet, he'd already shared more of himself with her than he had since Adrina.

Bridget took another step around him, startling him from his surprise.

He placed himself between her and the door. He could point out that his hadn't been a request. Remind her that she was in his employ and that appointment was part of her recently acquired responsibilities. Only, he didn't want her joining him through coercion and force. For then, he'd be just like many of his mother's former lovers who'd ordered her about. "Why?" he asked softly. "Why would you not wish to join me?"

Bridget hugged her journals close to her chest in a forlorn little embrace. Her eyes, usually windows into her thoughts and usual excitement and joy, were an opaque mirror that revealed nothing.

His stomach muscles clenched reflexively as he, at last, understood. She was a servant in his employ and he'd now taken her in his arms two times too many. *Oh, my God. I am my father.* "I see." On wooden legs, he stepped away from her.

Bridget tipped her head at a charming little angle. "What is it you think you see, my lord?" That question emerged reluctant.

There it was again. An additional reminder that he'd crossed an unforgiveable line with a woman on his staff.

He spoke in hushed tones, shame making his neck turn hot. "I've continued to force my attentions upon you. As such, I understand your reservations in accompanying me, anywhere." *However, I need you to.* It only reinforced the self-serving blood that flowed in his illegitimate veins.

CHAPTER 13

VAIL BELIEVED SHE DIDN'T WANT to be in his company. He'd somehow formed the opinion her refusing to join him was somehow a product of the burgeoning relationship between them.

Leave him to his erroneous supposition. It was far easier and required no explanation. He'd, after all, crafted the reason and provided the answer for her. Wordlessly, she stared after him as he retreated: tall, impossibly proud.

…*Deaf, ugly, and weak is what you are, Bridget*…

Those hateful, hurtful words that had been hurled by her siblings in equal measure whispered forward as she confronted her own weakness again where Vail Basingstoke, Lord Chilton, was concerned. For she could not allow him to stalk off and let him believe she'd found him wanting.

She briefly closed her eyes. "Vail," she called out. He stopped but did not turn back. "My not wishing to accompany you has nothing to do with…with… what *we* have done," she settled for. What was this that had formed between them in this short time? This inexplicable bond that wrought havoc on her senses and reason, in like measure. Registering that they now spoke in a hall of intimate matters, she cleared her throat. "I'd speak to you…alone." For a long moment she believed he'd deny her request.

Then with a terse nod, he urged her forward. They said nothing more until they reached his office. As soon as he'd closed the door behind them, Bridget clasped her hands close. He faced her and her throat worked. "Each time you kissed me, Vail, I wanted your embrace." She'd long ago ceased to believe that those tender exchanges could or would ever belong to her. Carefully depositing her work upon the nearby walnut console table, she forced herself over to him, erasing the distance even as it was far safer. "I was as much a participant as you. I'm as responsible and, as such, I take ownership of my actions." Somewhere along the way, she'd blurred her crimes with her pardoning his actions.

He looked at a point beyond the crown of her head. "My mother was a servant," he said unexpectedly. "She worked in a nobleman's employ as a nursemaid to that man's son and heir."

Knowing he needed to have this told, she gave him an encouraging silence.

A muscle moved at the corner of his mouth. "She was young and in awe of the devoted father who came and visited his son every day. That devotion went against everything she'd been led to believe or expect about noblemen." A humorous laugh escaped him; a darkly cynical expression of empty mirth so at odds with the affable gentleman he'd been around her. "My mother was, of course, too naïve to realize *she* was, in fact, the reason the duke came 'round."

"Your father," she said softly with a dawning understanding.

He nodded once and proceeded to speak in brisk, methodical tones. "He set her up as his mistress in town and, for two years, was faithful to her. The naiveté of that. To believe an unfaithful husband would be faithful to a mere mistress." He chuckled, giving his head a disgusted shake.

"Mayhap she loved him," she ventured, laying a hand on his sleeve.

The muscles bunched tightly under her grip, straining the fabric of his black jacket. "Then she was a bigger fool than I ever credited."

A kindred bond to that woman stirred within Bridget. "Because she loved where she ought not? One cannot control one's heart." She sadly smiled up at him. "If one did, then no one would ever suffer heartbreak and there'd only be happy marriages and joyous people and we both know that is not how the world truly is."

Vail stared at her with something akin to surprise. "You're a romantic."

She held her hands up to ward him off. "No," she said quickly. She'd only ever been logical and practical. "I've never been accused of being a romantic."

"And yet, not being accused of it doesn't make it not true," he accurately pointed out.

Bridget tightened her lips. He might believe she believed in love and fairytales and happily-ever-afters, like most other women, but she'd lived enough of life's ugliness to recognize the reality that was life. "Acknowledging that some people love and lose, and are capable of that emotion, doesn't make me a romantic. It makes me someone logical enough to see that love is real, just not a gift everyone receives. Your mother no doubt loved your father."

"Then she was a fool," he said without inflection. "He got a child on her."

"You," she said softly. "You wouldn't be here even now if she hadn't." And for his heroics at Waterloo and the siblings he cared for, and the servants he was kind to, the world would be colder without him in it.

Hard silver flecks blazed to life in his eyes. "And for the first year of my life, he was an attentive protector, still. He paid her visits and brought by gifts for me and for her. In the end, he had his man-of-affairs sever the arrangement, but not before he was generous enough," he spat, "to coordinate the services of her next lover."

Bridget recoiled. What must it be to love so deeply and then to be so callously turned out by the one you gave your heart to?

"Precisely," Vail said, misinterpreting the reason for her reaction. "That is the manner of reprobate my father was." His shoulders sagged. "And every time I hunger for you, every time I violate the moral code I hold myself to, I prove I am the same as him."

And then it made sense. He worried about becoming his father. Nay, he feared that he already was him. Bridget drifted over and, palming his cheek, forced his eyes down to hers. "You are not your father," she said simply.

He jerked. "You don't know that," he spoke in harsh tones, intended to push her away. "You cannot know that after but a week of living in my household." He dropped his voice to a low, angry whisper. "I've wanted to take you in my arms since I found you studying my bookshelves."

Butterflies danced in her belly. No one had ever looked upon her as one to be admired, as any sort of beauty. She'd simply only existed for her imperfections…that hideous crescent stamped by the Devil as a mark of the Hamiltons.

A pained laugh escaped him and he caught her gently by the shoulders. "Why must you have that besotted look over that?"

"Because you're the only one who has ever looked past my flaws." And that in and of itself marked him so very different than anyone else in Society. "I don't know your father but I know you enough to say you are not him," she said again. "Because you worry about becoming him. For that alone, you can never truly be like your sire. Where he turned the care of his child and former lover over to ruthless lords, you are one who loves and looks after those who share your blood."

A negating sound left his lips and she silenced it with her fingers. How could he not see that in entrusting his cherished work over to a woman most of Society had deemed unworthy and unfit, he was far greater than all those shameful lords?

Bridget gasped as he caught her wrist and brought it to his mouth, scorching her skin with the kiss he placed there. Little shivers radiated out, traveling up her arm, and wreaking havoc on her senses. "I need you there. Marlborough will not allow me to examine his collection without your presence."

Of course. Her heart sank, as he neatly steered them back to what had led to his revelations. Lord Marlborough and his collection and Vail's business. For the more she ventured out into Society, the more visible she became to the world. She'd existed as the Hamiltons' hidden, shameful secret and had only emerged to commit a criminal act. The fewer who knew who she was, the safer it was…not only for herself—but for Virgil and Nettie. "Vail," she began, needing him to understand, but unable to give him the truth.

He retained his hold upon her; a gentle, yet unyielding grip. "Bridget, I do need you there, but I also want you there."

He wanted her there with him. A week prior to this moment, she would have called him a liar. Life had proven that even her own kin didn't want her about. The inexplicable bond she'd formed with this man, however, challenged everything she'd previously believed—about the goodness a person was capable of—of how others viewed her or might view her.

"You enjoy your work," he pressed.

"Of course I do." Other than Virgil, examining precious literary classics had brought her the only joy she'd known in her hidden village of Leeds. Did he sense her weakening?

"And you appreciate literature."

Since she'd first read of Lord Marlborough's libraries and discussed it with Mr. Lowell, she'd yearned for so much as a glimpse of those rooms. And given she'd been a marquess' daughter, it should have been a simple journey afforded a woman of her station. But she'd never really belonged to that world. She'd been snipped from the fabric of that existence, with her parent's holding the threading needles.

"Why should you not come?"

If he were capable of the same perfidy as she and her brother, his own question would have set warning bells off for him. "Because… because servants don't accompany their employers to the homes of other noblemen," she cried, spinning away from him. Filled with a frantic restlessness, she began to pace. "By your own admission, lords have little use of maids and…" She stopped abruptly. "Society will note your peculiar relationship with your housekeeper," she said, presenting him with the only argument that might resonate, hating herself all the while for deliberately hurting him.

He gave a negligent wave. "I don't give a jot what they believe about me. I care more about what I know to be true."

Bridget bit the inside of her cheek hard enough to draw blood. How wholly unlike her father and brother this man was. Vail Basingstoke was a man of convictions and honor, and she stood before him a fraud in nearly every way. "Please, don't ask this of me," she implored.

He set his jaw and met her gaze resolutely. "It hardly matters what station you've been born to or the status of your rank or finances. A person's worth is defined by who they are." He'd made up his mind and had taken the decision from her.

Then, by the fierce glint in his determined eyes, it had never truly been a decision. He'd have settled for nothing but her acquiescence. She shuttered her expression, willing back the fear and panic that came in revealing herself before Polite Society. "Very well. I will accompany you," she said, even as her mind raced. None except for the servants in their family's Kent countryseat had known her and she knew what her parents had told them or the world in general after her disappearance with Virgil. A panicky laugh gurgled in her throat. That was assuming she'd even been anything more than a regretful afterthought.

Bridget started as Vail settled strong, reassuring hands upon her shoulders. "You're no mere servant. In the time you've been here, you've proven invaluable to me." Invaluable to him. Given that few had ever seen her existence as anything more than a burden, she should find a beautiful solace in his words.

I want more.

And it was folly and dangerous, not only because she'd never thought there could be more with a man such as Vail, rather because she wanted him—this one man she could never have anything with.

She froze. Afraid to move. Afraid to speak. Afraid to so much as breathe under the enormity of her folly. *Oh, God. I care for him.* A man she'd set out to deceive, who'd entrusted his business to her hands. In a short time, he'd come to matter. Her mind shied away from anything more.

"I have an appointment tomorrow," Vail was saying through her dread. She sent a prayer skyward that he'd restored them to the safe role of employer and servant. "We'll leave before noon."

We'll leave? Bridget closed her eyes. Of course Lucifer wouldn't allow her even a slight reprieve. "My responsibilities are here," she said weakly, in one last, desperate bid to extricate herself from that public visit.

He dusted his knuckles over that hideous crescent birthmark in a tender caress that threatened to shatter her. "With your skill and capabilities in handling literary texts, it would be a crime for you to take on any other role."

Why could he not let her carry on as a mere servant? Why must he involve her in his business dealings? It only enhanced the deviousness of her betrayal.

A knock sounded at the door and, as one, they looked to the entrance to where his brother, Mr. Winterly, stood. Cheeks flushed, Vail swiftly dropped his arm and backed away from her.

"This arrived a short while ago for you," the other man murmured, looking back and forth between them. He briefly settled his stare on Bridget's disheveled tresses.

Shame curled her toes reflexively.

Mr. Winterly held out a small folded sheet of vellum.

Stalking over, Vail claimed the page. With a slight, stiff bow, Mr. Winterly backed out of the room.

Vail flicked open that sheet and worked his gaze quickly over the words written there. He immediately folded it and stuffed it inside his jacket. Expression guarded, his firm lips set in an unforgiving line, and this towering figure before her was very much the ruthless businessman her brother had spoken of. "I have a meeting with a seller."

He owed her no explanations. "Of course," she forced herself to say, grateful for that wall he'd erected and the diversion that now called him away. She was grateful, so why did she feel this dejection at his abrupt departure. "I-I should return to cataloguing your most recent purchases."

He frowned. "It is your day off."

How many noblemen would note such a detail? How many would care?

"I enjoy my work here," she settled for, praying that would suffice. The alternative was further questions that served as unnecessary reminders of the young boy living alone with Nettie. "You should go, Vail. Your meeting." *Please, just go....*

With a hesitant nod, he turned on his heel and left.

As soon as he'd gone, a panicky laugh gurgled in her throat and she clamped a hand over her mouth to stifle that half-mad sound. All her life, she'd mourned that she was forced to conduct her work as a secret to Society for no other reason than because she'd been born female. Only to find the one man unafraid to acknowledge the role she played should be this one.

Reclaiming a spot at the mahogany desk, she resumed the work she'd left when Mr. Winterly had gone. Vail might have confided his fears that he would become his shameful father, but the truth remained, of her and him, only one of them shared their family's vile blood—and that was her.

Vail didn't deal in unscheduled meetings. To do so with buyers and sellers conveyed too much of an eagerness and jeopardized the profits one might earn. Such a lesson had been learned during his first transaction when he'd operated under a different set of rules...that punctuality demonstrated one's honor and character. That had been the last appointment he'd ever arrived on time to.

Taking those desperately requested meetings, however, was an altogether different matter. Early morn appointments and unexpected visits bespoke a seller's desperation and to not grant that one was the height of business folly.

Never before had he thought of declining one of those sessions. Until Bridget. What was it about the lady that made him want to damn the seller in his office and remain with her?

Mayhap it was her total lack of artifice. With her cleverness and acumen in the antique book industry she stood apart from the lords and ladies he dealt with daily. By her admissions and faint pleading, however, she didn't recognize her worth for what it was—greater than all those miserable peers who'd dare make her feel inferior. But it was also something he understood...because he'd once felt precisely as she had. As a boy, all Vail had been so very focused on was how different he was from the lords and ladies of Polite Society. He'd hated his lot and resented that he and his mother had been treated beneath those fancy members of the peerage. Too many nights he'd lain abed, staring at the plaster ceiling of a temporary home imagining himself becoming powerful like the duke who'd sired him.

In time, he'd found pride in the work he did and the battles he'd fought against Boney's men. When he'd returned from war and been titled for those acts of bravery, the last thing he'd given a jot about was Polite Society. He'd naively forgotten what it was to live on the fringes of that world as Bridget did.

And she didn't see her own inherent worth against those lesser people.

Reaching his office, Vail stopped at the edge of the doorway. To carry thoughts of Bridget into his meeting only posed a distraction. He forcibly thrust aside her visage and masking his features, entered the room. "Lord..."

The blonde-haired, cloaked woman at the center of the room, spun to face him.

Adrina.

"Vail," she greeted in her singsong voice that had so enthralled him as a young man. Tall, willowy, and in possession of a halo of golden curls, she'd always epitomized a flawless English lady. Now, he found himself preferring Bridget's understated beauty. Adrina cleared her throat. "It is so very good to see you." Three years away from thirty, she was older, more mature than the girl who'd married an old earl after Vail had gone off to war, and yet her golden tresses shimmered with the same shine. Only her eyes appeared harder, sadder. Once that would have gutted him.

"My lady," he said tightly. "I don't take meetings based on lies." He reached for the bell-pull but she rushed over in a rustle of black satin skirts.

"Don't," she pleaded. "I needed to speak to you."

Vail chuckled, the sound empty and mirthless to his own ears. "And here I thought no words between us were to ever be spoken again." He tossed back that sentence she'd etched in his memory the day he'd called upon her in London and learned she'd accepted the offer of an aging nobleman.

She winced. "I deserve that, but you must know, I *need* you to know I've thought of you and only you for the past eight years."

That utterance would have once sustained him. Life had changed him, however. It had made him stronger, harder, and, as such, Adrina may as well have been speaking on the weather or tedious *ton* gossip. "I have neither the time nor the inclination—"

"Please," she implored, again, holding out a hand. "It is not entirely a… personal call. I've brought a book."

He stilled, eying her warily. He'd met her, the village squire's eldest daughter when she'd been eighteen and he twenty. She'd had the brightest laugh and delighted in discussing gossip and visiting the milliner's, but never had she expressed a smidgeon of interest in a literary work.

The countess worked her eyes over his face and then rushed over to his desk. "My late husband's collection," she explained. "I'm…" She grimaced. "Required to sell his books." So, marrying her titled lord had not earned her a fortune. That realization brought no glee…just pity. Adrina's violet, doe eyes softened. "You were the only one whom I thought of…" She stretched the small leather copy toward him. "Who might help."

Vail searched for some emotion from that admission: joy, triumph. Instead, he fixed on her gloveless hand, gripping that book dangerously by the spine. Of course, he wouldn't expect her to know the proper handling. Few did…and yet Bridget was one of those who did. The first woman he'd ever known with that skill. Wordlessly, he collected the tome.

"I gathered one that held the greatest value," she murmured.

Not lifting his gaze, he assessed the age of the leather and shine of the etched leathering hinted at its newness, and flipping to the front page confirmed it as such. "I've no need for this work, my lady," he said without inflection. Even with their shared past, in this instance, she was no different than any other lord who stepped through his doors to sell him a *valuable* title. "I expect you can find someone else who might aid you in the sale of your late husband's collection."

Adrina lifted tear-luminescent eyes to his; twin pools of hurt. "The title, Vail. Look at the title."

He found the title. *Wordsworth's Poems.*

When he'd met this woman before him, he'd been so captivated, so convinced he'd fallen in love at first sight, that he'd enlisted his friend Huntly's aid to woo her. Poetry had been Huntly's solution. Mocking derision is what he'd been met with and pouts and pretty calls for baubles and ribbons. "It's hard to believe you've developed a sentimental appreciation for poetry now," he said dryly, holding that book out. "Byron," he reminded her. "It was Byron's earliest works I read to you from." The same day she'd urged him to seek out a commission from his father, the duke, for she could never wed a bastard without prospects. He'd humbled himself for her before that man he'd spend his life hating, and he resented himself as much as he did her for that faulty decision.

She jerked as though he'd struck her and then her tears fell freely, noisily. "I—I certainly understand y-you were hurt," she said, her soft weeping and words muffled by her palms. "B-but you needn't be cruel." Over her hands, she stared pointedly at him.

Swallowing a sigh, he fished out his kerchief and held it out.

The lady took the white scrap and proceeded to cry her sloppy tears into it. Mayhap he was as heartless as he'd been referred to by business partners and written of in the newspapers, for those well-timed crystalline drops left him unmoved. He remained coolly aloof until her tears dissolved into a shuddery hiccough.

"I am sorry you have regrets," he finally said. "But this," he motioned between them, "ended long, long ago." And he was better off for it. He knew that now. "Given that…" And the fact that he wanted nothing to do with her in the present. "It is better for the both of us if you find another buyer for the works you are intending to sell."

Her too plump lower lip trembled and he braced for another onslaught of her tears. But her sharp cheeks remained evenly set as she drifted over. That same cloying hint of jasmine that clung to her frequent missives, hung now on her willowy frame, oddly pungent. Pungent when there was a soft, sweet pureness to Bridget's floral scent. "Do you know what I believe, Vail?" she whispered in sultry tones, mature ones she'd acquired in their years apart. "I believe," she continued, gathering his lapels and stroking her fingertips over that fabric. "That you would send me to someone else because you want me as much now as you did then, and you fear yourself around me."

He stiffened and gathered her hands in his, setting them from his person. "I—"

Footsteps sounded in the hall. "Vail—"

He and Adrina looked to the doorway. Bridget, a journal in hand, jerked to a stop in the doorway. Her mouth formed a small circle of surprise that met her eyes as she lingered her gaze first on him then Adrina, and slowly back to Vail. "Oh. I… Forgive me, my lord," she said, her voice revealing not a hint of emotion.

He shook his head. "Mrs. Hamlet, Lady Buchanan was just leaving," he said, making the decision for that other woman.

Despite the terse command there, Adrina revealed that time and life had shaped her into an unapologetic noblewoman. "Mrs. Hamlet," she greeted. "And you are?"

It was on the tip of his tongue to tell her that she'd no right to come into his household and question anyone—particularly this woman before him—but Bridget quietly answered before he could bring forth the stinging rebuke.

"I am His Lordship's housekeeper." She dropped a belated, but respectful curtsy.

Adrina passed an up and down glance over her, lingering a horrified stare on Bridget's crescent-shaped birthmark. A lesser woman would have wilted under the regal noblewoman's censure. "His housekeeper?" A tinkling laugh escaped his former love's lips.

Bridget merely inched her chin up and met that dark stare.

Vail's hands curled reflexively into tight fists and fury blazed to life inside. This was the scorn she'd faced. Through it, she'd remained strong and unflinching. His admiration for her grew.

"Vail," the countess said, angling her body dismissively, giving Bridget the cut direct. "I want you to keep this," she spoke in hushed undertones, pushing that wholly unsentimental book into his hands. From the corner of his eye, he detected Bridget casting her focus to the mural overhead. "Please, think on what I've said."

Which part of it? Her collection he could do without, for the sheer reason it was his business to know the most well-stocked libraries and her late husband's was decidedly not one of them. And her presence in his life proved tedious for the reminders it raised of his own past mistakes. "My lady." He dropped a requisite bow.

She swept past him, the hint of jasmine lingering in the air as she took her leave.

Her leather journal held close, Bridget shifted back and forth on her feet. "Forgive me," she said somberly. "I've now interrupted two meetings."

"And both interruptions were welcome," he said truthfully, loud enough that she might hear him clearly from where she stood.

A hesitant smile tipped her lips. Where Adrina's even, plastered grins contained the same hint of artifice as her tears, Bridget's rang clear with sincerity. "Marlborough's?" she asked, dryly.

"Perhaps not at first, but certainly after." He motioned her forward.

She met him in the middle of the floor. Teasing smile aside, she opened the leather journal and turned it toward him. "I found this." He followed her point to the bottom of the page. "Lord Waters was slated to turn over an original first edition *Aphra Behn – Poetical Remains*."

"And?" he asked.

She shifted her ink-stained finger to the column beside it. "The title was originally published in 1698. By the markings, this copy is a second edition dated to 1699."

Vail traded Bridget the book in his hand for the records she held and skimmed the columns. Bloody hell. That was the price one paid for dealing with drunkards like that one. In the short time she'd been here, she'd singlehandedly identified two missteps in terms of the works he'd purchased, and also secured a meeting with Lord Marlborough he'd not have had a hope of having if it hadn't been for her.

He glanced over the top of the journal. Bridget eyed the tome in her hands. Had he not been closely studying her, he'd have failed to note the way she sniffed the edge of that copy. "Are you one of those who enjoys the smell of an old book?"

Gasping, she yanked her head up. Color splashed her cheeks. "Jasmine," she blurted. "It doesn't have the scent of leather or aged pages. It smells like…jasmine," she finished weakly.

"Yes." Adrina had always doused her skin in that strong, cloying scent. In his youth, it had been heady and seducing. Now, it reminded him of betrayal. He made to return his attention to the page.

"Who was she?" she asked. It was a brazen question that a proper lady would wonder about and perhaps probe servants over. Bridget, once again, revealed a candid honesty.

Handing back her records and accepting that book of poems, he settled for the simplest, most uncomplicated reply, "She is someone I knew when I was younger."

"I see." And by those two syllables, she spoke as one who, in fact, did. Bridget dropped another one of those formal curtsies. "I thought you should know about Lord Waters. Once again, it was not my intent to interrupt you, twice."

He searched his mind for a reason to keep her here. "Bridget," he called out as she reached the door. "Until our meeting tomorrow."

CHAPTER
14

STROLLING THE STREETS OF MAYFAIR on the way with Vail to an upcoming meeting, there were any number of things Bridget should be focused on: the peril of becoming someone familiar to Polite Society when she'd only entered their folds to steal from one of their own. The gawking stares directed at her cheek by unrepentantly bold passersby. Instead, all she could think about… was jasmine. She caught her lower lip between her teeth. Or rather, the scent of it. The same floral fragrance that had wafted from the note in his office.

Since she'd interrupted a second meeting of Vail's yesterday and stumbled upon him with a slender beauty who embodied beauty and perfection, she'd been unable to think of anything but that pair. Their bodies' positioning hinted at two people who'd shared… something. That mysterious note she'd spied upon his desk now indicated just what that *something* had been.

This was the woman he'd spoken of in the Portrait Room. She hadn't required him to confirm it to know it to be so. She was the woman Vail had fought a war for. And Bridget hated the woman with every fiber of her being.

With the Countess of Buchanan's perfect, cream white skin and flaxen curls, she was everything Bridget had never been, nor would ever be. Bridget had believed she'd found peace with who she was long, long ago. That she'd come to accept her imperfections. Only to stumble into Vail's meeting with a beauty to rival Aphrodite and be proven so wholly wrong. Despondent, she stared blankly ahead.

"…I discovered a copy of a *La Bibbia*…"

For she wasn't as at peace as she'd believed. She was filled with the same gripping, vicious resentment that some people were born perfect, without struggle, and then others, such as her flawed self, were born scarred and marked. Derided by Society for reasons beyond one's control, and forever reminded of one's defects daily in a mirror and in the whispers of strangers and—

"…and I used it for kindling earlier this morn…"

Vail's words at last penetrated her single-minded focus. She whipped her head up. "You found what?" she blurted. And then his latter words registered and she shot her eyebrows to her hairline. "And you did what?" she squawked.

He winked at her. "Neither," he drawled. "I was merely seeing when you might be paying attention."

She opened and closed her mouth several times. "So, you didn't obtain a copy of *La Bibbia, Tradotta in Lingua Toscana*? Because if you did—"

"I certainly wouldn't set it afire," he assured her. A glimmer danced in his eyes. "And not solely for monetary reasons but also because I'm not so ruthless that I'd burn an original edition of the bible." He followed that with a smile and she forced a matching one for his benefit.

Only, he wasn't ruthless. Despite what Archibald had shared in her cottage about the gentleman, there was nothing heartless about him. That evidence of his goodness chased away her false grin and filled her with a deeper sense of desolation.

"Come, Bridget," he murmured softly, dropping his head lower to hers. "I didn't bring you along today so you might feel sad."

Why had he brought her then? She wanted to hurl the frustrated question at him. Why couldn't he have simply allowed her to serve on as his housekeeper and never noticed that she was not only capable with antique books, but also hopelessly enthralled by the words contained within them. "I'm not sad," she quietly offered. *Liar.*

"That was belated," he correctly pointed out.

A handsome couple moving directly toward them snagged their

notice on Bridget's cheek. Such horror filled the delicate, blonde woman's eyes that, this time, that derision struck painfully in her chest. Directing her gaze forward, Bridget jutted her jaw out.

"I'm—"

"Don't," she rasped, digging her fingers into the soft-flesh of her palm. "Don't you dare." She'd not have his apologies or pity or—

He stopped walking and placed a gloved hand on her arm, halting her movements and forcing her to face him. "What did you believe I intended to say?"

They stood in the middle of the pavement. A passing gentleman tipped his hat to Vail, who ignored that polite greeting. She gave her head a terse shake, hating that he'd expose her this way before the whole of London's most powerful peers. She felt splayed open and on display.

His hard lips tightened. "I asked what—?"

"I don't want your apologies," she hissed. "I don't want your pity." She wanted him to treat her as he had from their first meeting where her hideous cheek and deafness didn't matter. But she was a fool. It always mattered and always would. Her solitary existence stood as proof of that.

He drew back, shock stamped in his features. "Is that what you believe I intended? To apologize? That I'd ever pity you?" Hurt filled that question. "What reason would I—"

"Don't do that," she pleaded. "At least don't pretend that I'm not different." She loved him for being more honest and forthright than any person she'd ever before known. She… Loved him? A buzzing filled her ears, like a swarm of angry bees that had been set free inside her mind.

Vail moved closer, so nothing more than a hairsbreadth separated them, pulling her from that panicky reverie. "You are correct," he said in hushed, solemn tones. "You are different." She winced. He'd given her that honesty, only to prove her a liar. She didn't want it from him…not in this. "You are different than any other woman I've ever known." The beautiful Lady Buchanan who'd staked a possessive hand upon his lapel, flashed behind her mind's eye, and the breath lodged sharply in her lungs. "You are more clever and more skilled than any I've known."

He appreciated her mind. It should be enough. And yet—she drifted her gaze past his shoulder—for the first time in her life, she wanted to be beautiful…for this man.

Vail moved his mouth closer to her right ear. "And you are beautiful…" She made a sound of protest, moving away. "In every way," he insisted.

"I know who I am, Vail. I confront myself every day in the mirror."

"And what do you see?" he answered, not allowing herself to speak further. "You see a mark upon your cheek? *You've* let that define you. Do you know what I see? What I saw the moment you stepped inside my office and found you there?"

Do not answer. Remind him of where I am and the strangers passing by, sick fascination over the couple conversing in the middle of a thoroughfare. She darted her tongue out, tracing her lips. "What?" she asked, unable to call the question back. Nor wanting to.

"I saw these flame-tinged strands." With his spare hand, he captured the errant curl she'd draped over her shoulder, rubbing it briefly. Her lashes fluttered wildly. The world was looking on. His actions were scandalous and the world would believe her to be his lover and she couldn't bring herself to care from this day on to Sunday if the Lord himself disapproved. "I saw the curve of your chin." He brushed his gloved knuckles over it. "Your eyes, pools that I could lose myself in. I was riveted in that instant." Her breath caught. Vail's thick, black lashes swept downward. "But it was and remains your mind and spirit that has captivated me."

All the air left her on a shuddery sigh.

His eyes went to her mouth and, for a long moment, she believed he'd kiss her here, and she wanted it, wanted it even though the gossip columns would be abuzz with tales of Lord Chilton and… A stranger to Society, embracing in the middle of Mayfair. Regret darkened his gaze and he straightened. "Come, we'll be late."

"You've still not said where we're going," she observed, falling in step beside him.

"No, I haven't."

At that veiled, secretive reply, she wrinkled her nose. "Is it to Lord Marlborough's?"

"Those details are still being worked out," he said, offering nothing more.

"Are you conducting a sale?" she pressed, gesturing to the velvet sack tucked in the nook of his left arm.

Vail offered her another one of those teasing winks. "No." He cradled the package in his arm with the same devotion she had Virgil.

At the thought of Virgil, a wave of wistfulness swept over her. All her life, she'd believed she was enough for him…that she and Nettie were the only family he needed. Now, walking beside Vail, a man who'd risen up from uncertain beginnings, and made a fortune and future for himself, she realized how horribly naïve she'd been. No matter how much she'd devoted herself to Virgil, he still so very desperately needed the influence of a man in his life.

"You've gone melancholy again."

She started. How very well he knew her. "I'm not sad," she lied. "I'm simply wondering after your mysterious appointment."

Her answer seemed to satisfy him, for he again grinned.

However, Vail had been correct. She ached with missing Virgil. At times, it was easy to lose herself in the distraction of her work and Archibald's scheming, for remembering him was too hard.

"Here we are," Vail announced, bringing her to a stop outside a white stucco townhouse. As he rapped on the front door, there should be a modicum of interest in the secretive visit. All she could think of, however, was the sobering truth: she could not have both Vail and Virgil in her life at the same time. Those two could never know one another and she could never have anything with the baron. Not that he'd truly indicated a desire for there to be more.

The front door was opened, interrupting her whirring thoughts. The young butler bowed and then smiled the way he might in greeting a familiar friend. "His Grace is expecting you," he explained, stepping aside to allow Vail and Bridget entry.

His Grace. A duke. One of those powerful peers just a step below royalty.

Helping them from their cloaks and turning them over to the waiting footmen, the butler guided them through the grandiose townhouse. With white, Italian marble floors and gold satin wallpaper, the household bespoke wealth. She peeked about, stealing glances at the gilded frames lining the halls. Her own family had once been of similar wealth and prestige, but all of that had faded with her brother's whoremongering and wagering. Bridget, shut away from the world, however, had known even less of that grandeur.

"Who is he?" she quietly asked, from the corner of her mouth, mindful of the servant several paces ahead. Was the gentleman another one of those fanatical collectors?

"This is not a business meeting," he murmured, close to her ear. His breath stirred the sensitive spot upon her neck and sent delicious shivers racing through her.

Then his words registered. It was *not* a business meeting.

"He is my closest friend in the world, like a brother to me." *...I found friendship... Oh, God, this was the man he'd found as a boy.* "The Duke of Huntly and I go back to..."

His words came as if from a great distance, with her mind slow to process and make sense of that revelation. His closest friend...a man who was like a brother to him was in fact—"The Duke of Huntly?" she repeated hoarsely, interrupting Vail mid-speak.

The butler cast a curious glance back.

"I assure you, Huntly is no more a pompous, self-righteous lord than I myself. He was born to modest beginnings and made his own way in the world. The only reason he found himself titled was through the death of a distant, distant relative."

The contents of her stomach revolted and she swallowed back the bile stinging her throat. The man Vail called another brother was, in fact, married to the woman Bridget's sister had nearly killed. Her legs weakened and she caught herself against the wall.

"Bridget?" Vail asked, quickly wrapping his arm around her waist and steadying her. "What is it?"

And then in her desperation, she gave him the absolute worst words. "I cannot be here." They were the truest ones and, yet, he'd hear nothing in them beyond her insecurity in being part of this foreign world.

Vail gave the butler a meaningful look and, averting his eyes, the servant faded to the end of the corridor. But she was aware of him, lingering there. "Come, love," he said with such a gentleness, it threatened to shatter her. "What is this about?"

"Vail..."

"Chilton!"

Her stomach lurched at the jovial greeting that echoed down the corridor. A tall gentleman with golden curls and an easy smile came forward, arms outstretched.

Bridget instantly shrank back, thankfully forgotten as the two men greeted one another. By the air of confidence and strength to him, there could be no doubting the gentleman before her was, in fact, the Duke of Huntly.

And my sister attempted to kill his wife.

The gentleman looked over to her and then back to Vail.

She immediately sank into a deferential curtsy. "Your Grace," she murmured, directing that greeting to the floor. How did one go about meeting the eyes of a man who'd been so terribly wronged by one's family?

"Huntly, may I present my…" His brow wrinkled. Yes, how did a nobleman otherwise go about introducing a mere servant he'd arrived with? "May I present Mrs. Hamlet," he settled for.

Bridget braced for a cool derision, welcomed it, particularly from this man.

The duke smiled. "Mrs. Hamlet, I am so happy you are able to join us."

Join us?

What in blazes? Her mind raced and she stared beseechingly at Vail. What was this exchange? Either ignoring or failing to note her gaze, he turned over the velvet sack in his hands. The other man widened his smile and collected it with a word of thanks. "Justina will thank you. *I* thank you."

"Think nothing of it," Vail assured. "May I have a moment with Mrs. Hamlet before we join you? We'll be along shortly."

"Of course," the duke murmured, taking his leave but not before Bridget spied the interest in his eyes.

"Huntly requested a copy from my collection for his wife to read from. Her Grace holds a salon inside her home." Her Grace. That young woman Marianne had been sent away to Bedlam for attempting to murder. "This visit is not motivated by my business or a need for your services, but rather simply one that I thought you'd enjoy."

And through the horror and shame of being in this household, her heart quivered. "Why must you be so bloody nice?" she whispered, blinking back a sheen of tears. "Why can't you," And Lord Huntly, "be a cold, unfeeling nobleman who looks down upon others outside your sphere?"

He stroked the pad of his thumb in a little circle over her right cheek. "You wouldn't want that and you don't deserve that."

He was wrong on both scores. Had he been cruel, her plans for him would have been easier and she should be the recipient of his loathing. *And I will be.*

Vail extended his elbow and waited.

She shook her head and he slowly let that limb fall to his side. "It is scandalous enough that I've joined you. What will the duke and duchess' guests think of a baron arriving with his housekeeper?" He needn't answer. Bridget knew precisely the opinion Society would form—that she was his lover.

"You should care less about Society's opinion and more about your own happiness," he said softly.

Bridget gave him a sad smile. "And this from the man who's dedicated his whole life to caring for others."

He frowned. "I've never complained or resented the role I've taken on."

She shook her head. "No. But you've also taken on the role of father for nine others, without a thought of your own happiness." Before he could speak, Bridget gestured around the hallway. "You'd bring me here and challenge me to find my own joy in life and, yet, all you do is work, Vail."

A muscle jumped at the corner of his eye. "I enjoy what I do," he said tightly, through his teeth.

"What do you enjoy about it exactly?" she challenged. "Every-thing can be bought, everything can be sold," she said into his silence. "That is what you said." She took his hands in hers and gave a light squeeze. "You have one of the largest collections in England and, yet, of all those books, you'd keep but one volume for yourself." She shook her head sadly. "And even that book is one that only reminds you of the darkness that exists in life."

He flinched, and the evidence of his tangible struggle hurt her like the physical lash she'd received from her brother for threaten-ing to shame him before all Society if he didn't allow her to care for Virgil. "Oh, Vail," she murmured, caressing his face with her gaze, memorizing each sharp angle, the slight curve of his aqui-line nose, his hard lips, all of it so when she was gone she'd carry him with her still. Before she did leave, she needed him to know the truth. "What happened to Erasmus was not your fault." She pressed her fingertips to his mouth, silencing his protest. "Having returned earlier and found him sooner could not have cured his heart. You gave him the best life you could have when you did and that is what matters most."

He clenched his eyes tight. "Him living mattered most."

"No," she said softly. "Knowing happiness while you are living is what is truly important. Otherwise, we're just surviving." Her throat worked spasmodically.

"Vail, are you…? Oh, forgive me."

They looked to the end of the hall to where a golden-haired, elegantly clad woman smiled uncertainly.

"Lady Justina," he greeted, his voice revealing none of the hoarsened emotion of before.

Lady Justina. The Duchess of Huntly. For a horrifying moment that hung on to forever, Bridget feared she'd been discovered for the fraud she was and that this young duchess knew Marianne's blood flowed in her veins.

She stiffened as the young duchess swept over with her hands outstretched. Bypassing Vail, she took Bridget's in her own. "I understand you're also an admirer of *Petrosinella*." Bridget blinked wildly. That is what she'd say? "His Lordship explained you also appreciate that work," she explained, answering that unspoken question. "He was good enough to loan me the edition so we might read from it," she said on a loud whisper. "And he thought you would wish to join me for the discussion."

Bridget's breath caught and she swiveled her head back to face Vail. He'd done this? "But I thought…I assumed…" That there had been something pertaining to one of his transactions. He, who'd claimed nothing mattered more than the sale of his collection would allow his friend's wife to read from it…and he'd invited her to take part. How was it possible to feel equal parts joy and equal parts shame at the same time?

Vail winked at her; that subtle movement of his eyes that was so patently his.

"I would be honored to join you," she said and allowed herself to be tugged along by the duchess.

CHAPTER
15

SEATED IN A SHELLBACK CHAIR at the back of Lady Justina's salon, Vail remained with his focus on where Bridget conversed with the young duchess at the front of the room. He took in the gathering of lords and ladies assembled, and assessed their every movement. If a single one of them gave her the cut direct, he'd destroy them.

"This is merely a reading and not a battle," Huntly drawled at his side.

He grunted noncommittally. For Bridget, who feared Society's reprisal, it may as well have been. Lady Justina motioned to a gentleman in the crowd. The tall, dark-clad future Viscount Waters came forward. Vail narrowed his eyes as introductions were made between the two. Once one of Society's most foppish dandies, Barrett had shed his satin-clad garments for dark ones, ceased using the oil in his hair, and now possessed a jaded hardness that marked him dangerous to a young lady. The gentleman said something that earned one of Bridget's coveted blushes.

A primitive rage simmered inside, threatening to boil over.

Bridget looked behind Mr. Barrett's shoulder and a little smile hovered on her lips; a secretive expression of mirth and warmth reserved solely for him. And some of the tension eased. Lady Justina spoke to her, calling her attention once more.

"There will, of course, be gossip." His friend casually observed.

Vail stiffened. "If her being here is a problem, we'll leave."

Huntly looked stricken. "Come," he scoffed. "Surely you do not take me as one who'd pass judgment on whose company you keep."

Whose company he kept. Somehow in hearing that, there was a wrongness to it. Huntly's word implied Vail's relationship with Bridget was something disrespectable. "She is in my employ and has an appreciation for literature. Whatever Society believes in her being here—"

"Being here with you."

"Then, they can go hang," he said tightly, rolling suddenly tense shoulders.

Huntly went silent. They stood shoulder-to-shoulder, gazes trained forward. It was his friend who broke the taut silence. "I merely intended to point out that the gossips will make something of your being together, regardless of the truth." He paused. "But given your protectiveness of the lady, as your friend, I would mention it does appear there is more there."

A flush heated Vail's neck. "Don't be…"

Bridget glanced over again in his direction and smiled. The sight of that easy grin, earned one from him in return.

"Well?" Huntly's droll question shattered the exchange.

Reluctantly he shifted his attention over to his friend. "Well, what?"

"This is the new housekeeper then."

He puzzled his brow. What in blazes did the other man know of Bridget?

"You didn't have to mention her. Servants talk and there's been gossip making its way around ballrooms." He cast Vail a sideways glance. "Though, I'd hope, as your best friend, should there be something with a lady you might at the very least mention it."

"There is nothing to mention," he said defensively, damning the gossips. Hating that Bridget was being spoken of about town.

"Servants whisper and nobles talk," Huntly casually noted. "She is not your lover, then?"

A muscle ticked irritatingly at the corner of his eye. The *ton* was gossiping about Bridget. He silently cursed loose-lipped servants. "She is not," he said frostily. *Though, I want her to be.* This woman he'd shared so much with.

He stared contemplatively at the woman in question. "But she matters enough that you'd bring her here to Justina's reading."

Huntly's was an observation more than anything. And a deuced accurate one. Then, this man and his sister had been the only friends he'd ever known in his life. Until Huntly, he'd believed other boys incapable of anything but cruelty and viciousness. The other man was correct…he had deserved more than veiled innuendos about…Bridget.

"She serves on my staff, hired by Edward as my housekeeper. But she has proven invaluable in her understanding and capability with valuable texts."

"Ahh," Huntly murmured, with a slight incline of his head.

Do not ask. Do not ask.

His friend, however, required no encouragement from Vail. "Is this the recent addition to your staff who called you away so quickly from your club at our last meeting."

Damn Huntly for being the clever bastard he was.

"She is," he bit out. The roomful of guests claimed their seats as Lady Justina took up position at the pedestal. When she began with her introduction of the reading, Vail spoke in hushed tones for his friend's ears. "I haven't made her my lover." Yet. He'd already come dangerously close and wanted to take her to his bed with an aching hunger no warm, eager body could satiate—except her. "I trust you should know me enough to know I've more honor than that." He followed Huntly to the two ends seats at the back row.

"If you care for her, then I wouldn't begrudge you a relationship with the lady, regardless of her position on your staff."

"I'd not be a lecher like my father," he shot back.

Huntly snorted. "I assure you, Ravenscourt wouldn't be worried after any lady's reputation and he'd certainly not have brought her along to a salon." When Vail made to protest, his friend spoke over him. "All I mean to say is if you care for the lady, you can expect support from Justina and from me."

The duchess paused in her reading and glanced pointedly over the heads of the guests to her husband.

Huntly touched a hand to his heart. "My apologies," he mouthed.

With a twinkle in her eyes, the lady resumed her reading.

Through the remainder of the afternoon, Huntly remained

quiet, with no more pressing Vail for information about Bridget. Yet, through the quiet of Lady Justina's reading and the discussion that ensued among the lords and ladies present, he stared contemplatively at the back of her head. Perched on the edge of her shellback chair, she hung on to every word read from that text. This kindred connection he had developed in their short time together went against the logical existence he'd formed for himself after Adrina's betrayal. Some businessmen made rotted transactions and lost. In reflecting upon Adrina's deceit, he'd gotten himself through the agony of heartbreak by likening their relationship to a failed venture. It had made him cautious of again letting any woman too close. And eventually, he'd found purpose in his business and his family.

What Huntly proposed, that there could be something more with Bridget, ran anathema to everything he trusted. So why did he want her, anyway?

Lord Langley stood and exited, clearing a place at the front of the hall.

"If you'll excuse me?" Huntly murmured. Not waiting for permission, he hurriedly stood and found a place nearer his wife.

Vail studied them. That closeness was one he'd naively hoped for—a family. Mayhap that is why he'd not allowed himself to see Adrina's avarice, because he'd been so fixed on attaining what he'd wanted. And mayhap—he looked to Bridget, now seated beside Huntly—mayhap, he might know that special bond, after all. He braced for the slithering of dread such vulnerability would bring—that did not come.

"May I claim this seat?" he stiffened. As though making a mockery of his hopeful thoughts, Lady Adrina hovered beside his chair in a cloud of fragrant jasmine.

She was as tenacious as a viper with its fangs out.

Lord Sandford turned back and frowned at them. Taking advantage of that distraction, Adrina swiftly slid into the chair. And all the earlier joy in being here was sucked clear of the room, leaving a vacuum of rotten memories and failed decisions in its place.

"Beautiful, is it not," she murmured, as Lady Justina resumed reading from a passage of *Petrosinella*.

"You've discovered a love of literature, then?"

"I have," she whispered. "You needn't look surprised, Vail." She glanced up at him through thick, golden lashes. "I've matured since you last knew me." Adrina stroked her fingertips over the plunging décolletage of her diaphanous silver gown. It was a scandalous piece that would have raised eyebrows at any ball or soiree. It was one that would leave no doubt as to her intentions, before a polite crowd of lords and ladies gathered for a reading.

Bored by her display, he looked forward.

"Oh, come, you might pretend to be indifferent," she said on a sultry, enticing whisper. She climbed her fingers up his thigh. "But there was once a time you could not keep your hands from me."

He caught her wrist just as she brushed the placard of his breeches. "Remember yourself, madam," he said crisply, finding Bridget.

She remained engrossed, hanging on to whatever words Lady Justina now read.

"What do you want?" he demanded in hushed tones.

"I want to begin again," she said, all artifice gone. The earlier desire replaced with a ragged pain. "I am not the same woman I was, Vail. I regretted every day of my marriage. But now, we can be together. You've a need of me. You're a baron and, with your business, you need a hostess." With her pronouncement and her recent visit and desperate notes, it at last made sense. *She* had need of him.

"Your husband left you in financial straits," he predicted.

She gave a small nod. "But that doesn't mean I don't love you and we cannot still benefit one another."

"You propose a business arrangement."

"Of a sort." She placed her lips close to his ear. "But based on love and with the same pleasure we once knew in one another's arms." Pleasure that had never entailed her giving herself to him completely—neither in body nor name. It should have been the proof that he would never have been enough and that she never would have married him. Now, with his title and wealth she'd deemed him worthy.

He fought back a wave of disgust. "We cannot ever be together," he said coolly, needing her to realize that what they'd had died long ago. "Nor do I have a wish to."

Tears filled her eyes and she recoiled. "Is this because of her?" She jerked her chin at the front of the room. "The housekeeper all Society is speaking of."

"This is about only us," he said, cautiously steering her away from mention of Bridget. A wounded former lover had the power of great evil. Huntly's wife had nearly been killed by one, as proof of it.

"Mark my words, Vail, she is as grasping as you took me for. I haven't trusted her since I heard your names tied together in a ballroom and had to see for myself if you'd been as ensnared as the gossips claimed. And they are." Pressing her breasts against his arm, she leaned up. "I was a climber," she whispered ominously. "I recognize one."

As if on cue, Bridget looked back. Her smile sank as she moved her gaze between him and Adrina, and then she swiftly jerked her attention forward. His heart thudded hard at the brief flash of hurt he'd spied there. "If you've come with warnings about Mrs. Hamlet, I'll have you know she has more integrity and honor than any other woman I've ever known. I think it best if you leave."

She tightened her mouth and then, with stiff movements, stood. "I see. If, however, you come to your senses, I am and will always be waiting for you. Good afternoon, my lord." With that, she swept off.

A round of applause went up about the room, signaling the end of the reading and discussion. Vail jumped up as Bridget spoke to the duchess and duke. With a smile he recognized as forced, she started for him. As she walked, he noted details that until Huntly's observation had previously escaped him: the sideways looks and stares that moved between him and Bridget. Suddenly, glad to be free of the room, when she approached, he held his arm out.

Not breaking stride, she marched past him, out into the hall.

Quickening his steps, he followed after her. "Bridget—"

"You cannot offer me your arm and you certainly cannot call me by my given name in public," she whispered. There was a tension to her slender frame that bespoke her disquiet.

And hating that, in this instance, she was correct—for her reputation did matter—he dropped his arm to his side and, this time, as they made the journey from Huntly's through Mayfair, and to his home, not another word was spoken.

Today had nearly been perfect.

If she'd been one of those fanciful sorts who'd allowed herself a dream, she'd have dreamed of a gentleman who'd not bring her flowers or recite prose, but rather one who'd brought her to a literary lecture.

And yet, Vail had escorted her to one of those very events, inside a duke's home, no less. As though she was his Societal equal in every way, and had a place beside him and dukes and duchesses.

Given the family she'd been born to, it was preposterous to think she belonged near any of those people. But for a small moment in time, she could have almost believed she could fit within that world, and be part of it, discussing literature with lords and ladies and having others interested in hearing her opinion as the duchess had.

Except, she'd not been one who'd ever taken part in pretend. Life had provided her with too many reasons to see with only logical eyes. And any illusions she'd briefly allowed herself had been shattered, first when presented with the kindness of the Duchess of Huntly, and reinforced a second time by the sight of Vail with his former love.

And never had she been more miserable.

Seated at the foot of the leather button sofa, her legs drawn to her chest, and her cheek resting on her skirts, Bridget stared at the copy of *Petrosinella* they'd brought back that afternoon. It had been returned to its proper stand and now awaited its sale to Lord Cartwright.

It was fitting for that volume to be resting out, a reminder of Vail's good-heartedness, a stark contrast to the evil she'd carry out against him.

"Do you never sleep, Mrs. Hamlet?"

She stiffened as Vail's loudly spoken words drifted over to her ear. It did not escape her notice, and hadn't, that since she'd revealed the truth about her partial deafness, he took care to speak more loudly when entering a room, and always positioned himself closer to her good ear. It only made her love him all the more. Uninvited, he settled himself beside her on the floor. "No," she confessed. Nor were her peculiar sleep habits the product of a guilty conscience and her search for the treasured Chaucer book. "Since I was a girl, my mind would always wander about the books I'd read, and I couldn't rest until I'd finished. And then after, my mind created stories of who those characters were."

Vail stretched his legs out and looped them at the ankles. "And as a woman?"

A clever man who saw everything, he'd noted that detail.

"As a woman, I focus on my work and…" *Virgil*. She sucked in a ragged breath, the ache of missing him hurt like a physical pain. "Surviving," she offered instead. How wrong it was that he should not know of the most important person in her life. With Virgil's skill in examining those books at her side, Vail would have only ever been impressed by the boy. Pride stirred in her breast, along with a pang of regret for a meeting that would never be.

"That is how you've lived these years then? Focusing solely on survival," he asked, answering his own question. It had been. Really for the whole of her life. "What of your family?" he asked quietly.

Just because one had blood family did not mean one had love and kindness and support. Vail and his siblings were just the fortunate ones who did. Bridget stared wistfully ahead. "When I was younger, I'd a lonely childhood. Books were like friends. I came across *The Description of Cooke-ham.*"

"Aemilia Lanyer," he murmured, and a smile pulled at her lips. Of course, he should know that book.

"She painted a world where even one who did not have family could have a home in a country manor. Only I didn't dream of a grand estate. I simply wanted a cottage surrounded by fields of flowers and there would be books and…" Her skin pricked with the feel of his gaze on her. She stopped her ramblings.

"This is the first you've ever spoken of your family." His was a quiet observation that sent warning bells of panic blaring. "Tell me about them."

She'd inadvertently brought herself down a dangerous path that could not be explored. Bridget cleared her throat. "Thank you for escorting me to meet your friends' home this morning," she said softly, reminding herself of the kind duke and duchess whose happiness her sister had sought to shatter.

Vail stood and she arched her neck back, studying his movements. She thought he'd leave. Instead, he wandered over to the rectangular table. "Did you enjoy Lady Justina's salon?" He directed that question over his shoulder, presenting his lips so she might see them. At that considerate gesture, she lost the last remaining piece of her intact heart to him. But then, that was who Vail was.

"I did," she said softly. "Very much." More than she'd had a right to. She'd allowed herself to forget the ugliness that bound her family to the duchess' and celebrated what it was to share a love of literature with another. Bridget pushed to her feet. "I..." Her words exploded on a gasp, as he picked the copy of *Petrosinella* in his bare hands and opened it. "What are you doing?" She did a search of the table and, finding a pair of white gloves at the far end, hurried to retrieve them and rushed back. "Lord Cartwright is coming to collect that title. You cannot—"

"Why this title?"

She stopped mid-sentence and blinked wildly. "I-I didn't coordinate the transaction. As such, I'm certain I couldn't say."

He favored her with a heart-stopping grin. "I don't give a jot for Cartwright. I meant you. What is it about this title," he held it aloft and she shot her hands out to rescue the copy from his careless grip. "That meant so much to you?" He moved the book further from her reach.

Bridget sighed. "Vail, you're going to—"

"I've told you everything," he said somberly. Without looking at what he did, he set the book down. "I've told you about my mother, my father, Adrina—" Hearing that name breathed into existence by him made the woman who sent him letters and sought him out in Polite Society too real. It struck like a serrated blade in the chest. "I've told you of Erasmus and my siblings." He searched a frantic gaze over her face. "And yet, you stop yourself from sharing details about your family and you cannot even tell me about your favorite book."

At the desperate edge there from this proud man, her heart wrenched. For the whole of her life, no one had wanted to acknowledge her existence and she'd ached at the solitariness of it all. Only to find the one person who wanted to know those parts of who she was and she couldn't share. Mayhap, this was to be the penance for her betrayal?

"My nursemaid read it to me when I was a girl," she said on a threadbare whisper, recalling Nettie's soothing voice as she'd cradled her on her lap, while her parents' muffled shouts and cries rattled around outside the nursery door. "My parents didn't have much use for me because," she traced the curve of that crescent-shape upon her cheek and Vail followed those movements. "When I was four and they learned I was partially deaf, then they had *no* use for me."

His face crumpled and, unable to confront the depth of that emotion, she returned her stare to the table. "The story is of a girl who never knew loving parents, who were wholly incapable of sacrificial love." Whereas she would have cut out her very heart with a dull knife if it would have kept Virgil safe. She slid her gaze briefly over to the copy of *Petrosinella*, the tale of a heroine who'd had a hero at her side to battle the world.

"I confess, listening to Lady Justina read from it, the tale is bleak."

Bridget gripped the edge of the table. "Only if you focus on the lack of love Petrosinella knew from her parents. But she found freedom. That is what the tale is truly of. So many in that book: her father, her mother, Petrosinella herself, are all enslaved but she finds a way out." It was that hope for freedom that had allowed Bridget to sell her soul to Archibald. "When she has a glimpse of the outside world, she'll sacrifice all." Whereas Bridget would be forced to retreat to her tower once more. Such a thought had once been a balm bringing with it peace. Now, it left her hollow inside. *I'll never again see him.* "One hour in port, the sailor freed from fears, forgets the tempests of a hundred years," she whispered to herself.

Vail pressed something cool into her hands and she glanced down in confusion.

"It is yours."

Her fingers curled reflexively around that leather volume. "I cannot," she rasped, setting the copy of *Petrosinella* aside. "*Everything* is for sale. You said it," she pleaded, needing him to be the ruthless businessman. Not this man who'd break with his values and compromise his reputation as a seller for her.

"Not this," he said simply.

Vail cupped her about the nape and covered her mouth in a tender meeting. She instantly melted against his chest. Reaching her arms about his neck, she pressed herself closer, returning his kiss. He deepened that embrace. Filling his hands with the swell of her buttocks, he anchored her against him, angling her head.

"You are a siren," he whispered, between kisses. "Taking you in my arms goes against my every moral fiber and paints me in my father's image. And even knowing this is wrong, I want you, anyway." Vail dragged his mouth over the column of her neck.

Moaning, she let her head fall back to better receive him. "This can only be right."

He guided her to the mahogany table at her back. A little gasp escaped her as he hitched her atop the edge. Claiming her mouth again, he parted her lips and slid his tongue inside. She instantly met him in a bold dance wanting to remember forever the taste and feel of him. Wanting this moment to be enough to last her until she was an old woman, alone, with nothing but these memories of them together. His breath rasping loudly, he searched his hands over her frame. He freed her breasts from the confines of her modest gown and explored that generous flesh.

Bridget's breath caught against his mouth as he palmed one of those mounds. "I-I always despaired of th-them being too large," she confessed breathlessly.

"Never," he groaned. He captured a peak between his thumb and forefinger and it pebbled under his ministrations. She let out a little mewling protest, when he drew back, but he only shifted his attentions lower to worship that bud.

"Vail," she moaned as he closed his mouth around it, suckling and teasing the flesh to life with his tongue. He moved over and bestowed the same focus on the other neglected tip.

"I forget every pledge I've made when you are near," he whispered. Bridget's heartbeat quickened. "I forget respectability and honor and want to only know you." He filled his palms with her breasts, bringing them together.

She arched into his touch. "Vail," she entreated.

He lifted his gaze to hers and she found the depth of her passion reflected back in his eyes. "Tell me to stop."

Growing up, Bridget had never thought to know the attentions of a gentleman…of any man. Marked as she was, she'd been reviled by her family and an oddity to the villagers. There'd certainly been no village boys eagerly stealing kisses.

As such, what occurred between men and women, the passion spoken about upon pages of ancient texts, recent ones, and gothic novels had been as much fiction as those books she'd read and worked with over the years. Vail Basingstoke, was the first person in the whole of her life who'd not fixated on the crescent marking on her face or the loss of hearing. In his arms, she was more than both those imperfections—she was beautiful.

His breath came hard and fast, matched in time to her own rhythm. An almost pained agony filled his jade-green eyes. With trembling fingers, she cupped his cheek and, leaning up, kissed him.

He stiffened and then, groaning, he devoured her mouth, tasting her as though he wished to brand her. Vail gathered the hem of her skirt and worked it up. She shifted, lifting her buttocks, as he pushed the blue skirts around her waist. The cool air slapped at her stocking-clad legs penetrating that thin fabric. A hiss exploded from her as he laid a possessive hand upon her calf. Leaning down, he drew that muscled limb to his lips. He placed a fleeting kiss along the inseam of her ankle and then higher, up to the lower portion of her leg. Her pulse quickened. Something in the flimsy divide presented by her stockings made his wicked exploration all the more forbidden.

"I-I hardly kn-knew a leg could feel like this," she rasped out, as he continued his seductive exploration of that limb. In reply, he parted her thighs and dropped a kiss along the inside of her legs. The heat at her center gave way to a molten wetness. Not knowing what she wanted, only knowing she needed his touch there, she lifted into his caress.

"So beautiful," he whispered, palming her through her under-garments.

She cried out, undulating slowly. Then, he worked her chemise down, until she lay bared from the waist down before him. There should be shame. He was her employer, a man she'd been sent to deceive and in the dead of night, on a table in his office, she opened herself to him, pleadingly, and yet there was none. A husky half-whimper, half-moan spilled past her parted lips as he found her with his fingers.

"Vail," she rasped in supplication. He parted her folds and teased the slick nub at her center. Bridget shot her hips off the desk. Sweat beading her brow, she lifted into that back and forth stroke. With every teasing caress, a restless pressure built inside. Her breath came in raspy little pants as she worked herself against his long, expert fingers. Wanting something. Needing it. Knowing only that he could show her.

He withdrew his fingers and she whimpered at the gaping loss of him. "I've wanted to explore you like this since the moment I caught you behind my desk," he breathed against her inner thigh. Her flesh quivered in response to the kiss that followed.

"I-I thought you wanted to sack me," she said, her voice faint and weak to her own ears.

"Sack you?" He briefly glanced up and her heart tripped at the charming half-grin on his lips. "I've wanted to kiss you," with each word, he trailed his lips higher, and higher, closer to the thatch of curls that concealed her wanton wetness. "I've wanted to touch you but never have I wanted to turn you out."

"Th-that is good," she said brokenly, her lashes fluttering. "Because I never want to leave." The staggering enormity of what she said froze them both for an instant as through the magic that was his touch, reality doused her like cold Thames water being tossed upon her naked body. For she didn't want to leave. She wanted to remain here with him.

Through thick hooded, dark lashes, Vail pierced her with a desire-laden stare. Wordlessly, he dropped a kiss atop her moist curls.

She cried out and, through the haze of befuddled hunger, reality melted away once more so only this remained. He slipped his tongue inside her slit, lapping at her. Bridget bit down hard on her lower lip and fell back, catching herself on her elbows. She lifted her hips in time to each hot, wicked stroke of his tongue. He slid his palms under her arching buttocks and dragged her closer to his mouth, his focused ministrations brought her higher and higher up a soaring precipice, until great keening moans spilled past her lips and her incoherent pleadings flooded her ears, in time to her beating heart. At the same time he suckled at her nub, he pushed a finger inside her channel.

She dimly registered him covering her with his muscled frame, and then reaching between them to free his shaft. He laid between her legs and thrust home.

Bright, blinding agony pulled a cry from her lips.

He stiffened; his breath came in desperate, ragged pants. "Bridget?" he asked, his voice hoarse with confusion and desire.

A tear squeezed out from beneath her lashes and she concentrated on breathing and the feel of him filling her.

All his muscles leapt with tension under her palms. "I don't understand? I thought you were married…?" Confusion spilled from his hungry gaze.

"Please don't stop," she begged, clutching at his sculpted chest. She didn't want to answer questions and what was more…she wanted to know all that came with this moment.

Sweat beaded his brow and then, clenching his eyes tight, he found her again with his fingers. That expert caress stirred the earlier longing and as he rekindled that desire, her hips of their own volition began to move.

His breath came harsh and hard, as he drew out and then pressed back inside, slowly. And as the initial pain dissipated, she felt other things: the slow, exquisite drag of him inside her tight channel, the pulsing at her core, as he pulled her higher and higher toward that ledge he'd brought her to earlier. Panting and moaning, her own incoherent pleas were muffled inside her head as she met him stroke for stroke.

He quickened his thrusts and Bridget wrapped her arms tight about him, holding on for all she was. Vail covered her mouth again, sliding his tongue in and out in rhythm to his hips. On a scream, she shattered in his arms. His body stiffened over hers and then Vail deepened his thrusts. He shouted his release to the rafters, filling her with his seed. Her channel pulsed around his throbbing length and he continued to pour himself inside.

And then with a harsh gasp, he collapsed atop her.

CHAPTER 16

MY GOD, SHE WAS A *virgin*.

His weight resting on his elbows, his chest heaving from the force of his release, Vail remained frozen—motionless.

It couldn't be.

There had to be another explanation why a widow was in possession of her virginity, still. Or had been. For he'd rutted between her legs, taking her atop a table like she was a corner street doxy.

Questions and confusion broke through the fog of desire and drew him into the cold, unwelcome world of reality. Stiffening, Vail shoved himself upright and, more slowly, Bridget dropped her legs over the edge of the table. Fingers shaking, she tried to right her garments.

Wordlessly, he pushed her hands away and saw to the task himself. He dragged a kerchief from his pocket and gently cleaned his seed and her blood from her center. She winced.

After her dress fluttered back into place, Vail dropped that rag to the floor. "You were a virgin," he said tightly, the pronouncement an obvious one that bore stating, anyway.

She gave her head a tight shake. "N–No." Her teeth chattered and she hugged her arms close to her chest, rubbing those limbs.

A thousand and one questions whirred around his mind, with not a single one taking root. She'd been a virgin. And somehow, this act that had gone against every moral he'd held himself to, grew in wretchedness. Nausea churned low in his belly. "You are not a widow."

She could not have been? Or could she have? Mayhap her husband had been a bookish man… He swiftly shoved the foolish idea back. Any man who called her wife could have never been married to her without knowing her mouth, breasts, and center the way Vail just had—the way only he had known.

"Bridget?" he snapped.

"I am not a widow," she confirmed, setting her feet on the floor. She took a step.

She was leaving?

Vail shot a hand around her forearm, catching it in a firm grip, and staying her retreat. "You are not leaving, madam," he said tersely.

If she'd never lain with a man that spoke to another lie. There'd been no Mr. Hamlet, devoted bookseller. "Why?" he managed to grit out.

Bridget skittered her gaze about, giving her the look of a cornered hare. "Because it is far easier existing in a world as a widow than it is as an unwed woman on her own."

That is what she'd been. A pang struck in the vicinity of his heart, but he thrust it back. All the earliest reservations he'd carried about this woman slid forward. "It is one thing to present that illusion to the world, madam." He understood those fears she raised, even as he'd not experienced them. "But you'd keep the truth from me?" Vail despised himself for the wounded edge to that query.

She hugged her arms about her waist in a lonely embrace. "There didn't present a time for me to make mention of it."

Restless, he stomped across the room. Rescuing the kerchief that contained the evidence of Bridget's innocence, he hurled it into the waste bin beside his desk.

A light knock sounded at the door. "Not now," he shouted. Bridget glanced around the room with frantic eyes. Why…why… she sought escape. *From me?* His nostrils flared as his fury only grew. "Perhaps when I shared everything about my bloody family and self, you might have made mention." He gritted his teeth so hard, pain radiated along his jawline.

Another knock landed on the door panel, this one more urgent.

"Bloody hell. Not now, Gavin," he thundered. He scraped a hand over his face. Now, he'd taken to yelling at his brother.

"B–But, Vail, it is a matter of import. Or that is the way I understand it. I wouldn't wish to be one who didn't..."

Cursing under his breath at that untimely interruption, Vail stalked across the room, and yanked the door open.

"...so it seemed better to simply intrude," Gavin finished. He blinked and then beamed at catching sight of Bridget. "Oh, hullo, Mrs. Hamlet. You're in there, too."

Bridget called out a weak greeting, lifting a hand for Gavin.

"Were you unable to sleep, Mrs. Hamlet? I wasn't as well, which is why I happened to be in the kitchens when someone came 'round back—"

"Gavin?" he asked impatiently.

"Oh, yes. Right. Right." Muttering under his breath, Gavin fished around one side of his jacket and then the other. His eyes brightened. "Here it is." He handed over the note. "It was delivered a short while ago for you. The young lad indicated it was to see your hands immediately. That is was a matter of import."

Vail unfolded the ivory sheet and quickly scanned the missive containing but one word and a name.

Urgent

Tabitha

Crumpling the page, he stuffed it inside his jacket. This was the letter sent when whisper of threat or danger was picked up in those streets of London's dregs. "My horse," he said tightly. Gavin rushed off, leaving him and Bridget alone. He eyed her with the same suspicion he'd shown at their first meeting. "This discussion is not over, madam."

She gave a shuddering nod.

Vail motioned to the door.

Bridget held her hands up. "I don't..."

"Out, madam. I have a meeting."

Her entire body jerked as though he'd run her through. Head held high, she marched past him and strode down the hall. After she'd gone, he pulled the door shut. Withdrawing his timepiece, he collected the special key that hung from the chain, and locked the door. He let the chain fall and slammed his fists against the door. Damn it. He'd hurt her with his orders and, yet, after what he'd discovered a short while ago, he had every reason to doubt her. And had he not been roiling with frustration and outrage over her lie, he'd have told her that whenever that note arrived, his Collection Rooms were locked.

There'd be time enough to sort through the tumult of this evening when they both were clear of head. And he, visiting King Street at this hour, and word from Tabitha could afford nothing but.

A short while later, his reins handed off to a waiting Jeremy, he found his way inside the Coaxing Tom. Vail blinked, adjusting his eyes to the thick cloud of cheroot smoke that hung over the gaming hell. From across the room, he found Tabitha. Perched on Mr. Barrett's lap, her lips close to his ear, she paused, as her gaze collided with Vail's. Without another word for her client, she hopped up, and sauntered through the club, expertly dodging the grasping hands of drunken patrons.

Twining her arms about his neck, she stretched up on tiptoe and sought his mouth. It was an act he'd participated in countless times, with no other purpose but deception in mind. Having just left Bridget's arms, however, it felt wrong and vile. He turned his head slightly and her kiss grazed his cheek.

"What is it?" he demanded in hushed tones, gathering her around the waist.

By the frown that reached her eyes, she'd detected his evasiveness. "Not here," she said, instead. Taking him by the hand, she cast him a come-hither stare and led him through the busy club to her private rooms.

As soon as she'd closed the door behind them, he pressed her again. "What is it?"

"Yar never impatient to the point of carelessness," she said, propping her hands on her hips. "Ya don't speak business on the hell floors."

No, he didn't. *By God, man. Clear your damned head.* "It is late," he offered, grimacing at the weakness of that.

Folding her arms at the middle, she plumped her enormous breasts up. "Does this 'ave anything to do with the lady whose got ya smitten?"

His face went hot and he resisted the urge to yank at his rumpled cravat. Word of Bridget had found its way to even these streets.

Bloody damned gossips. "Is that what you've called me here for? To speak about my new housekeeper?"

Tabitha said nothing for a long while and then whistled through her teeth. "It's true, then, isn't it? I never thought I'd see the day, Vail Basingstoke, the Bastard Baron and ruthless businessman, is smitten enough that he'd be thinking about a lady and not being called in the dead of night." There was nothing teasing there. Rather, pity coated her words. The prostitute shook her head sadly.

Disquieted, he squared his eyes on her face. "What is it?" he repeated, this time forcing aside thoughts of Bridget Hamlet.

"Two lords were 'ere earlier. Didn't get their names, but they were dressed fancy like and speaking the King's English like George himself."

Instantly alert, he pressed her for more. "What were they discussing?"

"Yar Chaucer."

That book slated for auction at the end of next week. It was estimated to bring more than one hundred thousand pounds to his purse and was coveted by all collectors. His ears immediately pricked up. "And?"

"And one of the nobs was saying to the other gent not to worry that 'ed have it for him." Tabitha hesitated and the regret deepened in her usually hard eyes. Unease churned in his belly and he couldn't get the proper words out to urge her to finish the damned telling. "Said all the gossip is that yar too busy lusting for the woman to know she's there to steal it from under yar nose."

His tongue felt heavy in his mouth, making it impossible to form words. "What woman?" he asked when he trusted himself to speak.

"Didn't say," Tabitha said gruffly. "Only that she'd been there less than three weeks and had found a place in yar bed." She paused. "Even though she's an ugly bit of baggage."

Been in his household three weeks...? There was one, and she'd ensnared him, but possessed a beauty that would have set a statue to weeping. It couldn't be her. It was impossible. He shook his head slowly as a dull humming filled his ears. "You're wrong." That denial emerged gravelly. "It's not..." It wasn't Bridget. And he'd certainly not stand here defending her to this woman, or any other.

He took a step toward the door and Tabitha moved away from it, holding a hand out. "Said she's ugly but no one knows more about books than her."

She may as well have kicked him hard in the belly. Vail staggered back a step. "Mm. Mm," he muttered, giving his head a frantic shake. "It's…whoever it might be, is not…"

…*The woman knows how to properly handle antique books. She not only knows how to care for them, but also has an appreciation for the contents within. And she fluently reads and speaks Latin, French, Italian, German, and Spanish…*

Vail froze as all the reservations which he'd buried roared to the surface, overwhelming him. Pacing the small confines of Tabitha's rooms, he pressed his fingertips against his temple and willed his thoughts to some semblance of order. *Think, man. Think.*

How did such a woman come to be in his employ? Stanwicke. Stanwicke, who'd provided the references and also sold him a counterfeit copy. Then all the details he'd not allowed himself to see before this moment rolled into one another. She'd been a virgin. She'd not been married. She'd never revealed a single piece about herself, until this night when he'd demanded some personal story.

And he *knew.*

Vail jolted to a stop.

Bridget Hamlet was a bloody, goddamned liar.

Bridget was a bloody, vile person.

In light of the suspicions she'd roused this night by lying in Vail's arms and the barely concealed fury before he'd parted, she could not remain here. He was too clever and would have questions, and piece together that she was nothing more than an imposter.

Tears clogged her throat and she choked them back. Useless. Tears had never solved a problem and they'd certainly never succeeded in erasing her hurts. They'd never ease the agony of leaving this household. She stopped outside his office.

Nay, not leaving his household—leaving him. Bridget laid her palms against the door and rested her forehead between them. *I cannot do this. I cannot steal from him. I need to take Virgil and go.*

She knocked her head silently against the wood panel. And where would she go? She'd not even two hundred pounds to her name, and a child and an old maid to look after. For a brief fleeting flash in time, she allowed herself the thought of laying this burden at Vail's feet. Of telling him all. He was a baron. An honorable lord, respected by the *ton*, with extensive connections all over England.

A wave of sadness assailed her and she shoved away from the door, resigned. In their world, a father would always have rights to his child before all others. It wouldn't matter that Archibald had forsaken the boy all those years ago or that Bridget had cared for him as a mother. The world would only recognize a powerful nobleman's right to his child…and his word won out above all—especially over that of a deaf, scarred sister. Not even Vail in all his strength and power could change the rules and laws that governed Society.

Bridget caught her lower lip painfully between her teeth. There was no other choice. Until she drew her last breath, Vail Basingstoke would hold every corner of her heart, but Virgil was the other half of her soul.

Fiddling with the ring of keys, she selected the corresponding one for his office. Bridget jammed the slip of metal in and the lock gave. She quickly let herself in. Blinking to drive back the dark of the room, she pushed the door slowly closed behind her.

He'd locked the doors to his Collection Rooms. It had been the first warning that he'd ceased to trust her—deservedly so. But it had also been the greatest indication that she needed to leave. *Now.* Heart pounding loud in her ears, she rushed over to Vail's orderly desk. Dropping into the folds of his leather seat, she yanked open the center drawer. She felt around the inside for a hint of metal. Scrunching her brow, she reached her hand further inside and searched around.

Nothing.

Bridget sank back in the chair. *Did you think he'd simply hide the book in plain sight?* Absently, she pulled out drawer after drawer, methodically searching them, and finding nothing. Shifting to the bottom left, and final one, she dug around. Empty.

Teaming with frustration, she jumped up. *Think. Think. Where would he keep something of such value that mattered so…*

She froze. Her heart thumped wildly. Quitting Vail's office, she moved out into the hallway, beating a familiar path, and then stopped outside the Portrait Room.

Swallowing hard, she forced herself on wooden legs forward to that peculiar throne-like mahogany chair…under Erasmus' painting.

She stopped, staring up at the smiling boy, joyous in his innocence. Yet, by what Vail had shared, the child had known great evil. And he'd still known happiness because of Vail. "I have to do this," she whispered to his memorialized self. There were no acts of heroism to see her with the fortunes Vail had known. There was no avenging sibling, swooping in to aid her. The world was remarkably limited in the opportunities it afforded women. Knowing that did not ease the guilt clogging her throat.

Kneeling beside the chair, she tugged at the edge of the seat. When there was no miraculous give, she bent, studying the underside of it. A strand of hair fell over her eye and she blew it back. She squinted and then a faint glitter of metal caught her eye.

Numb, she stretched a hand under and fiddled with that tiny latch.

The faint click sounded like a gunshot in the silence, as damning and evil. Fingers shaking, Bridget shoved the lid up and peered inside. Her stomach lurched and, even as she removed the velvet sack resting atop a feather pillow, she knew.

Bridget pressed her eyes closed, warring with herself. The instant she absconded with this book, her time with Vail would end, and she'd leave, dishonored…as deceitful as her brother and sister.

She slid the book out, hoping she was wrong and there was some other valuable work hidden in this cherished place.

All the air left her on an unsteady exhale.

The Canterbury Tales

"Of course, he would keep it here." Precisely where it belonged, under the portrait of his beloved brother, who'd known too much suffering.

"And tell me, where do you think it should be, Mrs. Hamlet?"

Her heart jumped into her throat and she went absolutely still. From where she sat on the floor of Vail's Portrait Room, she silently prayed that dry question—iced in steel—had merely been one she'd imagined of her own guilt. Prayed, that he was not there. Prayed, when she'd ceased praying long, long ago.

Vail shouted into the quiet. "Come, nothing to say?" She jumped at the thunderous boom of the door as it slammed.

Bridget squeezed her eyes shut. *He knows. My God, he knows.* She knew it implicitly without word of confirmation or even catching a glimpse of him. She knew it by the frosty contempt in his tone.

And I hate myself just as much.

At the eternal stretch of silence, Bridget popped her head over the bench separating them. Vail leaned against the doorway, arms folded, his right heel propped against the wall. He winged a midnight eyebrow upward. "Never tell me you're going to linger down there like a common thief, Mrs. Hamlet?"

And any shred of hope she'd had that he hadn't gleaned the purpose in her being here, in his household, died. "Vail," she said hoarsely. "I…" She glanced down at the book in her hands. *I have no words. I have no way of explaining this so you might understand.*

He shoved away from the door and stalked forward; a sleek panther pursuing its prey. Gooseflesh scoured her skin. Chewing at the inside of her cheek, she searched around, like the coward she was, for escape. Restoring the book to its proper sack, she set it aside and scrambled forward on her knees until Vail's legs lined up with her vision, blocking her retreat.

Tears filled her eyes and she stared blurrily through them.

"Tsk, tsk," he said, dropping to a knee beside her. "With your skill, you know better than to leave such a valuable text lying about."

She tried to draw a proper breath.

He tweaked her nose. "You should have told me you were merely looking for a book to read, Bridget."

He was toying with her the same way their kitchen cat did the mice inside their kitchen back in Leeds. Vail stretched out a gloved hand and, quaking, she came up on her knees and deposited that copy in his grip.

"Of all the books you might have chosen, I'd say it is peculiar you should come here for one." He sank his hip on the edge of the bench, that casual repose at odds with the fury teeming in his voice.

Unable to see him through the tears blinding her vision, she said nothing. What was there to say? He was deserved of his fury and condemnation.

"Do you know what I find interesting, Bridget?"

"What is that?" she managed to ask, her voice weak.

"Of all the books in my entire household you might have chosen, you, in fact, sneaked inside my Portrait Room," He waved the leather copy about. "You could have selected any title and you picked this one."

A sob stuck in her throat and she pressed a hand to her mouth to stifle it. *Tell him everything. Tell him about Virgil and Nettie and Archibald.* "I can explain," she whispered, struggling to her feet.

Where he'd once been tender and loving, all of that had faded, leaving this shadow of a man hardened by hatred. It gleamed in his eyes and iced his features. It poured from his heavily muscled frame, transforming him into a stranger. *I did this.* Knowing she was responsible for that change only deepened the agony rolling through her in waves.

"Tell me, Mrs. Hamlet. Tell me all."

That silken command sent the hair at the back of her neck up as a bleak desolation swept over her. He would never believe her now. And even if he did, he'd never care. Mayhap, he never would have. That realization didn't ease this slow, vicious breaking of her heart. She gave him the only words she could. "I'm so, so sorry."

His mask slipped, revealing a crack in his remarkable composure. But then he spoke, and it may as well have been a mere flicker of the shadows—or her own hopes. "Tell me what you are sorry for."

It was a demand that urged an answer that would see her in Newgate, if he so wished it. Her breath came in quick spurts, until stars danced behind her eyes. *I'm going to faint.* For the first time in her life, she was going to wilt on the floor. Numbly, she shot her hand out to steady herself on the desk, but her fingers found his thick calf instead. "I can't," she got out, her tongue heavy in her mouth, staring at her fingers upon his person. *Did we really make love only an hour ago?* Or had it been a lifetime ago that he'd gazed upon her with warmth and tenderness?

He chuckled and shoved aside her touch.

A keening moan worked its way up her throat.

"Tell me," he thundered, pounding his fist against his open palm.

Crying out, she jumped to her feet, and rushed to put the bench between them. Memories of the backhand Archibald dealt ten years ago when she'd ordered him to care for his child, flashed behind her mind's eye. *This is Vail. Even as he hates me, he'd still not put a hand to me.*

Her confidence in that faltered as he matched her steps. She retreated and he continued coming. "I-I came for the Ch-Chaucer," she confessed, her teeth chattering noisily. She stumbled over her hem, caught herself, and edged away from him. He deserved answers. "I was promised funds if I obtained it."

"Stole it." Those two syllables rolled off his tongue like a caress. Only the loathing underscoring them made a mockery of anything gentle.

"S-Stole it." She gave a juddering nod. Her knees knocked against the leather-winged chair before his desk and she toppled over the arm, landing inelegantly on her buttocks. Trapped. Once again, by a different gentleman. The end result had always been the same—her ruin. She'd just been naive enough to believe she could survive in a ruthless world. *I have failed Virgil. And I have wronged Vail.* She'd failed all those she loved.

He towered over her, immobile; a statue carved of stone and as icy cold.

Craning her head, she looked at him through her tears. "I needed the funds," she said blankly and then winced at the avariciousness of them. She struggled into a standing position.

He peeled his lip in a derisive sneer. "Well, it seems you are capable of telling the truth." Vail pointed to the door. "Move now, Mrs. Hamlet."

Dread kept her rooted to the floor. She clutched at her throat, more than half-fearing a constable waited outside that door. "Where are we going?" she whispered.

"Why, I'm showing you to your rooms." He paused. "Until I figure out just what to do with you."

CHAPTER 17

THE FOLLOWING MORNING, NOT EVEN seven hours after Bridget's betrayal and a sleepless night for Vail, silence reigned in his office.

His brother, Edward, was the first to speak. "I don't believe it." He echoed the very denial Vail had tossed out to Tabitha at the Coaxing Tom.

Vail grabbed his cup of coffee and took a sip of the fortifying brew. Horrid, rotted, stuff that he'd always despised, but had welcomed for the surge of energy it gave him. Until he'd tasted the cup Bridget brewed. He set his coffee down hard.

He spoke in deadened methodical tones. "She admitted as much. She came to steal the Chaucer. Promised funds." From whom she'd still not indicated. Vail shifted his attention to the other gentleman present: his brother, Colin, whom he'd summoned as the sun rose, stood against the wall, taking in the exchange with his usual quiet. "Two lords were overheard last evening speaking at the Coaxing Tom about a transaction. My contacts there gathered neither names nor details of when this exchange was to occur."

Silent as the grave, Colin flipped open his notepad and recorded several notes in his book. The scratch of his charcoal pencil grating in the tense quiet. "And your contacts at the Coaxing Tom?" he asked, all business in his tone and demeanor.

"Tabitha Sparks, a prostitute. And a street lad named Jeremy."

How am I this calm? How is my tone even when my bloody heart is shattered in ways Adrina hadn't even managed? Because I opened myself to Bridget. I splayed myself open and showed her my soul, and she shared nothing more than her lies.

Sucking in a slow breath, he looked away from his brothers' probing stares and glanced down at the floor. A vise squeezed about his chest cutting off the ability to draw proper breath into his lungs.

"I'll interview her after I've a chance to speak to your contacts," Colin directed that at his notebook. "Their facts will help me ferret out what she's keeping from you."

Ferret out. In the span of one day, Bridget Hamlet had gone from a woman he'd escorted to his friend's home and made love with, to a duplicitous creature the likes of which landed in Newgate.

"And where is she now?"

"In her chambers with a footman stationed outside her door."

"I can provide a guard," Colin said, stuffing his book back inside his jacket. He adjusted the lapels.

A guard. His gut, empty for anything but his black coffee, churned. Vail inclined his head in thanks and stared blankly as Colin left.

As soon as he'd gone, Edward turned to Vail. "You are certain?" He'd the same shattered look in his eyes that had greeted Vail that morning.

Unable to see that sentiment there without thinking of his own foolishness, he stalked over to the fireplace and dropped his hands atop the stone mantel. He stared blankly into the cold, empty grate. "She admitted it," he said hollowly. "She confessed to her complicity in the plan to steal the Chaucer."

I needed the funds.

And it surely spoke to his weakness that as she'd wept silent tears and pleaded with her eyes for him to understand, that he'd yearned to know the answer to why. That the need had come not from his business or fortunes, but rather the struggle she'd known that had brought her to this point.

The floorboards groaned indicating Edward moved. "This is my fault," Edward said hoarsely from just beyond his shoulder. "I am so sorry. I thought I'd found you the perfect housekeeper and, instead, I brought a thief into your midst."

A thief. Vail let the words roll around his mind and silently mouthed them, testing them on his tongue. Those two syllables, he'd been unable to bring himself to utter. "It is not your fault," he said tiredly. "She fooled us all." *And broke my heart.*

He fisted the edge of the mantel, gripping tight in a bid to keep himself upright. *My God, I loved her.* He would have fetched her a handful of stars if she'd but asked him. In the end, he'd made the same mistake he had with Adrina. He clenched his jaw. Never again. He'd build those same protective walls up and be damned if he ever let any bloody woman in again.

"You cannot go in there, my lord," Gavin's plaintive wail from the corridors cut across his tortured musings. "I've told you he's not accepting—"

"Oh, he'll see me," came Lord Marlborough's echoing warning. "By Christ, he'll see me."

Bloody hell. Jamming the heels of his palms into his eyes, he rubbed. What else could it possibly be? This day could not be any goddamned worse.

The door flew open and the earl stormed inside. With his flushed cheeks and quickened gait, there wasn't a thing sickly-looking about the ailing lord. He opened his mouth and broke into a paroxysm of coughing, shattering the illusion of wellness. Yanking out a kerchief, the older man glared at Gavin over the fabric.

Vail gave him a small nod and Gavin backed out of the room with a grateful glimmer in his eyes.

"You are not stepping foot inside my libraries, Chilton," he rasped, around the cloth.

And yet the day apparently was destined to dissolve into another horrid nightmare. "Fickle as always, I see," he said dryly, with feigned nonchalance.

"I invited you to bring your damned housekeeper to my household, not your bloody mistress," the earl barked, strength restored to his voice. "You would dare disrespect not only me but my daughters by bringing your lightskirt about?"

He was going to lose rights to the largest collection in England. Damning Bridget Hamlet for the thousandth time since he'd learned of her treachery, he searched for a blasted solution. "She is not my mistress and certainly not a lightskirt," he said between his teeth. Why it should matter how Marlborough or anyone else saw her was a mystery that could only be explained by the fact that he'd not slept in more than a day.

"I might not attend *ton* functions as I once did, but my eldest daughter was paid a visit by her friend, Lady Adrina." *Oh, bloody hell.* "She informed me of the manner of man I'd be doing business with."

Fury pumped through his veins. Hell hath no fury like a woman scorned. He'd seen the thirst for retribution in her eyes at Huntly's just yesterday. "Lady Adrina was ill-informed, as was the rest of Polite Society," he drawled, strolling over to his sideboard. His back presented to the fuming lord, he searched his mind for a way to appease Marlborough.

The earl snorted. "I don't believe it. I saw the way you looked at that lady." How? As though he'd been bewitched by her mind and her siren's ability to pull stories of his past from him? "No respectable man looks at his housekeeper the way you do Mrs. Hamlet." With every statement, the tenor of the earl's voice escalated until it thundered off the ceiling. "Or shows up with her in public at a duchess' salon, and then you think to come to my house, with my daughters and—"

"She's my wife."

It was harder to determine who was more shocked.

Vail, himself for that false utterance, his silent until now brother whose mouth fell open, or the earl with his angled head. "Come, again?"

To give his shaking hands a task, Vail poured first one brandy. *What in blazes have I done?* Except…as he went through the motions of splashing several fingerfuls into Marlborough's glass, he sorted out the situation with the duplicitous Mrs. Hamlet in his mind. Yes, she'd intended to steal from him, but she'd also proven immensely beneficial, by way of his business. His mind worked. As Adrina had pointed out, Vail required a hostess, particularly given his sister's upcoming entry into Polite Society, and equally as important were his hopes for Marlborough's libraries.

In fact, as long as he thought of it as nothing more than a business arrangement, it all made logical sense.

"Mrs. Hamlet is Mrs. Hamlet no more, but rather," he lifted his glass. "My baroness."

The earl thinned his eyes and stared at him through those narrow slots. "And why don't I know anything about this?"

Maintaining an evenness to his features, Vail shrugged. "I expect it's far more interesting for the *ton* to gossip about false rumors of me bedding my housekeeper, than to mention my marriage to the lady."

Lord Marlborough glanced over in Edward's direction. "This true, Winterly?"

Edward offered a lazy, unaffected grin. "Are you truly asking me whether Vail invented a wife to appease you, my lord?" He chuckled.

"Humph." The earl faced Vail squarely. "So, you've married the girl."

I will. He'd no choice. Not if he wanted to complete this transaction. He met Lord Marlborough's statement with silence. Vail had earned the collector's wrath for declining marriage to a different woman—the man's daughter—two years ago.

How ironic that Vail was as steeped in lies as Bridget. He battled back guilt. The falsities he'd fed Marlborough represented a means to an end.

Mayhap Bridget has her reasons, too…

He thrust back that unwanted niggling voice in his head.

The earl took a long sip of his drink. With a grimace, he set it down on the painted tray of the gold Louis XV table. "The appointment stands. I expect you tomorrow." He gave Vail a once over. "It's not every day I'm wrong. Marrying that one with her knowledge of literature and collecting? You're as clever as I took you for at our last meeting. See that you come with your new bride. She'll get on great with my daughter." Turning on his heel, the earl let himself out.

Vail winced, counted the ticking of the Morbier long-case clock, knowing what was coming from his brother. Knowing *precisely* what he'd say…

Edward made to speak, but he held a hand up, jerking his head toward the door. With the way his life had crumpled in the past day, he'd wager his entire fortune, titles, and estates that the earl was an earshot away from listening in and, thus, destroying Vail's hopes for that collection.

After several minutes passed in silence, Edward spoke on a hushed whisper. "The gentleman is expecting her to join his daughter? What in blazes are you thinking?"

"That I'm going to need a bloody marriage certificate from the archbishop," he muttered. He stalked over to his desk, amidst Edward's sputtering. Mayhap this wouldn't be as much a disaster as he'd originally feared. All he need do was wed the viper, have her join the damned meeting with Marlborough and the man's family, and then after Vail secured the collection, he could send her to the damned country until Catriona's Come Out, and then after his sisters were wed, he could be done with Bridget Hamlet.

Bridget sat in her rooms, perched on the edge of a needlepoint master chair, as she'd been sitting since she'd gone through her morning ablutions and faced the morning. Waiting for something to happen. Waiting for someone to come. Waiting for her fate to be decided.

Just waiting.

Since she'd been escorted to guest rooms high abovestairs in Vail's townhouse, dread had followed. She'd been a fool believing she'd any place involving herself in a scheme of deception. Even as she'd no choice, there'd also been no chance of her succeeding in the task. For despite being born to the Hamilton evil, she'd never been a master of treachery. Instead, she'd sat on the fringes; an outside observer to heinous acts committed by her siblings and parents unable to contemplate their iniquity. In one desperate instant where she'd sought to save her son, she'd allowed herself to descend into that pit. All the while failing to see that her discovery here had been inevitable.

Bridget focused on her impending fate. For that was far easier to confront than all she'd lost—him. It hadn't mattered whether he'd ever given any indication that he reciprocated her feelings; she loved him. She had come to London believing all noblemen were driven by their own material wants and pleasures, that they were men incapable of goodness. Then, in her first night living under Vail's roof, she'd found how very wrong she'd been. For he, with his love for his siblings and his dedication to them proved the depth of his heart.

"And I betrayed him." Bridget hugged her arms to her chest, squeezing tight. She'd been the one responsible for the darkness in his once warm eyes and the veneer of ice he'd donned, and she hated herself all the more for those changes she'd brought.

The rub of it was, if she could go back she was not sure she'd do anything differently. If her own welfare had been what Archibald had threatened her over then she would have told him to go hang, and awaited her fate. But ten years ago, when she'd been just a girl herself, she'd sacrificed her future and all when she took a motherless babe in as her own.

Restless, Bridget climbed to her feet and took up a place beside the window overlooking the London streets below. In the time since she'd awakened, she'd been periodically drawn to this very space, driven by an almost morbid fascination of just who she'd see below only to have those fears grow when a fierce blond stranger climbed the steps. She'd imagined him to be a constable come to cart her off to Newgate. Her fingers curled reflexively, leaving dagger-like crescents on her palms.

Just then, the front door opened, and she pressed her forehead to the crystal panel to catch a glimpse of who exited now.

Lord Marlborough stepped outside. He paused to adjust the brim of his John Bull top hat, and more than half-fearing he'd glance up and find her staring out, she jumped back.

How had she gone from joining Vail at Lord Marlborough's townhouse to…this?

A hard knock sounded at her door; the sound of it a perfunctory warning more than a polite request. Dread sent her heart climbing into her throat where it had largely been living since last evening, as she whipped about.

Vail entered and closed the door behind him. He stood there a long while, simply assessing her with the cool indifference he might a book he sought to purchase for his collection. She worked her gaze over his beloved frame, searching for a hint of the man he'd once been to her. Still impossibly beautiful, there was now a coldness that left her numb inside.

He steepled his index fingers and thumbs and tapped them silently together as he contemplated her. Through that scrutiny, Bridget remained silent and motionless. All the while she screamed inside wanting Vail back as he'd been. Wanting this exchange over with. Tired of the uncertainty of her fate, when it was at the very least his right to exact whichever cat and mouse game he played.

Suddenly, Vail ceased drumming his fingers. "Lord Marlborough paid an early morn visit."

She wetted her lips. Of course she knew, she'd been watching. "D-Did he?"

Letting his arms fall beside him, he stalked her with his long-legged strides. Where last evening she'd retreated, now she held firm. Mayhap it was exhaustion. Mayhap it was resignation. Or mayhap, she'd simply accepted punishment as her due, but she'd have him dole out whatever retribution he intended. For this horrifying uncertainty was far worse than at last confronting her actual fate. He stopped just beyond her shoulder and, lowering his head, whispered into her good ear, "Won't you ask why he came at this unfashionable hour?"

If one stripped away the steely words, and only knew his body's positioning and the delicious shivers his nearness still roused, even through her fear, one would take him for a teasing lover. *I want him to be that man, again.* And someday he would, but never with her. "Given everything," she said softly, her voice oddly calm. "It hardly seems the topic to remark upon."

"Given everything?" He chuckled and the frostiness to that sound scoured her heart. "Do you mean your treachery?"

The game continued. He was entitled to his fury and hatred of her, but he'd no longer have a willing participant in this. Bridget gave a shaky nod. Archibald and Marianne had taught her that hiding one's fear and meeting those games with directness inevitably quashed any fun the torturer received from them. "Yes," she forced herself to speak. "I referred to my treachery."

He jerked erect. But then he gathered a loose curl from over her shoulder. She stiffened as he toyed with that tress the way a lover might. The way he had so many other times before but then it *had* been with tenderness. "Ah, but what you don't realize is that everything since you've been here is connected to your duplicity." He raised that strand close to his aquiline nose and then suddenly released it, taking a step back. Had he forgotten himself in that moment? Had that gesture merged into something different, divorced of his hatred? "Everything, madam," he rasped, showing the first break in his composure. "Is a product of you being here.

Marlborough canceled the viewing."

She gasped, pressing a palm to her mouth. That coveted visit to the earl's libraries for the right to purchase. "Oh, Vail," she said stretching that same hand toward him.

He snorted. "Madam, spare me your wide, hurting eyes." Balling that palm into a fist, she forced it back down. "Society is all abuzz with talks of the servant I've made my whore…" He paused and flicked a stare over her. "That would be you."

He only sought to hurt her as he was hurting. She knew that. Understood he lashed out and yet she recoiled anyway at the vitriol there.

Vail dusted a speck of imagined dust from his sleeve. "Marlborough was incensed that I'd consider visiting him with my mistress."

"What did you tell him?" A proud man like the earl wouldn't care about Vail's protestations, but rather the appearance of things. Only he had never given a jot about how the world viewed him, or her, or them…or anything else.

"Pfft, I assured him that *you* are certainly not my mistress."

Had the emphasis been placed anywhere else it could not have hurt more than it did. Not wanting him to see his barb had stuck like an arrow in her heart, she glanced at the Aubusson carpet. He caught her by the chin and forced her gaze up to his. She winced at that harsh grip. Where Archibald had only dug his fingers tighter into her flesh when she'd shown that weakness, Vail gentled his hold, so that his fingers moved over her in a tender caress. "For you won't ever be my mistress," he breathed his head so close, his breath fanned her cheeks.

If she'd more respect she'd have hurled his words back and informed him that she'd never have wanted that dishonorable offer from him, anyway. Yet, where this man was concerned, all her pride was gone. For the truth was, she would have settled for the lesser place in his bed, if it had meant she held his heart. His gaze fell to her mouth, and her breath quickened and she felt it—through his hatred and his disgust for her—desire. He wanted her still. She fluttered her lashes and tilted her head back aching for his kiss.

He hovered his mouth close to hers. "You won't be my mistress, Bridget…" He paused. "That is your name, isn't it?" he asked with such derisiveness she turned cold. "Or is that another lie?"

"My name *is* Bridget," she said mournfully, never wishing more that she was someone else. *What will he say when he learns my sister attempted to murder Lady Justina?* Her stomach muscles clenched, viciously.

Vail flicked her nose in a mockingly playful gesture. "Yes, I informed Marlborough that you are, in fact...my wife."

His wife? Her hearing had always been rot. Yet she'd never imagined words, she'd simply failed to hear them. It had, however, sounded as though he'd said—"Beg pardon?" she blurted.

"My wife. The Baroness Chilton." His icy grin could have frozen the Thames. "Bridget Basingstoke, Lady Chilton."

Bridget Basingstoke. She rolled those two names joined together around her mind. How very right they were melded and, yet, for all that had transpired, so wholly wrong. Eying him warily, she retreated a step. "What game do you play, Vail?"

"This?" He tossed his arms wide. "This is no game. This, in fact, will turn out to be the only thing that was ever real." His jaw flexed. "I cannot have first right of purchase unless you're made respectable, Mrs. Hamlet. Marlborough insists you'd be a good friend for his daughter." He laughed, a cold, empty sound. "What wiles you possess that you so thoroughly wrapped so many around your finger."

Wiles. She wouldn't know the first thing about enticing a gentleman which is why Vail's interest had been so very hard to understand. Sifting through the words intended to wound, she focused on what she heard. "You want me to pretend to be your wife until you see that collection?"

"Pretend?" He drew back and then a beleaguered sigh escaped him. "Of course, given your propensity for lying that should be what you think."

Heat exploded on her cheeks and then the implications of his words took root. Why...why...he spoke of marrying her in truth? Bridget fisted and un-fisted the sides of her skirts. "What game is this?" He sought to wound her as she'd wounded him.

"This is no game, Bridget." She was Bridget again. Only all warmth remained gone from that use of her name, when before it had only ever been tender and gentle. "This is a business arrangement," he said bluntly. "I've need of a wife." He paused. "Specifically, *you*. You have a need of funds and I'd wager, a wish to stay out of Newgate?"

She flinched. "Are you threatening me into marriage?"

Vail flattened his lips into an unyielding line. "After I've had access to Marlborough's collections, you will have use of one of my country properties. Whenever I'm in need of a hostess, or introduce my sister to Society, you shall serve that role."

Marriage to Vail was the dream she'd never allowed herself, but not like this. He spoke in such chilled, methodical tones she walked away, rubbing her arms. What he offered was a cold union based on business when he'd already proven himself capable of such love and warmth. He deserved more. "You don't want this." Did she speak to him or herself? "Your business is important to you but if you did this thing…" She struggled to get the words out. "Marry me, you would grow to regret it. You'd deny yourself marriage one day to a woman you love." *A woman deserving of you.* When Bridget herself had never been worthy of him. The only place for a Hamilton was the pits of Hell with Lucifer for company.

Vail moved before her and she craned her neck back to meet his gaze. "I loved once before," *Adrina.* Her heart twisted, and he spoke, wrenching it all the more. "And I'll never love again."

Oh, God. Bridget pressed a hand to her chest and searched her palm for blood. For surely to be aching like this, there had to be a physical wound. "Vail," she implored, trying again, for his sake. For there could be no doubting that this was a decision he would one day, when the thirst for money and power faded, forever regret.

He pierced her with a hard stare and, from within those jade-green depths, a flash of pain broke through that harshness. "What do you want?"

"Want?"

"A fortune, madam? Fine satins and silks? Whatever you were willing to sell your soul for?"

My son. Virgil. The child who'd taught her to love. "I don't want anything from you, Vail," she said softly. Nothing that was material. She wanted what he could no longer give her.

"We wed tomorrow," he said coldly.

And with that, he left.

CHAPTER 18

"*...I*T WAS ORDAINED FOR THE *mutual society, help, and comfort, that the one ought to have of the other, both in prosperity and adversity. Into which holy estate these two persons present come now to be joined...*"

The hastily found vicar droned on the vows that would forever join Vail and Bridget together as man and wife.

Colin, Edward, Gavin, and Huntly stood on as silent witnesses. Only two of them knowing the treachery Bridget had intended to carry out and who, for it, recognized this union for the farce it was. Gavin stood, the sole smiling occupant in the room, and Huntly, his best man's face revealed nothing but a thinly veiled worry.

"*...I REQUIRE and charge you both, as ye will answer at the dreadful day of judgment when the secrets of all hearts shall be disclosed, that if either of you know any impediment, why ye may not be lawfully joined together in Matrimony, ye do now confess it...*"

Vail cast a sideways glance at his bride. Her complexion was gray and black circles under her eyes marked equally sleepless nights. No one would ever dare mistake her for a joyous, blushing bride.

"*...if any man do allege and declare any impediment, why they may not be coupled together in Matrimony, by God's Law, or the Laws of this Realm; and will be bound, and sufficient sureties with him, to the parties; or else put in a Caution...*"

Bridget's audible swallow reached his ears and he cast a sharp look at her. Did she intend to renege on this agreement? He dropped his lip alongside her ear. "We have a deal, madam."

The vicar paused and, pushing back his spectacles, looked at the bride and groom over the top of his Bible.

"I know," she whispered back. "You don't want to do this, Vail."

"No. But I need to." Motioning for the vicar to resume, the clergyman pressed ahead.

"Wilt thou love her, comfort her, honor, and keep her in sickness and in health; and, forsaking all other, keep thee only unto her, so long as ye both shall live?"

Love her. Forsake all others? He would have done it in truth and honor had she proven to be the woman he'd believed her to be.

"My lord?" the vicar prodded on a noisy whisper. "This is where you answer 'yes, I do'."

Feeling Bridget's pleading stare, he gritted out his affirmation.

Plowing ahead, the graying clergyman rushed through the remainder of those verses and vows, until it was done.

They were married.

As the vicar snapped his Bible shut and proceeded to ready the documents at the front table, Huntly joined him—them.

"My lady," he greeted for Vail's bride. He took one of her gloved hands and pressed a kiss atop it. "Allow me to congratulate you on your marriage. I'm honored to stand as witness."

Bridget offered a tremulous thanks and retreated several steps, glancing about—escape. Vail recognized that need to flee; too many men had worn it upon the battlefields of Europe.

The vicar cleared his throat and held out a pen. "My lord, we are ready to sign." He made a vague gesture to where Bridget now stood, speaking to Gavin.

Gavin spoke, gesticulating wildly, and then he tossed his arms around her in a hug, crushing her to him. Most ladies would have stiffened under that show of emotion. Bridget, however, returned that embrace, and said something that raised a laugh. Vail gnashed his teeth. He'd not soften where she was concerned. "The lady can sign after I've finished," he bit out.

Blinking like an owl startled from his perch, Vicar Alsop, hurriedly relinquished the pen into Vail's grip. Dipping it into the inkwell, he proceeded to scratch his name along the requisite places.

"Here," the vicar murmured. "And here…"

"What in blazes is going on?" At his side, Huntly spoke in hushed tones that barely registered.

"Not here," he said tightly, keeping his focus trained on his signing. Damn him for the weak fool he was, however, for instead being so attuned to the soft murmur of Bridget's husky contralto as she spoke, and for the effect it always had on him. And for the floral scent that filled his senses and made him think of country meadows in summer.

"And here, my lord," the vicar prodded, when he'd paused in his signing. He flipped to the next sheet. "Two more places."

Hastily inking his name on those final two spots, he dropped his pen and motioned over Edward. "See to…my…" *My wife. She is mine now until death parts us.* Why did that not usher in a deserved fury? "Her Ladyship," he corrected. "Have her readied for our visit with Marlborough."

Edward nodded and went to gather Bridget.

"What in bloody hell is going on?" Huntly demanded as they'd taken their leave of his office. Of like height, the duke easily matched his long strides. "What manner of wedding was that?"

"A necessary one," he muttered, stopping beside the Collections Room that had seen his world crumple before him last evening. He shoved the door open. "She deceived me," he said without preamble, staying whatever question had formed on Huntly's lips. "Found her in the Portrait Room with the Chaucer." Wanting the telling done as quickly as possible, he hurried through it. "As such, we've agreed to a formal business arrangement."

Huntly shook his head, a horrified glint in his eyes. "What have you done?" he whispered.

"Secured my business."

"At the expense of your own happiness?" his friend shot back.

Gathering a drink from the sideboard, he took a much needed sip. "Everything comes second to my business. Marlborough's libraries will fetch me a fortune."

"My God, listen to yourself. You have a fortune. Gobs of money."

"It's never enough." Not when there were nine siblings to look after and others to find.

Huntly stared at him and then shook his head slowly. "I know you, Chilton. You didn't need this money." Vail stiffened. "This is about more than Marlborough's collection," he spat. "You, who spoke to me of love and talked me out of my ill-decision, you never allowed me the same courtesy."

"Because you couldn't have changed my course. Just as I couldn't have changed yours." The only solution had been to wed Bridget.

"Pfft." Huntly slashed the air with a hand. "I don't believe that any more than you do. You married that young woman for a reason—"

"I just told you."

"—other than your business with Marlborough or your need of a hostess and every other rotted reason you've given."

"You're wrong," he said, taking a fortifying sip, even as Huntly's predictions wrought havoc on him. He couldn't be correct. To feel anything for her still would prove him thrice times a fool. He knew better than to feel anything for a schemer like Bridget.

His friend studied him and then shook his head sadly. "I'm right and I suspect, one day soon, you'll realize as much."

The thin thread of Vail's control snapped. He slammed his drink down on a scalloped table, sloshing liquid over the sides of the glass. "She is a bloody thief," he shouted. Those words, if overheard by one of his faithless servants, were enough to ruin…all. "She came here to steal from me," he said in quieter tones. "You expect that I should *care* for such a person?"

"I orchestrated a meeting with my wife with the intentions of breaking her heart and marrying her in a game of revenge. Do you think *she* should love such a person?" he countered.

A muscle jumped at the corner of Vail's eye. "It is different."

Some of the tension eased in Huntly's face and he snorted. "Because we've been friends since we were boys and you knew me longer? Why, you were even willing to help me."

He flinched. Yes, but that had been driven by a lifelong loyalty and also a sense that he could have talked his friend out of the cruel scheme he'd crafted.

"You can't pardon me so freely for my actions against Justina and not at least try and understand what drove your wife." Huntly's disapproval hung like a cloud over the room.

"She needed funds," he said tiredly, swiping a hand over his face.

The other man nodded. "Yes. You said as much." He held Vail's gaze. "Though, I suspect understanding *why* she required those funds is as important."

A knock sounded at the door and they looked up.

Gavin ducked his head inside. "V… Oh, hello, Huntly," he said with a wave for the duke, as though they'd just met for the first time that day.

Huntly inclined his head. "Lodge," he greeted.

Gavin looked back. "The carriage has been readied. Edward instructed me to tell you that Her Ladyship is finalizing her documents and will soon be aboard the carriage."

Nodding his thanks, Vail sent him along. "I thank you for your support," he said after he and Huntly were again alone. "But you're wrong in this."

"Perhaps." His friend smiled sadly. "But what if I'm correct?"

Bridget had never allowed herself dreams of a wedding day because she'd known the future that awaited her. Her parents had been abundantly clear and her sister decidedly cruel in reminding her frequently that the only fate for a deaf, marked lady was that of a spinster.

If she had, however, taken time to craft make-believes of what this moment would one day be, it certainly never would have been marked by the icy cold and silence of this day. She stared blankly down at Vail's elegant, black scrawled letters, and the empty spaces alongside them left for her mark.

The vicar cleared his throat—for a third time. "My lady?" he urged, casting a desperate glance over to the gentleman who stood at her side.

Not Vail. Not her husband.

Rather, his brother.

"Mrs… My lady," he swiftly amended, and though his urging was devoid of Vail's earlier hatred, neither was there warmth there, either. "Your signature is required."

"In multiple spots," the clergyman needlessly pointed out. "As soon as you add your name, my lady, it is done."

It was done, long, long ago. She'd always realized that. Vail had only just come to that understanding. She traced a trembling finger over the slight curve at the top of the V of his name. But it needn't be over for him. Even if he'd made this decision with his business and his siblings' best interest in mind, he'd one day come to hate her—all the more. He'd wake up and find himself trapped in a loveless marriage to a woman he hated, when there was surely a woman out there deserving of his love.

The vicar coughed loudly. Drawing in a breath, Bridget collected the pen and, with an unsteady grip, added her name beside his.

A short while later, it was done. She watched numbly as Vicar Alsop sprinkled some pounce upon her name.

"Come, my lady," Edward murmured at her side. "Vail instructed me to escort you to his carriage."

Managing a wooden nod, she fell into step beside him. She searched her mind for something to say to this other man whom she'd betrayed with her lies and purpose here. And anticipated a stinging rebuke from him.

Then, he proved himself more honorable than she deserved, for instead of recrimination, he offered her nothing but silence. After Gavin had helped her into her cloak, Edward escorted her out the doors to the waiting carriage. Ever the gentleman, he offered his hand to help her up.

She'd one foot inside when at last he spoke. "Vail cared for you."

Cared. One letter added to that word which so markedly changed it from something beautiful into something that gutted her. "I never meant to hurt him," she said softly. His features twisted into a reflection of his disgust. "Edward," she called, staying him as he made to go. "If I'd another choice, I would have never come here. I would have lived my life and certainly never brought pain to Vail."

He gave no outward indication that he'd heard. Her new brother-in-law remained like a sentry in wait. Settling inside the red velvet squabs of Vail's expensive carriage, she sat back, waiting.

A moment later, a large figure drew himself inside the entrance and claimed the seat opposite her. Vail's broad frame shrank the space of the otherwise large conveyance. As the door closed and the carriage rocked forward, air was sparse between them.

Given the fact that she'd still not sorted through what to do with her brother's threats and plans for her and Virgil, that is all that should matter and all she should focus on. And yet, every part of her was trained on the man across from her—a stranger for the way he now looked at her.

How was one to be around a person who so hated one? How was she to spend any of her days with this man who now stared at her as though she were an object he'd removed from the sole of his boot?

"What happens now?" she asked Vail. "What happens after Lord Marlborough's?" He'd mentioned sending her away. Mayhap that was her hope. That she and Virgil could disappear into one of her husband's obscure properties until Bridget sorted through the next pieces of her life with Virgil and Nettie. *But then you'll still have to explain to him about your...* Her mind spun.

"What happens now?" He laid his arms along the back of his seat. "I'll meet with Marlborough. You will entertain his daughters. Then, you'll need to be presented to Polite Society, properly, as my wife."

Presented to Society? Bridget scrambled forward to the edge of her seat and her knees brushed his, and heat radiated through her skirts from that brief contact. "But...but..." His plans went against everything she'd worked through in her mind. "I cannot." Her palms grew moist within the confines of her gloves. To face the *ton* and their censure. Theirs was a world she'd been born to but never belonged to.

"That is part of our arrangement."

"That you forced me to agree to," she bit out.

"Regardless, those are the terms struck. I'll not have a scandal attached to our marriage, given Catriona will be making her debut."

Why...why...he expected her to immerse herself in this world. She'd naively believed this upcoming meeting with the earl was to be the extent of their relationship—for now. *But this?* "Are you trying to humiliate me?" she asked tightly. "Is that the ultimate revenge you seek?"

His body turned to granite on the bench opposite her as he abandoned his casual repose. He dropped his hands on his knees and leaned forward. She gasped at the alacrity of that movement. "Let us be clear, madam," he seethed. "This was never a game. Not from our first meeting in my office to the night I discovered you in your act of treachery. Nor to the moment I demanded your hand in marriage. My regard for you..." Their chests rose and fell in a synchronic rhythm. "W-was also real, whereas you offered me nothing but lies from the start."

The carriage rocked to a sudden, jarring halt that sent her pitching forward.

Vail instantly caught her. He lingered his hands upon her, his hot touch piercing the fabric of her garments and burning her with the same desire she'd known in his arms yesterday. Back when he'd covered her with his body and moved within her, touching her to the core.

His driver pulled the door open and Vail instantly released her. Jumping out, he reached back and helped hand her down. He proffered his arm. "My lady," he murmured, with the same affable smile he'd worn days earlier. *Did I merely imagine that warmth?* Surely one who could don that easy grin was capable of the same artifice she herself had been rightly accused of. She made the mistake of looking into his eyes: to the steely warning there. It was his eyes. His eyes contained all the depth of his loathing for her.

"Smile," he commanded through his clenched teeth. "Come, madam, a liar such as you can surely do better than that," he said to her false effort.

I hate this. I hate everything about this. But Vail, however, had been correct. For the treachery she'd intended, this was something small she might do.

He guided her up the front steps and, before he could knock, the door was thrown open. They'd been expected, then. Bridget shrugged out of her cloak and gave her thanks to the footman who collected the muslin garment. "This way, if you will," the young butler encouraged, and led her and Vail through the marble halls that all stood a proud symbol of the earl's wealth.

As she walked at Vail's side, she gazed vacantly about at the heavy gold paintings and gilded hall tables with their Sevres-style celeste vases. Of all she'd wanted in life, this material extravagance had never been it. She'd wanted security and safety and… A family. Seemingly simple gifts, but the most precious ones. All these years, Archibald had threatened the life she'd made for herself with Virgil…

And I continue to let him…

Because she'd largely believed him invincible. As a marquess, even an impoverished one, he was a man of power and she? She was a deaf spinster. Or that is how she'd viewed herself. She'd only seen her own limitations. Vail had opened her eyes to her own self-worth; he'd shown her that her skill and wits were not simply a means to earn a handful of coins to feed her brother's vices but rather a testament to her intelligence.

Even the earl's request that she be here stood as proof. Some of the agony that had weighted her chest since Vail had discovered her in his Portrait Room, abated, leaving in its place strength.

She'd made herself a victim. She'd hidden herself away and allowed Archibald to hold sway over her every step. Why, she'd even agreed to commit a theft and had simply justified it in her head as an act that must be carried out. Self-loathing coated her tongue like acid. Her earlier thoughts when Vail had held her with affection in the guest room whispered forward. All these years she'd bemoaned the lack of family or friend to turn a burden over to. She'd even envied Vail's siblings for having an elder brother to rescue them. *I don't want to be rescued…* Her fingers clenched and unclenched reflexively. Not in this. To turn this burden over to Vail, a man who'd have hate shining in his eyes whenever he looked at her, would mark her just as weak. With a sense of absolute right-ness about what she must do, she brought her shoulders back.

The butler brought them to a stop outside a beautifully arched doorway with stained glass windows carved into the center. He lifted the iron hook at the top and knocked once.

"Let them in," the earl bellowed and, hiding the curvature of his lips, the butler admitted them.

All the air escaped Bridget on a swift exhalation and she pressed her hands to her heart. She'd never considered there could be anything more magnificent than Vail's collections, but this? Walls must have been taken down and the nearby townhouse purchased to expand this master library. In reverent awe, she tipped her head back and took in the shelving that ran from the floor to the mural that spanned the ceiling. "It is magnificent," she whispered. Feeling Vail's stare, she glanced over. His features, however, remained a careful mask. Did she merely imagine the regret that passed between them?

"Lord Chilton." A clear, pleasing voice slashed across that momentary connection. "It is a pleasure to see you again." The tall, slender beauty with midnight curls expertly arranged and kindly green eyes swept over, hands outstretched.

"Lady Clementina," he returned with his usual charm. "And it is a pleasure, always."

At that show of warmth, jealousy twisted low in her belly, like a venomous serpent poised to strike.

Her husband and Lord Marlborough's daughter spoke with such ease, it only highlighted all the parts she did not know about her husband. Their low murmurings impossible for her ears to detect, Bridget hovered, feeling like an interloper, despising the statuesque woman. A woman who'd be a perfect hostess, cultured, and clever. The kind of lady Vail Basingstoke should have married. It was wrong and petty but then that was why the sin of envy found one within the spheres of hell.

"May I present my wife?" *His wife*. She didn't feel like anything more than an albatross about his neck. "Bridget, Lady Chilton. Bridget, this is the Earl of Marlborough's daughter, Lady Clementina."

Bridget stiffened, as the stunning woman faced her. She touched her eyes briefly upon that hated crescent birthmark, but that same warmth transferred over from the lady's earlier exchange with Vail. "*You* are the woman I've heard so much about, my lady." Had that come from any other member of the *ton* it would have been a thinly veiled insult. There was such kindness in Lady Clementina's eyes that it made it impossible to hate her.

"She's the one," the earl said with a grunt.

"It says much about the one who can not only command my father's respect, but also bring him…" She tipped her head at Vail. "…up to scratch."

Up to scratch. This woman saw the myth Vail hoped the world would. The only place he had truly wished to send her was to the Devil. Unable to formulate the expected witty rejoinder, she offered a false smile. "It is a pleasure," she said softly.

"Come," the earl's daughter looped her arm through Bridget's. "So my blustery father might show your husband the collection he's been trying to for—" Lady Clementina cast a questioning look over in Vail's direction. A twinkle lit her eyes and the knots inside twisted all the more.

"Two years," he supplied.

How was it possible for this day to have gone from bad to worse, and now horrendous? Mayhap it was the hell of her world crumpling about her. Or mayhap it was the uncertainty of Virgil's future but Bridget fought back the urge to cry.

"My father indicated you've a love of literature. Shall we take a turn about the room, my lady?"

Out the door. The only place Bridget wished to go was out that beautiful arched door, and then on to Lambeth for her son, and off to Leeds so she could forget how she'd caused her own heartbreak. "That would be lovely," she managed, instead.

They proceeded to walk the perimeter of the expansive room. From the corner of her eye, Bridget followed Vail as he joined the earl at a leather, winged-chair. Resting his palms along the arms of that seat, he propped his ankle over his opposite knee. So sanguine he was, when Bridget had always struggled to come to terms with her differences.

"My father doesn't like anybody," the other woman confessed. "Quite despised Lord Chilton, too."

How could anyone hate such a gentleman? A man who'd risen up and been handed a title, but who chose to build a fortune with his own efforts?

"My father fancied a match between us," Lady Clementina confided.

Bridget stumbled, missing a step. The other woman helped steady her.

"I'm sorry," she said, concern lacing her tone. "I've startled you."

"No. No. Not at all." *Wounded me. Twisted the knife all the more, mayhap.* Startled had been the least of what Lord Marlborough's daughter had done.

"I expected you knew," the other woman persisted.

"I don't know anything about London Society." Her tone came out sharper than she intended and she curled her toes into the soles of her slippers. Bridget sighed. "Forgive me. I don't know anything of Polite Society," she repeated. "Much of my life has been away in the country...until now." *Until my brother forced me to abandon every comfort I'd made for myself. When I should have fought, forged my own path, just like Vail.*

"You are fortunate then," Lady Clementina murmured. "I quite despise it all, you know." She wrinkled her nose. "All that is, except the books. Though I suspect if one had a large enough estate house one might have all the books…" Her words trailed off. "My father wanted me to make a match with Lord Chilton, my lady," she said…for a *second* time.

A cinch squeezed at Bridget's already broken heart, draining the blood from that useless organ.

"Lord Chilton, however, did not want me."

It did not escape her notice that the other woman failed to speak of her own wishes.

"His heart was not engaged." Lady Clementina brought them to a stop at the opposite end of the hall, and surveyed her father and Vail engrossed in their discussion. "My father said he was mad for not wishing a union between our families, said anyone who'd not wed his daughter didn't deserve his books. Until he met you."

Bridget forced her gaze away from her husband, meeting the other woman's direct stare.

"Both of them. My father saw your understanding of literature and antique books and pardoned Lord Chilton." She smiled. "Which is why we're now here."

Bridget looked out once more.

Which is why they were now here.

CHAPTER
19

VAIL'S MEETING HAD BEEN A success. Nor had Bridget known as much from any words he'd shared, or because of a tangible excitement, but rather because of the smile and handshake he'd offered Lord Marlborough. That had been the last smile she'd seen from him that day, and also the last sight of him.

The house now quiet and her husband gone for the evening, she remained alone…more alone than she'd ever been. For in Leeds, there had been Virgil and Nettie. Her eyes slid involuntarily closed. Both of whom would have been expecting her, worrying after her. And coward that she was, she'd delayed this visit—until now.

Slipping out through the kitchen, and making her way from the mews, down the connecting alleys between Vail's townhouse and his neighbor, she quickened her step. More than half-fearing Edward, who'd been following her throughout the day, had noted her departing her chambers, she shot a look over her shoulder. The moon sent eerie shadows dancing off the brick walls as her only company.

She reached the end and, drawing her hood closer, Bridget stepped out. Having lived in the country for the whole of her seven and twenty years, much of her time had been spent walking. There were no phaetons or fancy carriages. Rather, there was an old sprigged curricle that had once belonged to her grandfather that Bridget drove to the village. Walking down the quiet streets of Mayfair, however, was vastly different. Even being the fashionable side of London, the roads were cold and damp.

Finding a hack at the corner of the thoroughfare, she handed over the coins clasped in her fist. "Five Lambeth Street," she instructed.

With a nod, the man took the coin and helped her up.

Soon, the carriage was rattling on, carrying her from Vail's home to the temporary residence Bridget had set up for her family. And for all the nervousness she'd felt over this upcoming meeting, tears pricked behind her lashes as a hungering to be with those very people filled her.

The carriage hadn't even come to a full stop at the small town-house before Bridget tossed the door open and jumped out. She grunted and shot her arms wide to steady herself. "Please wait." With the promise of more coin, she sprinted over the pavement and up the two steps. She knocked once.

The hair on the back of her neck stood as the sense of being watched swept her. Whipping about, she inventoried the darkened streets. Her driver, smoking a cheroot, stared back, the only figure about.

She turned back to again knock, when the door flew open. "Oh, saint's alive, girl." Nettie grabbed her by the hand and yanked her inside. She closed the door behind them.

Bridget collapsed into the familiar arms of her nursemaid and took the solace she offered.

"When you didn't come back I thought your brother. I thought…" She drew back quickly and, taking Bridget by the shoulders, searched her face. "Did he hurt you?"

"He didn't." Her voice emerged hoarse. "I hurt myself."

Flummoxed, the maid sputtered and then dragged her through the dark, narrow halls, onward until they reached the kitchen.

"Virgil?" she asked, as soon as Nettie pushed a cup of tea across the table.

"He's abed. Worried sick about you, girl. Convinced his uncle," she spat. "Found you and did something to you."

Her heart hitched. All these years she'd believed she'd kept her son from fear, only to find that at ten he was aware and fearful of Archibald's evil. "Why would he think that?"

"Said he had a feeling something was going to happen." And

something had. Blankly, Bridget stared into her drink. "What is it?"

"He caught me."

Nettie froze, the glass halfway to her lips.

"Lord Chilton. H-He came upon me with the book…" The teacup clattered in her hands and she dimly registered the other woman relieving her of it. And then the tears came. She broke down, giving in to the grief that had gripped her for two days now. Bridget covered her face with her hands and sobbed until her entire body shook and she thought she might break. She wept for all she'd lost and for all that could never have been anyway. She cried for hurting Vail. "I-I loved him," she rasped as her nursemaid gathered her close. "I-I fell in love with him."

"Shh." Nettie made nonsensical murmurings as she stroked the top of Bridget's head, the same way she had with Bridget as a child.

"He hates me. *Hates* me. And why shouldn't he?" she cried against her chest. Her nursemaid said nothing, just let Bridget weep until her tears faded to a shuddery hiccough. She sighed and sat back in her seat.

Nettie went to reclaim a spot on the opposite bench.

"He married me."

With a horrified gasp, the older woman fell into her seat. "Bridget?" It was an evidence of her upset that she'd strip the "Lady" from that address.

"I know. I know. I had no choice," she breathed, dragging her hands back and forth over her face. She proceeded to explain the terms Vail had put to her.

"Does he know…*everything?*"

Other than Bridget, Nettie, and Archibald, no one knew everything. It was far safer that way. Vail's palpable hatred for her now, only reinforced that. She let her silence serve as her answer.

"Mm. Bridget." Nettie stretched her hands across the wood plank dining table and gathered her hands, squeezing them. "What have you done, girl?"

"The only thing I could do."

"Then you need to tell him everything."

Tell him everything? Her mouth went dry. And risk Virgil's very life on the hope that Vail might put aside his hatred of her? To help a Hamilton? *You know he would…*

"Mama!" That excited cry pealed around the kitchen and Bridget instantly hopped up from her seat. She opened her arms and a bleary-eyed Virgil came racing across the room. He hurled himself against her, knocking them both back.

Finding her first laugh that day, she righted them both, and then hugged her son for all she was worth.

"Where were you?" he demanded, wresting out of her grip, indicating the precise moment he'd been restored from adoring child to perturbed older boy. "I thought we were for Hyde Park and you didn't come," he accused. "I thought something had happened to you. When you say you're going to be somewhere, you honor your word," he scolded, throwing a lesson she'd ingrained into him long ago, back into her face.

"I'm sorry," she entreated.

Virgil squinted in the dark and, leaning forward, he peered at her eyes. "Who hurt you?" he demanded, fisting and un-fisting his smaller hands.

Had he always seen this much? "No one," she said quickly. "I just missed you, is all."

He eyed her with a heavy dose of mistrust.

"Come," she said with a feigned smile. She glanced about for an apron and, shedding her cloak for that modest white scrap hanging on a hook, she donned it. "Nettie tells me you've missed my Shrewsbury."

Her son grinned. As she went through the motions of baking his favorite treat and being regaled with his tales of the week, she could almost believe they were back home and that her world had never fallen apart.

Vail sat at his back table at Brooke's because… he simply didn't wish to be home. His meeting had been a success with Marlborough and for all intents and purposes it was all he'd been searching for from the earl for the past two years.

And it didn't make him feel any damned better. It didn't do anything to ease the ache that had sprouted in his chest since he'd discovered Bridget's perfidy.

He stared into the contents of his brandy, lifting his head at the requisite moments that congratulations were called out. For all Society had, of course, learned of his marriage to Bridget. He wanted to hate her. He wanted to be filled with the righteous indignation he was entitled to since she'd crawled around Erasmus' painting with the Chaucer in hand. And he'd been content and able to do so.

Until damned Huntly.

… You can't pardon me so freely for my actions against Justina and not at least try and understand what drove your wife…

This betrayal, however, was different. It was black and… "White," he breathed.

…Life, much like color, doesn't exist in a neat, orderly way, no matter how much easier it might be to categorize it… People are no different. You cannot neatly file them as sinners or saints. We are all simply people, flawed by our own rights… surviving in an uncertain world…

He froze. She'd been trying to tell him. Mayhap it was his own need to make this woman who'd so captivated him into something she was not, but now every word she'd uttered rang with new meaning. Veiled statements that had offered unknown glimpses into who she was.

What had driven her? Those funds…those funds contained the answers to all the questions about Bridget's treachery, but in the immediacy of his own hurt sense of betrayal he'd failed to see there was more at play here.

And he needed to know all…before he passed judgment on his wife.

A shadow fell over his table and he looked up. His brother, Colin, met his stare with his usual somberness.

Vail swiftly set his glass down and motioned to the chair opposite him. "What did you discover?" he asked, after the younger man slid into the seat.

Not so much as moving his head, Colin shot a hand up, halting an approaching servant. The liveried footman with a tray and decanter shifted course to another table. "Nothing regarding the meeting at the Coaxing Tom."—Disappointment swamped him.—"Not yet," his brother corrected, that determined glimmer in his eyes one of the reasons Colin had risen to the ranks of one of London's best Runners. Dropping his elbows on the smooth mahogany surface, he leaned forward. "One of my men sent word that your wife was seen leaving your townhouse this evening."

Vail's heart thudded to a slow halt and then picked up a frantic beat. "What?" *I shouldn't have gone.* "And he let her go?" he gritted out, matching Colin's position. What if she was fleeing even now? And why did his stomach churn with dread at the thought of it? "By God, the whole bloody reason you had one of your men watch her is to prevent her from running away," he gritted out.

Colin shook his head. "Not when we can learn far more following her and determining where she's gone off to." Leaning back, he withdrew his small leather notebook and tugged out one of those pages. He slid it across the table.

Vail glanced down, staring blankly at the concise information scrawled there.

"It's an address. She's there now. I've two men stationed outside the residence. One at the front, the other at the back."

She'd waited until he'd gone out and then snuck out like a thief in the night. This paper and address contained answers to questions he had. But God help him for proving a bloody coward, he couldn't bring his legs to move. Feared what else he'd learn about her. Because if there'd been one lie, then what proof did he have that any of what they'd shared was real.

"Vail?" Colin prodded.

He swiped the page from the table and stuffed it inside his jacket. Standing, he started through the club, carefully sidestepping lords who moved into his path with goodwill wishes for the new bridegroom.

Bridegroom.

Everything about his marriage and his relationship with Bridget was a farce.

But I wish it wasn't. I wish I could go back to how it had nearly been the night we made love together.

Frustration, regret, and pain all roiled together, near crippling in their hold, and as he stepped out of Brooke's, he filled his lungs with the cool night air. Trying to settle his emotions. In vain.

Colin settled a hand on his shoulder, startling him. "I'll accompany you."

"I do not require assistance with…" *my wife.* He winced. For he had required help putting together the details surrounding her betrayal. This meeting, however, he'd handle alone. Vail collected his reins from a waiting street lad, turning over a heavy purse for the child. "You have men there," he said calmly, swinging himself into his seat.

Colin hesitated. "You're certain?"

Vail wasn't certain of anything more. Offering a brusque nod and a word of thanks, he urged Atlas forward. The streets were largely quiet at this late night hour. He leaned over his mount's shoulders and encouraged it to stretch its legs.

With a whinny of appreciation, the stallion lengthened its stride. Vail hung on to the reins, guiding him from the fashionable end of St. James Street. Soon, the roads gave way to narrow buildings, closer together. Those uneven structures, with their grime-covered windows and peeling plaster, revealed their age.

A chill skittered along his spine. What underhanded business had sent his wife fleeing here? Reaching the corner of Lambeth, he drew on the reins, slowing Atlas to a walk, and then he brought the horse to a stop. Vail swung his leg over and leapt down.

The full moon's glow cast a bright white light upon the dirty cobblestones and he peered through those shadows. His gaze collided with a child. Silently, he inclined his head. The boy hesitated and then rushed over. "Guv'nor?"

"I need you to care for my mount," he said in hushed tones. Offering the child several coins and the promise of more, Vail handed over Atlas' reins and then continued along the pavement. He did a search of the numbers displayed above each doorway… and then stopped.

His gaze climbed the townhouse. With just four front windows and in desperate need of repair to the roof, this was the place Bridget had gone. In these dangerous streets of Lambeth. The idea of her coming here, alone, unchaperoned to see to whatever underhanded business called her sent terror through him. He briefly closed his eyes. Anyone could come upon her in these streets and it didn't matter that she'd betrayed him, or how she'd cut him to the quick with his own suffering, the idea of her hurt knifed at Vail's insides.

He remained beside the gas lamp outside that townhouse so long that moments rolled over into minutes and then stretched on. What if Colin's men had been wrong? What if she was, even now, at home in their house, sleeping in her bed and he was here worrying for naught? What if—?

The front door of that townhouse finally opened and a small, cloaked figure stepped out. *Bridget.* His breath froze in his chest as he took in her furtive movements. She looked back over her shoulder and spoke to someone inside. Vail's feet twitched with the need to storm the twenty paces, climb those steps, and see just who that person was. But he'd never been one given to rashness: not since his days on the battlefield, nor in his business across London. And he'd not give in to that weakness now.

Bridget took the steps two at a time and settled her feet on the pavement. As soon as she started for the hack across the street, Vail leapt into movement. The driver caught his approaching figure and, not taking his gaze off Bridget's back, he pointed to the perch. That young man smartly complied.

Bridget reached for the door handle and, coming up behind her, Vail pressed his hand over hers, keeping that door in place.

His wife's shriek echoed around the streets of Lambeth and she spun about. Arm drawn back, he easily caught her ineffectual blow.

Vail curled his lips up in a slow, menacing smile. "Hello, my lady."

She flared her eyes, those cerulean pools hopelessly wide in her pale face. "Vail." There was a breathless accusation there. "What are you doing here?"

He folded his arms. "What am I doing here? The better question is what are you doing here, madam?"

Since he'd come upon her in the Portrait Room she'd been downcast, averting her eyes whenever he was near, and he'd missed her earlier shows of spirit. Given the transformation that had overtaken her since she'd revealed her duplicity, he expected more of that same woefulness. He should have already learned never to make assumptions where Bridget was concerned.

Glaring up at him, she propped her hands on her hips. "You followed me."

He'd not point out that there were, in fact, two men who'd trailed her here and another who'd reported back to Colin. "You haven't exactly given me reasons to trust you."

She tossed her hands up and a frustrated little cry escaped her. "I *married* you. You had your appointment with Marlborough; can I not have some freedoms?"

His patience snapped. He stuck his face close to hers. "No, you may not. And do you know why that is?" He took her by the shoulders and brought her up on her tiptoes. "Because women who confess to being thieves and then sneak about the streets of Lambeth lose those rights and privileges." Fear flashed in her eyes and she stared at his hands upon her person. Vail abruptly released her. *My God, what am I becoming?* "Who were you meeting?" he asked in flat tones.

"I'm not having this discussion here." She took a step toward the carriage and he blocked her path.

"Who?"

Bridget met that sharp demand with a stony silence. And at last, he accepted the unwanted truth he'd fought since Colin slid that note across the table—she'd met a man. Primitive rage pounded like a drum in his head and pulsed in his veins. Growling low in his throat, Vail spun back and stalked toward that hated townhouse.

"Vail," she shouted after him.

He did not break stride, but rather finished his march. Reaching the front door of that residence, he knocked hard.

"Vail," she cried, grabbing at his arm. "Stop."

Shrugging off her touch, he pounded. At his side, Bridget wept and, through those noisy tears, pleaded. She was determined to keep her secrets. She'd already made him for the fool. He would be damned if she made him a cuckold or—

The door opened and he froze mid-knock.

A plump, gray-haired woman stared back with a like shock as his own. What in blazes? She looked to Bridget. "My lady…what…?"

The sharp staccato of footsteps sounded down the corridor as a small boy came racing forward. He charged past the older woman, his eyes brightening. "Mama, you've come back."

Mama?

Stunned, Vail swung his gaze about, looking for the errant mother this child spoke of, and only finding one—Bridget. The boy tossed himself into her arms and she immediately held him close.

And the world ceased spinning. She had a child. By the looks of his size, he was near in age to Erasmus' years when he'd passed away. But…Vail glanced around, dazed. It was impossible. He'd been wrong about many things where Bridget was concerned, but there'd been no mistaking that the woman he'd made love to on his desk had been a virgin. He looked to his wife, but all her attention was reserved for the bright-eyed child in her arms.

"Who are you?"

Vail tried to scrap together a coherent reply to the boy's world-wary question as he tried to sort through this equally peculiar reunion and meeting. "Vail Basingstoke, Lord Chilton." *It was a bloody miracle that he was even certain of that, anymore.* "And who are you?" he asked the more important of the questions.

Bridget held his gaze over the child's head. "This is Virgil," she said softly. "My son."

CHAPTER
20

DESPITE THE LATE HOUR AND the frequent noisy yawns from Nettie, Virgil prattled the whole carriage ride from Lambeth to Mayfair. And never before had Bridget been gladder for his penchant for talking.

Her skin burned with the intensity of Vail's stare trained on her, just as it had been since he'd ushered her and her family into the hired hack. After the unexpected reunion on those porch steps, he'd instructed Virgil and Nettie to gather their belongings and return to the hack. Had his orders been harsh and cold, it would have been easier than the gentleness of his tone when he'd spoken to her family.

"That is why you didn't come today, then, isn't it, Mama?" Virgil piped in cheerfully. "All day I was angry with you for not visiting but you were really preparing to bring me and Nettie with you."

Opposite her, Nettie wrung her hands together frantically; a cryptic worry in her eyes.

Seemingly content without a reply on Bridget's part, Virgil swung his line of questioning to a stoic Vail. "You married my mother?" His earlier childlike excitement gone, Virgil looked at Vail through narrowed eyes.

He nodded slowly. "I did."

Her son frowned and glanced up at Bridget. "Is he a good man?"

Her throat worked painfully. "He is," she promised. The only male Virgil had in his life before this moment had been the thankfully fleeting visits from his father. How very much he deserved a man such as Vail. Yet, any hope of a family with him had been doomed from the moment Archibald had set foot inside her cottage with his demands.

Virgil continued to peer at the baron, searchingly. "Well?" he demanded. "Is my mother right? Are you a good man?"

Her husband carefully removed his gloves and stuffed them away in his pocket. "I can tell you that I am, but it is far wiser for you to look at a person's actions, rather than listen to their mere words," he murmured.

She flinched at that veiled indictment of her character.

Thankfully, Virgil abandoned that dangerous line of querying. "What about the gentleman who hired you to examine his collection? Does that mean you aren't going to be working for him, anymore?"

Vail sharpened his gaze at those revealing words.

"This is His Lordship," she said weakly, praying her son would reveal nothing else, uncertain how to stymie his words without attracting Vail's further notice. "He is—was—my employer."

Some of her son's earlier chill dissipated. "You like books like my mother, then?"

Vail nodded. "I do." He paused. "And do you have your mother's skill with those books?"

"I do." The little boy puffed out his chest, proudly. "I'm quite good at it, too. I started helping when Mr. Lowell first—"

"There'll be time enough for talk with His Lordship, later," Nettie murmured, with that interruption ending the free rush of information her son handed over at Bridget's expense.

Virgil again looked to her. "Does this mean we'll not have to be parted anymore? That we'll be together?"

She brushed a stray curl back from his brow. "That is just what it means," she said gently, giving him that assurance when she couldn't say that. At last, her son settled into silence and, with the noisy roll of the carriage through London, she stared out the window. The truth was, for Virgil's worrying and his questions, she didn't truly know what would come in the days ahead with Vail or Archibald. The only certainty was the uncertainty now facing them. In the past, where that would have riddled her with terror, having Vail in her life eased the fear that weighted her shoulders. He might hate her, but seeing him usher off an old maid and small child to a hack had proved he would always help. She caught her chin in her hand and stared out the window at the passing streets. Vail was not one who'd be able to deny others in need. She'd thought that kindness was a gift only extended to his brothers and sisters but tonight, helping Virgil inside the hack, she'd seen the truth of his character. Her heart filled with overflowing love for him.

They arrived at Vail's townhouse. Glad for the night cover that kept Society's prying eyes from their coming home, Bridget accepted Vail's hand. Next, he helped Nettie, then Virgil out. Rejoining the driver, coins were exchanged, and as Vail spoke with the man, Bridget pressed ahead with Nettie at her side.

"You need to tell him, girl," the nursemaid spoke in low tones.

Keeping her eyes on Virgil dashing ahead, she nodded. "I know. I will. I—"

"Should have told His Lordship before he found out for himself," Nettie chided, peeking over her shoulder. "He's a handsome one," she added, off-topic. "And kind to the boy."

"He will...*would* be good to him," she murmured.

The front doors were opened by the second-butler, Mr. Hammell. As he ushered their party in, several footmen rushed outside to assist with their meager bags. It was a testament to the professionalism of Vail's staff that not a single one of the servants gave an outward indication that there was anything extraordinary about their employer and his new bride arriving with a pair of strangers and their tattered possessions.

"Hammell," her husband said from over her shoulder as he entered. "Help Mr. Hamlet and...?"

"Nettie, Your Lordship. My name is Nettie," the old servant replied.

"Miss Nettie, to guest chambers until something more permanent can be readied for them."

That was it. Knowing nothing more than that these people were her family, even with all that had passed, he'd still make that offer? Her heart filled with love for him all over again.

Her son yawned loudly and scratched at his head. "My name

isn't Hamlet."

Vail sharpened his gaze on the boy.

"It's—"

Nettie promptly placed her palm over his mouth, muffling that reply. "The lad's tired. We'll speak more with His Lordship tomorrow." She favored him with the same quelling look she'd used on Bridget when she'd misbehaved.

Frowning around her hand, he muttered something, the words lost.

Vail's keen eyes missed nothing. He carefully took in every nuance of their language and their bodies' movements.

"If you'll follow me?" Hammell motioned to the stairway leading to the main suites and, grateful for that brief reprieve from her husband's questioning, she fell into step beside her son.

"My lady? If you would join me in my office?" Vail called out.

She jerked to a stop, her foot poised over the first stair. Of course, it was both foolish and wrong to expect she was deserving of a reprieve. Given he'd followed her and then everything he'd discovered, he would rightfully have questions—ones he was entitled to have answers to. Nonetheless, Bridget struggled to swallow around the unease choking off her throat.

Several steps ahead, Virgil looked down questioningly. She gave him a reassuring smile and then feeling much the way that ill-fated Queen of France had marching up those steps to the guillotine, Bridget turned back to join her husband.

"Vail," she began when they started ahead.

"Not a word, madam," he bit out. "Not a single bloody word." She flinched at the fury pulsing in his smooth baritone. "I'll not have this discussion before a houseful of servants."

Her heart sank. There were too many lies for them to overcome and certainly for him to forgive. That reality was etched in the granite-like set to his chiseled features and that telltale tick at the corner of his eye.

They reached his office and he drew the door open. She hesitated. "Get. Inside."

Flinching at that icy veneer that she'd come to despise, wanting him to be the man he'd been all her weeks here prior and just before in the hack with Virgil. On numb legs, she forced herself ahead.

Vail closed the door behind him with a quiet, ominous click. "Well?" he demanded, bringing her reluctantly back to face him. He leaned against the wood panel; arms folded, one leg propped in a negligent pose belied by the piercing intensity of his eyes and tone.

She'd an entire ride here to prepare a reply. Nay, she'd had nearly a month. But in that time, she'd not allowed herself the possibility of telling him the truth of who she was. Her tongue grew heavy in her mouth. *I am a Hamilton. I am from a family of attempted murderers and rapists, and*—Bridget pressed her eyes tightly closed. *I am the thief of the family.*

"A son," he spat the word like a profanity. "That child is no more your son than he is mine."

She recoiled. He could have struck her and it couldn't have hurt more. She'd given up everything for Virgil. "How dare you?" She charged forward, coming so close the tips of their shoes brushed.

"How dare me?" A mocking laugh burst from his lips. "Everything about you has been a lie." The fight seemed to go out of him. "Everything."

That agonized whisper ripped through her. He was hurting. *I did this to him. I have hurt him.* She was no different than Adrina. "You are right." His body coiled tight again. "I deserve that. Your condemnation and doubts." She dropped her voice to a whisper. "I may not be the woman who gave him life, but I have loved him and taken care of him as though I did. I held him when he was sick and cheered as he took his first steps and cried as he spoke his first word." Her chest heaved. "And I would *not* let you take the one thing I've done right in my l-life," her voice broke and she spoke around the tears clogging her throat. "And make it wrong."

Vail gripped her shoulders as he'd done at Lambeth, but this time there was gentleness there. "Then make me understand," he pleaded.

Forcing her eyes open, she searched for a proper place to begin. She sucked in a steadying breath. "My name is Bridget." She needed him to know that at least was true. "I was born to a noble family."

He instantly stiffened.

When still he said nothing, she pressed ahead with her hated telling. "My parents had little use for me." That much was true.

"When they saw…when they saw…" She briefly palmed her marked cheek. His gaze slid over to the crescent birthmark.

How many years she'd spent letting that mark define her? Vail had never looked upon it as though it had mattered in any way and, for it, she herself had ceased to believe it did. "It is a family one," she explained. "Every one of our ancestors was cursed with that crescent, but theirs were always here." She touched her opposite wrist.

Realizing that she rambled, Bridget immediately ceased, and let her arms fall. "When I was four, they learned I was partially deaf. It didn't matter I still had use of one of my ears. Lords didn't marry cripples," she repeated that hollow echo her father had hurled at her head. "I was…sent away to the country. I never left." After that moment, in the whole of her life there'd been just two times she'd gone anywhere—very briefly to London with her babe, and then back to Leeds, and now the time she'd spent here. Disquieted by his penetrating stare, she wandered to a nearby Tole tray table. Absently, she traced her fingertips over the rider painted in red.

"Who is your family?" he demanded.

She stilled. Of course, he'd ask that question. As a nobleman with business connections all over England he'd certainly expect to know a member of the peerage. And yet, the minute she revealed the truth to him she'd cease to matter to him.

"Bridget."

She started, having failed to note his approach. He stood a mere foot away, tension rolling from his frame in waves. Shaking her head, she continued with her own order of the telling. "One day, a young woman arrived at my family's countryseat." Bridget hugged herself as the remembered horror of that day assailed her. "She was weeping and ashen. She had a babe in her arms. She'd said my… my brother was…" Her teeth chattered at her family's propensity for evil. "That my brother had raped her."

Vail drew back, shock slackened his jaw.

"She threatened to kill the babe if he didn't take it." Bridget looked down at the floor, hating the earliest memories of her son's life. And yet, he was here because of them. And she could never, ever regret that he'd been given life.

What evil had his wife known?

…I suspect understanding why she required those funds, is as important…

This is what Huntly had spoken of.

The earlier fury that had sent him to his office with her, dulled with every revelation.

The lady was of the nobility. He'd known that nearly from their first meeting by her cultured tones and literary mind, but he'd allowed himself to believe that she was perhaps the daughter of an impoverished lesser lord. Mayhap a country squire as Adrina had been. He'd not, however, allowed himself…any of *this*.

This ruthlessness she spoke of: parents who'd shun their child and treat her as though she were dead to the world and a brother capable of the greatest evil.

Vail brushed his knuckles under her chin, forcing her gaze up. "And you took the babe in."

Bridget offered a shaky nod. "I-I brought him to London. It was the first I'd ever been there since I was a child. It was so noisy and dark and wet. It rained the minute the mail coach arrived and continued until…" She clamped her teeth tight stymieing her rambling. "He wouldn't take him," she whispered. "I couldn't reason with him. I couldn't make him do right. He said if I was so very worried about the babe, then…"

"You could take him," he quietly provided.

Biting her lower lip, she nodded.

What that must have been for her, a sheltered young woman, alone…with no resources. The air lodged in his chest. "How old were you?"

"Seventeen."

Seventeen. When most young women were making their Come Outs, sipping lemonade at Almack's and strolling Hyde Park, she'd been caring for a motherless babe. Where he? He'd been too busy wooing a grasping woman to look after anyone, except his own desiring.

"The boy…your son, Virgil is why you came here."

Tears welled in her eyes, and she nodded.

…People are no different. You cannot neatly file them as sinners or saints. We are all simply people, flawed by our own rights…surviving in an uncertain world…

She'd accused him of seeing the world in black and white, and for his insistence on the accuracy of that viewing of people and life around them, she'd been correct. There were shades of gray in between what he'd previously taken as certain truths.

He registered the absolute stillness and looked to his wife. A battle warred in her expressive eyes. "Oh, God." She searched about and then slid into a nearby King Louis XIV chair. "I want to tell you all," she explained pleadingly. "I want to tell you everything and know that it will be all right." A sob burst from her throat. "But how do I do that?" she begged. "How can I give you the answers you deserve if it might hurt my son?"

What battles she'd fought and continued to, on her own. Initially, he'd only wanted answers to assuage his own frustrations and anger. Now, he wanted to take the burden that she'd carried for too many years. Heart splitting in two, Vail stalked over and knelt beside her chair. He gathered her hands in his. "Tell me," he urged. "Not because you believe I deserve answers, tell me because you want me to share whatever this is."

"My brother…" She exhaled slowly through her compressed lips. In her eyes, he saw the battle she fought. Vail waited in silence, giving her the time she required. When she spoke, her voice emerged as a threadbare whisper. "My brother threatened to take Virgil if I did not… *steal* your Chaucer."

Vail sank back on his haunches. Given her earlier deception, everything Bridget gave him could be a lie. It could be a thief's attempt to play upon his sympathies and yet—

She eyed him warily. By the resignation he spied there, she expected him to doubt her. He sighed and dusted a hand over his face.

"Who is your family?" he asked again, quietly. Were they people he'd hosted at balls or conducted business with? His stomach churned at the prospect.

Bridget's face crumpled and she dropped her gaze once more. It was the second time he'd put that question to her and the second she'd evaded answering. Hugging her arms to her chest, she looked up, and held his stare. "My brother is the Marquess of Atbrooke."

The Marquess of Atbrooke.

Atbrooke.

More slimy than the worms he'd used for fishing as a lad, the man had been run off the Continent a couple of years earlier and had since returned. His love of whores, drink, and wagering was the only thing that called him to London. He'd not, however, been a man Vail had ever done business with. The man also had a sister—

All the air exploded from his lungs and burst from his lips. He jumped up. "Lady Marianne Carew." Huntly's former lover. A viper who'd attempted to kill Lady Justina. His stomach lurched. "This is your family," he repeated, sick, struggling to divorce who she was from the people whose blood she shared. He'd brought her into Nick and Justina's home as a guest. On the heel of that was shame. *I am not my father and neither is Bridget her family and yet…* He closed his eyes briefly, hating her connection to those fiends, anyway.

Bridget winced, saying nothing.

Struggling under the weight of all she'd revealed, Vail pressed his fingertips against his temples. What if they were just more lies? What if she were, in fact, as evil as her brother and sister and this tale was nothing more than a ploy to weaken him? He'd been made the fool two times now where a woman was concerned.

"Will you not say anything?" she pleaded.

"What would you have me say?" He no longer knew which way was up, down, or sideways, anymore.

Tears spiked her thick auburn lashes. "Anything. Tell me you hate me. Or tell me you believe me. Just say *something*."

In the end, he gave her the truth. "It is a lot to take in," he confessed. *And accept.*

Her lower lip trembled and she caught that plump flesh between her teeth, steadying it. "I know." She shoved to her feet. "I should see to Virgil."

"Of course." Bridget lingered, opening her mouth as though she wished to say more, but then left.

As soon as she'd gone, he unleashed a flood of curses. *Bloody, bloody hell.* This was who her family had to be? And yet, that would have mattered less had she come to him without lying about her identity…and a mountain full of secrets.

In desperate need of a drink, Vail stalked to his sideboard and poured himself a tall snifter. He took a long, slow swallow.

"So, you're my mother's husband."

He choked on his swallow, until tears streamed down his cheeks.

Glass in hand, he spun so quickly, sending liquid spilling over the side and splashing the floor.

Bridget's son slammed the door behind him and came rushing forward. "Look up," Virgil ordered. He took the snifter from Vail's grip and slapped him on the back with what he suspected was all his strength.

"L–Look up?" he managed to rasp out between choking, gasping breaths.

The small boy shrugged. "My mum always says it helps."

After Vail's paroxysm dissolved into a manageable, occasional cough he retrieved his drink and took another, smaller sip.

"My mum also says to drink a bit of water, but I expect that should do, as well." The little boy eyed the glass in his hand curiously. "Is that good?"

"Honestly?"

Virgil nodded.

"It's rot. But the more you drink it, the taste eventually grows upon you."

His nighttime visitor grunted. "Mum said that men who drink spirits aren't to be trusted and said I should never, ever drink it. Ever." By the rote-like deliverance, it was a familiar warning the boy had heard frequently uttered.

The glass trembled in Vail's hands as the solemnity of that boy's tone pierced the brief camaraderie. For with a handful of words, Virgil had offered an unwitting glimpse into Bridget's life. He searched the boy for some indication that he'd heard the discussion on his origins at the doorway but found none. Having only found his siblings when they were all largely grown, he'd little familiarity with children being underfoot and listening at keyholes. With Erasmus' difficulty comprehending and his struggle to hear, there'd been not even a thought that he might hear something he ought not. Searching for ground around this new person, he finally said, "Not all gentlemen who partake are bad. It is the ones who are unable to moderate themselves, who overindulge and let it consume them we should be wary of."

"Like my uncle."

It was a statement of fact. Vail stiffened.

The boy stuffed his hands inside his pockets, bringing Vail's attention to those modest, threadbare garments. They spoke to how this child and his family had lived. Vail tightened his grip around his snifter, hating the signs of struggle Bridget had known. "He drinks a lot," Virgil clarified.

"And does he come 'round a lot?" he asked, unashamedly pulling whatever he could from Bridget's son. Only more than wheedling information, there was a genuine need to know.

Virgil flattened his mouth into a hard line; that flash of cynicism counter to his otherwise innocent transparency. "Sometimes."

"And is he—?"

"You're looking for me to tell you about my family," the child said bluntly, with a shocking candidness and intuitiveness.

Vail blinked slowly.

"You want to know about my uncle? Why?" he asked, narrowing his eyes into thin slits.

Why? The immediate answer for Vail *should* be: that he didn't trust Atbrooke, Bridget, or any of this family. "Because I care about your mother," he said quietly, instead. *Because I love her. I loved her since the moment I came upon her in my office and she blurted out every last thought upon her lips.* The enormity of that hit him with the force of a fast-moving carriage. He didn't know if he could trust her. He didn't know if there were other lies that would come to light between them. But there was no understanding the heart.

Virgil spoke, breaking through that tumult. "You believe you can keep her safe…*us*, safe?" Color splashed the boy's cheeks. Was he ashamed in needing help? The sight of his pride and that devotion to his mother settled like a weight on Vail's chest.

"Do you believe you need to be kept safe?" he asked instead.

"Everyone does." Virgil rolled his small shoulders. Then, he glanced about, his eyes lighting up as he took in the shelving units. "Are these all your books?" he asked, as only a child was capable of moving off topic.

Vail followed his stare about the room. "Some of them."

The little boy wandered away from him and picked his way around the perimeter, going from shelf to shelf. "My mum loves to read." He paused beside one title and looked back. "She's always working and has to give them back afterward, but when Mr. Lowell brings them to her, I'll find her reading the passages at night, and not just evaluating the condition."

Vail didn't know who Mr. Lowell was, but the images the boy

drew forth, squeezed at his heart. Imaginings of a tired Bridget, sitting by a dying hearth, and reading, until that book was eventually taken back.

A memory slid forward of how Bridget had been her first day here, wholly captivated by the titles in his office. Her eyes had glowed with the same joy most women would have in looking upon a fine diamond.

"Can I look at your collections?" Virgil asked, the question emerging reluctantly.

"You have freedom to use whichever rooms you wish. My home is yours now." There was a lightness in his chest that came from that admission. "There'll also be tutors," he murmured, more to himself. He made a silent note to have Edward find the best for the lad. And in time, there would be Eton and Oxford...or Cambridge, should he wish it. He'd have every opportunity Vail himself hadn't.

Virgil shifted back and forth on his feet. "Thank you," he mumbled.

If he couldn't do right by this boy's mother, at least he could do right by the lad himself.

CHAPTER 21

"I HAVE INFORMATION."

Seated in his office, head bent over his ledgers, Vail looked up. Having revealed all Bridget had shared about Atbrooke, his brother had begun searching for the man's whereabouts and locating his contacts in London. And Vail, unsure how one was supposed to be around one's wife after everything she'd revealed, he had also steered clear of her.

Colin stood in the doorway, a grim set to his mouth. Vail slowly released his pen and urged him forward. He made to rise, but Colin waved him off. Gavin closed the door, leaving them alone.

"What is it?" he asked as Colin claimed one of the winged chairs opposite him.

"I've found a good deal about the family and their connections here in London." Flipping open his book, he turned it around.

His stomach muscles knotting, Vail had to make himself look at those pages. He reluctantly dragged his gaze over Colin's illegible handwriting, grateful when the other man turned it back to read from.

"She's lived in Leeds for nearly ten years." The year she'd taken in Virgil. That had proven accurate. "Prior to that, she lived in Yorkshire. The parents hired a nursemaid," Nettie, "to care for her and washed their hands of her. All of that proved accurate." She'd not been lying on those details. Ironically, after every fabrication and his own desire for the truth, he wished this had been one more falsity she'd fed him. Because he'd rather have found more lies than the truth of the agonizing existence she'd lived.

With every detail confirmed and with every new revelation, a boulder-like weight settled on his chest, restricting airflow and making it impossible to draw forth an even breath. Loathing for the parents who'd sired her and then forgotten her gripped him so strong he gave thanks they were dead and already writhing in hell for their sins against her.

"There is more," Colin, said, that somberness driving a wedge into Vail's tortured musings.

"Atbrooke secured work for the lady evaluating old texts. A…" Dipping his gaze, he searched through his notes.

"Mr. Lowell?"

"Yes," his brother confirmed. "In exchange for securing her work, Atbrooke received a portion of her payments."

A murderous rage simmered hot in his veins. It was fortunate for both him and Atbrooke that the bastard wasn't present for he would have run him through, and then gladly gone to Newgate for it.

"He's been on the Continent for two years, after he was run off by Viscount Wessex."

"Wessex?" Vail creased his brow. One of the most affable gents in London, the viscount never had a bad thing to say to anyone and there certainly weren't any dealings those two should have together.

"I haven't been able to find the connection between them, just enough to know there is no love lost between them." His brother proceeded to read methodically from his notes. "Recently returned from the Continent, he's been taking up residence at his various properties but there's nothing left to sell or wager. No one will extend him credit."

Which is why he's hatched the scheme to steal from me. It was a natural connection. Send him a young woman capable and skilled with antique texts, and she'd have access to a fortune at her fingertips.

"Which is why he could have hatched the scheme?" Colin murmured, snapping his book closed. "*Perhaps.*"

Unaware he'd uttered those earlier words, he looked up. "Do you have proof linking him?" Anything that Vail could coerce the man with and see him in prison over. The threat needed to be gone. Atbrooke needed to be gone. Until he was, there could never be any peace for Bridget and Virgil. Nor could he and his wife move forward as long as her brother lingered in the shadows, prepared to use her like a pawn. And having learned of the sacrifices she'd made and witnessing her love for the child, he'd no doubt she would make the same decisions she had—even if it involved stealing from him. Nor, if he were being honest with himself, could he hold that against her. Then Colin's earlier words registered. "Which is why he *could* have hatched the scheme? What are you saying, Colin?" he urged at his brother's silence.

The other man tossed his notebook down on a corner of Vail's desk. "I'm sorry, Vail. Thus far, all I have is Atbrooke's name. I have a motive, but I can't locate any people connecting him to the attempted theft." He paused, holding his stare. "There's only her."

There's only her.

Those three words lingered in the air, both damning and warning. Why…why…Colin was suggesting Bridget was guilty? Impossible. He shoved forward in his seat. "What about the two gentlemen meeting at the Coaxing Tom?" Someone had to know something. "Did you interview Tabitha?"

Colin frowned. Vail, however, had larger concerns than Colin's bruised ego at having his work questioned. "Numerous times. She provided descriptions which I've circulated to the men who were in the club that night. No one had names." Colin stared back, pityingly. "No one."

Vail thinned his eyes into narrow slits. "What?" he growled, at the suspicions there.

"Vail," he began.

"Just say it," he snapped. *Say what I'm already thinking.*

"The fact that her brother was a rotter," And she took his child in. "And the fact that she's been treated equally rottenly by her family doesn't mean anyone but the lady herself orchestrated the plan."

He sank back in his chair. "You're wrong," he said hollowly.

Colin dragged a hand through his hair. "If you were another client, I'd tell you to open your damned eyes. I'd not spare you from details or tolerate your questioning. But you *are* related to me and the career I have is because of you, but neither will I lie to you." He scraped his green eyes over Vail's office and then looked to him once more. "I've caught all manner of people, guilty of crimes: men, women, children. Lords, ladies. All of them," he said with a wave of his hand. "Do you know what I discovered in every case, from every person I apprehended?"

Unable to form a verbal reply, he shook his head woodenly.

"That desperation will make a person do desperate things."

…The story is of a girl who never knew loving parents, who were wholly incapable of sacrificial love…

It had been her, in every way. She'd been trying to tell him. He pressed his eyes closed. Did it even matter knowing? Did it matter what…rather, who had brought her into his household?

"I understand you care for her," Colin said gravely. *Love her. I love her.* "But sometimes the world is just black and white."

…One might see red and green and yellow and purple, but sometimes buried within are other shades… "Mm. Mm," he said, giving his head another firm shake. "You are wrong on this." Because what was the alternative? That even her love had been a lie? "You are wrong."

He wanted his brother to fight him. Wanted to pound his fists and drive out the uncertainty. Instead, Colin merely inclined his head. "I'm never wrong."

A knock sounded at the door and they looked as one.

"The Duke of Huntly," Gavin announced, letting Vail's best friend in. He'd arrived, Vail having put aside this task for two days now.

"I'll leave you to your visit," Colin said, collecting his items. "If you've need of me, send word."

"Of course."

Huntly claimed the seat just vacated by Colin. "What was that about?" he asked, astute when most lords would have missed the underlying tension between Vail and Colin's parting.

Needing to have it said, he spoke without preamble. "My wife is the sister of Lady Marianne Carew."

Huntly may as well have turned to stone. He sat, carved of granite, his eyes unblinking. "What?" that terse question emerged through tightly clenched lips. Did he expect the other man to be as forgiving of Bridget's crimes when he learned her true identity?

"She is Lord Atbrooke's eldest sister. She'd been shut away in the country." His hands formed involuntary fists on his lap. As he concluded the telling, he kept a careful eye on his friend's response. But for a slight paling of his skin, he gave no outward indication to the revelation.

"I…see," Huntly finally said. "It's a vile family."

He managed a jerky nod, hating that Bridget was part of it.

"My father killed himself."

Vail went still.

"Lord Rutland called in his loans and debt and my father? Hanged himself from above his desk. I concealed that from the world," he said quietly, unexpectedly.

My God. "I…I had no idea." These were the demons that had driven him to exact revenge on Lord Rutland.

"Your father? Some might argue is even more of a disgrace in how he cares for, or rather does not care for his offspring."

The other man was correct on that score.

"We're not our blood. We are our actions." There should be something freeing in that pardon but given Colin's visit and revelations, there could not be.

"Colin believes she acted without influence. That she's now passing blame to her brother."

"And what do you believe?" Huntly asked hooking his ankles together.

"I don't know," he confided, in pained tones. "I want to trust her. But had I not discovered her in the act and demanded her marriage, she'd be gone even now."

His friend grimaced. "In that, it is more complicated, and I can only—unhelpfully—say, that you have to trust what you know in your heart about the lady."

Shouts sounded in the hallway and the rapid beat of footfalls. The door flew open with such force it nearly slammed into Edward. Framed in the entrance, out of breath, a paper in his hands, he dropped his hands atop his knees. "Vail," he got out. "The Chaucer is gone."

"What?"

"And there is something else," he rushed forward, that page outstretched.

Dazed, trying to make sense of why Edward was brandishing a copy of his marriage certificate, he read those lines over and over…and then stopped at one name: Bridget Petrosinella Hamlet.

Not Bridget Hamilton.

His fingers clenched the edges of the page, wrinkling it.

By God, she'd used a false name.

They weren't married.

Two days later, Bridget didn't know what she'd expected in having revealed the truth of Virgil's parentage. But in sharing everything she had with Vail, she had abandoned the agreement to help Archibald. She'd put her trust in Vail and the hope that her wastrel brother wouldn't have truly set aside his wastrel ways to care for a child.

In short, she'd wagered with his life.

Nausea churned in her belly still and she fought the urge to cast up the contents of her stomach. With Nettie napping at her chair and Virgil playing spillikins on the floor before her, there was an air of familiarity to all this…and yet a sense of doom lingered in the air. It was silly, nonsensical worrying conjured of her mind, but also born of the uncertainty that now came as she awaited Archibald's next move.

Not only that, Vail had also become a stranger. Oh, he was polite and pleasant when they shared morning meals and supped together and he was kind toward her son, talking freely with him about his literary interests. But everything had changed since she'd revealed she was a Hamilton.

"Vail said I'll have a new tutor by the end of the week," Virgil directed that at the stick he carefully tried to extricate from another.

He'd already set to securing instructors for her son. No questions asked. No resentments held and carried over to the boy. Rather, he'd spend the necessary funds to hire that which she'd never been able to provide. Her throat moved spasmodically as she was filled with a renewed love and appreciation for the man he was.

"He *also* said that in the autumn I'd be able to go on to Eton." Virgil paused and looked up from his game. "But that they only let you in that school at certain times of the year."

A smile quivered on her lips. Vail had, and would continue to give Virgil everything she would have never, in the whole of her lifetime, have done for him.

Tossing aside the stick, Virgil popped up. "Is he angry at you?"

She stared unblinkingly. How had she failed to realize how perceptive he was? "No," she lied. She'd witnessed Vail's anger two days ago. But he was more than angry: hurt, disappointed, and wary. "Why would you think that?" she asked instead.

He shrugged. "You don't talk to one another." Virgil wrinkled his nose. "Not that I would want to talk to a girl, myself, but it just seems that you'd say something to each other."

She set aside the copy of Dante's *Inferno* she'd been reading and patted the spot next to her. "Come here," she urged. Virgil was old enough and astute enough that he was also entitled to some truth and answers. "Vail is a good man and I know that must be…confusing, given that you haven't had any in your life. But one day, I told him a lie…and so he's…." She searched her mind. "Cautious, now."

"What did you lie about?" Of course, no ten-year-old boy would be content to leave that detail unexplored.

Bridget sighed. "Someday, I'll explain it all to you. But for now, understand that he is entitled to his reservations. And when one tells a lie, one must work to gain back that trust. And it's not always easy. It's not ever easy." Nor did she even know if Vail wanted to repair what they'd shared this past month.

Virgil looked to the doorway and she followed his stare over. Her heart started.

He'd come. It was the first time he'd sought her out these past two days. "Vail," she breathed, hopping up.

Nettie snorted herself awake. "What is it? Where…?" Groggy, she joined Bridget on her feet, offering a lazy curtsy. "My lord."

"Virgil, Nettie, if you'll excuse us a moment?"

Her son hesitated and she gave his hand a gentle squeeze. "Run along. We'll talk more after." She looked to Nettie.

"Come along, lad," she repeated, gathering Virgil by the hand and ushering him out.

"Vail," she greeted. They'd made love. She'd shared more parts of herself than she ever had with another person, and yet she was more uncertain in this instance than she had been their first meeting.

He pulled the door shut, saying nothing.

She took in the grim set to his mouth. "What is it?" she asked, worry settling like a stone in her belly. For the first time since he'd entered, she noticed the paper in his hand.

"After you discovered the Chaucer, I never found a different hiding place for it."

He spoke of words that should have hinted at his trust. Bridget wetted her lips and met his vagueness with silence. All the while, an ominous chill rolled through her, freezing her from the inside out. "I don't…" She shook her head, searching for some reply. "I don't…"

"Edward just found me. The Chaucer is gone."

A dull humming filled her ears. That precious tome she'd been sent to steal had been gone. Then, the implications of what Vail danced around and suggested but didn't say. "You think I stole it," she breathed, her voice coming as if down a long hall.

"This is a copy of our marriage certificate."

She struggled to follow that abrupt shift and then did… Oh, God. Her gut clenched, and she sought to steady herself on the edge of the sofa.

"We're not married."

"No," she said on a broken whisper.

"You're not my wife," he repeated a different way, like one who sought to embed certain words on one's brain might.

"I did it for you." She willed him to understand. "I knew you'd regret it. I knew—"

"Do not put this lie on me, madam," he thundered and she cried out, stifling that agonized moan in her palm. "Colin came to visit. He found nothing linking Atbrooke to the theft. He found nothing about the gentleman whatsoever."

The air left her on a painful exhale. He didn't believe her. And why should he? What reason had she given him to trust her? She searched around, panicked, as her world crumpled about her all over again. She needed him to understand. Needed him to see that all the lies were not wholly tied. Bridget stretched a palm toward him. "I did not use Hamilton on the marriage certificates. You are correct."

He laughed emptily. "Of course, I am," he spat.

"But I did do it for you. I knew after you met with Marlborough and had that collection, you'd no more need for me." She just hadn't realized at the time that she'd also be freeing him for the earl's daughter; a woman certainly more deserving of him than Bridget herself.

"You thought it should be so easy?" he asked, stunned. "That you'd simply disappear and that the *ton* wouldn't ask about where my bloody wife had gone?" he bellowed again.

She jumped. "I just thought—"

"You thought of everything. Haven't you? All along."

"What are you saying?" she repeated, her voice hollow to her ears wanting him to put his belief out between them.

"The only certainty is my Chaucer is gone and I don't know about anything else."

The door opened and Edward entered. A flash of loathing filled his gaze when he looked at Bridget. "Your mount is readied."

"I'll be along shortly," he said tightly.

"Where are you going?" she asked achingly.

"To find my damned book, madam. We are through discussing this." With that, he stalked out of the room.

Go after him. Go tell him all. Bridget's legs gave out from under her and she slid into a heap on the floor, too numb for tears, too numb to think.

A small hand rested on her shoulder and she looked up blankly. "Virgil?" she whispered. Her heart raced. How much had he heard? "Why aren't you with Nettie?"

"I slipped off." He gulped loudly. "He's really angry now."

This time, over one crime she was not guilty of. "Yes," she confirmed, welcoming the press of his slender frame at her side, selfishly taking comfort there.

"I heard him," he confided in hushed tones. "*Yelling.* I thought before this that he might be different than Uncle Archibald."

"He is!" That truth burst from her. She'd not ever let her son, or any person link those two very different men. One was capable of only goodness who'd only been wronged in life. The other was sin incarnate.

"Well, he doesn't sound as though he's one who could take care of us."

Her already cracking heart, ripped all the more. She'd thought she'd shielded him, only finding now just how much she'd failed to insulate her son from the uncertainty that was the world. She sought to give him assurances that all would be well. That they'd have a home here still but could not even formulate the lie. Absently, she ran her fingers through his thick brown curls.

He angled away from her touch. "It's about the Chaucer?"

"Partly. It's…" She ripped her gaze down. What…?

His eyes formed round pools with fear emanating from their depths.

"What do you know of it?"

"I might know something of it," he said, his voice cracking. Going on her knees, she leaned down to meet his gaze. "I was visiting the mews last night and Uncle Archibald came by." Her stomach lurched. Oh, God. "He said…he told me that he'd take me away from you. That the only way to be sure I never left you was if I found him that book." A moan tore from her throat and she dragged her son into her arms.

"I'm in trouble, aren't I? The baron is going to see me hanged."

"He's not," she said her mind whirring. "When did you give it to him?"

"This morning." She strained to pick up his small voice. "I don't want to live with him," he whimpered.

"Never." Grabbing his hands, she pulled Virgil to his feet and squeezed them gently. "You will never, ever live with him. Ever." She flattened her lips. She needed to retrieve that book for Vail… and end this once and for all.

"What are you doing?" her son asked as she slid into a nearby secretaire, and rifled through the desk.

She'd brought this to Vail's life. She'd set it to rights. Dipping a pen in the crystal inkwell, she hastily scratched a note. "I'm going to see your uncle." He made a sound of protest. "Stop," she commanded, that firmness seemed to penetrate his worrying. Focused on the words she wrote, she spoke to her son. "I will return. I promise. I always do. If I don't return by tomorrow morning," she paused. "You are to give this to His Lordship."

"What is it?" he asked, as she sprinkled pounce upon the ink.

Bridget blew on it. "'Tis a letter that you're only to give if I don't return."

"But you'll return," he pleaded.

Vail had given her everything. She would do this for him. She set her jaw. "Always."

CHAPTER
22

DUSTY, TIRED, AND NUMB, VAIL jumped down from his mount and tossed the reins to a waiting servant.

Through his brother's revelation about the Chaucer, he'd set out for some hint of Lord Atbrooke. And mayhap it spoke to his own weakness, but he'd spent the day searching out that gentleman, looking for some proof of what Bridget had said. All his contacts in the lower ends of London and in every damned hell had revealed nothing. The man may as well be a damned specter.

Entering through the doors as Gavin pulled them open, he shrugged out of his cloak. "D-Did you find it," Gavin whispered.

He shook his head once. "No."

Of course, everyone, his siblings included, would expect that Vail was off looking for that coveted volume up for auction next week. All he'd ever thought about his entire adult life was his business and his fortunes. It had been Bridget who'd shown him that something more mattered…if one focused only on providing for one's family, one lost every moment one had with them, too.

"It's fine," he said quietly, squeezing Gavin's shoulder. "It really is. It is just a book."

His brother nodded and, head down, shuffled off.

Vail stared after his retreating frame letting those words settle in his mind. The Chaucer was just a book. It was one of value that would fetch a fortune, but the words inside that particular copy didn't truly mean anything to him. Rather, what that book represented was what had brought Bridget into his life…and now what was threatening to tear her out of it.

He stared briefly up the curved staircase, wanting to go to her. *Go to her, then.* This woman he wasn't truly married to.

I did it for you.

She'd freed him. Only, she'd made the decision as to what he needed, and again fed him a lie. Tired, he shifted direction and sought out his office.

As soon as he closed the door, his eyes found the small figure perched on the chair at his desk; Virgil's small form swallowed impossibly by the leather folds. "Virgil," he greeted, thrusting aside his own melancholy.

"My lord."

Seated as he was, with his arms layered upon the desk and a folded sheet of parchment resting under his folded hands, Vail had a glimpse of the man Virgil would one day grow into. The boy made to stand, but he waved him back into the chair.

"Thank you, sir. My lord."

"Just Vail. Please, just Vail."

The boy's Adam's apple bobbed. "Do you know the problem with being a child, sir…Vail?"

"Oh, I remember any number of them," he confessed, sitting in the chair across from him.

"Yes, that's true." He scrunched up his little brow. "Everyone thinks you don't hear what's going on or don't understand it. And so, they speak freely around you. I know she's not my mother."

Vail stilled. Oh, God. Had he and Bridget in their discussions revealed the truth to the boy?

"Knew for some time. Overheard Nettie. She's got looser lips than my mum. I heard what you said to her. The night we came here as a family." A family. That is what they were. Or, that is what Vail wanted with her—with them. It's what he'd always been in search of; since before he was younger than the boy across from him.

His chest tightened with the dream for more with both Bridget and this small boy. "Which part?" he asked hoarsely, more than half-fearing the answer.

"Calling her a liar." If looks could kill Vail would have been dead at this boy's feet—and deservedly so. "Saying I wasn't her son."

Gutted by what he'd casually tossed out, he hung his head.

"I don't need you to make her feel bad for it, either. About taking me in and lying to me." Vail winced, properly shamed and humbled by a ten-year-old child. Virgil jutted his chin out and met Vail's gaze with a ruthless promise in his eyes that revealed the strength of his character and the man he'd one day be. "She may not have birthed me, but she's loved me as her own, and I'll not have you, bastard, baron, businessman, dare make her feel less. Sometimes lies are important. Even I know that." Virgil slid the page under his hands toward Vail.

"What is this?" he asked when he trusted himself to speak.

"I was to give it to you if my mum didn't return by tomorrow."

Vail ceased to breathe. "What?" he asked, that question faint.

"*I* took your book," he said, his earlier bravado gone. "I found it and turned it over to my un…to *him*…thought he'd go away and figured you certainly wouldn't go poor for missing it." He glanced about the stocked shelves. Then Virgil's bravado crumpled and his lower lip trembled slightly, revealing the truth and reminder that he was just a boy. "He'll hurt her, sir. And I don't know if I can trust you, but I think you're able to help her and so I'd ask you to do so."

Vail's heart rattled against his ribcage. As terror swamped his senses, he fought for calm. The little boy staring back reflected his own dread. Bridget hadn't been made for the ruthlessness Vail witnessed daily from his clients. She wasn't a match for Atbrooke's evil. "I'll bring her back," he promised. "Run along."

After Bridget's son had gone, Vail tore open the letter written in Bridget's hand.

My dearest Vail,

I've told so many lies it's hard to ask you to sort through what is the truth. I have loved you since the moment you came upon me in the Portrait Room. You are all that is good.—His throat constricted—*"I did not steal the Chaucer, but I did come to rob you. That is true. My brother won't rest until he has that book, but we've taken so much I'd not let him have this, too."*

An agonized groan tore from his chest, better suited a wounded beast. It meant nothing. She was his everything.

"If anything were to happen to me, I ask you to please care for Virgil. Ever Yours,
Bridget

He squeezed his eyes shut. "Damn you, Bridget." Tearing from the room, he shouted the house down for his horse...and her nursemaid, Nettie.

Her life had, in a way, come full circle.

Bridget returned to this hated place of sadness and irresponsibility and evil. One where she was turned back ten years earlier, without a coin to help her, and only a foundling babe in need of a family.

Carefully picking her way through the side alley connecting the two buildings, she found her way, not this time through the front door of this townhouse but the kitchens. A cool breeze stole through the mews and she huddled deeper inside her cloak. Shifting the velvet sack in her arms, she pressed the door handle and let herself in.

As she closed the heavy panel behind her, she blinked, adjusting her eyes to the dimly lit space, and then found a lone servant sprawled at the kitchen table. Head down, a tankard beside his arm, the servant snored. Biting the inside of her cheek, she tiptoed past the young man from the kitchens.

For all her brother's vices and all he'd cost their family, the lack of reliable, underfoot servants was the one gift he'd given. Bridget drifted through the hallways. This townhouse had been home to her for the first four years of her life and yet the memories here were so fleeting, filled only with the distant echo of her parents' derisive words and her brother's jeering laughter.

No good had ever come from her being in London. Even her time with Vail, who'd forever hold her heart, had been marked by darkness.

But then, mayhap that was simply the way of the Hamiltons. That it could not be purged from who they were and was destined to follow them. Thrusting aside her useless regrets, she began her search. Bridget moved from room to darkened room. The same sofas and curtains hung, now tears and faded colors marked their age. The porcelain vases and fripperies gone, no doubt sold by her wastrel brother. Empty, faded paint marked places on the walls where portraits once hung. The barrenness of her family's town-house made her search easy.

As every room revealed nothing more than dust and ancient memories, her frustration mounted.

She reached the end of another hall. "Think," she mouthed. Holding her velvet sack, she did a slow circle. What was important to Archibald? What had been anything he could have never lived without?

Nothing. Nothing mattered. He'd always been too busy whoring, drinking and…

Bridget stopped mid-turn. Her eyes flew wide. Spinning left, she started down the corridor. She entered the billiards room, doing a sweep. The red velvet table, though faded, still gleamed from the shine on the mahogany wood. The crystal chandeliers sparkled. She honed her gaze on the sideboard in the corner.

And the sideboard was well-stocked. Heart knocking wildly with a growing hope, she set down her bag. Dropping to her knees, she did a search under the table, stretching her arms, she felt about. She bumped her head on the bottom of the sideboard and grunted as her chignon came loose and her hair fell about her shoulders and waist.

Nothing.

She shoved up onto her knees and froze, as her gaze collided with the small silver circle on the sideboard door. Palms shaking, she tugged it open.

Bridget's eyes slid closed and she sent a brief prayer skyward. She made quick work of switching out the newer edition of Chaucer's work with the prized one Vail had going to auction and placed it inside the gold velvet bag. Crawling under the billiards table, she frantically scanned the floorboards, looking for and finding one specific plank. Digging her nails into the faint cracks along the slide, she lifted the board and tucked Vail's book inside. It gave with a satisfying click. Scrambling out, she rushed back to close the door of the sideboard.

"Tsk, tsk." Bridget froze, her fingers damningly on the door of her brother's liquor case as a hated voice drifted over to her good ear. Dread stuck in her throat and held her motionless. "Stealing from one's sibling. Why, you *are* a Hamilton. If it weren't me you were stealing from, I would say I was proud. Get up," he clipped out, yanking her up by her upper arm.

He forced a cold smile; the only one she'd seen her brother don in the whole of his miserable life. "Archibald," she greeted, angling her chin up, defiantly. "I would say it is a pleasure but it has never—" He backhanded her across the cheek.

Bridget cried out and went flying backward. She caught herself against the wall. Stars danced behind her eyes and she blinked them back.

"You were always useless," he said, his tone hopelessly bored like one speaking on the weather. He strolled toward her and, legs shaking, she retreated. "And here I thought I'd found one single task you could accomplish. I asked that you get me that damned book and you couldn't even do that. My son, however, proves he's very much my child."

Fury burned hot through her veins. "He is not your son, you bastard," she hissed.

Archibald shot out his other palm, catching her again on the cheek. She went down hard on her knees. Pain shot along her jaw. Cradling her cheek, the metallic hint of blood tinged her mouth, flooding her senses.

Her brother grinned.

Refusing to give him any more satisfaction, she let her hand fall back to her side. "I'm not letting you do this."

"I already did it." Bridget darted around him making for the velvet sack, crying out as he wrenched her arm high behind her back. "I'm taking it and leaving tonight." Gathering her by her hair, he drove her forehead into the edge of the billiards table.

A piteous moan spilled from her lips as she battled the inky blackness pulling at the corners of her vision. Not wanting to give in to that darkness, she fought it, as under the table a pair of legs appeared in the doorway. And it must have been the effects of Archibald's blows, but through the agony pounding at her head, Vail's face drifted over—lined with fury and yet tender at the same time.

The pull proved too great—and she pitched forward, slipping into unconsciousness.

Nettie had gathered the one place Bridget had likely gone. She'd come here. To confront her brother and rescue a damned book Vail would just as gladly set fire to if it meant she would be safe.

Now, he did a quick sweep of Atbrooke's billiards room. "Where is my wife?"

"N-Not sure what you're talking about, Ch-Chilton," the marquess stammered from the opposite end of the table. He yanked at his lapels. "C-Certainly not the thing entering a man's home. Baron or no, I-I'm a marquess and can have a constable called."

Vail laid his palms on the opposite end of the table. "Wrong response," he whispered and started forward.

The marquess squeaked as Vail approached; a predator with his prey in sight.

"S-stop there," that shaky command emerged as a desperate plea.

Vail continued coming and then stopped. His heart stopped beating and sank to his stomach and dropped down to his toes. *"Bridget."*

She lay sprawled face-first with half of her body concealed under the table and her legs jutting out.

"Sh-she came to steal from me," Lord Atbrooke's voice was pitched high. "Anyone would say—ahh."

With a thunderous roar, Vail charged forward and, gripping the other man by the throat, he propelled him to the floor. Drawing back his fist he drove it into the other man's nose. The satisfying crack melded with the man's agonized screams. A sticky stream of blood coated Vail's hands as he rained down blow after blow, knocking the marquess' head against the hardwood floor. Wanting him to hurt as he'd hurt Bridget and her son over the years. Wanting to kill him and yet wanting him to live all at the same time so he could happily torture him until he drew his last breath.

"Vail." Colin's voice penetrated, as if from a distance, through the fog of hatred, madness, and bloodlust. Snarling, Vail grabbed Atbrooke by the throat and choked his limp frame. "Vail." Hands scrabbled with his back and he fought against the hold, wrestling free of that grip.

Colin slapped him hard across the face, wrenching him back

from the precipice of madness. Chest heaving, Vail struggled to get air into his lungs. He blinked wildly. So this is what it was to go mad. Releasing the marquess, the man's body fell with a satisfying thump and Vail scrambled on his knees over to Bridget.

"No. No. No." He moaned. With fingers that shook, he gently drew her out from under the table and cradled her on his lap. Limp like that cloth doll Erasmus had once played with, she sagged against his chest. Keening like a wounded beast, he searched her neck for the beat of her pulse. His eyes slid closed as he found it, steady and strong. "Bridget," he pleaded, brushing back the tangle of curls from her face. The air left him on a swift exhale. A large knot, now turning purple, marred the center of her noble brow. Blood leaked from the corners of her mouth. "Nooooo," he groaned, his earlier relief fading. He'd seen too many men fall and eventually draw their final breath from nothing more than a blow to the head.

"Take her out of here," Colin urged. "I'll handle Atbrooke."

Gently lifting Bridget, he shoved to a stand. She moaned, as her head rolled into his chest.

"Oh, God. I'm so, so sorry." For so much. This was the depth of evil she'd lived with. A brother who would have killed her to secure his own future. She'd never had a choice.

"Vail."

Bridget's voice, weak and strained, froze him. "Yes, love?"

"It's under…" Her words broke off.

"Stop. We'll talk later." There were so many words to be said.

"No," she pleaded. "Th-there is a board… under the billiards. Your book…" And she went limp once more.

Panic threatened to engulf him as he searched for a pulse. "Don't you dare die," he rasped. "For a bloody book." She'd threaten him with the prospect of eternal loneliness and the loss of her for a damned book. Nothing mattered more than her. Tears blurred his vision and he blinked them back.

Colin settled a hand on his shoulder and squeezed. "Take her and go. She needs a doctor."

Colin's steady, assured voice pulled him back from the brink of madness. With Bridget in his arms, he rushed through the marquess' townhouse, past portraits he'd not noted when he'd entered. A noble family: a mother, father, a son, and daughter…and yet there was another child missing from all those portraits.

He wanted to rail at the ugliness that existed in her parents' soul. He yearned to take a knife to each painting and drag the blade through those people who'd cast her out.

Throat working, he glanced at the pale woman in his arms. Then, mayhap with the evil her brother would have carried out against her this day in the name of his greed, she'd been spared a more dangerous fate than had she lived in their midst.

Reaching his carriage, not relinquishing Bridget to his driver's care, Vail climbed inside. "H-Home," he managed, that one word breaking. Seated on the bench with her on his lap, he turned his attention back to her. The knot on her forehead had already turned a vicious shade of purple and blood continued to trickle from her mouth. With shaking hands, he yanked out his kerchief and gently brushed away the blood from her lips. "Oh, Bridget," he whispered achingly. "What have you done?"

A piteous moan escaped her and he froze.

Her lashes fluttered, revealing pain-laden eyes. "Vail. It was you."

He strained to hear her faint words. "Did you think I would not come for you?" Except, when the Chaucer went missing, he'd shown his doubt. How he hated himself for not having trusted her in this. He dusted his knuckles along her jaw.

"I didn't..." She winced, closing her eyes again.

"Shh," he pleaded. They'd talk later. They had forever. He'd show her that.

"I didn't want you to come."

For a moment, he thought he'd misheard her. She hadn't wanted...?

"I n-needed to do this." Bridget touched her fingers to his cheek. "For you."

"For me," he echoed, his voice curiously blank. He sank back in his seat. She'd have sacrificed her life to prove herself.

"I wanted to tell you—" The carriage hit a bump and an agonized moan filtered around the carriage.

His worry swelled. "Not now," he said quietly. "Rest. We'll talk later."

And once more, Bridget slid into unconsciousness.

CHAPTER 23

Seven days later

"THAT GENTLEMAN NEVER LEFT YOUR side for the two days you were unconscious."

No, he hadn't. Through the haze of confusion and pain, reality and pretend blurred in and out, shifting out of focus. But Bridget had known he was there. But neither since she'd awakened had he come 'round, either.

Curled on her side, her gaze trained on the satin wallpaper, a little smile played about her mouth. She winced. Her lips still split and bruised from Archibald's blows protested that slight gesture.

That was the manner of man Vail was. He'd do for anyone and everyone.

Her gaze wandered to the trunks sitting in the corner. "He ordered my belongings packed, Nettie," she said gently, even as her heart was breaking. "Why would he do that?" Unless he intended to send her away.

Her nursemaid tossed her hands up. "I don't know. Mayhap because you went silent when the boy was around. Mayhap because you two are young fools who don't have the sense to talk about everything between you."

Given how life was, how was Nettie still capable of that optimism? "Oh, Nettie," she said, patting her hand lovingly.

"Bah, don't patronize me, girl. I know you took several knocks on your head, dear, but I know you still hear me," Nettie scolded, stroking the top of Bridget's head.

She rolled onto her back and stared up at the mural. "What is there to say? He is honorable and good and…" *Everything I am not.*

Nettie ceased her gentle strokes. "Stop that now, gel," she scolded. "That boy loves you."

Loved me.

She stared at the bucolic scene overhead. "I do not doubt he cares for me. I do not doubt that there might have even been love between us, but sometimes love is not enough. Sometimes the lies are too great and—"

"Pfft, what do you know of it, gel?"

"I know that I love him," she said simply. "I know that I want him to be happy—"

"And you think that you are the one to decide what makes him happy."

A tentative knock sounded at the door. Virgil peeked his head in. Worry filled his eyes as it had since she'd first found him at her side. "Mum?"

Sitting up amidst Nettie's protests, she motioned him over. "Mum cannot lie here like a slugabed forever."

Virgil sidled over slowly and then rushed the remaining distance. He cuddled against her side, much the way he had as a small babe who'd awakened from a nightmare. "I knew he'd hurt you," he said forlornly.

Bridget caught Nettie's eye. The older woman nodded and wordlessly let herself out of the room. Alone with her son, she squeezed his narrow shoulders. "He won't hurt us ever again, Virgil," she said solemnly. "He's gone." Because of Vail. His brother, Colin, had not only recovered the stolen Chaucer, but he'd personally escorted Archibald to a ship bound for the penal colonies where he'd pay the penance for his crimes. Some of them. The others could only ever be atoned in hell.

Her son leaned back. "Because of Vail?"

She nodded. "Because of Vail." Vail, who'd saved her in every way a woman could be saved. He'd taught Bridget her own strength and beauty and he'd vanquished her dragons. Much like the ones within those fairytales she read to Virgil. She sighed. Alas, life was not, nor could ever be a fairytale. It was hard and complicated and ugly. And in some fleeting moments, laughter, love and happiness were sprinkled in to sustain a person.

Virgil edged away from her. "I want to stay here." With a hard set to his mouth, he glanced over at the packed trunks.

"Oh, love. Sometimes we have to leave, even when it's hard."

"Or when you're a coward," he muttered.

She bit the inside of her cheek to keep from telling him that Vail hadn't given her an indication that he wished her to remain. Since she'd awakened four days ago, he'd inquired after her well-being and shared the details of her brother's fate, but there had been no words of love. No pleas for her to stay. "Run—"

"Along," he groused. "I know. I know." He hopped up and sprinted over to her window. Shoving back the heavy curtains, he let sunlight stream in.

"What—?"

"Your room is dreary," he mumbled under his breath. Using all his strength, he shoved the panel up. A soothing spring breeze filtered into the room, rustling the curtains. "Everyone can use a bit of sunshine." With a smile, he offered her a jaunty wave.

"Did anyone ever tell you, you're a smart lad?" she called out.

"You," he said, not bothering to look back. "All the time."

The door slammed behind him, shaking the frame, and she managed her first real smile that week. With the occasional gust of wind her only company, she sighed and looked over at her trunks. Her smile faded. And with Nettie and Virgil gone, she let her earlier show crumple. Covering her still bruised face, she wept into her palms. She didn't want to leave. She loved Vail. She loved him for caring as he did for so many. She loved him for being a man who didn't think anything of hiring a woman to work with his business. And she wanted all of him. Wanted—

"Bridget. Bridget. Let down your hair."

Her breath lodged in her throat. *What?* Blinking slowly, she came to her feet. Unsteady from the days she'd spent in bed, she made her way to the opened window.

And her heart swelled.

A half-sob, half-laugh escaped her. "Vail?" she whispered incredulously, leaning out. "My God, what are you doing?" An enormous ladder braced against the front of the townhouse, Vail made a slow climb to her rooms.

"Bridget. Bridget."

A tear slid down her cheek. Followed by another and another. "You do know the prince tumbled to the ground and lost his vision," she called out; her heart burning with love for this man.

"Did he end up with his princess?" Vail paused in his ascent and directed that question upward.

"He did."

He grinned. "Then, that is all that matters."

Bridget stared at the soaring distance between Vail and the ground. Passersby remained motionless in the street, voyeurs, all their focus trained on the baron. Her stomach lurched. His brothers, Edward and Colin, positioned at the base, steadying the ladder. The Duke of Huntly stood supervising, pausing to lift his hand in greeting. Bridget returned the wave.

She gasped as Vail reached the top. "May I?"

Wordless, she backed up, allowing him to heft himself over the ledge. "What are you doing, Vail? You could have—"

He cupped her about the nape and took her lips in a gentle meeting. "I love you," he breathed against her mouth. He loved her? Her heart started. "I'll scale walls, I'll fight dragons, but you are my Petrosinella." His eyes darkened. "The day you went to face your brother, you forgot the story." Vail touched his nose to hers. "They fight dragons together. Marry me." He paused, offering her a heart-stopping grin. "Again."

He offered her everything she'd believed could never be hers. A gift she'd thought herself undeserving of. "But I don't understand....my trunks. You ordered them packed."

"I'd have us leave this place, together."

"But where…?"

He placed a finger gently to her lips. "Come with me."

All the doubts, fears, and sadness that had filled her, lifted, so there was only them. "Do you think we'll live happily ever after?" she asked hoarsely.

Vail touched his brow to hers. "As long as we are a family together, you, Virgil, me, we shall."

A tremulous smile hovered on her lips.

"Is that a yes?"

She nodded. "That is a yes."

Four Hours Later

"Have we arrived yet?"

Virgil's giggle cut across the carriage. "You've asked that seventeen times, Mama."

From over the satin blindfold Vail had delicately tied over her eyes an hour or so earlier, Bridget shot her eyebrows up. "Have I?"

"Yes," her son confirmed.

"Then we shall consider ourselves even for all the twenty-three times you asked from our journey to London." She stretched her arms out searchingly and found her son's side.

Virgil snorted with laughter as she tickled him. "S-Stop. T-Tell her to stop, V-Vail." He squirmed out of her reach.

"I would not dare presume to order your mother about," her husband drawled at her side. Vail folded an arm around her shoulder and brought her close. He lowered his lips near her ear and whispered into it. "We are, however, *very* close."

Her husband. Bridget tested that word in her mind. Despite the lies and treachery that had brought her into his life, he'd found forgiveness in his heart and loved her still. And he'd proven that love earlier that morning by marrying her—for real, this time.

"And you still will not tell me—?" The carriage rolled to a stop.

"We're here," Virgil cried excitedly, clapping his hands.

"We've arrived, Your Lordship," the driver echoed from outside the conveyance. The click of the door sounded in the quiet. Virgil streaked past her; his little legs brushing her skirts.

"Virgil, be—*careful*," she finished, the thump of his small feet striking gravel.

His excited laughter grew distant and Bridget tilted her head up toward Vail. "Now, may I...?"

He'd already begun loosening the strip of fabric. She blinked several times and then winced at the blinding flash of sunlight that spilled through the doorway. "We're here," he said softly, stepping out of the carriage. He reached inside and helped her out.

"Where…?" Bridget's question faded to silence and she touched a hand to her chest. A sea of yellow wildflowers blanketed the nearby fields and meadows, and nestled deep back amongst them was a stucco cottage.

Her husband lifted her fingertips to his mouth and pressed a kiss to them. "Lanyer didn't have the right of it. A manor, a cottage, a townhouse can only be a home if there is a family within it." He gently squeezed her fingers. "Let this be a place we come to…a home, together. I want you in every part of my life: my business, in London, *here*. I—"

Bridget hurled herself into Vail's arms and he instantly folded her in his embrace. "I love you," she breathed. "Home is wherever you are."

"Nay, home is where *we* are," he whispered, claiming her mouth.

And with Virgil's laughter filtering around the countryside, Bridget smiled and welcomed the rest of her life with both Vail and Virgil at her side.

THE END

OTHER BOOKS BY
CHRISTI CALDWELL

"TO ENCHANT A WICKED DUKE"
Book 13 in the "Heart of a Duke" Series by Christi Caldwell

A Devil in Disguise

Years ago, when Nick Tallings, the recent Duke of Huntly, watched his family destroyed at the hands of a merciless nobleman, he vowed revenge. But his efforts had been futile, as his enemy, Lord Rutland is without weakness.

Until now…

With his rival finally happily married, Nick is able to set his ruthless scheme into motion. His plot hinges upon Lord Rutland's innocent, empty-headed sister-in-law, Justina Barrett. Nick will ruin her, marry her, and then leave her brokenhearted.

A Lady Dreaming of Love

From the moment Justina Barrett makes her Come Out, she is labeled a Diamond. Even with her ruthless father determined to sell her off to the highest bidder, Justina never gives up on her hope for a good, honorable gentleman who values her wit more than her looks.

A Not-So-Chance Meeting

Nick's ploy to ensnare Justina falls neatly into place in the streets of London. With each carefully orchestrated encounter, he slips further and further inside the lady's heart, never anticipating that Justina, with her quick wit and strength, will break down his own defenses. As Nick's plans begins to unravel, he's left to determine which is more important—Justina's love or his vow for vengeance. But can Justina ever forgive the duke who deceived her?

"ONE WINTER WITH A BARON"
Book 12 in the "Heart of a Duke" Series by Christi Caldwell

A clever spinster:

Content with her spinster lifestyle, Miss Sybil Cunning wants to prove that a future as an unmarried woman is the only life for her. As a bluestocking who values hard, empirical data, Sybil needs help with her research. Nolan Pratt, Baron Webb, one of society's most scandalous rakes, is the perfect gentleman to help her. After all, he inspires fear in proper mothers and desire within their daughters.

A notorious rake:

Society may be aware of Nolan Pratt, Baron's Webb's wicked ways, but what he has carefully hidden is his miserable handling of his family's finances. When Sybil presents him the opportunity to earn much-needed funds, he can't refuse.

A winter to remember:

However, what begins as a business arrangement becomes something more and with every meeting, Sybil slips inside his heart. Can this clever woman look beneath the veneer of a coldhearted rake to see the man Nolan truly is?

"TO REDEEM A RAKE"
Book 11 in the "Heart of a Duke" Series by Christi Caldwell

He's spent years scandalizing society.
Now, this rake must change his ways.

Society's most infamous scoundrel, Daniel Winterbourne, the Earl of Montfort, has been promised a small fortune if he can relinquish his wayward, carousing lifestyle. And behaving means he must also help find a respectable companion for his youngest sister—someone who will guide her and whom she can emulate. However, Daniel knows no such woman. But when he encounters a childhood friend, Daniel believes she may just be the answer to all of his problems.

Having been secretly humiliated by an unscrupulous blackguard years earlier, Miss Daphne Smith dreams of finding work at Ladies of Hope, an institution that provides an education for disabled women. With her sordid past and a disfigured leg, few opportunities arise for a woman such as she. Knowing Daniel's history, she wishes to avoid him, but working for his sister is exactly the stepping stone she needs.

Their attraction intensifies as Daniel and Daphne grow closer, preparing his sister for the London Season. But Daniel must resist his desire for a woman tarnished by scandal while Daphne is reminded of the boy she once knew. Can society's most notorious rake redeem his reputation and become the man Daphne deserves?

"To Woo a Widow"
Book 10 in the "Heart of a Duke" Series by Christi Caldwell

They see a brokenhearted widow.
She's far from shattered.

Lady Philippa Winston is never marrying again. After her late husband's cruelty that she kept so well hidden, she has no desire to search for love.

Years ago, Miles Brookfield, the Marquess of Guilford, made a frivolous vow he never thought would come to fruition—he promised to marry his mother's goddaughter if he was unwed by the age of thirty. Now, to his dismay, he's faced with honoring that pledge. But when he encounters the beautiful and intriguing Lady Philippa, Miles knows his true path in life. It's up to him to break down every belief Philippa carries about gentlemen, proving that not only is love real, but that he is the man deserving of her sheltered heart.

Will Philippa let down her guard and allow Miles to woo a widow in desperate need of his love?

"The Lure of a Rake"
Book 9 in the "Heart of a Duke" Series by Christi Caldwell

A Lady Dreaming of Love

Lady Genevieve Farendale has a scandalous past. Jilted at the altar years earlier and exiled by her family, she's now returned to London to prove she can be a proper lady. Even though she's not given up on the hope of marrying for love, she's wary of trusting again. Then she meets Cedric Falcot, the Marquess of St. Albans whose seductive ways set her heart aflutter. But with her sordid history, Genevieve knows a rake can also easily destroy her.

An Unlikely Pairing

What begins as a chance encounter between Cedric and Genevieve becomes something more. As they continue to meet, passions stir. But with Genevieve's hope for true love, she fears Cedric will be unable to give up his wayward lifestyle. After all, Cedric has spent years protecting his heart, and keeping everyone out. Slowly, she chips away at all the walls he's built, but when he falters, Genevieve can't offer him redemption. Now, it's up to Cedric to prove to Genevieve that the love of a man is far more powerful than the lure of a rake.

"To Trust a Rogue"
Book 8 in the "Heart of a Duke" Series by Christi Caldwell

A rogue

Marcus, the Viscount Wessex has carefully crafted the image of rogue and charmer for Polite Society. Under that façade, however, dwells a man whose dreams were shattered almost eight years earlier by a young lady who captured his heart, pledged her love, and then left him, with nothing more than a curt note.

A widow

Eight years earlier, faced with no other choice, Mrs. Eleanor Collins, fled London and the only man she ever loved, Marcus, Viscount Wessex. She has now returned to serve as a companion for her elderly aunt with a daughter in tow. Even though they're next door neighbors, there is little reason for her to move in the same circles as Marcus, just in case, she vows to avoid him, for he reminds her of all she lost when she left.

Reunited

As their paths continue to cross, Marcus finds his desire for Eleanor just as strong, but he learned long ago she's not to be trusted. He will offer her a place in his bed, but not anything more. Only, Eleanor has no interest in this new, roguish man. The more time they spend together, the protective wall they've constructed to keep the other out, begin to break. With all the betrayals and secrets between them, Marcus has to open his heart again. And Eleanor must decide if it's ever safe to trust a rogue.

"To Wed His Christmas Lady"
Book 7 in the "Heart of a Duke" Series by Christi Caldwell

She's longing to be loved:

Lady Cara Falcot has only served one purpose to her loathsome father—to increase his power through a marriage to the future Duke of Billingsley. As such, she's built protective walls about her heart, and presents an icy facade to the world around her. Journeying home from her finishing school for the Christmas holidays, Cara's carriage is stranded during a winter storm. She's forced to tarry at a ramshackle inn, where she immediately antagonizes another patron—William.

He's avoiding his duty in favor of one last adventure:

William Hargrove, the Marquess of Grafton has wanted only one thing in life—to avoid the future match his parents would have him make to a cold, duke's daughter. He's returning home from a blissful eight years of traveling the world to see to his responsibilities. But when a winter storm interrupts his trip and lands him at a falling-down inn, he's forced to share company with a commanding Lady Cara who initially reminds him exactly of the woman he so desperately wants to avoid.

A Christmas snowstorm ushers in the spirit of the season:

At the holiday time, these two people who despise each other due to first perceptions are offered renewed beginnings and fresh starts. As this gruff stranger breaks down the walls she's built about herself, Cara has to determine whether she can truly open her heart to trusting that any man is capable of good and that she herself is capable of love. And William has to set aside all previous thoughts he's carried of the polished ladies like Cara, to be the man to show her that love.

THE HEART OF A SCOUNDREL

Book 6 in the "Heart of a Duke" Series by Christi Caldwell

Ruthless, wicked, and dark, the Marquess of Rutland rouses terror in the breast of ladies and nobleman alike. All Edmund wants in life is power. After he was publically humiliated by his one love Lady Margaret, he vowed vengeance, using Margaret's niece, as his pawn. Except, he's thwarted by another, more enticing target—Miss Phoebe Barrett.

Miss Phoebe Barrett knows precisely the shame she's been born to. Because her father is a shocking letch she's learned to form her own opinions on a person's worth. After a chance meeting with the Marquess of Rutland, she is captivated by the mysterious man. He, too, is a victim of society's scorn, but the more encounters she has with Edmund, the more she knows there is powerful depth and emotion to the jaded marquess.

The lady wreaks havoc on Edmund's plans for revenge and he finds he wants Phoebe, at all costs. As she's drawn into the darkness of his world, Phoebe risks being destroyed by Edmund's ruthlessness. And Phoebe who desires love at all costs, has to determine if she can ever truly trust the heart of a scoundrel.

"TO LOVE A LORD"
Book 5 in the "Heart of a Duke" Series by Christi Caldwell

All she wants is security:

The last place finishing school instructor Mrs. Jane Munroe belongs, is in polite Society. Vowing to never wed, she's been scuttled around from post to post. Now she finds herself in the Marquess of Waverly's household. She's never met a nobleman she liked, and when she meets the pompous, arrogant marquess, she remembers why. But soon, she discovers Gabriel is unlike any gentleman she's ever known.

All he wants is a companion for his sister:

What Gabriel finds himself with instead, is a fiery spirited, bespectacled woman who entices him at every corner and challenges his age-old vow to never trust his heart to a woman. But... there is something suspicious about his sister's companion. And he is determined to find out just what it is.

All they need is each other:

As Gabriel and Jane confront the truth of their feelings, the lies and secrets between them begin to unravel. And Jane is left to decide whether or not it is ever truly safe to love a lord.

"LOVED BY A DUKE"
Book 4 in the "Heart of a Duke" Series by Christi Caldwell

For ten years, Lady Daisy Meadows has been in love with Auric, the Duke of Crawford. Ever since his gallant rescue years earlier, Daisy knew she was destined to be his Duchess. Unfortunately, Auric sees her as his best friend's sister and nothing more. But perhaps, if she can manage to find the fabled heart of a duke pendant, she will win over the heart of her duke.

Auric, the Duke of Crawford enjoys Daisy's company. The last thing he is interested in however, is pursuing a romance with a woman he's known since she was in leading strings. This season, Daisy is turning up in the oddest places and he cannot help but notice that she is no longer a girl. But Auric wouldn't do something as foolhardy as to fall in love with Daisy. He couldn't. Not with the guilt he carries over his past sins… Not when he has no right to her heart…But perhaps, just perhaps, she can forgive the past and trust that he'd forever cherish her heart—but will she let him?

"The Love of a Rogue"
Book 3 in the "Heart of a Duke" Series by Christi Caldwell

Lady Imogen Moore hasn't had an easy time of it since she made her Come Out. With her betrothed, a powerful duke breaking it off to wed her sister, she's become the *tons* favorite piece of gossip. Never again wanting to experience the pain of a broken heart, she's resolved to make a match with a polite, respectable gentleman. The last thing she wants is another reckless rogue.

Lord Alex Edgerton has a problem. His brother, tired of Alex's carousing has charged him with chaperoning their remaining, unwed sister about *ton* events. Shopping? No, thank you. Attending the theatre? He'd rather be at Forbidden Pleasures with a scantily clad beauty upon his lap. The task of *chaperone* becomes even more of a bother when his sister drags along her dearest friend, Lady Imogen to social functions. The last thing he wants in his life is a young, innocent English miss.

Except, as Alex and Imogen are thrown together, passions flare and Alex comes to find he not only wants Imogen in his bed, but also in his heart. Yet now he must convince Imogen to risk all, on the heart of a rogue.

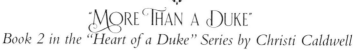

"More Than a Duke"
Book 2 in the "Heart of a Duke" Series by Christi Caldwell

Polite Society doesn't take Lady Anne Adamson seriously. However, Anne isn't just another pretty young miss. When she discovers her father betrayed her mother's love and her family descended into poverty, Anne comes up with a plan to marry a respectable, powerful, and honorable gentleman—a man nothing like her philandering father.

Armed with the heart of a duke pendant, fabled to land the wearer a duke's heart, she decides to enlist the aid of the notorious Harry, 6th Earl of Stanhope. A scoundrel with a scandalous past, he is the last gentleman she'd ever wed…however, his reputation marks him the perfect man to school her in the art of seduction so she might ensnare the illustrious Duke of Crawford.

Harry, the Earl of Stanhope is a jaded, cynical rogue who lives for his own pleasures. Having been thrown over by the only woman he ever loved so she could wed a duke, he's not at all surprised when Lady Anne approaches him with her scheme to capture another duke's affection. He's come to appreciate that all women are in fact greedy, title-grasping, self-indulgent creatures. And with Anne's history of grating on his every last nerve, she is the last woman he'd ever agree to school in the art of seduction. Only his friendship with the lady's sister compels him to help.

What begins as a pretend courtship, born of lessons on seduction, becomes something more leaving Anne to decide if she can give her heart to a reckless rogue, and Harry must decide if he's willing to again trust in a lady's love.

"FOR LOVE OF THE DUKE"
First Full-Length Book in the "Heart of a Duke" Series
by Christi Caldwell

After the tragic death of his wife, Jasper, the 8th Duke of Bainbridge buried himself away in the dark cold walls of his home, Castle Blackwood. When he's coaxed out of his self-imposed exile to attend the amusements of the Frost Fair, his life is irrevocably changed by his fateful meeting with Lady Katherine Adamson.

With her tight brown ringlets and silly white-ruffled gowns, Lady Katherine Adamson has found her dance card empty for two Seasons. After her father's passing, Katherine learned the unreliability of men, and is determined to depend on no one, except herself. Until she meets Jasper…

In a desperate bid to avoid a match arranged by her family, Katherine makes the Duke of Bainbridge a shocking proposition—one that he accepts.

Only, as Katherine begins to love Jasper, she finds the arrangement agreed upon is not enough. And Jasper is left to decide if protecting his heart is more important than fighting for Katherine's love.

"IN NEED OF A DUKE"
A Prequel Novella to "The Heart of a Duke" Series
by Christi Caldwell

In Need of a Duke: (Author's Note: This is a prequel novella to "The Heart of a Duke" series by Christi Caldwell. It was originally available in "The Heart of a Duke" Collection and is now being published as an individual novella.

~★~

It features a new prologue and epilogue.

Years earlier, a gypsy woman passed to Lady Aldora Adamson and her friends a heart pendant that promised them each the heart of a duke.

Now, a young lady, with her family facing ruin and scandal, Lady Aldora doesn't have time for mythical stories about cheap baubles. She needs to save her sisters and brother by marrying a titled gentleman with wealth and power to his name. She sets her bespectacled sights upon the Marquess of St. James.

Turned out by his father after a tragic scandal, Lord Michael Knightly has grown into a powerful, but self-made man. With the whispers and stares that still follow him, he would rather be any-where but London…

Until he meets Lady Aldora, a young woman who mistakes him for his brother, the Marquess of St. James. The connection between Aldora and Michael is immediate and as they come to know one another, Aldora's feelings for Michael war with her sisterly responsibilities. With her family's dire situation, a man of Michael's scandalous past will never do.

Ultimately, Aldora must choose between her responsibilities as a sister and her love for Michael.

"ONCE A WALLFLOWER, AT LAST HIS LOVE"
Book 6 in the Scandalous Seasons Series

Responsible, practical Miss Hermione Rogers, has been craft-ing stories as the notorious Mr. Michael Michaelmas and selling them for a meager wage to support her siblings. The only real way to ensure her family's ruinous debts are paid, however, is to marry. Tall, thin, and plain, she has no expectation of success. In London for her first Season she seizes the chance to write the tale of a brooding duke. In her research, she finds Sebastian Fitzhugh, the 5th Duke of Mallen, who unfortunately is perfectly affable, charming, and so nicely… configured… he takes her breath away. He lacks all the character traits she needs for her story, but alas, any duke will have to do.

Sebastian Fitzhugh, the 5th Duke of Mallen has been deceived so many times during the high-stakes game of courtship, he's lost faith in Society women. Yet, after a chance encounter with Hermione, he finds himself intrigued. Not a woman he'd normally consider beautiful, the young lady's practical bent, her forthright nature and her tendency to turn up in the oddest places has his interests… roused. He'd like to trust her, he'd like to do a whole lot more with her too, but should he?

"A Marquess For Christmas"
Book 5 in the Scandalous Seasons Series

Lady Patrina Tidemore gave up on the ridiculous notion of true love after having her heart shattered and her trust destroyed by a black-hearted cad. Used as a pawn in a game of revenge against her brother, Patrina returns to London from a failed elopement with a tattered reputation and little hope for a respectable match. The only peace she finds is in her solitude on the cold winter days at Hyde Park. And even that is yanked from her by two little hellions who just happen to have a devastatingly handsome, but coldly aloof father, the Marquess of Beaufort. Something about the lord stirs the dreams she'd once carried for an honorable gentleman's love.

Weston Aldridge, the 4th Marquess of Beaufort was deceived and betrayed by his late wife. In her faithlessness, he's come to view women as self-serving, indulgent creatures. Except, after a series of chance encounters with Patrina, he comes to appreciate how uniquely different she is than all women he's ever known.

At the Christmastide season, a time of hope and new beginnings, Patrina and Weston, unexpectedly learn true love in one another. However, as Patrina's scandalous past threatens their future and the happiness of his children, they are both left to determine if love is enough.

"Always a Rogue, Forever Her Love"
Book 4 in the Scandalous Seasons Series

Miss Juliet Marshville is spitting mad. With one guardian missing, and the other singularly uninterested in her fate, she is at the mercy of her wastrel brother who loses her beloved childhood home to a man known as Sin. Determined to reclaim control of Rosecliff Cottage and her own fate, Juliet arranges a meeting with the notorious rogue and demands the return of her property.

Jonathan Tidemore, 5th Earl of Sinclair, known to the *ton* as Sin, is exceptionally lucky in life and at the gaming tables. He has just one problem. Well…four, really. His incorrigible sisters have driven off yet another governess. This time, however, his mother demands he find an appropriate replacement.

When Miss Juliet Marshville boldly demands the return of her precious cottage, he takes advantage of his sudden good fortune and puts an offer to her; turn his sisters into proper English ladies, and he'll return Rosecliff Cottage to Juliet's possession.

Jonathan comes to appreciate Juliet's spirit, courage, and clever wit, and decides to claim the fiery beauty as his mistress. Juliet, however, will be mistress for no man. Nor could she ever love a man who callously stole her home in a game of cards. As Jonathan begins to see Juliet as more than a spirited beauty to warm his bed, he realizes she could be a lady he could love the rest of his life, if only he can convince the proud Juliet that he's worthy of her hand and heart.

"Always Proper, Suddenly Scandalous"
Book 3 in the Scandalous Seasons Series

Geoffrey Winters, Viscount Redbrooke was not always the hard, unrelenting lord driven by propriety. After a tragic mistake, he resolved to honor his responsibility to the Redbrooke line and live a life, free of scandal. Knowing his duty is to wed a proper, respectable English miss, he selects Lady Beatrice Dennington, daughter of the Duke of Somerset, the perfect woman for him. Until he meets Miss Abigail Stone…

To distance herself from a personal scandal, Abigail Stone flees America to visit her uncle, the Duke of Somerset. Determined to never trust a man again, she is helplessly intrigued by the hard, too-proper Geoffrey. With his strict appreciation for decorum and order, he is nothing like the man' she's always dreamed of.

Abigail is everything Geoffrey does not need. She upends his carefully ordered world at every encounter. As they begin to care for one another, Abigail carefully guards the secret that resulted in her journey to England.

Only, if Geoffrey learns the truth about Abigail, he must decide which he holds most dear: his place in Society or Abigail's place in his heart.

"NEVER COURTED, SUDDENLY WED"
Book 2 in the Scandalous Seasons Series

Christopher Ansley, Earl of Waxham, has constructed a perfect image for the *ton*–the ladies love him and his company is desired by all. Only two people know the truth about Waxham's secret. Unfortunately, one of them is Miss Sophie Winters.

Sophie Winters has known Christopher since she was in leading strings. As children, they delighted in tormenting each other. Now at two and twenty, she still has a tendency to find herself in scrapes, and her marital prospects are slim.

When his father threatens to expose his shame to the *ton*, unless he weds Sophie for her dowry, Christopher concocts a plan to remain a bachelor. What he didn't plan on was falling in love with the lively, impetuous Sophie. As secrets are exposed, will Christopher's love be enough when she discovers his role in his father's scheme?

"Forever Betrothed, Never the Bride"
Book 1 in the Scandalous Seasons Series

Hopeless romantic Lady Emmaline Fitzhugh is tired of sitting with the wallflowers, waiting for her betrothed to come to his senses and marry her. When Emmaline reads one too many reports of his scandalous liaisons in the gossip rags, she takes matters into her own hands.

War-torn veteran Lord Drake devotes himself to forgetting his days on the Peninsula through an endless round of meaningless associations. He no longer wants to feel anything, but Lady Emmaline is making it hard to maintain a state of numbness. With her zest for life, she awakens his passion and desire for love.

The one woman Drake has spent the better part of his life avoiding is now the only woman he needs, but he is no longer a man worthy of his Emmaline. It is up to her to show him the healing power of love.

"A Season of Hope"
A Danby Novella

Five years ago when her love, Marcus Wheatley, failed to return from fighting Napoleon's forces, Lady Olivia Foster buried her heart. Unable to betray Marcus's memory, Olivia has gone out of her way to run off prospective suitors. At three and twenty she considers herself firmly on the shelf. Her father, however, disagrees and accepts an offer for Olivia's hand in marriage. Yet it's Christmas, when anything can happen…

Olivia receives a well-timed summons from her grandfather, the Duke of Danby, and eagerly embraces the reprieve from her betrothal.

Only, when Olivia arrives at Danby Castle she realizes the

Christmas season represents hope, second chances, and even miracles.

"Winning a Lady's Heart"
A Danby Novella

Author's Note: This is a novella that was originally available in A Summons From The Castle (The Regency Christmas Summons Collection). It is being published as an individual novella.

~★~

For Lady Alexandra, being the source of a cold, calculated wager is bad enough…but when it is waged by Nathaniel Michael Winters, 5th Earl of Pembroke, the man she's in love with, it results in a broken heart, the scandal of the season, and a summons from her grandfather – the Duke of Danby.

To escape Society's gossip, she hurries to her meeting with the duke, determined to put memories of the earl far behind. Except the duke has other plans for Alexandra…plans which include the 5th Earl of Pembroke!

"Tempted by a Lady's Smile"
Book 4 in the "Lords of Honor" Series

Richard Jonas has loved but one woman—a woman who belongs to his brother. Refusing to suffer any longer, he evades his family in order to barricade his heart from unrequited love. While attending a friend's summer party, Richard's approach to love is changed after sharing a passionate and life-altering kiss with a vibrant and mysterious woman. Believing he was incapable of loving again, Richard finds himself tempted by a young lady determined to marry his best friend.

Gemma Reed has not been treated kindly by the *ton*. Often disregarded for her appearance and interests unlike those of a proper lady, Gemma heads to house party to win the heart of Lord West-field, the man she's loved for years. But her plan is set off course by the tempting and intriguing, Richard Jonas.

A chance meeting creates a new path for Richard and Gemma to forage—but can two people, scorned and shunned by those they've loved from afar, let down their guards to find true happiness?

"Rescued By a Lady's Love"
Book 3 in the "Lords of Honor" Series

Destitute and determined to finally be free of any man's shackles, Lily Benedict sets out to salvage her honor. With no choice but to commit a crime that will save her from her past, she enters the home of the recluse, Derek Winters, the new Duke of Blackthorne. But entering the "Beast of Blackthorne's" lair proves more threatening than she ever imagined.

With half a face and a mangled leg, Derek—once rugged and charming—only exists within the confines of his home. Shunned by society, Derek is leery of the hauntingly beautiful Lily Benedict. As time passes, she slips past his defenses, reminding him how to live again. But when Lily's sordid past comes back, threatening her life, it's up to Derek to find the strength to become the hero he once was. Can they overcome the darkness of their sins to find a life of love and redemption?

"Captivated by a Lady's Charm"
Book 2 in the "Lords of Honor" Series

In need of a wife…
Christian Villiers, the Marquess of St. Cyr, despises the role he's been cast into as fortune hunter but requires the funds to keep his marquisate solvent. Yet, the sins of his past cloud his future, pre-

venting him from seeing beyond his fateful actions at the Battle of Toulouse. For he knows inevitably it will catch up with him, and everyone will remember his actions on the battlefield that cost so many so much—particularly his best friend.

In want of a husband…

Lady Prudence Tidemore's life is plagued by familial scandals, which makes her own marital prospects rather grim. Surely there is one gentleman of the ton who can look past her family and see just her and all she has to offer?

When Prudence runs into Christian on a London street, the charming, roguish gentleman immediately captures her attention. But then a chance meeting becomes a waltz, and now…

A Perfect Match…

All she must do is convince Christian to forget the cold requirements he has for his future marchioness. But the demons in his past prevent him from turning himself over to love. One thing is certain—Prudence wants the marquess and is determined to have him in her life, now and forever. It's just a matter of convincing Christian he wants the same.

"Seduced By a Lady's Heart"
Book 1 in the "Lords of Honor" Series

You met Lieutenant Lucien Jones in "Forever Betrothed, Never the Bride" when he was a broken soldier returned from fighting Boney's forces. This is his story of triumph and happily-ever-after!

~★~

Lieutenant Lucien Jones, son of a viscount, returned from war, to find his wife and child dead. Blaming his father for the commission that sent him off to fight Boney's forces, he was content to languish at London Hospital… until offered employment on the Marquess of Drake's staff. Through his position, Lucien found purpose in life and is content to keep his past buried.

Lady Eloise Yardley has loved Lucien since they were children. Having long ago given up on the dream of him, she married another. Years later, she is a young, lonely widow who does not fit in with the ton. When Lucien's family enlists her aid to reunite father and son, she leaps at the opportunity to not only aid her former friend, but to also escape London.

Lucien doesn't know what scheme Eloise has concocted, but knowing her as he does, when she pays a visit to his employer, he knows she's up to something. The last thing he wants is the temptation that this new, older, mature Eloise presents; a tantalizing reminder of happier times and peace.

Yet Eloise is determined to win Lucien's love once and for all… if only Lucien can set aside the pain of his past and risk all on a lady's heart.

"ONLY FOR THEIR LOVE"
Book 3 in the "The Theodosia Sword" Series

Miss Carol Cresswall bore witness to her parents' loveless union and is determined to avoid that same miserable fate. Her mother has altogether different plans—plans that include a match between Carol and Lord Gregory Renshaw. Despite his wealth and power, Carol has no interest in marrying a pompous man who goes out of his way to ignore her. Now, with their families coming together for the Christmastide season it's her mother's last-ditch effort to get them together. And Carol plans to avoid Gregory at all costs.

Lord Gregory Renshaw has no intentions of falling prey to his mother's schemes to marry him off to a proper debutante she's picked out. Over the years, he has carefully sidestepped all endeavors to be matched with any of the grasping ladies.

But a sudden Christmastide Scandal has the potential show Carol and Gregory that they've spent years running from the one thing they've always needed.

"Only For Her Honor"
Book 2 in the "The Theodosia Sword" Series

A wounded soldier:

When Captain Lucas Rayne returned from fighting Boney's forces, he was a shell of a man. A recluse who doesn't leave his family's estate, he's content to shut himself away. Until he meets Eve…

A woman alone in the world:

Eve Ormond spent most of her life following the drum alongside her late father. When his shameful actions bring death and pain to English soldiers, Eve is forced back to England, an outcast. With no family or marital prospects she needs employment and finds it in Captain Lucas Rayne's home. A man whose life was ruined by her father, Eve has no place inside his household. With few options available, however, Eve takes the post. What she never anticipates is how with their every meeting, this honorable, hurting soldier slips inside her heart.

The Secrets Between Them:

The more time Lucas spends with Eve, he remembers what it is to be alive and he lets the walls protecting his heart down. When the secrets between them come to light will their love be enough? Or are they two destined for heartbreak?

"Only For His Lady"
Book 1 in the "The Theodosia Sword" Series

A curse. A sword. And the thief who stole her heart.

The Rayne family is trapped in a rut of bad luck. And now, it's up to Lady Theodosia Rayne to steal back the Theodosia sword, a gladius that was pilfered by the rival, loathed Renshaw family.

Hopefully, recovering the stolen sword will break the cycle and reverse her family's fate.

Damian Renshaw, the Duke of Devlin, is feared by all—all, that is, except Lady Theodosia, the brazen spitfire who enters his home and wrestles an ancient relic from his wall. Intrigued by the vivacious woman, Devlin has no intentions of relinquishing the sword to her.

As Theodosia and Damian battle for ownership, passion ignites. Now, they are torn between their age-old feud and the fire that burns between them. Can two forbidden lovers find a way to make amends before their families' war tears them apart?

"MY LADY OF DECEPTION"
Book 1 in the "Brethren of the Lords" Series

This dark, sweeping Regency novel was previously only offered as part of the limited edition box sets: "From the Ballroom and Beyond", "Romancing the Rogue", and "Dark Deceptions". Now, available for the first time on its own, exclusively through Amazon is "My Lady of Deception".

~★~

Everybody has a secret. Some are more dangerous than others.

For Georgina Wilcox, only child of the notorious traitor known as "The Fox", there are too many secrets to count. However, after her interference results in great tragedy, she resolves to never help another… until she meets Adam Markham.

Lord Adam Markham is captured by The Fox. Imprisoned, Adam loses everything he holds dear. As his days in captivity grow, he finds himself fascinated by the young maid, Georgina, who cares for him.

When the carefully crafted lies she's built between them begin to crumble, Georgina realizes she will do anything to prove her love and loyalty to Adam—even it means at the expense of her own life.

NON-FICTION WORKS BY
CHRISTI CALDWELL

Uninterrupted Joy: Memoir: My Journey through Infertility, Pregnancy, and Special Needs

The following journey was never intended for publication. It was written from a mother, to her unborn child. The words detailed her struggle through infertility and the joy of finally being pregnant. A stunning revelation at her son's birth opened a world of both fear and discovery. This is the story of one mother's love and hope and…her quest for uninterrupted joy.

BIOGRAPHY

Christi Caldwell is the bestselling author of historical romance novels set in the Regency era. Christi blames Judith McNaught's "Whitney, My Love," for luring her into the world of historical romance. While sitting in her graduate school apartment at the University of Connecticut, Christi decided to set aside her notes and try her hand at writing romance. She believes the most perfect heroes and heroines have imperfections and rather enjoys tormenting them before crafting a well-deserved happily ever after!

When Christi isn't writing the stories of flawed heroes and heroines, she can be found in her Southern Connecticut home chasing around her eight-year-old son, and caring for twin princesses-in-training!

Visit *www.christicaldwellauthor.com* to learn more about what Christi is working on, or join her on Facebook at Christi Caldwell Author, and Twitter *@ChristiCaldwell*

Made in the USA
Middletown, DE
15 June 2017